Tyler Anne Snell lives in South Alabama with her same-named husband, their artist kiddo, four mini 'lions' and a burning desire to meet Kurt Russell. Her superpowers include binge-watching TV and herding cats. When she isn't writing thrilling mysteries and romance, she's reading everything she can get her hands on. How she gets through each day starts and ends with a big cup of coffee. Visit her at tylerannesnell.com

Cindi Myers is the author of more than seventy-five novels. When she's not plotting new romance storylines, she enjoys skiing, gardening, cooking, crafting and daydreaming. A lover of small-town life, she lives with her husband and two spoiled dogs in the Colorado mountains.

Also by Tyler Anne Snell

Manhunt
Toxin Alert
Dangerous Recall

Small Town Last Stand
Search for the Truth
The Deputy's Secret Double
Against the Clock

The Saving Kelby Creek Series
Cold Case Captive
Retracing the Investigation

Also by Cindi Myers

K-9 Avalanche Rescue
Danger Zone

Eagle Mountain: Unsolved Mysteries
Canyon Killer
Wilderness Search
Peak Suspicion
High Country Escape

Eagle Mountain: Criminal History
Mile High Mystery
Twin Jeopardy

Discover more at millsandboon.co.uk

A DEATH AT THE WEDDING

TYLER ANNE SNELL

EXPLOSIVE EVIDENCE

CINDI MYERS

MILLS & BOON

All rights reserved including the right of reproduction in whole or in part in any form. This edition is published by arrangement with Harlequin Enterprises ULC.

This is a work of fiction. Names, characters, places, locations and incidents are purely fictional and bear no relationship to any real life individuals, living or dead, or to any actual places, business establishments, locations, events or incidents. Any resemblance is entirely coincidental.

Without limiting the exclusive rights of any author, contributor or the publisher of this publication, any unauthorised use of this publication to train generative artificial intelligence (AI) technologies is expressly prohibited. HarperCollins also exercise their rights under Article 4(3) of the Digital Single Market Directive 2019/790 and expressly reserve this publication from the text and data mining exception.

® and ™ are trademarks owned and used by the trademark owner and/or its licensee. Trademarks marked with ® are registered with the United Kingdom Patent Office and/or the Office for Harmonisation in the Internal Market and in other countries.

First Published in Great Britain 2026
by Mills & Boon, an imprint of HarperCollins*Publishers* Ltd
1 London Bridge Street, London, SE1 9GF

www.harpercollins.co.uk

HarperCollins*Publishers*
Macken House, 39/40 Mayor Street Upper,
Dublin 1, D01 C9W8, Ireland

A Death at the Wedding © 2026 Tyler Anne Snell
Explosive Evidence © 2026 Cynthia Myers

ISBN: 978-0-263-42024-1

0326

Printed and Bound in the UK using 100% Renewable Electricity at
CPI Group (UK) Ltd, Croydon, CR0 4YY

A DEATH AT THE WEDDING

TYLER ANNE SNELL

This book is for Tyler, Dad, Mike, Hana, Damon and sometimes Brian. There was a lot going on when this book was written, but Core Group gave me the fun giggles I needed every night to start over fresh again in the morning. Thanks for the laughs, screams and inside jokes.

Chapter One

Evelyn Myers wasn't book smart. She didn't have any school trophies or impressive college accolades. Her skills were average, her ability to solve math equations low, and to say she was uncoordinated was like saying it got dark at night. Eve wasn't a standout from the crowd. She was in it, trying to get from point A to point B while counting down the minutes until she could get home and take off her bra.

Her only notable exception, however, was enough to change absolutely everything for the worse.

Eve had a soft spot for trouble.

Which was why she was wearing a wedding dress beneath her coat and leaning against the McCoy County Sheriff Department's front desk with a smile that had been idling as long as Mrs. Jane had been trying to find the man she'd come calling for.

"Darius—I mean, Detective Williams is out on a call," Mrs. Jane said after she placed the phone back on its ancient cradle. It was as outdated as the interior of the building, but it wasn't like the small as small town of Seven Roads, Georgia, should have been expected to meet the current times with vigor.

Eve hadn't been back in town since she was twelve, and

now at thirty-five she was sure as spit boiling on the sidewalk in summer that the dust on top of the vending machine in the lobby hadn't been cleaned since she had been living with her daddy in that old house on Maple.

"Do you know if he'll back anytime soon?" Eve asked. She subtly pulled her coat even tighter over a dress that cost more than her last apartment's rent. Mrs. Jane might not have recognized the little girl who had been a local all those years ago, but the wedding dress would be a dead giveaway to the fact that now she was Mrs. Keys-To-Be.

Eve Myers was unimpressive. But the family Eve Myers was marrying into had a net worth of almost half a billion dollars, spearheaded by the absolute stud of a bachelor named Scott Keys. Very impressive.

Even though she wasn't marrying Scott, she *was* marrying his little brother, Mitchell.

The running joke in the media was she was getting the keys to the castle, not the entire kingdom.

But standing there, staring at Mrs. Jane trying to find an excuse to shoo her away, Eve could tell she was as unimpressive to the woman as the frayed carpet beneath their feet.

"You'll just have to leave your name and number, sweetie," Mrs. Jane settled on, some spice to her Southern syrup. "That's the best I can do if you don't have an appointment with him already. He's a very busy man. He's the only detective in the county, you know."

Eve didn't need the Darius Williams who was a detective.

She needed the Darius Williams who owed her a favor.

Eve sighed out heavy. Her wedding dress sure was tight.

"Leaving all that isn't going to do me any good right now." She tapped the counter with her knuckle twice. "I'll see myself out now."

Mrs. Jane looked like she wanted to say something, but

Eve's attention flitted to the giant analog clock above the double doors leading outside.

It was almost four o'clock.

Which meant five wasn't far behind.

An hour and a half until I get married. Eve growled out at herself. *You sure did make a mess of things, huh?*

If she had known this morning what she did now, she could have avoided this whole thing. Instead, Eve pressed out into the cold of a true rare Georgia winter. She was wondering if Darius still lived out on Maple—wondered if his mama had kept her promise—but knew even if she ran out there, he was working. Seeing the old house wouldn't do a dang thing other than help her reminisce.

Eve pulled her coat closer and chided herself for not being the kind of woman who came up with backup plans when a couple walking past caught her attention.

The man she didn't recognize, but his deputy's uniform read *Gavin*. The woman, at least a foot shorter and a pregnant belly wider, was dressed sharply in slacks, a sweater and a leather jacket. A badge was clipped onto her exposed belt, but Eve couldn't see any name on her. Not that she needed shiny metal to recognize Wildcard Rose Little. A town menace to some, a hero to many, especially over the last few years. No one messed with the petite woman without regretting it. The same had been just as true when they were in first grade and Danny Ripken had refused to let Rose on his dodgeball team during recess. He'd called her *too little, just like your name* and had laughed a whole lot at what he thought had been a Grade A insult.

Rose had given him a few moments with it before pegging him in the face with a rubber ball. His nose had busted like a mighty geyser, followed by giant crocodile tears. Rose hadn't been finished.

"Did that hurt, just a little?"

One question filled with a sea of sass.

It had been enough to get Rose picked first for teams in dodgeball after, and now years later, the memory had made it easy to spot the adult version of that small spitfire.

She rubbed at her pregnant belly and kept on, not at all recognizing Eve.

But Eve had locked in on the first mention of their only detective's name. The second mention came quickly after.

"Darius said they were headed back from the hospital with the paperwork for the request, but we all know it's going to be a pain in the backside. Last time…"

Rose's words trailed away as she and Deputy Gavin made it to the department's front steps. Their retreating backs took the hope that had been snuffed out by Mrs. Jane and fanned it back to life.

The hospital.

Lane Medical.

With only one road connecting it to Seven Roads.

Eve jumped into her hatchback and was off in a flash toward County Road 22.

If she'd had a phone, if she'd had his number now, if she knew without a doubt that he wouldn't hang up on her the second she asked—

Eve growled out in frustration again.

The only chance she had was to look Darius Williams right in the eye and remind him of one old, simple truth.

Darius was hers.

And she needed his help.

The second Eve was on County 22, she pressed the gas pedal to the floorboard.

Chapter Two

Darius Williams was late getting on the road because, despite years of working relatively solo, he had begrudgingly taken on not one but *two* busybodies under his worn, tired and slightly annoyed wings.

Annoyed, not because they were a handful by themselves.

No. Annoyed because Oil was sitting in the back seat and arguing with Water in the passenger's seat.

The water portion of the problematic duo was sitting shotgun and rolling her eyes. She had a notebook open on her lap, notes neatly written out in tight rows and a fancy book bag at her feet. Winnie Collins, the little girl that the McCoy County Sheriff's Department had watched grow up alongside her young and extremely talkative father, Price, through the years.

Now she was about to graduate college, a budding professional in a pantsuit and a shocking reminder that time did indeed go fast when you weren't paying attention.

Though Darius couldn't help but see the preteen in her at the added huff she sent toward the oil portion of the duo in the back seat.

Darius hadn't watched Theo Weaver grow up, but he had caught the tail end of his teenager years after the sheriff had taken him in. Now he was a year out of college and had been officially adopted by the Weaver brood.

Which meant that Darius had somehow gone from the only detective in the county to the only detective in the county who had been talked into helping the oldest children of the McCoy County Sheriff's Department's most beloved.

Some of the newer hires might have balked at the pressure.

Darius, thirty-six, no kids and single, simply wanted turn up the radio to drown out their bickering.

Instead, he kept quiet as Winnie went for another pound of flesh from Theo in the back seat.

"Listen, I'm not saying *you're* wrong," she said. "I'm just saying *I'm* right. So do you want to keep talking about it or just agree to move on with the facts?"

"The *facts*?" Theo repeated, voice pitching higher and not at all showing signs of moving on. Darius heard the resulting rustling of the laptop bag that had been constantly glued to the boy's side. "Do you need to see the data again? I have it all right here, in plain text *and* code. All you have are *feelings*."

"Feelings?" Winnie shot back. "You mean my *experiences* with other human beings? You know, those things you can't talk to without getting on every single one of their nerves?"

Darius finally made it out onto County Road 22, but he knew the ten-minute drive to the sheriff's department would be the end of him if he didn't stop the young'uns from slandering one another.

So he cleared his throat.

Despite their drive to prove the other wrong, both Winnie and Theo quieted in an instant. At times like this Darius didn't mind the reputation he had gotten as the stonehearted dealer of death, an extremely dramatic depiction of a homicide detective, if you asked him.

"Having both the feelings *and* facts when you're trying to answer a question isn't a bad thing," he said. "When I solve a case I look for evidence *and* the story that fills the spaces in between. The head and the heart. If you don't have one, there's no point in having the other."

"But we're not looking at a homicide case," Theo pointed out. "We're trying to figure out if the new pharmaceutical company is actually doing their jobs or not. That puts me neck-deep in data, and data doesn't need a story."

"Data *plus* interviews from the admin, former patients and staff who worked in the research annex where the drug study was taking place *creates* a story," Winnie returned just as quickly. "One you are, for whatever reason, ignoring because you think facts and figures are never, ever wrong."

Darius stifled a sigh. He hadn't solved the problem but instead thrown more fuel on the fire. He rolled his eyes to County 22 through the windshield.

Then that eye roll went to nothing but focused attention.

A little hatchback was parked on the shoulder of road, emergency lights on, and driver's-side door wide open. A woman was standing in the middle of the road, coat pulled tight around her.

"Look alive," he told the kids.

Darius wasn't in a cruiser, but he reached for the walkie-talkie that was always in his personal vehicle, just in case. He slowed, taking in the details as his passengers did the same but with volume. Their feud turned to joint observation in a snap.

"She doesn't look hurt," Theo said from the back seat. "No blood or open wounds. The vehicle seems to be in one piece. The tires aren't flat. At least not the ones I can see."

He was right. The hatchback was facing the same direction as traffic but from there didn't seem to be any obvious reason it was disabled.

"She doesn't look distressed either," Winnie added. "Maybe a little excited?"

Darius put down his radio.

He agreed.

The woman didn't look worried or hurt or even a bit stressed.

She did, however, look familiar.

It was an odd feeling that pressed against Darius as he put on his hazards and pulled over onto the side of the road.

Seven Roads was a small town; McCoy County was bigger, but the faces rarely changed. He had been a career local, born to a woman born to the town, and had rarely left the county limits since. Where they were now wasn't exactly a hot spot of tourism or even a well-traveled road from simple passers-through.

Maybe she was a relative or friend visiting?

Maybe she was new to town?

Maybe she was just lost.

Either way she wasn't missing an inch of him. Her stare burrowed into him as he pulled to the shoulder.

Then she smiled.

Darius hesitated for the briefest of moments. That smile? It...

The woman started toward them, her pace obviously slower than the easy-to-see excitement spreading through her.

Darius left the engine running and handed the walkie-talkie to Winnie. The girl took it but threw out one last observation before he had the door open.

"She's wearing a wedding dress!"

The woman's steps were slow, but her coat fell open at the movement. She didn't try to cover herself back up as the white fabric became unmistakable against the backdrop of the old county road.

Why would a woman wearing a wedding dress be in the middle of County 22?

"Stay here."

Winnie and Theo were quiet as Darius left the warmth of vehicle for the crisp cold of the Georgia winter. It would turn his nose red if he stayed out in it for more than a few minutes. The woman had to have been waiting for a bit: her nose was red as she approached him.

That didn't seem to dull her excitement.

She stopped a few feet short and put her hands on her hips. The smile of excitement switched to an undeniable mischievousness in a flash.

"Well, if it isn't Darius Williams." She tilted her head to the side. "I was getting a little worried you'd somehow found a new way back to town since I've been gone."

His brow rose in question.

The woman seemed to be in her own world. Her gaze swept up from his feet to his eyes.

"I can tell you for sure the one thing that changed is how tall you are," she continued. "You outgrew me by almost a foot. Not sure if I like that, to be honest."

Darius had been the only detective in McCoy County for years. He hadn't seen a lot of things compared to bigger counties or cities—nothing that had left him speechless or staggering, at least—and even outside of work his surprises, scares and startles hadn't been much at all. Nothing to write home about. Nothing to flip, rock or shake his world.

He could take a hit.

He could dole one out too.

He could button up his emotions, and he could unleash hell, if need be.

Even walking up to a woman waving him down in a wedding dress wasn't enough to move the needle on his radar from *cautious* to *confused*.

But then the stranger moved her hand up above her head to emphasize how he was taller.

And that's how he saw the small scar along the side of it.

It instantly reminded him of the scar on his back, jagged and uneven. Darker than his olive skin color and easy to spot if he wasn't careful with the sleeves of his shirt.

If the location were different, it would almost look like they had tried to match—

Darius's eyes flashed to the woman's face.

At first the woman had been nothing but average. Nice-looking in a pleasant, fine way. Green eyes, brunette. Hairstyle that might be expected for a wedding and a smile that was all right. A woman who might not stop traffic but could stop one driver.

But now?

Darius saw something else entirely.

Someone else.

The scar seemed to be the secret password to unlocking an entirely new version of the woman standing in the road, wearing a wedding dress.

"Evie?"

The name came out of his mouth on reflex.

"I guess some things always look the same no matter how long it's been." She nodded and then dropped her hand with a little shake. Like it was the most normal interaction in the world, she continued with a smile still. "Though, I guess you might not have figured it out had I been in a crowd. So I'm not sure this counts all that much."

Her shoulders tightened, and her smile disappeared, all before Darius could mumble out a word in response. She tucked her hand and its scar into one of her coat pockets.

The scar that matched Darius's.

The scar that had changed his life.

The scar that would have been much worse had a little girl named Evelyn Myers not protected him with everything she had.

Now, scar out of sight, there might have been a fully grown woman standing across from him, but Darius couldn't help but feel like he was staring into the determined pine-green eyes of the same little girl next door back then.

"I have never once asked for it but, you, Darius Williams, owe me a favor," she said, smile absolutely wiped clean. Her next words were spoken with a familiar resolve that gave him no space for a response. Not that he would have known what to say if he'd had the time to do so.

"My wedding is in an hour…and I need you to stop it."

Chapter Three

There was something to be said for the passage of time. One day there was a gangly boy, subconscious and a little too quiet—wearing clothes that were a little too big—and the next there was a man standing in the place of his memory. Not completely unfamiliar, but absolutely not the same small boy Eve had met in the space between their houses when she was just as young.

Time hadn't paused because Eve had left.

Instead, it had built a boy into a man.

And it had apparently taken care to make that man quite the looker.

Darius Williams was one heck of a sight. There were no two ways about that. Built like a capital T, his upper body was wrapped in a button-up and corduroy jacket that fit him like a glove, and his Levi jeans hugged him right comfortable like an old friend. There wasn't a scrap of fabric on him that didn't fit him. Not an inch of awkward to see. In fact, Eve couldn't help but think if Darius ever wanted to leave the life of law enforcement behind, then he could make one heck of a living out of modeling denim for the masses.

It was obvious that he worked out or ate right or a little of both, she had decided as he'd walked across the asphalt to meet her.

And that was to speak nothing of the fine form that face of his was. Eve could see the boy she used to know in the coloring of his dark eyes and the overly serious set of his matching brow, but the rest had taken to growing up mighty fine. His jaw competed with the seriousness of his expression—hard and slightly intimidating—and he had undoubtedly grown into his nose. Though, it looked like it might have been broken in the time since Eve had seen it last. There was also a small scar at the top of his lip, barely noticeable but there all the same.

Eve saw it with ease before he had even stopped across from her.

Its corners never pulled up from its frown.

She had started to mentally comment on the slight wave of his dark hair—and how it, too, was a far cry from the buzz cut he'd been forced to keep as a kid—when a new reality had hit her beneath the smile she couldn't help but give when seeing him after all these years.

Darius hadn't recognized her.

Only after she had mentioned his height had she seen the connections start to form.

If she had had more time, Eve would have smarted at that. It wasn't like she had changed all that much since her preteen years. Her hair was still just as middle-of-the-road brown as it had been then. Her eyes, a muddling hazel. A few freckles, a jawline that was nowhere near as cutting and eyebrows that still rarely pulled together with such severity. While she had been cute when she was a kid, that cuteness had only grown into ordinary as an adult. It was, after all, one reason the gossip had been wholly unkind to her once it had been announced that she, an average woman on all fronts, was marrying into the Keys family.

Still, Eve couldn't help but feel a little sting at being overlooked by him.

But there was a time and place to think longer on such things, and as the wind bit into the skin above the cut of her wedding dress, Eve reminded herself that now certainly wasn't it.

Her last words still hung heavy in the air between them.

"My wedding is in an hour...and I need you to stop it."

Darius looked just as serious as before, if only a bit confused on top of that.

He finally responded, but it was only one word.

"What?"

Eve reined in all thoughts of the little boy whose voice had never been that strong and barreled into her bottom line.

"I'm marrying Mitchell Keys at the old library downtown at five thirty," she said. "The wedding planner acts like we're an army unit going to war, so I'm sure that's a hard five thirty, and even if I try to stall she'll find a way to cut my metaphorical legs off. So if you can't get there before and find a reason to stop it from starting, then you have until five fifty to do something. After that we're saying *I do* and being told to awkwardly kiss in front of everyone."

Darius was wearing a watch. Eve went for it. He was faster and batted her hand away.

"I'm sorry but I'm going to need more than that," he said, holding his wrist up and away.

Eve still tilted her head to see the face of the watch. The minute hand was a little too close to the two.

She had wasted more time than she had thought waiting for Darius to show up.

"There's not enough time to get into specifics. I just need the wedding to stop." She also needed to leave. The drive back would eat up at least ten minutes. She was already playing way too close to the line.

Darius didn't understand, and although she knew that was a valid reaction, that didn't mean knowing fixed the issue.

"Why don't you just stop your own wedding?" Darius's expression hardened ever so slightly. "Unless you're being forced to go through with it?"

Eve could understand that worry with the Keys family involved—what couldn't a family so wealthy get away with?—but this problem was solely hers.

"I'm not being forced, but I can't stop it myself." Eve grabbed his wrist to steady her gaze at his watch. Darius let her this time. She indeed had read it right originally.

Which meant she had to leave.

Now.

"Why not? What's going on, Evelyn?"

She didn't like the use of her full name, but Eve let his wrist go and took a step back.

"I don't care what you do to stop it, but please don't let anyone know that I asked you to do it." Eve watched as confusion washed over Darius's face. She didn't have time to explain so she reiterated the only point she had to convince him. "You do this and we're even, Darius."

Eve turned so quickly that her coat slapped closed against her chest. She didn't wait to see what his next move was. She didn't look back at him at all, in fact, as she started her engine and got back onto County. For the second time that day she pushed the gas pedal all the way down.

THERE WAS A road that was old, weathered and worn that only a few locals knew about. Most of those called it the Twig.

Just take the Twig, they might say. *If it's dry out and your tires are fine, use the Twig to shave off some time.*

Darius's tires and truck were fine—it paid that the department had their very own on-call mechanic in Rose's husband—and the rain hadn't been coming all that much since the cold snap had snapped at them in the last week. Taking the

Twig from County wouldn't get him stranded or find him in any inconvenience. It would simply take him from the big road to the mouth of Harper's Hill, a neighborhood that was a hop, skip and a jump away from the church on Main's parking lot.

Which just so happened to be across the way from the building that had once housed the Seven Roads Library.

Darius tightened his grip around the steering wheel. He hadn't moved the truck an inch since watching Eve drive off. The kids in his car hadn't moved either. Only their mouths had gone to work and, to be fair, each question had been valid.

"What's going on? What did she say? Where is she going? Are we following?" Theo's questions had come out in short, consistent bursts, concerned about the current situation and what came next.

Winnie had been more people-oriented in her queries.

"Do you know her? Are you all right?" she had asked on the boy's heels.

Darius hadn't yet answered anyone. Instead, since sitting back in the driver's seat, he had been doing everything in his power to calm down.

Evelyn Myers was back.

Evelyn Myers *was back*.

And she was getting married.

Darius felt his own jaw start to ache. He let his too-tight grip on the steering wheel go and rubbed a thumb beneath his chin.

You, Darius Williams, owe me a favor.

He did. He really did.

Darius checked his mirrors and pulled onto County. He didn't answer either kid's question. Instead, he flipped the script.

"What do you two know about a wedding going on today in town today?" he asked.

Theo was fast with a reply.

"The younger Keys brother is getting married, and the entire town is blowing it out of proportion. Wait. Was that the bride?"

Darius nodded toward Winnie. She didn't miss the direction.

"It's a big deal because Scott Keys is the groom's brother."

"Scott Keys," Darius repeated. The name was familiar, but he couldn't place it.

Winnie helped him out.

"He's known as the White Knight of Small-town Living," she started. "He finds ways to invest or bring in jobs that help rebuild more rural, forgotten or failing small towns. He had a few interviews at the steel mill here before he announced that his brother would be getting married in Seven Roads. Nothing's been confirmed, but the hope is that he's about to white-knight Seven Roads."

"But it's his brother getting married, Mitchell?"

That name wasn't at all familiar.

Regardless, Darius didn't like it.

Out of his periphery, he saw Winnie nod.

"He doesn't have a fun nickname or really any kind of popularity other than being called Scott Keys's brother. His media presence, at least, is pretty low."

"My bet is that his wedding wouldn't be that big of a deal if he wasn't marrying the White Knight's assistant," Theo tacked on.

"She's Scott Keys's assistant?" Darius asked.

There was a small silence. He bet the two kids shared a look.

"The bride-to-be is, yeah," Winnie answered after the moment. "She used to be a local… Is that how you know her? From when she lived here as a kid?"

Darius nodded, but even he knew it was tight.

"She was my neighbor."

Theo made a noise. Out of his periphery, Darius saw Winnie swat back at Theo.

"So that *was* her just now?" he asked. "What did she want? Was she waiting for you? Is there something between—"

"Theo," Winnie hissed.

"What? Don't act like you weren't asking me a billion questions while he was out there talking to her—"

Darius saw it up ahead and to the left. If you didn't know it was there, it would be easy to drive by. He glanced at the truck's clock.

If he wanted to get to the old library in time, the Twig was his only option.

But did that mean he was actually going to—

"Son of a—" Darius turned the wheel and bumped along into the Twig. Whatever Winnie and Theo were arguing about, they stopped.

"What are you doing?" Theo asked, but Winnie proved that she was less analytical than the boy. She had already made the jump to the more human problem of the equation.

"Are we going to the wedding?"

Darius cussed a good cuss.

"No," he decided. "We're not."

Despite good tires and an engine that could move mountains, the Twig bounced them good and dirty as he continued driving it.

"Well, we sure aren't going to the department this way," Theo pointed out.

Darius was growing hot under the collar. Bothered every bump and divot they drove over, annoyance growing like the clouds of sand his tires kicked up into the air.

Theo was right. He was heading in the opposite direction.

He cussed low again.

It wasn't like hiding it from them would do him any good. Darius was out of time to do anything other than floor it to the library. Plus, he couldn't just drop them off on the side of the road. Not only had he promised to watch out for the two, it just wasn't good policy to ditch the sheriff's son and one of their star deputy's daughters on the side of the road.

Though, for a moment, Darius did entertain the idea.

He would have preferred not to have an audience for what he couldn't believe he was entertaining.

"We're going to the wedding," he finally caved.

"Oh, so the bride just invited you," Theo guessed.

Darius tilted his head a little, trying to figure out exactly how to say what he needed to—and exactly what it was that he himself intended to do.

Without wanting to, he recalled the distinct smell of blood. So strong he had to fight the urge to touch the scar on his back.

He wasn't in that room anymore.

He wasn't that kid anymore.

There was no blade, no blood and no terror gripping his chest so tight he could barely breathe.

There was no girl with her arms around him, bleeding too, but not at all scared.

Yet, even though he wasn't thirteen anymore, there was the smell of blood filling his nose.

But, then, there was also bubble gum.

Faint but still a memory that had endured over the years.

The anger in Darius, the frustration and confusion, the feeling he couldn't quite define, floated away.

He took a deep breath.

Then he let it out.

"We're not going to watch the wedding," he told his passengers. "We're going to stop it."

Chapter Four

If Eve were being honest with herself, she hadn't spent much time in her youth imagining her future wedding, and the few bouts of fancy she had given herself as a kid had only ever gone one way.

Something small in the backyard, daisies and a sunflower or two around an arch her dad built, and some of those nice folding white chairs she had seen at Mrs. Dunphy's garage sale pushed in between her old refrigerator and the electoral box in the wall, sitting pretty on the lawn. There wouldn't be a lot of people there—of her own family, all she needed was her dad anyways—but there would be enough that they would have to buy a party platter from the home-cooking restaurant on Main for the reception.

Eve would wear some pretty white dress that poofed at the bottom and maybe put her hair up some nice-looking way. She'd paint her nails blue to match her groom's tie.

The groom, of course, would be the boy next door.

A little nervous but smiling wide like he did when they were watching movies or sneaking out to the Becker Farm's creek or passing notes between their windows.

Eve would walk down the aisle toward Darius without an ounce of hesitation because their wedding was inevitable.

She *had*, after all, made it very clear that he was hers for life, and wasn't that just another way to say *husband and wife*?

Now, though, reality showed Eve something quite different.

She wasn't strolling down the grass aisle of her backyard, arm looped around her father's, with sunflowers and daisies and a few guests in attendance. There was no poof to her tight designer dress. Her nails weren't painted a fun blue, and the groom certainly wasn't Darius Williams.

The Seven Roads Library had suffered a fire in the early nineties, and while it been repaired since, the main room no longer resembled its former glory. Instead of a large room filled with shelves and books and a librarian's desk, there was an expansive space surrounded by exposed brick, laid out in refurbished hardwoods, and a partially domed ceiling of glass.

The sunlight poured through that ceiling and made a design in shadows against a wooden arch at the end of the room. One that had *not* been custom-made by her dad but instead bought with Keys money.

The same Keys money that had the once-big room now feeling claustrophobic. They might have been in Seven Roads, not exactly the prime spot for upscale socializing, but almost every suit and dress in attendance had made the trip without fuss.

And they weren't there for the man in the tux Eve was walking toward.

No, they were there for the man at his side, movie-star smile warming an already-attractive face.

Scott Keys.

The White Knight.

Always wrapped in philanthropist glory, something designer and charm.

Everyone wanted him; some wanted to be him.
Eve wanted to destroy him.
And so did the man standing next to the altar.
Eve smiled at Mitchell as the wedding march ended. He met her at the one step up in the room, holding his arm out. He wasn't unattractive, but it was hard to see what made him shine while constantly being in his brother's shadow.

He had blue eyes that looked nice with his tan and obediently straight brown hair, while his fashion sense felt more natural than showy. When they had first met he had been wearing earrings in both ears and a bomber jacket that had felt extremely stylish. But that had felt like a lifetime ago.

Now, even at his own wedding, he wore a tuxedo that visibly paled in comparison to his brother's.

His eyes, though, they were kind as they took her in.

"You look beautiful, Evelyn," he whispered. She took his arm as she nodded to the compliment.

"You're pretty snazzy too," she returned.

A smile flashed across his face, not at all the same one he'd been wearing a moment ago. A genuine one of appreciation.

Not romantic love.

Because, even though they were both there of their own accord, neither one of them had actually planned on getting this far. Their plan had only included the ruse of dating, of getting engaged, not wedding bells and library chapels.

That had been Scott's idea.

"Family is the most important thing in this world," he'd told them, holding out his mother's ring to Mitchell. "It's the greatest wealth you can attain, so why not go ahead and become wealthier?"

Mitchell had had no choice to propose then—another part of his life taken over by his brother.

Six months later, and the memory still made Eve's blood start to boil.

Scott Keys was a man standing on a pedestal of his own making.

And she desperately wanted to knock him off it.

Mitchell's smile tightened as they stopped at their designated spots across from the man who had been ordained, hired and picked by Scott. He squeezed her arm once before letting go.

Eve understood that quick grip.

He wanted to know if they were really going to go through with the wedding. If she had managed to find the solution to their problem. If wherever she had snuck out to and gone that afternoon had borne any fruit, so to speak.

The man between them asked them to face one another.

Eve used the time to glance back down the aisle and at the double doors she had just walked through.

She didn't want divine intervention to stop their sham marriage.

She wanted Darius Williams to bust through those doors.

Eve mentally sighed.

How dramatic would that have been? she thought. Seeing Darius bust through those doors yelling "I object!"

It would make everything seem like a movie and earn Eve a chance to escape the problem that she had, in part, created.

Darius, however, didn't burst through the doors, and she turned around to listen to the officiant. The part where someone could object came and went without a peep. The vows came next, and Mitchell—not one given to public speaking like his brother—struggled through his.

Eve kept smiling through it all, even though the hope that Darius would show up was starting to fade.

Had she been too nostalgic? Had the request been too outrageous? Had their past stayed firmly rooted in the past?

Despite herself, Eve started to think about what happened next.

The honeymoon.

For completely different reasons, it made her blood run cold.

She resisted the urge to look over Mitchell's shoulder. His brother would also still be, no doubt, smiling too.

Neither one of them meant it.

"Now, Evelyn, it's time to read your vows." The officiant's voice sliced through her thoughts like a machete through butter. While there were many things that affected others, Eve had always had a way of going with the flow. Sadness, fear, anger…they rolled off her shoulders like water, and she just kept going.

But now, there was a coldness in her stomach that was starting to spread.

She shouldn't have let it get this far. She shouldn't have—

A loud bang sounded through the main room. Mitchell jumped, while a flurry of gasps and mutterings sprang from the guests. Eve, though, whipped her head around to look at the double doors.

The coldness in her warmed in an instant.

The doors were closing and standing in front of them was the little boy who owed her a favor.

Darius.

He'd come, and just in time too.

Eve was wondering how he would play the next part when the door opened again.

It was a man she didn't recognize. The star-shaped badge at his hip, however, was easy to see even from her spot at the altar.

The sheriff of McCoy County had a tight smile.
Darius wasn't smiling at all.

"WHEN I SAID stop the wedding at all costs, this isn't what I had in mind."

Eve's voice was small, but there was no shake or tremor to it. All things considered, it was impressive. Not many could see a dead body and manage some humor.

They were standing next to the mouth of a small hallway that fed from the old library's main lobby and into the area that used to house offices and the break room. The wedding party was spread between those rooms now. Mitchell Keys was in the break room with his brother.

A man wearing a gray suit was dead on the bench seat next to the closed double doors a few feet from them.

Eve cut her gaze away from the man and back to Darius. Again, he felt impressed at her composure. Then again, maybe it wasn't all that surprising. This was Evelyn Myers, after all. Even as a kid she'd had a habit of not blanching.

"His name is Gary Whittaker," she said, voice back to a normal volume. "He's the Keyses' family lawyer. Or was, I guess."

Darius had a pad of paper out, a pen in his other hand, but he didn't write anything down. Like the young Eve had had a habit of not swerving at whatever game of chicken she had been forced into, the young Darius also had his own habit of remembering everything the girl said.

He suspected time hadn't changed that ingrained skill.

Still, for appearance's sake, he held on to both.

"Family lawyer, huh?" he said. "Pretty close, I guess, to come to an out-of-town wedding."

Eve shrugged.

"When you have enough money, even the lawyers get

close enough to become part of the family. He was at almost just as many family events as I was."

"So you were friends?"

Darius didn't have to look back at the body to know the details. Once he had rushed into the lobby and noticed the man, it had been hard not to take it all in.

A man who appeared to be in his late fifties, early sixties, slumped over on a worn and weathered wooden bench. Not at all worn and weathered was his suit, charcoal gray, with a white button-up shirt beneath it. The white was pristine in all places except where it had come untucked at his waist. It was stained crimson.

The bullet wound that had most likely killed him was hidden beneath his coat.

For Eve, not much had changed about her appearance since Darius had seen her at County 22. Her coat was gone, and her hair had been pinned up. Another quick look down at her dress, and Darius couldn't help but think that the Eve of their younger years would have disliked such an uncomfortably tight thing.

He buttoned that line of thought as Eve sighed out long.

"I wouldn't call us *friends*, but we were familiar," she said. "As Scott Keys's personal assistant, I had more cause to run into him than most. Especially since he helped out with the philanthropy side of things."

She shook her head—not even a strand of hair moved.

"I don't know why anyone would want to kill him, though. Or why they would kill him and then put him here."

She motioned toward the late Gary Whittaker.

"And before you ask how I know he was killed somewhere else and then moved after, it's because there's not more blood," she added. "If anyone other than you had found him, they might not even have noticed he'd been shot at all."

She was right.

There was no blood around the victim. Not even a drop. He had been shot elsewhere and moved.

But why?

"When's the last time you talked to or saw Mr. Whittaker?" Darius asked.

He had to raise his voice a little to compensate for the chatter taking place across the room from them. The county coroner, Martin Blues, a newly hired crime scene investigator, and Deputy Gavin were professional when it came to their jobs. They were also social about it too. Darius had already had to skirt Martin on two other cases after the younger man had tried talking sports over a dead body. He understood trying to bring brevity into a heavy situation, but even the less-than-social Darius knew there was a time and a place.

Eve didn't seem to mind the new distraction. Her brow furrowed, and her frown deepened.

"The last time I saw Gary was back at the company."

"In Atlanta?"

She nodded.

"Scott had a meeting with a Green Suit and asked Gary to sit in. I didn't sit with them but ended up walking Gary to his car in the parking garage. He talked about the upcoming wedding and *his* wedding to his now ex-wife, but it was all just small talk."

Darius tilted his head to the side a little.

"*Green Suit?*" he asked. "Is that some kind of business term I'm not familiar with?"

Darius had the distinct impression that Eve almost rolled her eyes at that but held it in.

"Green Suits are what I secretly call the businessmen who don't mind donating or investing big money to the Keys

Foundation but, for whatever reason, don't like a little ol' assistant like me being in the room." She already had her arms crossed over her chest, but Darius noticed she tightened the stance. "It's the only time I'm okay with being a little passive-aggressive."

One of the office doors behind them opened. Darius kept his spot next to Eve but angled around to see whose heavy footsteps were headed their way.

It wasn't long before the sheriff's long face was staring right at him.

"Miss Myers, if you would excuse us for a moment, I need to have a talk with Detective Williams."

Sheriff Liam Weaver was a large, solid man of muscle and steel, but when he needed to cut his ingrained intimidation down, the smile his wife had helped him find over the years did the trick. His long face softened with the small upturn of his lips as he told Eve she could return to the wedding party.

Eve glanced at Darius but nodded and left without another word.

No sooner than he heard one of the doors shut behind them than the sheriff's smile all but disappeared.

"The talk with Scott Keys went that well?" Darius asked.

Liam's jaw tightened for a moment.

"He's not the Keys brother I'm worried about," he said after a moment. His already-low voice grumbled lower. "What all do you know about Mitchell Keys?"

That surprised Darius.

He answered with honesty.

"Only what the kids told me earlier. He's the younger, unpopular one of the two."

And Eve's future husband.

"Why?" Darius added.

Liam glanced across the room. Martin seemed to be done

with his initial pass. Darius would talk to him next, then go from there. Starting with retracing the man's steps and hopefully finding where he'd been killed. Then he would—

"I think Mitchell Keys might be our killer," Liam said, halting all of Darius's future plans in an instant.

"What?"

The sheriff sighed. He wasn't looking at Darius when he explained. Which was good, because Darius's usual composure momentarily cracked at what he said next.

"And I think there's a good possibility that the bride-to-be might have helped him do it."

Chapter Five

Eve was happy to get out of her wedding dress and slip back into more comfortable clothes. The slightly oversize knit sweater hung past the waist of her jeans while her tennis shoes felt like an apology to her poor feet. She had never been a heels type of girl, and yet she'd had to endure the tall traps she had promptly thrown back into her bag once she had entered the bridal party dressing room. The bobby pins forcing her hair into a headache-inducing tight hold were more of a production to get rid of. She only managed to pull half of them out before deciding the ones on top could stay until the last vestiges of adrenaline had disappeared. Because, ever since seeing Gary slumped over in the lobby, dead, Eve had felt like ants were crawling beneath her skin.

She felt for Gary. And she worried for her plan.

Not to mention the Darius of it all. After he and the sheriff had interrupted the wedding, she had believed a wonderful excuse was coming her way—something that would put a hiccup large enough in the proceedings that she would have more time to do what she needed.

But a murder?

That hadn't been even remotely on her list of possibilities.

A knock on the suite door sounded. Eve checked her reflection in the mirror to make sure she didn't look as chaotic as she felt and scooped up her bag. No matter who was at the door, she had already decided that she wouldn't be going back to the old library anytime soon. Especially not for her own wedding.

A familiar and not-at-all-liked face was frowning so severely that Eve had to fight the impulsive urge to shut the door as soon as she had opened it.

Maria Sanderson was a few years younger than Eve but acted as if she had lived twenty more lives than her at any given moment. Her confidence came from two places and two places only: her husband's money, and a lifetime of having everything she wanted handed to her. It was a slightly harsh assessment that Eve had made after meeting the wife of Scott Keys's best friend, Toby. But now, a year later, she stood steadfast in her opinion.

Maria had never liked a pragmatic, daily worker like Eve. The gossip that came with Eve, though? That was worth more than any friendship.

Maria was already talking the moment the door opened.

"I can't believe someone died at your wedding!" Maria followed Eve out of the room and down the hallway. She was still in her designer dress and covered in various accessories that sparkled even under the library's old fluorescent lights. Eve didn't miss the woman's gaze down at her now very underwhelmingly average outfit. On a normal day it would have most likely prompted a backhanded compliment of some sort. Today, however, Maria hurried past any veiled or not-so-veiled insult.

"Well, I guess calling it a wedding is generous, all things considered," she said. "The ceremony didn't even finish, and I'm guessing that rescheduling for later tonight isn't in the cards either, huh?"

Maria might have liked gossip, but she wasn't giving Eve

any space to provide a word. Her heels clicked and echoed through the hallway around them.

"The sheriff already told us all to go back to the hotel," she continued. "Toby already left to talk to management about extending our stay. He wanted to go with the sheriff and Scott to Gary's room to look around, but I told him we should probably take care of the guests who didn't want to stay here more than a day, you know? Just in case they're needed with the investigation."

While Maria had been talking, Eve had been inching them toward the library's lobby. Pointing out that a man's death was more important than a guest's potential discomfort didn't seem the right play, though Eve felt the urge to say it all the same. But unlike Maria, she knew there was a time and place for things.

Right now? All Eve wanted to do was talk to only two people. Maria was neither one of those people.

Still, Eve couldn't deny she was glad for the mini-update on what had happened in the time she had been sequestered to the bridal party dressing room to change.

Namely, finding where one of the two people she wanted to see next had gone.

"Is Mitchell with Scott and the sheriff?" Eve asked. "I can't get him on the phone."

Maria's eyes widened. Her lipstick's deep red looked oddly off-putting. The fluorescent lights really weren't doing anyone favors here.

"He's probably at the police station or department or whatever it's called. I saw him leave, but he got into a police car with some man in a uniform."

Eve paused in her short stride.

"He left in one of their cars?"

Maria nodded.

"Don't worry. He was sitting in the front seat, or else I would have said something, believe you me."

Why had Mitchell gotten into a deputy's cruiser at all? Why hadn't he gone with Scott and the sheriff?

Eve felt her brow knit together. Maria noticed but didn't understand the emotion behind it.

The diamond of her wedding ring had swiveled downward. It pinched a little as she patted Eve's shoulder.

"Don't you worry, I'll be talking to Toby and Scott about getting you two married as soon as possible so we can get back to civilization."

Eve didn't have the mental space to point out that Maria had just insulted her hometown and, instead, finally made her way out into the lobby.

After waiting in the offices for half an hour, then escaping to change, the old library's lobby had apparently been emptied. Gary's body was gone, and in its place some caution tape and a sign had been put up. All personnel and law enforcement were gone.

All but one.

Maria let out a little breath as both women saw Darius. There was definitely no denying he had more than grown up. Leaning against the wall next to one of the open front doors, he looked like he had stepped out of a magazine. Modeling denim, Eve couldn't help but think quick.

Maria must have also appreciated the sight.

When Darius pushed off the wall and came toward them, she cleared her throat ever so slightly. Then that too-dark lipstick moved into a sharklike smile.

Darius gave her a small nod, but his gaze didn't move from Eve. Which was good, considering he was one of the two people she was hoping to talk to now.

"Mrs. Keys, I was wondering if you wouldn't mind coming

with me for a statement at the department?" He sure looked like Darius, but the voice and name change certainly threw Eve for a mental loop. She felt her brow fly high in question.

Maria beat her to a response.

"Miss Myers, actually," she corrected. "Sadly, the ceremony was cut short, so she's still Myers. Miss Myers."

This time, Darius looked her way. He didn't smile but did step back to open one of the doors even more wide.

"Even more of a reason to get going." He motioned for Eve to go through the door. She gladly accepted the directive.

"I'll be going now, Maria. Let me know if anything else happens, okay?"

Maria wasn't used to being brushed off, and normally Eve would have been more polite with it, but given the circumstances, she assumed the faux pas would be overlooked.

Darius, however, addressed Maria's presence the second they were in his truck.

"I don't like her," he said, grabbing at his seat belt. Eve followed suit but added in a snort.

"If you showed her your bank statements, she wouldn't like you either."

Darius made a sound of mock pain.

"Way to leg-sweep me there, Eve."

Eve didn't scramble for any kind of apology.

"Scott Keys might be *rich* rich, but Maria is married to his best friend Toby. And Toby? Already had six figures in his bank account before he exited the womb."

Not that Maria was much different. While she wasn't the stereotypical trust-fund baby, her mother had married a business tycoon in Texas. As far as Eve knew, neither woman had wanted for a thing after that.

Darius started the engine and had them aimed out of the

parking lot, all while shifting expressions. His obvious distaste for Maria's attitude smoothed a frown into a neutral middle expression.

"If you're not a fan either, why was she one of your bridesmaids? Or, I guess, *maid of honor*."

That surprised Eve.

"I guess you're still good at the details," she said. "I didn't think there was time to look around before you and the sheriff shut everything down."

In fact, other than a quick look between Eve and Darius while they were on opposite sides of the aisle, Darius hadn't met her gaze again until they were each pulled out of the offices to talk.

"Just because I was stopping your wedding didn't mean I wasn't paying attention."

His tone was as matter-as-fact as they came. It bothered Eve.

Part of her had expected him to show up, part of her knew it had been a ridiculous request. Regardless, shouldn't he have been asking more questions?

Even without poor Gary's death, she would have expected more than inquires about Maria Sanderson.

But who was she to nitpick?

"When Scott realized I wasn't planning on having any bridesmaids, he thought it would be a good to ask Maria since she loves big, social events. Janice and Renee, the bridesmaids, are from the foundation."

"The foundation? You mean the Keys Foundation?"

Eve nodded.

"So you work with them, then."

"Yes. Coworkers."

They were driving across Main Street. Eve didn't take in the scenery. She knew Seven Roads had changed; she didn't need to know how much. What she had to do next was too important for her to worry about the outside world.

Even when it came to Darius.

"When can I see Mitchell? I haven't been able to talk to him since you pulled me out to talk earlier."

"We're going to him right now."

His neutral tone pricked a little.

Eve looked sidelong at him.

"I heard that Scott was helping the sheriff. Did they find something? Do you know what happened to Gary?"

Darius didn't look her way, even as they slowed to a stop at a red light.

"We're working a lead right now."

Eve waited for more.

She didn't get it.

"What's the lead?"

Darius kept his eyes right on the road. The badge on the chain around his neck still shone in the fading sunlight.

For the first time since being back in Seven Roads, Eve saw the boy next door for what he was now.

A man of the law.

And, she realized too late, that his offer to take her to the department might not have had anything to do with their past at all.

"Darius, what's the lead?"

In profile she watched him clench his jaw. It took a moment for him to answer.

And it wasn't even an answer at all.

"Let's wait until we're at the department."

IT WAS HARD to tell who was the most unhappy in the room. There was Liam with his thumbs hooked into his belt loops, brows drawn in and lips thin, standing at the head of the meeting room table. His chair was empty behind him. He didn't seem like he was going to use it anytime soon.

Price wasn't as robust in his aggravation. He had come into the room and sat down at his usual spot next to Rose. Despite her promotion, she looked more at ease next to the deputy, like old times. One hand was on her belly, the other was balled on top of the table.

Deputy Gavin, usually quiet, sat across from Darius with a frown.

The sheriff spoke first.

"I know we've been through a lot of tricky cases over the last few years, but I have to point out that this one is a bit more complicated than I would like. And we need to make sure we keep everything—*everything*—aboveboard. No breaking the rules for the greater good. No going rogue. No missed check-ins because we're all friends here. Got it?"

He pressed his fingertips down onto the tabletop but let his gaze sweep over each of them until everyone had nodded.

Darius also dipped his chin too.

Liam didn't seem as convinced. Still, he moved on.

"As of right now we still haven't found where Gary Whittaker was killed, but according to Doc Ernest, the cause of death was from the shot to his gut. Wherever he was before, he bled a lot. That's where I need you two to use your powers that come with being long-time locals." The sheriff motioned to Rose and Price. Even though Darius had also been born, raised and mostly stayed within the Seven Roads's zip code, Price had a penchant for gossip, and Rose had a way with locations. Her husband, the only local mechanic, also had proven to be an asset when it came to local information-gathering.

"He was staying at the new hotel with the rest of the wedding party and last seen this morning in the lobby. Doc Ernest says he hasn't been dead for more than a few hours. Wherever he was killed, we need to find it."

Rose nodded.

Price looked to Darius.

"Have you talked to the brother yet? Mitchell Keys?" he asked. "I heard it's not looking that great for him."

Darius hadn't.

Which led to one of the complications the sheriff now sighed about.

Rose picked up on the tension quickly.

"What? Let me guess. He started yelling for a lawyer?"

Liam shook his head.

"No," he answered. "His fiancée."

Darius felt the same flash of annoyance as he had when Mitchell had said the same thing to him no less than half an hour beforehand.

"What?" Price asked.

"He's refusing to say anything until he can talk to his fiancée, not a lawyer, not his brother. Just Miss Myers. And he wants to talk to her privately first."

Price snorted.

"Well, that's not suspicious or anything," he said.

The sheriff nodded.

"I agree. And normally we wouldn't even entertain that idea but—" Liam looked to Darius "—Detective Williams has done something that he apparently has never done before during the span of his entire career that's made me rethink our next steps."

Three heads turned in sync.

Darius didn't think it was that big of a deal.

Yet, he straightened his back as he spoke.

"I vouched for her. I vouched for Evelyn Myers."

Chapter Six

Her phone died sometime between arriving at the sheriff's department and being told to wait in Darius's office. It was unfortunate timing. And annoying.

Darius had left the small box of a room what felt like hours ago, but Eve logically knew it was probably closer to twenty minutes she sat there alone.

Unlike the boy she had once spent all her time with, this adult version called Detective Williams seemed to be more fond of debilitating silences instead of idle chatter. Once he made it clear that he wasn't going to give her a crumb of information about Mitchell or Gary's death, he had gone quiet in the truck. It had forced Eve to play around in her own head while she waited to arrive at their destination.

That play hadn't lasted long.

She kept bumping up against two problems, and neither one of them had an easy solution.

Gary had been shot and moved to the wedding ceremony, right? That meant something. But what? And who would do it?

The other problem was Eve's whole reason for the wedding in the first place. She had thought stopping the ceremony would give her what she needed to finally, *finally* take the almighty White Knight down.

Now?

Now she was sitting in the sheriff's department, her only partner in crime holed up somewhere else within the building, most likely a nervous wreck.

Not for the first time since Darius told her to stay in his office, Eve glanced at the door.

Maybe if she slipped out and went looking for Mitchell herself, no one would notice: she wasn't wearing her wedding dress anymore. It wasn't like she was anyone of consequence when it came to the guests she had been standing in front of a few hours ago.

Eve chewed on her lip, this time really contemplating the move, when the doorknob turned under her gaze.

Darius had a folder in one hand. He used the other to point to her mouth.

"Whatever bad idea you and that poor lip you always chew on have, go ahead and park it here," he said. "Let me remind you you're at a sheriff's department and not some movie theater you can go sneaking around in."

Eve blew out her own exasperation. She decided rolling her eyes was too much, but she knew her tone let him know it was missing.

"I'm not some kid anymore. I don't need you telling me what I should or shouldn't do."

Darius snorted. He took his seat opposite her. The framed picture she had already studied at length that sat between them showed Darius in the middle of a group of people at what looked like a mechanic's shop. Some of those faces Eve recognized as the law, others seemed to be their partners and children. Darius was sandwiched between an extremely tall man and a teenaged girl with pretty blond hair.

She didn't think the girl was his daughter, and several glances at his ring finger made her believe that Darius was single.

Or, at least, not married.

She wouldn't put it past him to leave the rest of his sentimental pictures at home. He had never been a big sharer, after all.

But, shared past or not, the present was more important than figuring out his current relationship status.

She needed to talk to Mitchell.

So she made sure he heard that need one more time.

"Can I see Mitchell now?"

Darius leaned back in his chair a little. The folder didn't leave his hand.

"Which is what your fiancé keeps saying too. Minus the seeing part. Instead, he keeps saying *talk*. 'I need to talk to Evelyn.'"

She felt a fake smile trying to hurry and hide her rising anxiousness. Darius had always been good at seeing through the few times she had put on a fake smile as kids.

Now wasn't the time to see if that skill still worked.

"There's nothing wrong with wanting to see or talk to me after something like this happened," she pointed out.

Darius was quick, but his words felt like they were lounging.

"No, not strange at all, but what has a few of us scratching our heads is who he won't let us talk to."

Eve felt her eyebrow rise.

"Who? Scott?" She shook her head a little. "You know Mitchell is his own man and doesn't constantly need his brother for everything." Eve didn't like how Darius looked so comfortable all of a sudden. To push her own point home, she contrasted his stance. She crossed her arms over her chest.

Darius's expression was impassive.

"Men with money and backing like the Keys typically call for a lawyer first."

"Gary Whittaker is the Keyses' family lawyer. You can see why he wouldn't be asking for him."

Even to her own ears Eve heard her voice go sharp.

Darius didn't budge.

"And, again, men with money and backing like the Keys can surely find themselves another lawyer when needed."

In hindsight, Eve would realize she had glossed over how the last word changed the entire situation. Mitchell needed a lawyer, not wanted one.

He *needed* one.

But Eve didn't hear the meaning in the moment. Instead, she simply doubled down.

"Maybe he needs me more. Now, can I see him or not?"

Darius was quiet a moment. Then he rapped the desktop with his knuckle twice.

"Yeah, you can, but under one condition."

"And what's that, Detective?"

Darius didn't skip a beat with his answer.

"I have to be with you."

A heaviness settled against Eve's chest. That would make talking impossible. Or maybe not. She looked into those dark eyes and wondered how much she could get past them.

Sure, they had once been inseparable, but then they had indeed gone their own ways.

Darius might have known her then. That didn't mean he knew her now.

"Only you?" she clarified.

Darius nodded.

Eve's anxiety spiked. She would also realize later that, in that moment, she also was skimming over one very obvious fact.

She *also* wasn't being given a choice.

Eve let out a small breath. Then she agreed.

"Let's go."

THE ROOM HAD a whiteboard against the wall on one side, a long table with chairs tucked underneath it in the middle, and Mitchell Keys in a tux against the back wall.

During Darius's career he had seen all kinds of people waiting in the big room. Victims, loved ones, witnesses, colleagues and suspects he didn't want to spook with an actual interrogation room. He had walked alongside them, let them lead or sat in his usual chair, waiting for them to be brought in.

He had seen reactions from every angle.

Sadness. Anger. Happiness. Apathy. Confusion. Exhaustion.

It all blended in a carousel of memory.

So he shouldn't have been surprised at the reaction the ill-fated, almost-married couple gave when Eve walked into the room ahead of him.

And yet, Darius couldn't help but pause in the doorway.

Mitchell Keys might not have been the same as his brother, but so far he had been holding himself with a rigidness that was nearly contagious. Anxiety and a twitch beneath the skin just itching to get out. Darius had expected that anxiety to lessen at the sight of Eve because that was what he believed to be a normal reaction. To see the woman you were supposed to marry after a tragedy kept it from happening? After you clearly hadn't been able to talk anything out with each other?

Never mind being the number one suspect in a homicide investigation.

However, the second Mitchell laid eyes on Eve, there was only one emotion that was so palpable that Darius nearly felt it too.

Relief.

Undeniable and absolute relief.

So much so that the man who had once had a decent height to him, lost an inch or so as he sagged into an exhale. In one moment he was taut, a rubber band ready to snap, in the next he was melted ice cream, pooling on the old carpet floor.

And Eve's reaction to *his* reaction was just as surprising.

She didn't mirror the relief. Not one bit.

In fact, when the couple met each other in the middle of the room, the tension that had fallen from Mitchell seemed to be freezing up into Eve. Like he had passed the buck through simple eye contact. Her shoulders were straight as a board by the time she reached him.

For the third time in the span of seconds, Darius was surprised.

Instead of some kind of intimate embrace or kiss, Eve simply reached her hands out and grabbed his.

Then she patted them.

It reminded Darius of a grandparent trying to assure a child who had just been scolded by a parent. Protective and loving.

She's not in love with him.

The thought flashed into Darius's mind in the steps between the doorway to his usual chair at the table. By the time he was settled into it, he decided the unprompted suspicion was, in fact, true.

Even if Eve hadn't asked him to stop the wedding, he would have drawn the same conclusion.

However, adding in the wedding itself: the social, easy-to-talk-to Eve had had no friends standing at her side; the bridesmaids were associates and hand-me-downs from Scott Keys; her family also wasn't in the audience. No Drake Myers, a father she had loved dearly when they were kids. No aunt. No cousins. No one.

Just a room filled with fancy outfits and concern at the interruption.

But not concern for Eve.

Even now, her fiancé wasn't the one offering reassurance. It was Eve who was comforting him.

Darius didn't know what it could possibly be, but he knew then that Eve was up to something. Given her genuine shock at Gary Whittaker's death, he didn't think a homicide was a part of whatever she was doing.

The jury on Mitchell Keys, however, was still out for Darius. It was why he and the sheriff had made sure that at least one of them would be in the room when the two reunited. Something that Mitchell didn't seem to mind at all. His gaze was glued to Eve's.

"How are you holding up?" she asked the groom. "My phone died, or else I would have already called."

Mitchell shook his head. While the sheriff had spent most of his time talking to the man, Darius had introduced himself at the library. He hadn't been verbose or charming then. Just simple.

Now there was a softness to his words. There was affection, but again, it wasn't what Darius had expected from a future husband.

"Scott was holding my phone for the ceremony, and I didn't get a chance to grab it back before he went off with the sheriff," he explained to her. "When I tried to call from one of the phones here, they wouldn't let me."

Darius switched his gaze to Eve at that.

Her shoulders stayed tight.

"It's okay. Everything is going to be fine." Eve gave one more hand pat. Instead of pulling away after, she kept her hand right on top of Mitchell's. From her profile, Darius could see her open her mouth a little and then close it. She waited a beat, then finally chose the words she seemed to want to say. "Everything we were going to do? We're still going to get it done. This only pauses our plans, not ends them, okay?"

Darius felt his eyebrow rise.

Mitchell nodded.

His *Okay* was just as soft as before.

Darius would have expected more talk between them, but Eve turned to face him, dropping Mitchell's hands in the process. Her voice changed yet again. This time, it was a tone he recognized.

Determination.

Pure and true.

"We have things to do," she said. "So what do we need to give you before we can leave? A written statement?"

Like Darius knew that Eve wasn't in love with Mitchell Keys, he knew right then and there that Eve truly hadn't put together one and one yet. That he hadn't taken her to the department to be reunited with her fiancé or simply do paperwork.

He wasn't her childhood friend right now.

He was Detective Williams.

A part of him didn't like the feeling.

The other part domed his fingers on top of the table.

He met Eve's stare head on.

"The only way he's leaving is if he has an alibi."

Eve's eyebrows slammed together in complete confusion.

"An alibi?" she repeated. "For what?"

Darius felt the weight of his badge against his chest. His answer was as clear as could be.

"For the murder of Gary Whittaker."

Chapter Seven

She wasn't a small woman, but she wasn't big either. Eve was average. Compared to Darius? Maybe that average lost a few inches. Physically, at least. She had to tilt her chin up to meet his eye but didn't need to put too much space between them to get a good angle to do it.

She jogged for exercise when she had the time and was toned in some places, squishier in others. The muscles Darius had built since he was a kid had even the toughest of hers beat three to zero.

He had the law hanging around his neck in a badge. Eve had Scott Keys's personal passwords memorized.

The differences in their divide were easy to see. Where one shone, the other flickered; where one ran, the other stood. And in the years since they had last seen each other, Eve felt like she had been the one who had stood the most still.

Yet height, muscles, past, present, badge or not, Eve felt confident that there was one area that little kid Eve still reigned supreme over Darius.

She had a mouth on her.

A Southern one, to boot.

And an angry Southern mouth? It yelled faster than it thought and sounded off with a syrup that could choke you if you weren't prepared.

Eve couldn't tell now if Darius had expected it, but she knew Mitchell hadn't. The moment her volume rose above her average height, she felt one of his hands at the back of her elbow.

It did nothing to calm her.

"And here I thought you were just trying to be nice to an old friend, but it turns out you were just buttering me up to lob an absolutely ridiculous accusation at my fiancé *on our wedding day*," Eve started in. "No wonder you were waiting for me at the library and offering me rides! Also, I track you down to ask you for help, and now I'm having to defend myself not even a few hours later? The absolute gall of you, Darius Fitzgerald Williams!"

Mitchell did a little squeeze against her skin.

Darius simply sighed out.

"I never buttered you up or lobbed anything at you, and I'm not being ridiculous," he said. "In fact, as you just said yourself, you were the one who came to find me. Not the other way around."

He left out the part where the reason she had come looking for him in the first place was to ask to *stop* the wedding she had just become defensive about. If Eve hadn't been so hot under the collar, she would have thought nice on the kindness of not pointing that out in mixed company.

Darius leaned forward a little and kept on before she could get rolling again.

"I'm asking a question about a current homicide case." Darius pointed over her shoulder but kept her stare. "And, if I say so myself, I'm being pretty polite about doing it here first and not throwing both of you into an uncomfortable interrogation room to do it. So, if you would stop using my full name like I owe you money and take a breath and a seat, we can get this all moving somewhere other than right into a fight. Does that sound good to you, Evelyn Rebecca Myers?"

Eve's nostrils flared. Her face scrunched. Both acts were like stretching before really starting to run. If she had been twelve, she would have kept going, louder than sin, but Eve the adult had picked up a little decorum in the last decade or so.

She also was starting to remember where she was and who was behind her.

If she had been solo in the same situation, she would have summoned more spitfire.

But she wasn't by herself.

Mitchell needed her, and no murder accusation was going to make her stop protecting him.

"You don't owe me money, you owe me *you*," Eve finally muttered, pulling back the chair closest to her. Darius didn't react to talk of their childhood promise and only watched as she settled across from him. He waited for Mitchell to do the same. Then he split his attention between both.

"While we haven't found the location where Mr. Whittaker was killed, we've been able to get his time of death down to earlier today, somewhere between noon and two o'clock," he started. "Since he was obviously moved to the location of the ceremony, it's hard to ignore the theory that it was a premediated event and not a crime of passion or one of opportunity. Which is why we looked at the wedding party for any information that might point us in a solid direction to start."

There was something to be said about dark eyes locking in on a target. Eve suppressed a little shiver as Darius moved his attention to Mitchell.

"And several fingers pointed your way, Mr. Keys," he said. "So now that Miss Myers is by your side, let me ask where you were today between the hours of twelve and two."

Mitchell had never been good at hiding his emotions; he was especially bad at hiding his anxiety. Eve knew the moment the question finished that he was already stressed about his answer. His body language, the hesitation in answering...

She also knew before he said a word that he was going to lie.

"I was in my hotel room. With Eve."

The lie was short. Its aftereffects were going to ripple far.

"You were in your hotel room," Darius repeated, tone impassive. "With Eve."

Mitchell nodded.

"I-I'm not big into crowds like my brother is. I was nervous and needed someone to help me calm down."

"So you asked to see the bride before the wedding. That's bad luck, you know."

Mitchell nodded again. The movement was stiff.

"I know, but seeing her always makes me feel better."

Like the lie, this truth was also short, but Eve knew it was genuine. She would have felt the warmth from it, had a coldness not started to spread throughout her body.

The fact of the matter was she hadn't been with Mitchell from noon until two. She hadn't seen him in person until she had been walking down the aisle toward him.

But could Darius prove that? Was there evidence he already had that Mitchell was lying? Had someone seen him or her out and about without the other during that time?

Instead of immediately agreeing, Eve tried to steer the conversation in a different direction.

"Mitchell had over two hundred people who can put him at the altar around the time when Gary was moved to the lobby," she pointed out. "He couldn't have done that. At least one of us would have noticed if he had stepped out mid vows."

Darius was quick.

"Just because he didn't move the body doesn't mean he didn't have anything to do with Mr. Whittaker's death."

"So you're saying you think he killed Gary and then—what?" she said. "Then, he had someone place poor Gary in the lobby after the ceremony started? Why? That makes no sense."

"I'm not saying anything at the moment," Darius shot back. "I was *asking* where Mr. Keys here was during the hours between twelve and two today. And now I'm asking *you* the same question."

Darius's expression remained impassive. His tone, however, had hardened.

Eve matched his energy.

"Mitchell already answered that," she replied.

"But you didn't." Darius leaned forward, those dark eyes on a new target. "So let me be clear in what I'm asking now so you can be just as clear with your answer. Where were you, Eve, during the hours of twelve and two today?"

Eve could picture the house in front of her. She could feel the grass under her bare feet. She could smell smoke coming from somewhere in the neighborhood, probably someone grilling in their backyard. She remembered shivering at the cold but not as bad as she would later, since she hadn't yet changed into her wedding dress yet.

Her childhood home.

That's where she had been earlier that day, still undecided about what to do next to get out of the wedding. To stop from being legally tied to the Keyses. To instead use the change in their crumbling plan to her and Mitchell's advantage.

She had just been staring and thinking about the present and future. Then, without realizing it, nostalgia from the past had swept her worries away for a while. Only a glance at her watch later had pulled her from her quiet recollection.

Whatever plan she would make would have to come after she donned her wedding dress.

So at 1:42 p.m., she had left the front lawn of her childhood home and hurried over to the bridal party's dressing room at the old library to get ready. No thoughts of using Darius had crept in until she had taken off her engagement ring and caught sight of the scar on her hand.

Before that?

She hadn't seen or talked to Mitchell at all during those two hours.

It was one thing to not correct Darius about Mitchell's lie.

It was another to lie directly to his face.

But Eve wasn't back in town to reminisce about the boy she had once promised to take care of for the rest of their lives. She was there to stop a man filled with greed, malice and power.

Eve took in a deep breath. She released it as she spoke clearly.

"I was with Mitchell Keys in his hotel room."

And, just like that, Eve lied to become a murder suspect's alibi.

However, the worst part?

She knew that Darius knew it too.

HE WASN'T ONE to pitch a fit but there he was—pitching it.

Darius threw his bag down against the couch. Like the rest of the furniture in his house, it wasn't new, but it definitely wasn't worn either. He rarely spent time lounging around, and that went double for lounging around in his home. If there was any one spot in all of Seven Roads that was worn because of him, it was his desk chair at the office or the strip of carpet that ran in front of his desk at home.

He was a man who was used to living in his work, pacing in his home, and only using his off time to do the necessities in life.

It was how he had been living between the walls of his childhood home since he had been the last one left.

Pitching a fit? Throwing a tantrum? Being annoyed enough to throw his bag and then start cussing?

That was the part of his work and life routine that was abnormal.

As was the fact of someone already inside of the house, answering back.

Theo Weaver hurried into the living room with a frying pan in one hand, a cell phone in the other and an expression that looked split between caution and fear. Add in the fact that he was wearing the joke apron his dad had bought Darius a few years back that read *Don't kiss the chef, I have trust issues* and the sight might have been comical enough to force Darius to see the humor in it.

Instead, he grumbled deep.

It was the first time since Theo had moved into his guest bedroom after his graduation that Darius had legitimately forgotten that he now had a temporary roommate.

One who was, unfortunately, very smart.

Trying to avoid the obvious wouldn't work here.

Theo's wide eyes lost their worry. He lowered his phone but kept the frying pan level.

"Are we good?" he asked in greeting. Theo eyed the bag Darius had just thrown. Darius ran a hand through his hair and took a beat to crack his neck to the side.

"Sorry," he said. "It's been a day."

Darius belatedly looked around for signs of another bag or purse. Theo caught the sweep.

"Winnie already left," he said. "She said she couldn't concentrate on her interviews after everything that's been going on." He smirked. "Between you and me, I think she just wanted to go gab with her dad and JJ about the whole wedding drama."

Darius suppressed another grumble and followed Theo into the kitchen.

"Winnie doesn't like gossiping," he reminded the boy. "It's one of the better traits of yours that you share with her. You two only give what you need to, and even then, it's like an act of God to get information out of you. I can't imagine if you two ever made another human together."

Theo made a noise of disgust.

Darius didn't think it was genuine, but he let his joke lie.

A bowl filled with scrambled eggs, sausage and other little things was on the counter. Darius was surprised to see a second one next to it.

"Winnie told me to make you whatever I was having for dinner and put it in the fridge just in case, but I guess your timing worked out," Theo explained. "Though, honestly, I thought you wouldn't leave the department at all tonight."

Darius felt some of the anger in him release a little. He gave the boy a pat on the shoulder and a quick thanks. He made a mental note to return the favor to Winnie sometime soon. For all their fights and youthful annoyances, there was no denying these kids were thoughtful.

They settled into the small dining nook and ate their breakfast-for-dinner bowls in silence. Darius might have vented a little, but his shoulders lined with a tension that seemed to seep downward and spread. It was only after Theo placed his fork into his empty bowl that Theo addressed it.

"I'm guessing the Mitchell Keys lead didn't pan out," he said, as neutral as the sheriff when he was being matter-of-fact. Darius glared. Theo raised his hands in self-defense.

"Winnie and I might be stars in the tight-lipped department but that can't be said for a good majority of McCoy County's finest. Try as everyone might, some information slips out."

Darius knew that no matter how hard he tried to keep a lid on the investigation Theo was right. Details and information would get out.

That's why he hadn't yelled at Eve right then and there in the meeting room.

You're lying, he'd wanted to shout.

But, for one, he had never yelled at Eve a day in his life, and he wanted to take that achievement to the grave. And, for two, if anyone found out that Eve was lying about an alibi—an alibi in a murder investigation, to boot?

Darius shook his head now even at the thought.

It would get out. It would put suspicion on her. It could ruin her.

But what if she is involved? What if she's covering for Mitchell?

These two thoughts had been on repeat since he'd had to let the couple leave. Darius hadn't for a moment thought Eve had killed Gary or had a hand in his death, but would she really cover for Mitchell if *he* had?

It was a question that grated against Darius.

Maybe he had been wrong about her relationship with the younger Keys brother. Maybe she was in love with him. She was, he believed, lying to law enforcement for him. That wasn't some typical friendly thing to do, was it?

Theo was still looking at him.

Darius sighed out and let his fork clink into the bowl beneath his hands.

"Everyone in the wedding party alibied out," he skirted. "Almost all the guests came into town right before the wedding. There were only six who could have been here during the kill window. And, of those six, none had connections to Mr. Whittaker."

"And no one knows where he was actually killed yet," Theo added. Again, he raised his hands in defense. This time he added a smirk. "You can blame me hearing that from the sheriff himself. He pulled me and Blake into a video call to ask us career locals about places around here y'all might have not thought about."

If it had been anyone else other than Blake, Liam's wife, Theo's adoptive mother, and one of the fiercest former sheriffs he had ever known, Darius might have taken offense at asking outside of the department for help. Instead, he knew to be grateful she had taken time out of her own job to try and give them more than they had.

Which was still almost nothing, if Darius were being honest.

"I'm assuming, since I haven't been called in, that nothing came from that conversation?" he asked.

Theo made a gun with his hand.

"Bingo. Blake couldn't think of anything y'all had missed, and now that she's been back in town for years, she's more of an expert on this town than me."

Darius rubbed at his neck. Sighing wasn't going to do a thing, but he felt the urge again.

So there was a strong possibility that it happened outside of Seven Roads, making an already-difficult search even more so.

"This is one of those few times I wish a victim had been more into social media," Darius said after a moment. "Mr. Whittaker's last few days have been hard to pin down. We can't even confirm yet when he first got into town. He's not married or in a relationship either, so there's no one who seems to have had a good itinerary for him leading up to the wedding. Usually social media can help us with things like that."

For the next few minutes, they went back and forth with questions and answers that Darius had, for the most part, already gone over back at the department. No new insights sprang up, and no missing information shook loose.

Darius's patience, however, dissolved into a tiredness that he decided not to ignore any longer. He warned Theo not to stay up too late, washed his dishes and only paused in the kitchen doorway as an afterthought.

"You and Winnie never asked about it, but I want to explain."

Theo turned his way, bowl in one hand, dish soap in the other. His eyebrow rose. Darius, so sure in every word he spoke about work, felt an uncomfortableness ease into an explanation he hadn't originally intended to give.

"Evelyn Myers used to live in the house next door," he started, motioning to the house outside to the right. "We were friends as kids until her dad got a job up north and they moved. Today was the first day I'd seen her since then."

"And she thought you two were still close enough to ask you to stop her wedding?"

It was a fair question for anyone to ask, and Darius couldn't fault the boy for his bluntness.

In return, he gave a simple answer.

"I'm not sure why she wanted the wedding stopped, but I owed her a favor, so I was going to do it."

"That's a big favor to ask," Theo said. "She must have really done something big for it to hold water all these years."

Again, Darius stuck to a truth that was as honest as they came.

He nodded.

"She saved my life."

He didn't explain further, and Theo didn't pry past that. Darius moved down the same hallway he'd walked since he had learned how to walk but paused at the door on the right. It was Theo's room now: years ago it had been his.

Part of Darius was glad to have moved to the main bedroom at the end of the hall—it was bigger, he'd updated it, and there was an attached private bathroom that was nice too—but sometimes when his mind went to the past, he missed the one thing that his new room didn't have.

The view from its window had been one of a kind.

This time, Darius did sigh.

It came out low and long enough to carry him back to the present.

That night he fell asleep quickly.

In the morning, he was up before his alarm went off at seven.

Despite forgetting to turn the heat on, he was surprisingly warm.

Then that warmth moved.

Someone was next to him in bed.

Darius's eyes were open in a flash. Adrenaline exploded in his veins, and every muscle he had seemed ready to spring into action. It was only by the grace of God that he recognized who it was pressed against his side before his fight instincts fully kicked in.

The person in question was unbothered by the internal struggle.

Then again, Evelyn Myers had always been a heavy sleeper.

Chapter Eight

Raina Myers was a nice, fair woman. She wasn't unkind or abusive, didn't cuss or yell. Paid full price, donated to charity, and always drove the speed limit. Her grades had been good, her friends happy, and even though her parents had died young, she had been old enough to cherish them. Most everyone who knew Raina even believed that the love she'd shared with her parents would transfer to her future children after she had married.

So it took longer than it would have otherwise for most to admit—in hushed waves of gossip—that those people were wrong. Raina might have been a nice, fair woman, but when it came to being a mother, she'd decided she didn't have time for it.

That's why the smallest Myers was still outside long after the sun had gone down the first time she met Darius Williams.

The then-seven-year-old had been trying to run away and had been horrible at it. Something that the six-year-old Eve had had to point out.

"You'll hurt your leg if you do it that way."

Her voice had been small but easy to hear in the side yard between their houses. She had a bat in one hand while the other should have held a softball had she not lost it. She had decided to play golf with the two and had realized quickly that the porch lights and streetlamp in the distance weren't doing the best to illuminate her makeshift golf course.

It had been quite the shock to see the neighbor's window slide open and a boy around her age start trying to climb out.

He, on the other hand, seemed to be much more shocked. Once her voice broke through the quiet of the night air, his backward climb out of the window turned into more of a downward spiral. It wasn't that far of a drop, but the angle was all wrong, and Eve knew all too well that it was the angles that got you most of the time. She'd once jumped from the back of a pickup truck with ease but had misstepped on the porch stairs and landed wrong enough to twist her ankle.

She'd cried for a long time after that.

Now she knew to watch for angles.

The boy was going to hurt himself if he fell the way he was going, so Eve dropped her bat and closed the space between them just in time to become a pillow.

She tried to stop his fall but instead met him as he fell backward. They hit the grass with a little more than a thud. Eve had her arms wrapped around from his back to his chest and kept her hold a few moments after everything had stilled.

He wasn't heavy enough to knock the breath out of her, but the book bag that he had thrown out of the window before his scurry down looked like it would have done the trick had he been wearing it.

Eve glanced at it as the boy rolled off her to the side and sprang up to his feet. His eyes were wide and dark as they were finally about to take her in.

"You—you're the girl—" he pointed to her house "—you're the neighbor."

Eve laughed and stood, dusting off her jeans.

She pointed to the window opposite the one he had just fallen from.

"Eve Myers. That's my room." She gave him a questioning look. "Who are you? I haven't seen you before."

The couple who had moved into the house next door had done so while Eve had been at school. Or maybe when she was out at the park. Maybe it had been when she was trying to sneak onto the Becker farmland that wasn't too far from where they were now.

Either way, she hadn't known the new owners had any kids.

Suddenly, she found herself extremely excited at the prospect.

The boy was shy in his nod.

He rubbed at his arm.

"I start school next week. My name's Darius."

The rising excitement was too much for the small Eve. She dropped her bat and jumped up and down in place.

"*Finally*, I can have someone to play with," she exclaimed. "I get so bored here by myself! What are you doing now? Do you want to play golf?"

She scooped the bat back up and held it out like a queen presenting a knight with his sword.

"I'll let you go first," she added. "We just have to find the ball. I was hitting it in the front yard, but it rolled to the street, and I think I hit it a little too hard to get it back, and it *sounded* like it might have hit that gutter…"

Eve rattled off all the possible trajectories she believed her ratty softball had gone, half expecting him to stop her and half expecting him to ignore her if she managed to finish her train of thought.

However, the boy who had just fallen out of the window turned those wide eyes and their dark gaze around to the unexplored space between the houses. Eve followed him as he walked over to the tall parts of the grass toward the back corners and bent over slightly.

By the time she realized he was searching for the ball, he had found it.

Darius presented the surrogate golf ball to Eve without comment.

Eve was grinning ear to ear as she took it.

"This is going to be so much fun!"

The next few minutes she explained her rules, gave Darius some tips and challenged the boy to a new game. And that's what they did for next hour or so. Chatted and played. Eve didn't ask why he had been trying to leave, and Darius didn't ask why no one seemed to notice that Eve had already been gone.

It was only when Eve yawned out big that she decided her bed was calling her name.

"Do you need me to help you climb back in?" Darius asked, pointing to her bedroom window.

Eve shook her head.

"I can just go through the front door," she said. "No one will notice."

Eve nodded to the window across from hers.

"Want me to help you climb?"

Darius seemed tall enough to be able to do it himself now that he wasn't going backward.

"I can pull myself back in," he said.

Eve was so excited that the boy had chosen not to complete his plan of running away that she threw her arms around him in a quick hug. He stiffened in her embrace and still looked uncomfortable after she let go.

But Eve didn't care. She finally had someone to talk to.

She tossed the bat and ball into the grass and pointed once again to her window.

"I'll open my curtain when I get inside so you can see me!"

And that's just what she did. After running through her house, slowing slightly at her mother's door, and then bounding into her bedroom, Eve flung open her bedroom curtain and looked out.

Darius sure was impressive. He was already back inside his room. His window was still open. Eve was impatient as she opened hers too.

"Do you want to play tomorrow?" she asked, trying not to be too loud.

"I'm grounded for the weekend," he called back. "I can't leave the house."

Nothing was going to—or could—stop the excitement that Darius's sudden existence had unlocked in her. Not even his parents.

"Don't worry," Eve yell-whispered. "I'll come to you."

The next night that's exactly what she did. When his parents went to their bedroom, Darius unlocked his window to find a green-eyed girl staring up at him. He pulled her and the bag of toys up the wall and over the windowsill with relative ease.

After that, it became a routine. Darius kept his window unlocked, and whether it was daytime or not, there was always an Eve who eventually crawled on through. Sometimes they would play, sometimes they would just talk. As they got older, the foot of his bed became their dedicated homework-and-study spot. When things at their respective homes became difficult, the time spent in his room became longer.

Then, one night, Eve hadn't left.

A storm had made her empty house seem terrifying for

once, and Darius had done what he did best and knew what she needed without asking. He'd given her his bed and made a pallet for himself on the floor next to it. Eve had fallen asleep to the sound of his voice while the storm raged on outside.

That was how Eve realized there was only one thing in her life that was certain, and that one thing was Darius Williams.

HER HAIR WAS WILD, thrown across his pillow and arm like an escapee finally sensing freedom. Her clothes were a little more restrained. She was wearing jeans, a black tank top and socks with rainbows printed on them. Darius only knew this because the side of her that wasn't touching him was partially uncovered.

Eve was a kicker in her sleep.

But he only knew that from having seen her thrash around from a safe spot on his floor when they were kids.

He'd never experienced it in his bed.

With him in it.

Eve's little movements turned into a big stretch and yawn. Darius, unsure of exactly what to do, waited until her eyelids slowly opened.

She blinked a few times before angling her head to the side to look up at him.

When the green met his dark, he reacted instinctually.

"What the hell, Eve!"

Like some shy teenage boy, he bolted upright. The sheet and blanket slid down his bare upper body. He clutched at them, pulling then back up. The memory of him silently trying to decide what top to wear after his shower the night before—and ultimately deciding not to wear anything at all—flashed through his mind.

Thank goodness he'd opted for bottoms, at the very least.

Eve also sat up but with way less effort and concern. She rubbed at her hair and then motioned to the closed bedroom door.

"What the hell right back at you, Darius," she said. "I almost climbed into the wrong dang room with another whole man in it! Since when did you change rooms?"

Darius couldn't believe what he was hearing.

"Since I bought the house after Dad moved to Montana— Wait. You tried to get into Theo's room? Did he see you?"

Eve was fast with that. "No! Once I realized the window was locked, I finally really looked through the gap in the curtain and realized he was too young to be your grumpy butt. Who is he?" For the first time since waking up, she finally showed some form of panic. "Wait. Is he *your kid*? You're not married! I checked!"

Her voice had gone high. On reflex Darius slapped a hand over her mouth.

"Stop crowing so loud, woman," he hissed. "And no, not married, and no, not my kid. He's Sheriff Weaver's boy."

Darius had enough muscle memory in him to know that he better let go quick before she bit him, so he dropped his hand with a warning look thrown her way for good measure.

To her credit, she adjusted her volume.

"The sheriff's son? Why are you living with the sheriff's son? Is the sheriff the one who moved in next door?"

Darius held up his hand in a *Stop* gesture.

"Theo just graduated college and is interning," he explained. "He has a lot of young siblings at home and wanted a little more quiet when he came back to town. I offered my spare room until he could save a little more money for his own place. And no, the sheriff isn't the one who bought the house next door."

Eve flopped back in the bed like she owned it.

"Well, if there's one thing you're good at, it's being quiet," she said. "Playing hide-and-seek with you as kids was harder than any waitressing job I've had since."

"That's only because when it was your turn to hide, you couldn't stop giggling," he pointed out. "I didn't need to be good at hide-and-seek. I just needed to wait for you to give up because you were bored."

She tapped her feet together and didn't disagree.

Then Darius came back to his senses.

He turned to face her completely. The top sheet and cover fell again at the movement. This time he didn't bother with them.

"Eve," he said, voice stern, "why are you here? In my house. *In my bed?*"

She sat up in a flash, clearly offended.

"What?" She pointed to the floor beside the bed. "Did you expect me to sleep on the floor like when we were kids? Not to point out the obvious, but this bed is gigantic compared to your old bed. There's plenty of room for like three of me to fit here." She swept her hand over her lap and toward him to, he assumed, show all the space there was around them. However, there were two problems with that.

One, there was no space between them. Or, at least, there hadn't been when they'd first woken up. Two, her hand paused in midair. Her gaze did not.

It was as obvious as the moon in the night sky that Eve had just put together the fact that Darius wasn't wearing anything above the waist.

"Wow. I guess you turned into one of those guys who exercises, huh? Look at all these muscles. And here I thought I was in good-enough shape."

She reached out her hand, and he knew with every bone

in his body that her intention was to feel said muscles. Because she was Eve and he was Darius and, a long time ago, they were Eve and Darius. She was comfortable with him; he'd built a door in the wall that always was around him for her.

Being this close was nothing for them.

Yet, just as he could see the old scar along the side of her hand, Darius could see the engagement ring on her finger.

Both were quick reminders that time had indeed separated them.

Darius caught her hand before she could make contact with his chest.

When he spoke, his words had a warning carefully carved into the tone.

"Eve, tell me right now why you're here."

Her hand was warm in his.

The rest of her went tense.

With one look, Darius knew she had finally come around to being serious. Talk of their past, of their friendship, of the years between then and now all went to the back burner.

Eve sighed out sharply.

Her words came out steady.

"I think I know who killed Gary Whittaker."

Darius's eyebrows rose.

"Who?"

Eve didn't flinch.

"Me," she said. "I think it was me."

Chapter Nine

He was still mad. Big mad. Mad enough that even sitting in the cab of his truck half an hour after her admission, Darius was still giving her the cold shoulder.

And Eve couldn't take it anymore.

"I said I was sorry," she tried. "I'm big enough to admit that maybe I crossed a line by coming to you with this now."

Darius snorted.

"You mean breaking and entering into my house and bed and then casually telling me you've been lying about a homicide case? Eve, you couldn't even turn around and see the line you've crossed, because it's so far back."

He turned off the engine and slid the key into his front pocket.

"The window was unlocked so it was entering, not breaking. And I lied to you about Gary because I didn't even think about it until last night when I was in bed. So it wasn't really a lie. It was just a connection that I hadn't made yet." She held up her finger. "Though, I have to remind you, as soon as I made it, I came over to you."

"And instead of waking me up, you got under my sheets."

The memory of the bare-chested Darius popped into Eve's head so quick that she stumbled in her response.

"I—Well—I—" She took a breath. Her cheeks grew

warm. Darius was a looker, no contest, but she hadn't expected looking *at* him like that would do as much as it had done to her. Eve fought the urge to try and wipe the blush that was no doubt turning her cheeks as red as a Stop sign and powered through her defense. "I figured it was better to let you sleep since this didn't seem like a problem that would get worse with a few hours. Plus, if I'm being honest, I haven't been getting the best sleep over the last month or so, and your bed is a memory foam. It would have been harder to stay awake."

An expression she couldn't read flashed across his face before Darius turned to look out the windshield. In all of Seven Roads this was probably the one spot he hadn't expected her to direct them toward.

To be fair, it had been a surprise to Eve too when she had thought about it.

"You said you think you got Gary Whittaker killed here?"

The former Grayton Steel Mill, now owned by a company called Bellview Tech, stood sentry at the edge of Seven Roads as it had since the town's inception. The small town could survive the earth cracking in two beneath them, but they couldn't make it a week if the steel mill ever went out of business. Even Eve knew this, despite being away for years.

As the employer for most of Seven Roads, it would probably outlast all of them, their children and their children.

It was one reason why she knew Darius was so hesitant to believe that Gary Whittaker had been killed inside the back quarter of the mill's residence hall. Gary wasn't a local. He would have had no reason to be at the steel mill, never mind the residence hall.

"Most of the dorms are empty, minus a few night workers and the weekend crews who come in twice a month," he added before she could answer. "There's no reason Gary should have been here."

The residence halls were in two long buildings wrapped in brick abutting the edge of one of the steel mill's wire fences. They were parked at the side of the dirt road that led in from the main one. It looked as unused as the buildings themselves.

Eve squared her jaw.

"Because I told someone once this is the last place even a local would go for trouble."

"Someone? Do you mean Mitchell?"

Eve opened the truck door. All humor and teasing she'd had in her for the man behind the wheel was gone. The blush at her cheeks had already cooled before the cold outside met her.

"If I'm right, I'll explain everything," she said skirting his retort. "Until then, can you trust me?"

She formed it as a question but didn't wait for an answer. Eve shut the door before he could respond. She was crossing the line again, she was sure. A detective was asking her valid and reasonable questions.

And she was telling him all hands inside the cart until the ride has come to a complete stop.

Even if he hadn't been the law, it was asking a lot given the situation.

What could she do but go forward?

Darius, at least, didn't fight her on it. He walked around the hood of the truck and fixed his belt. In between Eve sneaking back out of his window and across the side yard to his truck and him leaving the house, he had put himself into a good pair of jeans and a gray-and-black bomber jacket. Along with his height, it created a look of casual but potent intimidation.

That went double when his voice ground out low.

"Let's go, then."

The gate wasn't anything to speak of, and the same went for any security cameras or guards in the area. Darius commented on it as he nudged the gate open with his shoulder and motioned her through.

"Theo used to work here part-time in the cafeteria and said the new management cares as much as the old crew about keeping the back quarter guarded."

"So they don't care at all either."

He nodded.

"No reason to waste money watching nothing," he said. "Honestly, I'm surprised they haven't shut this entire section down. Or at least demolished it to build something else here. The new company that took it over seems to have more than enough funds to do it."

So she had been right after all. Her off-the-cuff story about the residence halls had stayed true even after she had left town.

"Dad used to hate staying in them during his long shifts," she said. "He said he imagined it was like being in a college dorm, but instead of a bunch of guys goofing around and having fun in their gym shorts, the men's residence hall was filled with grouchy men in sweaty coveralls. And they always stole his lunch out of the fridge."

Darius slowed as they approached the first pathway leading to the women's residence hall to their right. She quieted. Other than their footsteps, there were no other sounds.

The one-story building was an eerie setting against the cold silence.

She waited for Darius to make a silent decision. Once he kept moving to the path that led to the men's residence hall to the left, she followed.

Her stomach started to twist as they got closer. Her nerves sharpened. Eve almost jumped when Darius spoke low again.

"How is your dad doing?" he asked. "I didn't see him at the wedding."

Eve had been asked countless times over the last few months why her father wasn't attending the wedding. Why her family wasn't there. If she realized how sad that would look in pictures. In the press.

Or how lucky she was to have no one there but Scott Keys and his family and associates.

She had had the same stock responses ready to go until they had become a reflex instead of a response.

It's why the lie almost came out first.

Eve ran her thumb across the scar on her hand and pulled the truth out instead. At least, the truth about why he wasn't there.

"He didn't know about it, actually. The wedding, I mean." Darius's wide eyes swung her way at that. "That sounds bad, but it's not that big of a deal. He's met Mitchell and knows we're engaged but never has been a fan of these flashy kinds of events. So I decided not to bother him with it."

"Not to bother your dad with your wedding?"

Eve winced at the guilt that came from hearing that come right back to her.

"There's layers to the situation," she tried.

Darius's eyebrow went sky-high.

"Layers," he deadpanned.

She nodded.

"Yeah. You know every relationship is different with their own layers. Their own issues or complications. That's me and Mitchell. No need to pull in my dad for something like this."

They walked up the steps of the men's residence hall,

but he stopped at the door. Eve thought he was about to do some nifty law-enforcement move before entering a potential crime scene. Instead, he turned to face her head on.

"Complications like you and Mitchell not actually being a real couple."

The lie never had a chance to form.

The truth was already in between them before Eve could clock it.

"Yeah."

Darius didn't flinch.

She opened her mouth to take it back, to try to cover it up—to do something—but all Eve could do was stare.

A different kind of blush crawled up her neck. Embarrassment.

She wanted to ask how he had figured it out so quickly, and she knew there was no way to convince him otherwise now, when something finally cut through the silence around them.

A car door shut in the distance behind them.

They both turned toward the direction of the gate. From where they were standing they couldn't see the gate itself, never mind what car had pulled up.

Darius's hand went to the inside of his jacket.

"Are you expecting anyone out here?" he asked.

Eve shook her head.

"I wasn't even expecting us to be out here until late last night."

She heard a button click as his hand moved within the jacket's folds.

"And no one knows you're out here?" Darius added. "What about Mitchell? You said you told him about this place once."

She shook her head again. The sound of metal moving

rattled from the direction they were staring. Someone had gone through the gate.

"No one knows I'm out here," she said, dropping her voice to a whisper. Darius had turned, and with the movement he pulled his service weapon from his shoulder holster. He kept it down as she grabbed at the elbow of his other arm.

Eve realized a few beats too late what he had said.

The need to correct him rose with an anxiousness that made her stomach grow cold.

"And it was Scott I told about this place by accident, not Mitchell."

Footsteps could be heard crunching over some of the leaves that had been brave and quick enough to fall and change with the burst of cold weather. Soon whoever was coming would be in their field of vision.

However, Darius turned to her so fast that Eve nearly yelled in surprise.

When he spoke, his voice was so deep that the rumble felt like it went right through the fabric of his jacket and into the cold of her fingers.

"You're after Scott, not Mitchell."

Another truth, though there were some nuances missing. Now she could hear the footfalls. Still, it felt important to correct him once more.

"We're both after him," she clarified. "It's the only way we can take him down."

"Why?"

Relief flooded out with Eve's next truth. Finally, she could tell someone else.

"Because all Scott Keys is is a monster in a suit."

Darius's eyes didn't widen. He didn't look shocked or mad or concerned. He didn't look like the boy next door, and he didn't look like the only detective in town.

He was just a man standing in front of a woman, looking as calm as could be wrapped up in a jacket and denim.

So before the gunshot went through them both, Eve couldn't help but feel a sense of contentedness.

No matter why she was back in Seven Roads, it just felt nice to be standing on a front porch with a good man like Darius Williams.

HE KILLED THE man behind Eve in the time it took to blink. The hunting rifle in his hands hit the ground as his head tipped backward.

Darius didn't have time to watch the unknown man's body fall.

There was still the person approaching from the gate.

Darius used his free arm to swoop behind Eve to keep her upright and spun around enough to get his own gun aimed and ready.

The person who had been so noisy was already there with her own gun raised high. Darius's body acted on an instinct that was much faster than any bullet would be. He threw himself and Eve back into the residence hall door with enough power that the old wood splintered at the bolt.

A gunshot cut through the air as the door gave way.

Where he should have had the time to find his balance, and Eve along with him, the world just kept turning.

He felt the floor beneath his feet crack no more than a few steps into the room. A yellow caution sticker on part of the broken door caught the corner of his eye. All Darius could do was hold Eve tight as the floor gave way.

And what he thought would be a quick fall into some kind of crawl space turned into a long plummet into darkness.

Chapter Ten

Eve ran through the hallway, one hand pressed hard on her shoulder, and the other holding a gun. Darius labored behind, his wheezing becoming more pronounced the farther they went into whatever maze they had fallen into. She wanted to stop, to check all his injuries, but there wasn't any time.

Whoever the second shooter was might have followed them. Though, their way down into the underground corridor had been less than ideal.

Eve had still been processing the fact that she had been shot when the two of them had collided against debris and concrete. Or, really, Darius had. He'd taken the brunt of the impact beneath him.

It's why she was the one holding the gun.

"My—my hand isn't working," were his first words once they both realized they were still relatively in one piece.

Their only stroke of good luck had been the sliver of light that had shown the hallway they were now currently stumbling through. Darius must have also spotted it. They pulled themselves up together, only pausing long enough for Eve to pick up the gun.

Now she was heading in the direction of the female residence hall, sure that they had stumbled into an old storage system or water-pump holding corridor that had long since been boarded-up.

That was, until she almost hit a wall.

"Hold on," she breathed out. Eve felt Darius's body heat against her back. She used the arm holding his gun to rub it against the stone in front of her. "This is a dead end? We need a light."

"My phone is in my pocket." Darius kept his voice low too, but the sturdiness in it had crumbled. He was in pain. *Pain* pain. "G-get it for me."

Wherever they were was quiet enough that the simple action of placing the gun at her feet and feeling for his phone were as loud as yelling.

Which was good because that meant they should be able to hear their pursuer if they came their way.

Eve managed to pull the phone from his pocket with one hand, careful to keep her other pressing against the wound on her shoulder. Her hand was soaked, and she knew it would hurt like hell once her adrenaline started to ebb.

But now wasn't the time to mentally hover.

Instead, she felt a wave of gratefulness at the fact that Darius had the same model phone as her. Eve had the flashlight function on and working within seconds.

Darius was smart to shy away from its beam.

From the quick flash she was still able to see a lot of blood.

"There's...there's two ways to go," Darius breathed out.

Eve and her pounding heart turned to give the discovery more light. They had, in fact, run into a dead end whereupon you had to turn left or right.

"Where *are* we?" she asked herself.

The light showed a path to the right that was almost identical to the one to the left. No sign of life either way. Both dark and seemingly endless. The path to the right had a few wooden-looking crates stacked on one side. The other to the left looked like it sloped slightly downward.

Eve motioned to the left.

"This would go toward the main part of the mill? The other way would be toward the woods? I don't... I don't know where we are."

Darius's body heat intensified as it pressed into her back. The sudden weight made her stumble into the stone wall.

"Sorry, I—" Darius was close enough that her hair moved at his words, but he couldn't have sounded farther away.

"Darius? What's wrong?"

His head dropped to the top of her good shoulder, weighing it down enough that she had trouble turning to face him. Eve wasn't able to get the light directly on his face, but she saw enough to know asking what was wrong had been a silly question.

Everything was wrong.

He was in undeniable pain.

And that pain had a terrifying consequence.

"I-I'm not dying, but I am...going to pass out," he managed. With each word she felt him become heavier. Eve let go of her shoulder to try and help somehow, but Darius's remaining bit of strength went to him pushing her hand right on back.

"Keep pressure on it." He slid off her and hit the ground before Eve could stop him.

"Darius? Darius!"

In the dim light Eve saw his eyes close. They didn't open again.

Panic as pure and solid as the ground beneath her feet grabbed ahold of Eve as she grabbed ahold of Darius. There wasn't much she could do other than keep him from falling over totally, and even that was met with half success. He was lying more than sitting. And so still.

"I'll get you help," she told him, whispering as she fumbled to get the phone back on. There was no service, but she sent out the phone's SOS, meant to go through whenever it did come back on. It would put a tracking pin on their location and alert the authorities.

Eve glanced back down at Darius.

She knew she had taken a shot, but now she wondered if Darius had too. Or had the fall been enough?

"I'll get you help," she repeated.

A feeling of déjà vu mingled with her rising panic as she found the gun again and switched hands. The pain in her shoulder was starting to turn her stomach. Her side hurt too. So did her head.

Who was after them?

Why?

Was it Scott?

Was it people who worked for him?

Was it Gary's killer?

There was no time to figure it out.

Eve hovered in the cross-section of the pathways. She needed to get out to get help, but neither direction had light or sound coming from them. The way to the right might lead to the woods and an exterior exit…or it could dead end. For all the times her father had spoken about his work, Eve herself had never walked the mill to know for sure where every entrance and exit was.

The way to the left went in the direction of the heart of the steel mill… But wouldn't that mean the way out was probably farther away? And who was to say it was even accessible? Was where they were now even open to the general public, or had bad luck shown them a forgotten series of rooms?

There could be help in either direction, or there could be nothing, and Eve would have wasted Darius's time.

Eve turned back toward the way they had come.

Escaping into the darkness then had been about getting cover.

Now it was about getting out.

Eve flexed her grip around the butt of the gun. She tossed Darius's cell phone on the ground next to him.

"Don't die," she ordered him.

Then Eve ran full-tilt toward what she hoped was a good choice.

RAFE WAS DEAD. Dead as dead could be.

Lana moved along the old brick building and paused by its door, glancing in the direction of where the man lay prone. His gun, a thing that looked as old as the mill they had been circling, was at his side, but there were no signs he was going for it.

That man, that damned lawman, had gone and killed him true and through in one shot.

And her shot?

Well, Lana had been slower to it.

When she'd been asked to follow Detective Williams, she hadn't expected to find a Mrs. And when they had come all the way here, of all places? Lana thought it was better to keep at least one of them alive to get some answers.

That's the only reason she'd pulled her shot.

The reason the two had tucked into the building?

Lana saw the blood on the porch and guessed that for all Rafe was bad at, his first shot must have landed somewhere. But which one had taken it?

She didn't need to peek through the door to see if the couple were waiting for her right inside. The door was in pieces and gave a clear view of a confusing development.

The floor was gone.

Some of it, at least.

Lana held her gun out, ready to squeeze the trigger, and took a tentative step toward the hole in the hardwood. Sunlight from uncovered windows in the ground-level room gave just enough light to show there was an entirely different room hidden below. An old metal hunk of machinery could be seen at one side while a whole lot of nothing could be seen around the rest of the debris that had caved in.

The couple who had done the falling were nowhere to be seen.

Blood was, though.

That seemed to be the only easy thing to make out from her vantage point at the edge.

Lana held her breath. She cocked her head to the side a little.

No talking.

No rustling.

They had to have survived the fall, or else she would have seen their bodies. Maybe they were hiding in a part of the room she couldn't see?

Lana resisted the urge to sigh.

It would have been a whole lot nicer had Rafe not died.

She could have made him go down below and figure out their situation. But he had died the way he'd foolishly lived: impulsively.

That wasn't how Lana worked.

She kept her gun ready but lowered it to her side and looked around the rest of the aboveground space. She hadn't been there before but knew no one came around this part of the mill anymore. Whether they were paid to avoid it or just did it naturally, she didn't know or care. Her only job had been to follow, watch and report back.

Shoot if needed, only kill if you were told.

The room was large and open and looked to be a storage area that had been converted to hold several sleeping spaces. Rusted and broken iron bunk beds were positioned throughout the back end of the space. Nearest her seemed to have been a more general hangout spot. A couch that hadn't fallen below sagged low against the wall to her left. The wall to the right had a fogged window that looked out at another building in the distance.

She wasn't sure what building that was and, honestly, didn't care.

What she needed to do was figure out if the detective was still alive.

Lana was light and cautious with her steps around the opening in the floor until she made it to the back end of the main room. There were two closed doors, and both complained with metallic whines as she opened them.

The smell of mold hung heavy in the communal bathroom behind the first. The second held more of the same but with an added slight rot, which made sense considering it was a small, obviously forgotten kitchen. In neither room was there a set of stairs or another door that could lead to the room below.

Knowing there wasn't a back door, Lana opened a window over the sink. She climbed through it with ease and walked along the back wall of the building.

There were no stairs or exterior way to enter whatever room her mark had fallen into. At least not that she could see.

Lana turned toward the fence and the woods just beyond it. Would there be an access point there, or would she have to go in the other direction?

Maybe there wasn't an access point at all.

The mill was old, most of it repurposed instead of replaced as far as she had seen. They weren't in the working part either. Maybe they had closed up whatever they hadn't needed in order to skirt any liability issues.

Not that she cared.

She shouldn't have accepted the job to come to a place like Seven Roads.

Lana gave up her search for an easier way into whatever pit had formed beneath the detective's feet and instead looped back to the front door. When she went back inside, she holstered her gun and took a more conclusive look at her obstacle. She pulled her cell phone out and turned the flashlight function on. It didn't do much, but she could now guess the drop was about eight feet down. There didn't seem to be anything to help with that descent either, at least not from its concrete floor up to her.

Lana glanced around the dorm room around her. An industrial complex surely had something she could use to get down there without having to scale around like an acrobatic. Rope or a ladder or maybe if she could push one of the bunk-bed frames over the edge she could use it to drop onto and then climb back out of. Or maybe—

Lana had moved her gaze back to the hole as she went through potential plans.

The beam of light that was faint but clear enough was still empty. However, all thoughts stuttered to a stop when she realized that just outside of its scope was something she hadn't seen before.

At first, she thought it was the detective, but the shape was all wrong. Smaller.

The woman, she realized.

Not only had the woman survived a potential shot from

Rafe and the fall, she had managed to collect a gun in the process.

And that gun was aimed up and right at Lana.

Her words carried with absolute clarity despite the open floor between them.

"Throw me your clip and then your gun or I'll shoot," she yelled up. "You've got ten seconds."

The woman was covered in dirt and blood. Her clothes were torn. Her hair a mess.

Her words were stone.

Despite herself, Lana was impressed.

But she was no fool.

The woman was at a disadvantage no matter how determined her voice sounded.

However, Lana wasn't going to test her patience.

She threw herself backward as far as she could.

No sooner than she lost sight of the hole than three gunshots shot out from it.

Lana might have stayed to see if she could run out the woman's clip, but another sound had entered the area.

Someone was coming. Their footfalls were loud in the silence that followed the last gunfire.

If there was someone other than her and Rafe, Lana hadn't been told about them. Which meant she wasn't going to take her chances that the detective or his woman had had the chance to call in backup.

Lana didn't sigh as she backtracked with quiet speed. She only handled problems that were listed in her contract. Whoever that woman was hadn't been on that list.

Though, as she disappeared into the woods behind the mill, she bet she would be soon.

Until then, Lana did what she did best.

She disappeared.

Chapter Eleven

Something had gone wrong.

It was the first thought Darius had before he opened his eyes, and it was only reinforced when he took in the room around him.

He was at the hospital.

Well, *in* the hospital.

A dull pain radiated up his left arm. A little pinch at his hand too. He couldn't see the bag or its label at the top of the IV pole, but he recognized the sound of digital monitors beeping. Over the last seven years or so, members of the McCoy County Sheriff's Department had been in and out of the hospital multiple times because of one case or another.

The hospital staff already knew most of them from living in such a confined area, but by now most had gone from a polite *hello* to the doctors and nurses to an easy first-name-basis chat.

However, in the last seven years, Darius hadn't been a patient. Only a visitor and a detective on the job.

He'd never been a patient who had, he guessed, gone through some sort of surgery. Darius looked down his left side. Instead of wearing a shirt, there were various bandages stuck to and wrapped around his arm, chest and shoulder.

He also guessed his ribs had a wrap, but he couldn't confirm it visually. A blanket was wrapped around him.

On top of that blanket a hand rested on his thigh.

There was a small bandage and tape holding an IV to the back of the hand. Darius followed the tube with his eyes until he had to turn his head slightly to his right. Someone was in the hospital bed with him, body pressed along the side of his, head laid back with the incline of the bed, and mouth wide open.

Darius must have been coming off some medication.

It took him way too long to worry about Eve.

He was glad that once his brain caught up to worry, she was already there with him.

She was resting above his blankets and wearing a hospital gown that stopped at her calves. Her rainbow socks were gone.

Darius continued tracing the plastic tube from her IV to the metal pole standing on the other side of the bed. He moved his head slightly to get a better view of the reason she needed it in the first place.

Eve had been shot. He knew the moment it happened because a pain he had never known before tore through him the second she had fallen against him. It wasn't until he had been in the room below the residence hall that he had guessed the same bullet had gone into him too.

He hadn't cared then. He didn't care now either.

Bandages peeked out of the top of Eve's gown, but he couldn't get a good view of how much of her was covered. Darius's own IV tube pulled as he gently moved the collar of her gown away a little.

There were no ulterior motives in the move—simply the need to see proof that it wasn't as bad as he had imagined at the time.

Eve didn't stir at the adjustment.

However, someone else did.

Theo stood from a chair near the foot of the hospital bed. There was a couch on the wall next to them. It was occupied by another sleeping woman. Winnie had a blanket wrapped around her.

Theo had a look of panic wrapped around him.

He put his finger to his lips and hurried over to Darius's side.

"Literally both of them just fell asleep," Theo whispered, so close that Darius could smell coffee on the boy's breath. "If you can, keep it down."

Normally, Darius would have been a little grumpy at the command, but it was obvious what had happened wasn't exactly normal. Darius took his advice to heart. He turned his head slowly, trying not to move Eve in the process. He waited a beat to make sure he succeeded in the attempt.

He only spoke once he confirmed her breathing was even.

"What time is it?"

Darius's mouth was dry. His throat hurt a little too. He managed to keep his voice low despite the uncomfortable feeling.

Theo didn't need to look at his phone or find a clock.

"Just after three in the morning. You've been out since yesterday." He frowned. "You lost a lot of blood. You had to have surgery too." His finger hovered next to the bandage on Darius's shoulder. "They had to dig a bullet out of you."

Darius understood why he was running slower now. He really was medicated. It explained the haze and the dull pain.

"I'm guessing they got it out?"

Theo nodded.

He pointed to Darius's side.

"You have some pretty intense bruising around there—we guess where you took the impact from the fall through the floor—and there's also some bad gashes around your thigh area. But other than where you were shot, there's no stitches. At least, the doctor didn't tell us if there were."

When he said the word *us*, his gaze went to Winnie on the couch.

Darius waited for him to look back before asking the part of the situation he didn't understand.

"What about her? Eve. Is she okay?"

Theo nodded again.

"The bullet that lodged into you went through her first, but she got lucky at the angle," he said. "It went clear through and didn't do any permanent damage. The doctor even clocked her recovery time at a few weeks as long as she takes her antibiotics."

Anger seared through Darius.

Eve being shot hadn't been *lucky* in his book.

Not at all.

"The man who did it?" he asked, jaw clenching.

Theo lowered his voice just a bit more.

"Died instantly. Never had a chance to shoot his gun again."

It hadn't been the first time Darius had had to take a life in the line of duty. That didn't mean he was used to it. But seeing as how the man had made the first move—that move being to shoot Eve—he wasn't overly upset about it.

"What about the second shooter? The woman."

"A woman carjacked Mr. Gleason at the gas station next to the mill around the time I got down to you and Eve. They caught her on camera and have an APB out on her and the car." He shook his head. "So far nothing, but the entire department is on it."

The last thing Darius remembered before blacking out was being in the dark with Eve in a tunnel beneath the residence hall. His eyebrow raised in question.

"When you got down to us?"

Theo went from frowning to brandishing a sheepish smile. He pulled at his earlobe in a fidgeting gesture.

"I kind of followed you yesterday morning."

Darius almost tilted his head to the side at that.

"You followed us... What do you mean?"

Eve had gone back out of his bedroom window the morning before while Darius had gone through the house, acting like everything was normal. He hadn't seen Theo at all.

That sheepish smile grew a little.

"Winnie convinced me to run a half-marathon with her in a few months, so I've been training before breakfast. I was out running and came back in time to see a lady coming out of your window. I almost said something until I realized it was Miss Myers. I, uh, hid to see what she was up to. Then when you came out and got into your truck with her... I got curious." His smile dropped. "I would have gotten to you sooner, but by the time I got out to the road, I had to guess where you'd gone. I guessed the right direction, and when I heard the first shots, I was close enough to the back-road turn. Sorry."

Darius wasn't sure why he was apologizing.

He said as much.

"It sounds like I should be thanking you. I'm guessing the second shooter took off because you showed up. You get us out of that room too?"

Theo looked pleased, even though he shook his head.

"I called Dad and EMTs before going down there to check on you." He motioned in Eve's direction. "I tried to get her out first, but she refused to even try until you could come with her. Lucky for all of us that Rose's husband was close to us. He was the one who helped get you up the ladder we got from the main building."

James was Seven Roads's only mechanic. He was also a muscled mountain of a man. If there was anyone who could get Darius as dead weight up a ladder, it was definitely him.

Still, he didn't overlook what had been Theo's obvious effort.

"Thank you," Darius said, "for helping to get us."

Theo's cheeks turned a little red. He waved a dismissive hand through the air.

"Just trying to be a good tenant to my landlord is all. It was no biggie."

They finally got to the part of the conversation that was, indeed, a biggie. Darius knew that Theo felt it too. He cleared his throat but managed to stay as quiet as he had been.

His gaze moved to Eve.

"She wouldn't tell me—or anyone—why you two were there at the steel mill," he said. "All she would say is that you were the one who needed to answer the questions. Dad got mad at her, but I think that was more because of Scott Keys."

Darius felt that anger rise in him again.

Before they had been attacked, he had finally put together that Eve wasn't interested in Mitchell but rather his brother.

And not in a romantic way.

He hadn't had time to consider what was actually going on.

"Scott Keys? What was he doing?"

Theo rolled his eyes.

"Kicking up a fuss so loud that Dad and Blake had to pull in some lawyers."

That didn't make sense. Why was Scott kicking up a fuss

at the sheriff when it seemed like the sheriff was the one also trying to find the bad guy? Theo must have picked up on the question. He answered it without Darius having to ask. Though, there was some hesitation in it.

"Mr. Keys seems to think that Miss Myers has an intimate relationship with you...and that's causing some issues."

Darius felt his eyes widen.

"An intimate relationship," he repeated.

Theo nodded.

"And he doesn't even know about the whole sneaking-out-of-your-window thing yesterday morning either."

It was Darius's turn to roll his eyes.

"I'm not having an affair with Eve," he started. "And even if I were, us getting attacked at the steel mill while there's still a homicide investigation going on doesn't really fit into a sexy rendezvous scenario, does it?"

"That's what Dad said too, but Mr. Keys still seemed pretty mad. Winnie pulled me back to the waiting room while they left to go to the department, so I'm not sure how that all resolved. No one has been here to see either one of you except us and Mitchell since visiting hours ended."

In all the information dump, Darius had forgotten to wonder where Eve's fiancé—real or fake—currently was.

And why Eve herself was in *his* bed.

Thankfully, Theo kept his answering streak going.

"Miss Myers's room is next door, and Mitchell Keys was in there sleeping last I saw. She said that he knew where she was when she came in here an hour or so ago and that it was okay." That sheepish look came back. "I worried about her getting into bed with you and also that Mr. Keys would be mad, but Miss Myers told me something that made Winnie give me The Look. You know, the don't-ask-any-more-questions look. They fell asleep not too long after that."

Darius noted the boy's cheeks had reddened again.

"She said something *to you*, the pragmatic one, that made you think it was okay for her to hop into my hospital bed while we *both* are injured and one of us in engaged to a very rich, well-connected man?" Darius had a hard time with that one. Winnie he could see letting it slide because she had, no doubt, picked up on the fact that Darius and Eve were close.

Or *had* been close.

But Theo?

He usually took a lot more convincing. Which was why Darius wasn't surprised or all that offended that the boy had followed them the day before.

Now he shrugged a little and nodded to Eve.

"She said you were hers," he said, matter-of-factly. "And between us, she was very convincing."

THE YOUNG MAN named Theo had a nice voice that would have been good for narrating books or hosting podcasts. At first, Eve accepted his whisper-talking in tandem with Darius's deep drone like it was white noise.

Which was good, considering she felt she was still in need of a mighty nap.

Only when that white noise became words she could follow did she remember where she was.

And who had finally woken up.

Excitement nearly made Eve open her eyes to detail out as much of Darius as she could before slinging a barrage of questions his way. How was he feeling? Did his shoulder hurt? What about his side? Did he want water? Did he need a doctor?

She managed to keep the desire to a thought only.

She liked Theo for what he had done, but Eve still wasn't ready to let him into the secret.

The secret she was finally ready to tell Darius, despite swearing to keep him and anyone else out of it.

While the two men spoke quietly at her side, Eve took a chance and moved slightly. When no one reacted, she used her hand's new position to place her thumb against Darius's leg. She applied a quick three pulses of pressure.

The man didn't move a muscle.

Did he not get the hint?

A few moments passed by, Eve readied to do it again, but Darius apparently had understood the assignment.

"Hey, why don't you go ahead and take Winnie home?" he said when their conversation paused. "I know for a fact that those couches are uncomfortable as all get-out, and since I'm clearly okay now, there's no reason for her to suffer on it and for you to do the same on a chair."

There was some initial pushback at the suggestion. That pushback doubled when Winnie herself was woken. It was obvious that neither of them wanted to leave, but eventually Darius won out with a compromise. They would leave for only a little while, get some sleep and be back as soon as visiting hours started again.

No discussions happened past that.

Theo and Winnie said hushed good-byes before their quiet footfalls finally left the room.

The second the door closed, Eve opened her eyes.

It was no surprise that Darius was already looking at her.

"Climbing through windows and climbing into beds," he said. "I'm almost scared to see what habit you'll pick up next."

Eve suppressed an eye roll.

Mainly because there had been a specific reason why she was there now. It wasn't just concern.

It was necessity.

And she cut right to the chase.

"We need to get our stories on the same page right now," she said.

Darius's dark brow rose.

"About the real reason you're with Mitchell Keys," he guessed.

She nodded.

"And why I think it's time I officially ask for your help."

Chapter Twelve

"I kind of lied about why we left Seven Roads when we were kids."

Eve was staring at the wall across from them. The hospital room's TV had been off since Darius had been wheeled in after his surgery. No one had thought to turn it on after, even on low. Darius had never been someone who could sit in front of a TV with any real enthusiasm. He was more of a book or hands-on-project kind of guy. He had never been much of a fan of noise.

If Eve had to guess, she thought those ways of his hadn't exactly changed over the years. He was single, living in his childhood home, working a job that forced him to ask more questions than answer. The only surprise was that he had taken on a roommate. Though, the younger man also seemed prone to talking less than more. At least until the young woman, Winnie, was in the room.

The three of them had spoken quietly earlier beneath the TV no one had even thought to turn on.

Then again, who was Eve to say if Darius had or hadn't changed since they were kids? She had been gone.

Did people really change all that much from when they were kids?

Circumstances forced action—but change? Real change?

It was a question Eve had wondered throughout the years, usually in the quiet of the night, staring at the bedroom ceiling and trying to remember the little girl who had once lived in Seven Roads.

Now Eve let out a breath. This was a story she needed to tell him—she knew that—but that didn't mean she was eager to do it.

Regardless of her feelings, Darius gave her the space to work through them. He was quiet as she tried to figure out the best entry point to the origin of her lie.

He didn't even question why she was sharing his hospital bed.

He didn't say anything at all.

Eve had already heard a bit of gossip in town about people often calling him cold.

That she didn't understand.

Darius Williams had always been warm to her.

It was one of the reasons she hadn't wanted to leave Seven Roads as a kid.

It was one of the reasons a part of her was glad to finally be able to explain why she had.

Eve adjusted her gaze to the spot across the room where the wall met the ceiling. Her memory yanked her back into the past.

"I didn't know Dad was sick until we were in Texas," she started, eyes straight ahead. "Maybe because he was never really at the house because of work when we were here, or maybe because, by the time he did start to hang around after Mom left, I was so used to being by myself I just didn't see the signs. So when we got to Houston and he told me he'd been accepted into a drug study—his last chance at surviving—our life here in Seven Roads just kind of disappeared."

Eve picked at the fabric of her hospital gown.

She didn't like hospitals, doctors or medical clinics, but over the last decade or so, she had more than gotten used to them.

"I won't get too into the details because he's okay now, but back then, even with the drug trial, he was really sick," Eve continued. "You know Mom, once she left here that was it for us as a family. And remember Aunt Pat? She'd just had her third kid. The rest of Dad's family wasn't exactly dependable to start with either. So when things started getting really bad, I realized it would be just me taking care of Dad."

There was still an anxiety there. An imprint of the terror in Eve's chest when she finally understood that the position of sole caregiver would have to go to her. That her father dying wasn't something she could avoid or ignore. That she couldn't simply give him encouragement or a hug as she passed by. That the man she had barely seen because of his work throughout her young life was now the person who needed her most.

And it had all happened so quickly too.

One week she had been climbing through Darius's window, a lonely but happy preteen, the next she was standing in a small apartment in Texas with a father who was staring at death, asking her to hold his hand.

"We finally started getting really promising results around the time I turned sixteen," Eve continued. "When I was eighteen, Dad was given the all clear. He still has to take meds for the rest of his life, but the shortened life expectancy we'd kept hearing about every year was finally extended."

For the first time in years, he had been smiling too. It had been better than any present Eve could have gotten for officially becoming an adult.

At the same time, that happiness had seesawed with a new, uncomfortable weight.

"But by that point, it had been almost eight years," she said. "Eight years of me taking care of him. Of always being on call. Being there every minute I could. Chores and exercise. Tracking medicines and making doctor visits. Having to deal with financial problems, picking up after-school jobs to help fill the gap."

Eight years of a childhood that hadn't been childlike at all.

Eight years of realizing that the only taste of a childhood she'd had at all was because of the man sitting next to her now.

"So when it was time to graduate high school and head to college, I couldn't just leave." Guilt mingled in with the feeling of being medicated. It was an old, worn and beaten kind of shame. The shame of a lie told so much that, at times, Eve had forgotten it was a lie at all. "I didn't tell Dad that's why I decided not to go to college. He'd just started dating for the first time since Mom left and was trying to find some normal... So I lied and told him I'd rather work."

Waitressing, tending bar, seasonal cashier jobs, odds-and-ends gigs like cleaning and babysitting. Just anything and everything she could do to help with the bills and debt that had piled up Eve did for the next ten years.

"It wasn't until Dad got remarried to my stepmom and moved out of that small apartment that I really realized we had finally done it. We'd gotten him out of this exhausting situation where it felt like he'd been trying to climb out of some never-ending hole for years. But that's when I really understood the part I'd really played in helping him get out of it."

Eve sighed.

"I hadn't pulled him out, I'd pushed him out. Which meant I was still there when he was able to finally walk away." She listed her next points lazily off on the fingers still resting against Darius's leg. "I had no real friends, no real career, no life goal or dreams I was running toward. My romantic relationships came down to a handful of dates scattered between weekend shifts and overtime, and even though I managed to get an apartment that wasn't all that bad, it was just a place I went to for sleep."

Eve snorted, a bit of self-loathing in the sound.

It was another feeling she never would forget.

Over thirty years old and she felt like she was a kid again, standing at the beginning of adulthood without a clue about what to do first.

The spot on the wall Eve had been staring at blurred slightly.

She cleared her throat and continued.

"I tried to slow down after that," she said. "I tried making friends, find a relationship that meant something, figure out career things and if I even had dreams. Then, through one of Dad's old friends he'd made from his treatment days, I learned about some work the Keys Foundation had done with a medical project in a small town in Alabama. I checked their social media and found a press release about Scott Keys, praising small-town medical studies. When he named-dropped the hospital's new research annex that was in Seven Roads—well, I was sure it was fate."

"I applied for a job at the foundation's headquarters in Atlanta, got an interview and probably was the most excited I had been in years." Eve laughed, but it was short and not at all humorous. "Though, with my résumé, or lack thereof, they told me on the spot that I wasn't a good fit. Now, believe me, I understand their reasoning. I was underqualified for sure. But to go all that way, just to be told I wasn't good enough? It was rough."

The small hope Eve had had?

It had disappeared into the night air then.

"I went to the bar later, ready to drown my sorrows in drinks I couldn't really afford, when I ran into a group of guys being rowdy in a nearby alley. Three guys against one, and the one guy who was being pushed around didn't look like he could hit a wet paper bag stuck on the sidewalk."

At this part, Eve felt a smile curve up the corner of her lips. It was genuine.

Darius finally spoke.

"Let me guess. You jumped in to help the one," he said.

Eve laughed a little. She nodded.

"I went in there all loud and fast—you know, not giving them a second to really think—and finally made enough space to get the guy and run." If it had been a movie, their escape would have been in slow motion Eve had thought even then. Dramatic but fun. Low stakes that, in the moment, had felt so high. "Once we were clear of them, he treated me to a nice meal that I was in no mood to refuse. We chatted all night before I had to go back to my hotel and we'd had a good time, but there were no plans to see each other again or talk, even. So when I got a call early the next morning to come in for another interview with the Keys Foundation, I was surprised as all get-out to see him there. Standing all smart and proper in a suit."

"Mitchell Keys," Darius guessed.

Eve nodded.

"Mitchell had gone back that night after our dinner and told Scott about my so-called daring rescue. Scott had wanted to meet me before I left town, so what I thought was an interview with HR for a job at their headquarters ended up being a meal with the big boss himself. Before that meal was even finished, he hired me to be his personal assistant." At the time, Eve had been so surprised her mouth had flopped open like a fish out of water. It had been the first bit of hope she'd had in years. "Scott said I was good under pressure, and if I could handle an issue like that with his brother discreetly, then working with a high-profiler like himself would be easy. So I became his assistant."

Again if it had been a movie, that would have been the beginning of a beautiful ending.

Down-on-her-luck, listless daughter finally finds purpose and drive again. Meets not one but two kind men who care. Finds purpose in work, love and life.

Life fulfilled.

Future bright.

But that wasn't what happened next.

There was no need to pad the rest of the past with emotional asides and deep, life-changing epiphanies.

Now Eve was at the fact portion of her problems.

"Out of all the work that Scott did, I took the most interest in his involvement in anything medical, and when he started meeting with a man named Horace Clare, owner of Clare Biometrics, I couldn't help but pay attention."

"Clare Bio," Darius echoed. His low rumble vibrated against her as he spoke. "The company that's about to use the research annex here for a new pharmaceutical trial? I didn't know that the Keys Foundation had anything to do with them. I've only heard Scott wanted to invest in the town, but not how."

Eve nodded.

"He's been looking into ways to boost the economy by bringing in new business, using the research annex and whatever study they do as a good example of how small towns can do big things."

"His whole Small Town White Knight shtick."

She nodded again.

"I thought his meetings with Horace were related to Clare Bio being the new company to move into the research annex," Eve continued. "And that it was all happy coincidence that I, his new assistant, had lived in the same town as a kid. I was wrong."

Eve finally turned face the man next to her. Darius did the same. His brow was drawn in.

"Scott had been interested in Seven Roads before he met me, before he met Horace and way before he made it known publicly that he was investing in the town."

Darius's eyebrow rose high.

"What? Why?"

Eve lowered her voice, glancing at the closed door just past him.

"I think he's been the reason behind all of the town's problems these past few years."

Darius also glanced at the door. When his gaze was back on her, he looked as cold as the town rumors claimed.

"What do you mean all our problems? Do you mean our past cases? Because, as much as I'd like to blame one person for all of them, even the big investigations we've gone through over the last few years have been cut-and-dried once we got all our ducks in a row."

Eve had known about the department's big cases over the last decade simply because she had been keeping tabs on a certain detective's career. At least, for the most part. That task had become much easier thanks to a few key investigations and their outcomes making the national news.

That's why Eve hadn't intended on telling Darius, or anyone else, her discovery until she had concrete evidence. Her belief, her accusation, would change everything. Without proof, though? She knew she sounded delusional.

Staring now at a man who had a successful career as a detective in part because of these past wild cases, she felt some nerves start to twist in her stomach.

She wiggled a little like the physical move could dislodge the new feeling.

It didn't.

She continued anyways.

There was no point in keeping it in any longer.

Darius had taken a bullet because of her.

The truth would hurt less.

She hoped.

"I think he's the reason he got the White Knight of Smalltown Living nickname in the first place."

Darius's eyebrow lifted once more.

"He gave himself the nickname?"

Eve shook her head.

Her answer felt as loud in mostly dark hospital room as the gunshot had.

"I think Scott Keys destroys small towns just so he can save them." Eve made sure to hold Darius's gaze. He sure was handsome. She let out a small breath. "And I think he's only coming to save Seven Roads now…because he's spent the last several years slowly destroying it."

Chapter Thirteen

The town was in an uproar and, for the first time it had nothing to do with the danger or mystery that had taken place within its limits.

No one really cared about the still-unknown woman shooter who had carjacked Mr. Gleason while he was pumping premium or that, while his car had reappeared in the next county over, she hadn't.

No one seemed to care about the shooter who had died at the steel mill being identified as a Rafe Bailey—a do-anything for hire with a long jacket of various criminal activities and time spent in several county jails and one state prison—or the fact that still no one knew who had hired him.

And when it came to the steel mill itself—the largest employer of the entire town, and the one stretch of space in all of Seven Roads that most residents had been to at least once—almost no one spoke about the boarded-up, blocked-off and hidden network of old rooms beneath that had been partially discovered after the shooting.

Some did speak to the fact that the shooting in question had resulted in the injuries of the only McCoy County detective and the Keyses' almost-bride, but most of those people chattering were working at the sheriff's department. One of their own had been hurt, and they had no one in custody to answer for it. A gnawing problem that kept their focus on the things that mattered most.

Talk of Gary Whittaker's homicide case, still without a lead, hadn't completely died down, but the shock value's stock had never risen too high to begin with, since he had been an outsider.

Instead, the gossip that blew every other piece of news out of the water for the town locals kept to one bit of information that had leaked in the aftermath of all the hubbub.

The rumored breakup of Evelyn Myers and Mitchell Keys.

It was one thing for the wedding to be postponed because of a homicide. But for the bride-to-be to be caught out with another man the day after with no public explanation, not to mention the extra layer of rumor that Scott Keys had made such a stink at the sheriff's department, demanding that same man be fired... Who cared about Gary Whittaker?

Who cared about the missing shooter?

Who cared why there had been a shooting at all?

Darius, a week later, believed he could have left the town in ruins if they could only see who met him in his living room after finally being released from the hospital.

Eve, sitting cross-legged in front of a laptop on his couch, nearly fell over as she tried to undo herself to stand. Mitchell, sitting next to her, managed to catch the water bottle she'd had sitting next to her before it fell to the floor.

"I didn't think you were getting released until this afternoon," Eve exclaimed, righting herself. Mitchell gave her a little push for extra stability. She didn't address it. Her gaze went over his shoulder to the hallway leading to the front door. "How did you get here? Did you drive? Is that allowed? I mean, I know it's mainly the one side of you that's all hurt, but surely that's still not allowed. You know, I got a flu shot in the backside once, and it hurt like all heck just driving back a few blocks, so I bet a bullet wound would—"

Darius held up one hand in a *stop* gesture and interrupted the raging flow of thoughts.

"Theo's outside with my bag," he said. "He'll be in after he finishes telling Liam I'm out and home. My phone's juice is low, or else I'd do it."

He added in the last part because he had a feeling Eve was about to grill him on why he hadn't called her.

Which would have been another awkward exchange in front of her fiancé if it weren't for the fact that both had already set the story straight for him back at the hospital.

"The fight that Eve helped rescue me from when we first met was with my ex-boyfriend's *new* boyfriend and his friends," Mitchell had explained, sitting on the couch next to Darius's hospital bed. "They were under the impression that I was trying to get back with him after we ran into each other earlier that day by accident. They accused me of using my money and influence to try and win him back. I...got a little heated at that, and that's when they remembered it was three against one."

Mitchell had shared a look with Eve that was clear in its gratitude. She'd accepted it from her spot on the edge of Darius's bed with a little nod.

Then Mitchell's attention had fastened on Darius again. There it had stayed for the remainder of his explanation.

"If that isn't an indication of the important part—I'm gay," he'd clarified. "But I've never come out to most of my family or the public, and so far I've managed to keep it a secret, despite people like those guys trying to make me pay for whatever imagined slights they think I've committed."

"So Scott doesn't know," Darius had had to make sure.

Mitchell had nodded.

"Our father was a very traditional man, who made it very clear that to inherit the family money and business an heir had to be just as traditional. While I've never been in the running for being the CEO or taking a seat on any board since Scott is older, my mother's deathbed wish was to make sure I at least inherited my share of the money when my father did pass. Which meant the easiest thing I could do was leave the idea of *traditional* on the table, at least for a few years." He'd sighed out long at that. "Those few years turned into over a decade, and then Dad got sick, and I realized the idea of not admitting who I am just to get money...felt too wrong to keep going. So I decided to finally come out, and I was so nervous that I invited one of the few friends I had over to help me practice what I was going to say."

Mitchell had been tensing slowly Darius had noticed. At that part, his shoulders had become a hard line of obvious stress.

"In hindsight I shouldn't have picked a hotel as a meeting place but we were working out of town so it seemed practical," he continued. "Scott saw me go into a room, with a man, and assumed we were there for other things. And when my friend left, Scott came in to—I thought—talk too."

Eve had balled her hand into a fist. Her jaw had tightened. She'd been mad.

Darius had understood why after Mitchell stood, turned around, and lifted his shirt.

Scars—so many different lengths and depths and severity—had been spread across the skin of his back, a horrifying series of stamps of the past. Even Darius had felt his own anger rise at the sight.

"The mere idea that I had kept a secret from him, sent Scott into a rage," Mitchell had started again after a moment. He'd turned around, face fallen. "He didn't care if I was gay—he didn't even ask—but the thought that I might have been trying to 'scam him out' of what would have been all rightfully his? He was so angry that he didn't even give me a chance to confirm or deny if I dated men or not. If it wasn't for Eve, I'm not sure what would have happened had I actually told him the truth."

Eve's jaw had unclenched then.

"I had already been working for Scott for a while and saw him break from schedule," she'd jumped in. "I followed him, worried I'd somehow made a scheduling mistake, and when I realized what was happening, I said what I thought would be the most helpful in the moment—that Mitchell wasn't secretly dating men but secretly dating me instead."

"And, even though I had been planning on telling the truth up until then, I saw something in my brother that scared me to lie along with her." Mitchell had lowered his voice. It had made his next confession all the more sinister-sounding. "A man who would do anything and everything for power, for money, for status, even kill his own brother for even the chance of getting slightly more of it all."

Eve's expression had softened but her words were still as harsh as they had been before.

"I had just found out that the foundation had money coming out of and going into accounts I couldn't identify or trace when they should have been going into various originations, specifically the drug trial that during which my father's friend had died. I had been planning on asking, assuming it was some kind of clerical issue, but then I saw what he did to Mitchell. And how, even after I caught him in the act, he buttoned up like it was nothing after he accepted our lie. He even smiled."

Eve had shaken her head.

"So I opened up to Mitchell instead, and for the last

six months, we've been doing our own investigation into the missing money, and *two* months ago we finally had a breakthrough."

"But before we could do anything with it, Scott told me I needed to marry Eve," Mitchell had added. "Not that I should or might want to, that I *had* to."

"Right when you two found something that might expose him," Darius had underlined.

They'd nodded in tandem.

"We're worried that he found something out but can't figure out what that might be," Eve had said.

"And we were worried Scott was setting us up somehow. Why else would he want me to marry all of a sudden?"

This was when Darius finally understood the lie Eve had told him the day of the wedding.

"Which is why I met with Gary Whittaker once before we came to Seven Roads," Mitchell had said, sheepish in his confession. "I wanted to know the full extent of what it meant for Eve and me to be married and what she would legally be able to do, wondering if there was a reason in there that we could find for the sudden rush down the aisle."

"It was like I lit a fire beneath him and asked him to sit on it," Mitchell had continued after a bewildered expression had crossed over his face. "He became angry and said he wouldn't answer any family questions without the family there—without Scott there. Which only made *me* panic, and I reeled everything back in and wrote it off as prewedding nerves. It seemed to calm him down, but then when I tried to talk to him last week, he looked like he was seeing a ghost."

"When you saw him last week," Darius had repeated.

The conspiratorial partners had glanced away from him at that.

Mitchell took his blame well despite it.

"I met Gary for lunch the day he was killed, just after noon."

Darius had looked at Eve for that. She'd met his gaze too, less enthused to admit her part in what had happened next.

"Which I didn't know about because I was too busy trying to stop the wedding, so when I was asked about where Mitchell was later… I lied and said I was with him."

The rest of the conversation had been short, but Darius couldn't deny he had felt something in him shift at finally knowing the why behind Eve's lie. It wasn't that she was in love with Mitchell or held him on some pedestal because of his fortune, status and connection to his older, much more popular brother.

She had been trying to help a friend.

A friend who swore up and down that Gary had been alive when he'd left his hotel room around twelve twenty.

There was no evidence or way to confirm Mitchell's story, but despite himself Darius believed him. Maybe, he realized, because Eve did.

After that, Darius might have stayed in the hospital, but Gary Whittaker's homicide case had done something he hadn't expected it to do.

It had gone backward.

Back before the day of the wedding, or the arrival of the wedding party in Seven Roads, or the engagement, or the lie told to Scott about Eve and Mitchell's secret relationship. Because, they might not have had proof yet, but Darius had had a hard time believing it had been a coincidence that Gary had been killed after talking with Mitchell.

And, for the first time since the murder, Darius had a lead he knew would go somewhere.

It just was a matter of how to approach it.

Now standing in his living room and staring at the fake couple who had spent the last half of a year trying to topple a man steeped in money and power, Darius had a plan.

One it was time to share.

"You think Scott is using his money from the foundation to fund more sinister activities. I think you're right. And I've come up with a plan that I think will prove it."

Darius had spent the last several days in the hospital pouring over all the notes Eve and Mitchell had made on their investigation. Their breakthrough had been less of a breakthrough and more of a hunch that someone in the wedding party had helped with Scott's less-than-legal intentions.

As of that morning, Darius believed he'd finally bridged that hunch to what would be a tangible piece of evidence.

If they played their cards right.

Eve's eyes had widened as she waited for his explanation.

Instead, he knew he was about to get her anger next.

"But I'll only help on one condition." Darius pointed to the woman standing in front of him. "You don't leave my side. Not once and not for anything."

"What? Why?" Darius noted her reddening cheeks, but he didn't wait to see if it was from annoyance or something else.

Instead, he narrowed his eyes at her and made sure the aim of his finger stayed true.

"Because you, Evelyn Myers, have a talent for getting into trouble. Whether you're making it or falling into it. So until we get this entire thing settled, you aren't leaving my sights. Agree now, or else you two can leave and I'll let you figure it all out on your own."

That, of course, was a lie.

And like the fake alibi she'd given Darius before, he knew that *Eve* knew it was a lie too.

Still, she'd never been one with the personality to accept an ultimatum easily. Her nostrils flared a little as she took a moment to let his nonthreat linger.

Mitchell was smart enough to also stay quiet behind her.

Darius was finding that he was liking the man more and more.

After a moment, Eve let out a quick breath of defeat.

"Fine," she gave in. "Until we can prove the White Knight of Small-town Living is the villain in disguise, I'm all yours, Detective Williams."

Chapter Fourteen

Lunch was served by Theo, moving around the small kitchen with ease while bickering with the young woman named Winnie even more. They were talking about the best practices to train for a half-marathon one moment, and the next they were fussing about the proper way to make a sandwich worthy of a specialty shop.

Mitchell threw in his two cents worth from his spot at the kitchen counter about what he thought were the best trimmings for said perfect sandwich, and this, somehow, transitioned into a conversation about the local coffee shop. What constituted the perfect drink came next. Eve let her attention wander to the man sitting opposite her while their debate started.

Darius seemed uncomfortable.

And it wasn't with the current company chattering in his kitchen.

Something in him was hurting or, at least, bothering him. Eve had already seen him adjust his shoulder twice, and his drawn brow hadn't relaxed since he'd arrived home.

She couldn't blame him.

Not only had he been shot and gone through surgery and recovery in the hospital, he had also spent those days studying the chaotic notes Eve and Mitchell had taken on a story that, if broken, would at the very least turn the town upside-down.

Then he had come home and gone right to work.

There was no rest for the wicked; there was no rest for detectives who knew Eve Myers.

A problem that Eve understood was tricky.

What if she hadn't come back to Seven Roads, at least until they'd had concrete evidence of Scott's wrongdoings?

Darius wouldn't be sitting across from her, wounded and working in secret. Setting his rules, his procedures, aside for a case that wasn't even technically a case.

Because keeping everything on the down-low was the other stipulation that everyone in the kitchen had agreed upon.

Their deep dive into Scott Keys, the fake relationship between Eve and Mitchell and the connection to Gary Whittaker and his murder were all pieces of information that they alone knew about.

It was another point of pressure that Eve had inadvertently applied to her former boy next door.

She hadn't even asked him to keep such a complicated secret once he had taken her bullet. Yet the straight-as-an-arrow lawman had done so.

It made Eve's stomach twist a little. The memory of his one condition being that she couldn't leave his side—well, that made her stomach feel a different kind of way.

That feeling, and a sudden warmth crawling up her neck, made Darius's gaze suddenly pulling up to meet hers only intensify.

Eve tried to play it off.

She tapped the table's top beneath her finger.

"Out of all the furniture you got rid of from when we were kids, I'm glad this one didn't make the cut," she tried. "I've always liked this table."

Darius snorted.

"You only like this table because of how much my mother loved it."

Eve couldn't deny that. She shrugged. The sandwiches might not have been finished, but Winnie had clearly decided it was time to enter a more interesting conversation. She was smiling as she sat down to Eve's right, her back against the wall so she could keep an eye on Theo's progress, Eve assumed.

"Theo said you two were neighbors," she said. "I didn't realize you were close to Darius's parents too."

At this Darius's snort turned into a little chuckle.

Winnie's smile faded a bit. It probably didn't help that Eve must have looked offended.

"Close in distance but never in spirit," she clarified. "My time spent in this house was out of sight and mind of those two."

Winnie's eyebrow rose as Theo started to hand out plates of food. Mitchell joined him. He looked as perplexed as they did.

"But you like this table because his mother loved it?" Theo repeated. "Doesn't that imply that you feel a fondness for her since she felt a fondness for it?"

Darius let out a bite of laughter again but decided to help out.

He tapped the table's top.

"Put on your phone's flashlight and look underneath."

Winnie, Theo and Mitchell did just that.

Mitchell was the one to read the words that had been scratched into the wood in little-kid handwriting.

"Eve Myers owns this table. Jon D. can bite tires."

Three faces emerged with varying expressions of delight and confusion.

Eve thought it was telling of their personalities who asked the following questions.

"You wrote this?" Mitchell asked. "How old were you?"

Eve didn't have to think long.

"I was a persistent eight-year-old, who thankfully got a little better with my handwriting."

Winnie was next.

"You claimed the table as yours because you *didn't* like his mother," she said. "Did she ever see this?"

Darius answered that with a resounding *no*.

"For almost two years she sat at this table never knowing that little Eve the terror had defamed one of her favorite pieces of furniture."

Theo only seemed concerned about the last part.

"Who's Jon D. and why can he *bite tires*?" he asked.

At this Darius's mouth shut and thinned into a line.

In all honesty, Eve had forgotten she had added in a mention of Jon D. Even before what he'd done when they were ten, she had already greatly disliked the boy. She sobered a little for her answer, trying to be as discreet as possible. She might not have been around for the last twenty years or so, but she had a feeling that Darius hadn't been chatty about the origin of the scar on his back.

The scar on her own hand felt oddly heavy as she answered.

"He was a boy who lived down the street and who only came during the summer breaks to stay with his grandparents," she explained. "He decided to make it his personal mission every summer to make our lives miserable. Around the time I scratched that in, he was at a level seven out of ten on the annoyance scale. If you'd given me a few years I'd have written in a lot worse."

Darius didn't add anything to that.

The rest of the table seemed to take the hint. They fell into a communal silence as each ate their food. It wasn't until a few contented sighs and the sight of empty plates later that the silence was broken.

Eve was the one to do it.

"So how do we prove that Scott has been destroying small towns before he saves them? What did you find that we didn't?"

Everyone's gaze waved over to the man at the head of the table.

Darius didn't flinch at the dramatic, yet valid, questions. Instead, he seemed more than ready for them.

"You and Mitchell built your investigation on timing, right? Scott meeting with key individuals in one town before and after something inherently goes wrong, only to be able to fix that exact thing that went wrong." Eve nodded, not that he needed the confirmation. Her notes had looked like a madwoman's rantings and ravings as she had tracked Scott over the past ten years as best she could through financial transactions, planners, press releases and gossip.

"There was a lot of overlap of him being at the scene of the crime before the crime happened and then directly after," she confirmed.

"Like what's been happening with Clare Biometrics," Winnie added.

Eve had been the one to personally tell Winnie and Theo everything she knew, while Darius had been in the hospital. However, she was starting to realize that Winnie had a knack for making sure everyone was on the same page. It seemed to be a trait that Theo appreciated too.

Eve nodded.

"The last pharmaceutical company that had used the research annex, Camden Pharmaceuticals, was ruined by corruption, and after the investigations and the company being shut down and having to leave, the whole thing was a big hit against Seven Roads and the county's future growth. Until Horace took an interest in it and decided to go on contract with Clare Biometrics for the next ten years," Eve said. "Horace Clare coming to town created excitement and created a positive outlook for Seven Roads, which is what Scott claims had *him* become interested in the town."

"Which seems harmless until you realize that Scott had met with one of the higher-ups of Camden Pharmaceuticals twice before they moved to Seven Roads," Mitchell added.

"Which, again, might not seem like anything if you look at it as an isolated event, but of the three small towns that Scott has been praised for supposedly saving, there have been similar situations like this," Eve added.

It was Darius's turn to nod. He domed his fingers on top of the table.

"The breakthrough you and Mitchell say you made right before Scott insisted on the two of you getting married was finding the flight plans for Scott's best friend, Toby Sanderson," he underlined.

Mitchell and Eve confirmed that.

"We realized from the big uproars that happened in the second small town he was praised with saving that Scott hadn't met with anyone but his best friend and fellow rich socialite Toby Sanderson had," she said. "And he'd gone there on his private jet. We had finally gotten our hands on a copy of those flight records when Scott told Mitchell to propose."

"Then Mitchell reached out to Gary Whittaker about the legal side of being married, since he was the family lawyer," Darius said. He looked to Winnie and Theo. While he had agreed, begrudgingly, to let them in on what was happening, he hadn't been able to talk to them at the hospital for any real length of time.

Theo let him know that this information was something that they already knew.

"Which seemed to freak Mr. Whittaker out," Theo finished.

"A feeling he still had when Mitchell went to meet with Gary the day of the wedding," Winnie said. "Right before he was killed *somewhere* within an hour-and-a-half radius of the diner here in town where he and Mitchell met."

Despite their harrowing time spent at the steel mill, the site of Gary's murder was still a mystery, as was his killer.

Darius moved his hand to tap the top of the table, bringing their attention back to him.

"So let's assume that finding the flight plans and linking Toby Sanderson to Scott's plans alerted Scott in some way, leading him to force Mitchell to marry Eve—though, I'd like to point out we aren't sure that's what happened because the motive there is unclear," Darius started. "Meeting with the family lawyer only for him to be killed right after seems like too much of a coincidence given our original assumption. I think that either Gary knew something about Scott that he shouldn't have known, or Scott believed that Mitchell told Gary something he shouldn't have known. And then suddenly two guns-for-hire come for me and Eve the next day?"

Darius shook his head.

"I think there's a disconnect between the two sides of what we all assume is connected to the White Knight of Small-town Living," he continued. "Scott doesn't know what Mitchell has found out and, like us, is probably only making guesses and reacting to opportunities as fast as he can."

He paused long enough to jab the tabletop once, but that was enough to make what he said next the star of the show.

"So I want us to make an opportunity of our own that will make him so nervous he'll be forced to react," he said. "Then he's ours."

THE PLAN TO entrap a millionaire savior by using his best friend to admit to a conspiracy that had been at least ten years in the making wasn't all that complicated.

The sleeping arrangements that night, however, were.

At least they felt that way to Darius, who'd spent more minutes than he should have staring at his closet before his shower. He chose a full outfit for his sleepwear, a black T-shirt and some sweatpants, and took care to make sure each piece was perfectly in place after slipping into bed once his bandages had been changed and his medicine had been taken.

Theo helped with the latter part of the routine, hanging around in Darius's bedroom until he was satisfied that he had helped enough. Then he went to the living room and, Darius had no doubt, instantly went to sleep on the couch. Apparently, he hadn't been getting that much sleep while Darius was in the hospital. Darius made note that, once everything was said and done, he would have to do something for the boy. Winnie too. They might have been young, but they could give most of the adults he'd met in his life a run for their money when it came to being considerate.

A good example of that was Theo giving his room to Eve for the night.

Something she had lightly huffed about.

"I don't want to put you out," she'd told Theo after Winnie had left and Mitchell was wrapping up to go too.

Theo had waved the thought off. Mitchell had offered to get him a room at the hotel where he was staying—and where Eve had, in name, also been staying—but Theo had refused to leave Darius, still hurt, alone.

Though, there was never any real danger in that worry.

He'd made it clear that Eve wasn't going to leave his side and she had been just as vocal about staying put. Her suitcase had already been in his room when he'd come back from the hospital.

Now that suitcase was down the hall in his childhood bedroom.

And Darius was staring up at the ceiling, wondering if the anxiousness he was feeling in him was warranted or not.

Half an hour after the house quieted and he was searching for the sleep that was trying to elude him, Darius was silently grateful for his thinking ahead about his sleepwear choice.

The bedroom door didn't squeak, but the floorboard just outside of it did.

Darius kept his eyes closed as the soft clicks of the door opening and closing preceded the soft shuffles of feet wrapped in socks.

He still didn't open his eyes when the mattress sank lightly beside him a few moments later.

Eve took care not to touch him this time, though she did speak.

"Let me stay for a bit," she whispered at his shoulder. "It feels weird to sleep in this house without you."

Because he knew Eve, Darius understood the statement was innocent in nature. She had, after all, spent most of her nights asleep in the same house with him next to her on the floor as kids.

But also because he knew Eve, Darius understood something else the moment she made the comment.

He hadn't just guessed that Eve would climb into his bed that night.

Darius realized he had been hoping that she would.

Mitchell never went to his hotel. Everyone inside thought he had—and he certainly thought he was going to as well—but the second he made it to his rental's driver-side door, something heavy hit his back.

The pain was a lot to handle and, in trying to suppress it, his yell internalized. All that came out of his mouth before the woman attempted the hit again was a gasp. Not even an impressive one. The cicadas in the summer would have been louder.

Regardless of his initial reaction, the second hit was enough to make the lights go out.

When he opened his eyes again, head throbbing and stomach ready to be sick, he was in a room with a woman sitting across from him in an upholstered chair.

She was young, but confidence made her feel much older than him.

Mitchell's voice wobbled as he spoke.

"Wh-who are you?"

The woman had a gun on her lap, gloves on her hands and a clear look of annoyance on her face.

Her voice was as smooth as silk.

"Someone who was starting to get worried that I might have hit you a little too hard," she said. "The second time. The first I misjudged how tall you were. Don't worry, I have your number now."

She wasn't holding the gun, and as she crossed her legs, it moved over her thighs like a ship at sea. Mitchell couldn't help but watch the movement with a stomach that felt more than motion sickness.

The woman caught his concerned gaze and glanced down at the weapon too.

"Oh, don't worry, I'm not going to use this." She pointed down at the terrifying black metal. "I'm actually here so

I don't *have* to use it at all. Because, believe me, it would be easier if I could, but, well, that's now how this plays out tonight."

"What do you mean?" Mitchell asked, voice still wobbling but at least loud enough to not be ignored. "Wh-where am I?"

He knew he was in a house, a living room, but there was nothing in his surroundings that led him to believe someone had been living in it. The furniture that was around was hidden by dust covers, the walls around them were bare, and despite the cold outside, the heater was obviously turned off and had been for a while. Even the chair he was splayed across felt rigid and cold.

However, despite the lack of life around him, Mitchell couldn't help but feel it was familiar.

The only person who knew the answer for sure smiled at him.

"I'd be less worried about where you are now and more concerned about where you're going next." That smile didn't change, but her gloved hand moved just enough that she could point down at the gun in her lap. "Because this gun?"

Pain was radiating across Mitchell's body, his stomach felt ready to empty at any moment, and neither could compete with the rising fear in his chest.

However, when the woman spoke again, every fiber of his attention attached to her words.

"It's not mine, Mr. Keys," she said. "It's yours. And I'm here to make sure you use it. So why don't we go ahead and get this job going."

Chapter Fifteen

There was a lot, she guessed, that they could have said. Eve, in bed at Darius's side, careful to keep her distance. Darius, in bed at Eve's side, polite enough to not comment on the fact that she had once again invaded his space. Yet, neither one spoke after she adjusted the blanket around her neck, trying to get warm.

And after that?

She fell asleep to silence.

It wasn't until she opened her eyes again that she finally felt the need to say something to the boy next door, now a man with a badge and a six-pack.

Mainly because, when she woke, the space Eve had been careful to give him had disappeared somewhere in the night. That chiseled upper body she had been in awe of the week before? She no longer wondered if it felt as impressive as it looked.

Eve woke up on top of it, her chin on his shoulder, her chest and stomach against his, and one leg pulled over him like she was his personal seat belt, and he wasn't going anywhere unless he unbuckled.

But it didn't seem like he had been trying to undo said seat belt during his shut-eye either. One of his hands—

warm and big—was resting on the bare skin of her thigh, her shorts having shifted during sleep. The other hand and arm that weren't bandaged had wrapped around Eve to accommodate her position. She felt his fingers flex on her lower back as he also stirred from sleep.

For all the years she had slept in the same room with Darius Williams, waking up in such a position was a first.

A first that felt extremely *intimate*.

Eve might have just woken from sleep, but she was immediately and keenly aware that there was something else she could feel beneath the fabric of both of their sleeping attire. Something just south of the muscles she had been admiring.

Her face heated—her body heated—and she readied to apologize for stepping over a line she herself had drawn to give the man a boundary from her.

But something was wrong.

The hand on her thigh tightened, and her chest rumbled as Darius spoke three words, low.

"Eve, go hide."

It was the equivalent to ice water being thrown onto her face. Any vestiges of sleep, or thoughts of Darius's body, turned into alert obedience. Eve unbuckled herself from Darius and slid out of bed on swift but quiet feet. By the time she was crossing the threshold of the attached bathroom, Darius was already on his feet, heading for the gun on hand.

If it wasn't for the small light on in the bathroom behind her, Eve wouldn't have been able to see his expression.

But she could, and it let her know absolutely one thing without any context: their quiet night was about to take a turn.

Darius motioned for her to go deeper into the bathroom, a simple point-and-go. She wanted to ask what had woken him, what he had heard, what he thought was happening. Instead, she backed up and watched as he slowly turned the doorknob.

Eve held her breath. Part of her had expected to jump. But nothing, and no one came through.

That didn't stop Darius.

He raised his gun and moved into the dark hallway. Before he was out of sight, he reached back and locked the bedroom door from the inside.

Eve held out her hand to stop him. He disappeared before she could.

The small light in the bathroom did nothing to alleviate how dark the room felt after the soft click of the door closing.

Eve closed the space between it and her on bare feet. She didn't unlock the door—she didn't even touch it. Instead, she leaned close to it and listened.

Her heart was beating too loudly, racing since she had realized Darius had gone into fight mode. Her breathing, too, was off. Too fast, too distracting.

She couldn't hear anything but herself.

Eve put a hand to her chest, closed her eyes and took a deep breath.

It helped.

There was nothing at first, but then she heard a faint sound of movement.

Eve tilted her head, trying to figure out exactly where it might be coming from.

Too far away to be from the hallway bathroom or Darius's childhood bedroom. Close enough, though, that it couldn't have been the foyer or the living room.

The kitchen?

Maybe Theo had gotten up for a late-night snack? Or maybe he had risen early to go do his marathon training?

Eve realized she didn't know what time it was, just when she realized her Theo theory was most likely wrong.

The faint noise in the distance turned into something breaking. Glass shattering. A loud thump. Something scraping against hardwood.

Then, worse.

Silence.

Eve's eyes flashed opened.

Hearing a gunshot would have been more surprising.

She strained to hear something—anything.

No one spoke.

Eve reached for the doorknob.

Surely if it had been Theo that Darius had run in to they would have said something or—

Footsteps.

Eve stopped her hand midair.

They were coming down the hallway.

Maybe it was Darius.

Maybe he had come to explain what was happening.

Creak.

The floorboard outside of the door—the one Darius wouldn't have stepped on—sounded.

But Darius didn't say a word.

The doorknob, however, started to turn. It stopped at the engaged lock.

If it were Darius, this would at the very least be the first time he would say it was him. Let her know to unlock it. Called out to Eve, giving an all clear.

Instead, the silence was only broken by another twist of the doorknob.

Eve hadn't realized she was already backing up on reflex.

It made running for the window even easier when the sound of frustration went from trying the lock to someone trying to break down the door.

DARIUS PLACED HIS gun in the kitchen sink. To say he was unhappy was an understatement.

The second shooter from the steel mill, the woman who had gotten away, had now found her way back into his life.

Into his home.

And she, and the gun she had pressed against Theo's back, had backed him into a corner in the kitchen.

He hadn't yet seen the second person in his home, but he sure heard him trying with everything he had to get into the main bedroom.

"I don't know what this is, but I can tell you that he has no part in it," Darius said, aggravated. Theo's deep frown seemed to mimic the feeling. Both men were angry and trying to put a lid on that rising rage so they could all come out of this safely.

The woman wasn't taller than the boy but had angled herself to where she could see Darius clearly from his side without losing the upper hand.

Without the gun trained on him, she would have looked all but normal among them. Casually dressed, somewhere between their ages, and a pleasant-enough smile without context. Though, even without the gun in her hand, two glaring details would have eventually shattered the image.

For one thing, her lip was busted, blood dripping down her chin, and two, she was wearing black gloves.

Normal didn't seem to be on her docket.

She nodded to Theo, whose eyebrow had a nasty gash with a matching blood drip, and kept her smile tight.

"You just voluntarily put your only weapon in the kitchen

sink," she pointed out. "He might not have been a piece on the game board, but you can't argue the results of using him."

She was right.

Even as he had walked into the living room following the sounds of her and Theo's scuffle, Darius hadn't had the time or the space to go on the defense or offense. Not without risking Theo's life.

Never mind having to deal with whoever was trying to break down the bedroom door.

If the lock hadn't held, Darius wouldn't have cared if there was space or not for him to move. He would have found a way to get back to Eve come hell or high water.

But the lock and the door were holding.

Which would give Eve enough time to hide or escape.

She was, as history had shown, good at climbing in and out of windows.

"What do you want?" Darius asked. He was hoping to stall for time to figure out a plan that got everyone he cared about out of harm's way. "Why are you here?"

The woman used her free hand to wipe some of the blood away from her chin. She sighed.

"I'm running into more complications than I intended, that's why." Her hold on her weapon and aim didn't waver while she multitasked.

"Then, quit," Darius said. "Tell me who you're working for, what game they wanted you to play, and then leave. Cancel whatever deal you made, whatever contract you entered, and go."

The woman's eyes widened in obvious surprise.

She said as much.

"The honest, rule-following Detective Williams giving me an out?" She shook her head a little. "Well, that wasn't on my bingo card for this trip, that's for sure."

Darius shrugged. He pointed at Theo.

"You holding me and my friends hostage in my house wasn't on my bingo card either," he pointed out. "Putting my gun in my sink was also something I didn't plan for. We all gain some and lose some in this."

The mystery man who had kept plowing into the bedroom door finally made progress. Before the woman could respond, the sound of splintering wood sent a new surge of adrenaline through Darius.

He didn't need to see into the hallway to know that the bedroom door was no longer hanging on its hinges.

Along with adrenaline, anger flooded his system.

He bit out a warning.

"Pull him back," he said. "Now."

The woman's smile was like the slithering of a snake. It twisted into one that indicated that she wouldn't take his order.

"I might consider this one," she said, motioning to Theo. "But everyone else needs to stay. Sorry."

She wasn't sorry, and Darius wasn't going to just stand there.

He could go backward for his gun in the sink or close the space between the woman and Theo in an attempt to disarm her. Then, he could deal with the man in his room. By then the backup that Eve had no doubt called would arrive to assist. The only variable he would have to worry about was Theo and, Theo's tensing body language probably meant he was about to try to make some kind of move to help.

Darius felt the muscles in his legs tighten in anticipation.

His fingers wanted to flex, ready to retrieve his weapon.

All he had to do now was make the first—

A body flew into view from the hallway, crashing into the woman with a loud yell and toppling her and her gun to the floor. The gun went off, but the shot embedded into the ceiling.

Darius moved quickly.

Before Theo could turn around to figure out what had happened, Darius was pushing him deeper into the kitchen.

"The sink!" he yelled.

Darius didn't wait to see if the boy understood. Instead, he joined the current fray happening in the space between the kitchen and the hallway.

And the person who had not, in fact, escaped to call for help.

Eve had attached to the woman's side like a koala. Legs wrapped around her, one arm trying to pull back the woman's neck, the other wildly flailing to try to get to the gun still in her hand.

While Darius had been surprised at her sudden appearance, their attacker looked completely taken aback by it. Her reflexes had probably kept the gun in her hand, but the rest of her didn't appear to be on the offense.

Not that she would have been able to do anything for long. Eve was too close to her—to the gun—and there was someone else in the house that, one step into the hallway, would have a clear view of Eve.

He needed the upper hand now.

Darius dropped down and grabbed the woman's wrist.

Then he broke it.

She yelled out in pain as the gun dropped from her grip and clattered to the ground.

Darius had it in his hand within a heartbeat.

Which was good because he had to pivot even more quickly.

Darius dropped his hold on the woman and switched his hand over to Eve. Timing wasn't on his side. He trained his new gun down the hallway on the bedroom door, hoping the man who had gone searching inside was slower than him.

He wasn't.

The man came out of the main bedroom, gun already up.

Darius shot the second he could. He missed but knew he would.

He was too busy yanking Eve by the shirt backward into the kitchen with all the force he had.

The sound of fabric tearing was overshadowed by the man's returning fire.

"Stop!" the woman on the ground yelled out.

The man didn't listen. Darius jumped backward into the kitchen, out of sight, while the man continued to unload his clip with no obvious regard for his partner lying in the way.

She tried to make herself flat, yelling out for the man to stop, eyes closing at each shot. Pain already etched into every syllable from her broken wrist.

Whoever the man down the hall was, he was unaffected.

Darius wasn't.

He reached down to grab the woman's leg and pulled her back with him into the kitchen. She didn't fight him, but she sure yelled.

Darius didn't join her as the man thundered into view, eyes wide and gun up.

The fact of the matter was Darius had already decided to pull the trigger the second he saw the gunman. He had been after Eve, and he had no issues about shooting at her, at his partner, and obviously no issues with killing Darius too.

This was no longer a defensive play.

He was only waiting for a kill shot.

So the nanosecond the man showed his face—sharp lines and stubble and rage—Darius's index finger flexed, pulling the trigger with certainty.

The gun, however, had other plans.
For the first time in Darius's career, his gun jammed.
The shot that tore through the house after was deafening.

Chapter Sixteen

Eve only saw one of three things that happened all at once.

The woman lying on the floor between Darius's legs gave the man a look of such acute concern that, for that moment, it seemed she had forgotten to be angry or in pain or that fighting them might have been in her best interest.

Instead, it was worry.

She could see something that Eve, at Darius's back, couldn't see.

And that was before the shot went off.

After her gaze went from concern to blatant confusion.

Then Eve's attention split to the other two things that had happened while her focus had strayed.

A heavy thud and a slight shake of the foundation let her know that the man in the hallway had taken the single shot. At least, Eve knew it wasn't Darius. Her hands were already against his back, as if touching him let her know he was still standing. Theo had been more proactive.

He had his own gun up and was already standing at Darius's side, yelling out commands.

It confused Eve at first.

Maybe their attacker was still trying to fight? But then, why wasn't Darius moving from his spot?

Beneath her hands she could still feel the man's tension.

When it lessened, it was her sign to finally get back to reality.

Eve stepped to the side, between the two men, to size up the situation, but Darius was faster. She saw only a sliver of the attacker on the floor, blood already on the hardwood, before his hand covered her eyes.

"Don't look," he said, voice low.

Normally, she would have bucked at the command, but another voice cut her off.

"H-he's dead, isn't he?" It was a man's small voice, breaking slightly and coming from the hallway. A voice that shouldn't have been there at all.

"Mitchell?"

Mitchell made a small noise of confirmation.

"He is," Darius answered. "Theo, keep your gun on her. Mitchell, give me yours. Evelyn, turn around."

Using her full first name did the trick. Eve turned and lost the warmth of Darius's hand. The kitchen window on the far side of the room showed nothing but darkness as the rest of the people shifted around.

Darius secured Mitchell's gun, Theo secured the woman, and Mitchell appeared at Eve's side as they started making calls.

Eve would have paid more attention to it all had she not focused so completely on Mitchell when he came into view.

His face was black and blue, there was dry blood at his hairline, and there was broken and bloodied duct tape at his wrist.

"What happened?" Eve asked, hands flitting up. She didn't touch him when he flinched.

His voice was loud enough to carry to the room around them. His gaze went over Eve's shoulder. He was incredibly pale.

"She grabbed me outside when I was leaving earlier. She said I needed to come back a-and kill Detective Williams and—" Mitchell's voice broke. He took a breath. He was more quiet than before when he continued. "And you. She said that I needed to kill you."

Darius swore behind Eve.

The woman remained quiet on the floor.

Whatever fight she had had in her earlier was gone.

Mitchell shook his head.

"She said I had to be the one to do it—only me—but I said no. Never." His voice hardened. "I tried to fight her, to stop her, but that man showed up, and I guess he got me good. I woke up on the floor alone. I rushed over after and found a gun on the floor in there. I-I used it."

"My gun," Theo explained, voice as solid as Darius's had been. "I heard them breaking in and didn't have time to do anything other than defend. She got the upper hand and disarmed me. I barely had time to react." Regret laced his tone.

Darius picked up on it.

"You made enough noise to alert me," he assured him. "You gave me the time to come out and Eve enough time to escape."

Mitchell returned his gaze to Eve. His eyebrow arched.

Eve could feel Darius's unasked question hanging in the air around them.

Sirens started up in the distance. They mingled in with her sigh.

"There was no way I was leaving everyone behind." She shrugged. "I went out one bedroom window and came in through another."

It was the truth. The second she had realized the man outside of the locked bedroom door wasn't Darius was the moment Eve had gone through the main window. After that there had been no other path for her to take other than to go to her favorite window. She had climbed into Darius's childhood bedroom like a gentle breeze easing its way across a summer day. No one had heard her. Not until she had wanted to be heard.

A talking point she would get an earful about from Darius later, she was sure.

"Where was she keeping you?" he asked now.

Mitchell thumbed over his shoulder. The movement made him wince. Still, he promptly answered.

"The house next door."

"The house next door?" Eve repeated. "My house?"

Mitchell nodded.

"It's empty," Darius added.

The sirens were becoming louder. Backup was about to arrive.

It seemed to apply a new sense of pressure to the woman on the floor.

"If I were you, I'd think real quick about what happens next," she said. "You can either tell the truth and get us all killed, or you can lie and buy yourselves more time to figure out what I won't tell you. Because I guarantee you that you can't do both."

Eve couldn't see the woman still, but she easily heard the smile in her voice.

Just like she heard the anger in Darius's when he responded without hesitation.

"I suggest you shut your mouth," he said, frost on every word. "You lost any shot at bargaining with me the second you threatened *her*."

"I now see where my fatal flaw was with this one," the woman replied just as quickly. "I thought Miss Myers was insignificant."

She snorted.

"Judging by the look on your face, Detective, I guess we were dead wrong about that."

WINNE CAME IN CONCERNED. After glancing at Theo's beaten face, she left the kitchen angry. She took several even, quick steps back into the living room where their mystery woman was being cuffed.

Then Winnie slapped her across the face.

It was so loud it echoed.

"That's for hurting them," she exclaimed.

Her father, Price, had been the first responder on scene and was the one currently working on the woman's handcuffs. His surprise was instant and mirrored in Theo, who rushed to Winnie's side.

For a moment, Darius thought the move was unnecessary.

But then he noted her balled up hands, her widening stance and the absolute mask of anger that covered her face.

Winnie was about to attack again.

This time probably giving more than one slap.

It was a guess that proved to be correct as the young woman launched herself again at the hired hand.

Then everyone was yelling.

The woman at Price, Price at Winnie, Winnie at Theo for grabbing her, and Theo at Winnie for fighting *him* to get to the woman.

It was chaos.

And perfect for Darius.

He took a step back and quickly and quietly addressed Mitchell. Eve, at his side, listened in with a slight head tilt.

"You came over here earlier tonight because Eve and I are having an affair," Darius said, hurriedly. "You decided to end things and were attacked when leaving."

Mitchell's eyes widened.

"What?"

Darius continued, ignoring the question.

"Instead of asking for a lawyer, ask for your brother," he said. "Tell him you're afraid of me and my job in the department. Really lean into that. Got it?"

Mitchell didn't immediately answer.

Eve did it for him.

"I'll refuse to see Scott to really sell it," she added. "If they want to question me alone, I'll only ask for you."

Darius nodded.

"That'll work."

Mitchell still looked confused.

Eve patted his arm but kept her gaze on Darius.

"We've got this," she assured him.

THREE HOURS LATER and she'd proved herself right. Not only did Mitchell make a show about their alleged affair, he outright refused to answer any more questions without his brother Scott present.

Eve was the same but less flashy with it.

When she gave her statement, she did so with the sheriff and Darius at her side.

Though, the sheriff wasn't at all pleased with the situation.

He finally voiced his displeasure during a small window of quiet as everyone waited for Scott to arrive.

Liam was leaning against the wall, outside the sheriff department's bathroom, with a long face and an even longer sigh leaking out. Darius didn't miss the glance he cast around the hallways to make sure they were alone before he spoke.

"I haven't known you as long as most of the people here have, but I can confidently say that you having an affair with an almost-married woman doesn't seem to be in line with your character."

His sheriff's badge would have had a glint to it had they been out in the sun. Instead, the fluorescents made it look dull. The lack of luster wasn't reflected in the wearer. Liam had been tightly strung since seeing his son sporting blood and bruises.

He had been the only one, in fact, who hadn't reprimanded Winnie for her pointed attack on the woman who had caused it.

At any other time, Darius would have appreciated the enthusiasm.

Now he hoped to avoid its consequences.

"If it was any other woman, I wouldn't be in this situation," Darius said, telling the truth without all the details as dressings.

"But she's your childhood friend. Your former next-door neighbor."

The sheriff's words were calculated. Blunt.

Their relationship was a two-way street. Liam knew Darius was holding something back, just as Darius knew that Liam was trying to get him to admit to it.

But he couldn't.

Not yet.

So Darius stuck to the truth he could tell. The truth that might best help the sheriff understand why he was acting out of character. Or, really, why acting out of character for Eve was as in character as he could ever be.

First Darius cleared his throat.

Then he told the sheriff a story only three people in the world knew about.

The story of why, even as a boy, he would do anything for Evelyn Myers.

"When we were younger, before Eve moved, there was a boy who lived in the neighborhood who really, really didn't like me," Darius started. "Even now, two decades later, I have no idea why he hated me as much as he did. I wasn't mean to him, didn't ignore him, never fanned the flames when he still tried to bully me. He just didn't like me. Every summer he spent with his grandmother, he would find ways to peck at me. Not Eve—who, by the way, tried to fight him multiple times in my name—just me."

The heaviness of memory pressed into Darius's back.

He was uncomfortable, but he continued.

"Then one summer, something in him changed. He wasn't just some annoying kid who was annoyed by me, he was angry. And then that anger almost killed me." Liam's eyes widened a little. It was enough to verify that the man really hadn't known the story. That there hadn't been a thread of town gossip about him that Darius had managed to miss the past several years.

He was glad for it.

This was his and Eve's story. It wasn't some cheap tale to give out for some kind of shock value or as a way to break boredom.

"Before the steel mill ruled this town by itself, there was a tractor-supply company that employed a lot of the town," Darius explained. "They had two locations—the main office, and a warehouse where they stored equipment and occasionally did maintenance. The warehouse was rarely staffed unless someone actively needed to use what was inside or do a pickup. It was also two miles from my house. Which is how Jon got me there on foot and alone."

Darius shook his head, unable to avoid the anger he had at himself for being so stupid back then.

He said as much now.

"I was naive enough to believe him when he said he and Eve had found something that they wanted to show me," he continued. "The second he said Eve was there, I was already anxious that I wasn't, so I followed him into the warehouse without blinking an eye. But she wasn't there, and Jon attacked. He got the upper hand, and before I knew it, I was tied up to an old industrial rotary tiller." Darius laughed. It was in bitter disbelief, even all these years later. "He had jerry-rigged the tiller to twist the rope until it broke or until I was pulled up to the first blade."

"My God," the sheriff interrupted.

Darius understood the knee-jerk reaction. The horror, the sudden escalation of it all, had made it feel like he had been placed in a tub of ice in the moment. It wasn't until the tiller turned on and started to drag him backward that young Darius pushed his shock aside to fight against the rope.

"No matter how much he hated me, he couldn't stomach watching whatever happened next. He left when I was a foot away from the first blade." Darius shook his head a little. He could still feel the twisting panic in his stomach like it had only happened yesterday. "The rope was for industrial use, and the knot he'd tied was surprisingly effective. I couldn't untie it, and I couldn't miss that first blade, no matter how much I moved."

It had been the single most terrifying moment of his existence.

He would die alone, in a terrible way, on the floor of a warehouse his dad and police would never think to look in, while his mother would never care to look for him at all.

The quiet son of parents who were never there, gone missing at the hands of a bully down the road.

Darius smiled.

"But I had Eve."

Warmth spread over that twisting terror in his gut.

The scariest moment of his young life held hands with one of the most profound.

"She got worried when I wasn't home, and instead of waiting around to know the reason, she went directly to Jon's house."

"How did she know he was behind it?" Liam asked. It was a genuine question, no suspicion that it might have warranted from an outsider.

Darius couldn't help but give a little laugh.

"Because she said she knew I wouldn't just leave her behind without a word," he answered. "A little kid with an overwhelming sense of confidence in her friend's loyalty to her."

"She was right."

Darius nodded.

"Jon's grandmother told her the direction we had headed in, and she took off running," he continued. "She didn't stop, not even when she passed Jon. She just kept going until she said she heard me screaming. She broke a window with a rock and found me just as the first blade was cutting into my back."

For all the serious bluster he had clung to during his career—and in most of his personal life too—Darius broke his own character and let the sheriff see something he wasn't even sure Eve had seen before.

He let Liam see him as that scared little boy on the warehouse floor.

With wide eyes, still able to fill with the absolute adoration and wonder he'd had for the little girl who had come to him covered in sweat and worry, he looked at his sheriff with every wall he'd built through the years completely down.

"Eve pulled the blade off my back just far enough to slide

her hand in between and, as the blade went into her hand, she used the other one to help me untie the knot. And, when we finally got it undone and I was able to move away, do you know what the first thing she said was?" Darius didn't give him the time to answer. "She was angry she hadn't gotten there sooner."

Her hand bleeding, hair plastered to her face and neck from sweat, dirt pressed into her clothes, shards of glass still embedded in one of her shoes, and all she had been was angry at herself for not running faster.

"I never told her that, in that moment, all that fear and pain and panic I had been feeling just went away. Instead, what I felt was nothing but pride." The warmth from the moment spread through Darius, just as warm as it had as a kid. "Pride in her for being so brave and selfless. And pride in myself because, for the first time in my life, I was able to feel worthy. That something I had done had earned the unwavering love of the girl from next door."

Darius shook his head.

"That moment is the entire reason I got into law enforcement," he admitted. "She gave me a gift, and I wanted to spread that to as many people as possible to honor it. To honor her. Even after she left town and we lost touch, I never for one second forgot her. She's why I help people. She's why I try to save them. She's why, even if I can't, I'll make sure I bring whoever hurt them to justice in the end. Liam, she *is* my why."

The sheriff's expression gave nothing away.

Darius waited, knowing they were already back to the present before he asked his question.

"So the point of you telling me that story is—what? That you're not going to tell me what really is going on with you, her and the Keyses?"

Darius felt his walls rise back and settle into place again. There was no smile, no adoration in his eyes and no warmth left in his chest.

There was anger now.

"This is me telling you that there isn't anything I wouldn't do for that woman." Darius felt that anger rise. He lowered his voice, but the feeling behind it was still just as clear and loud as if he had been yelling. "And that's why, if I were you, I'd break Scott Keys before it's my turn to get to him."

Chapter Seventeen

Scott Keys was wearing his Italian leather.

That's how Eve knew that he had come to the department for blood.

"What the media will never tell you about Scott Keys is that he actually dislikes people calling him *rich*."

Eve stepped back from her spot next to the window in the break room door, no longer able to see Scott after he disappeared into a meeting room down the hall. She had only seen a sliver of him but could have spotted that outfit from space if given a glimpse.

She explained her statement to Darius and Theo, both behind her with coffees in hand.

"You can't earn respect if you pay for it, and he believes the same goes for any reputation worth having," she continued. "He wants people to see him as the charming philanthropist and not the bored trust-fund baby who likes attention. So when it comes to what he wears in public, he's always been careful to pick clothes that look nice but aren't too flashy or too easy a reminder of his inherited wealth."

Eve tapped the door, pointing in the direction of the meeting room where the sheriff was waiting.

"What he's wearing right now is more expensive than

the department's salaries combined. And that's not even factoring in the shoes. Those were custom-made *in* Italy."

"Which means he's not trying to be humble right now," Darius guessed.

Eve shook her head.

"No. Right now I think he's trying to remind us that we're not on the same page as him. Not even the same book."

It had been another hour since they had arrived at the department and gone over their initial statements. The woman who had attacked them was under lock and key at the hospital, while the man who had been killed had been identified as Brae Lee, a frequent flyer at a jail two counties over for offenses that ranged from drunk-and-disorderlies to a smattering of petty thefts. He hadn't had a history of violence, but his ex-wife had been quick to let them know that in the last two years his entire personality had seemed to change.

"The man stumbled through life with nothing but cheap beer and excuses until he lost his job, our house and me," she had said on the phone, voice clear even on Speaker. "Then one day he disappears only to show up with his back straight and his pockets lined with cash. Said he found some good luck and would keep having it as long as he did some traveling and kept his mouth shut." There had been a pause. Eve had imagined the woman had shaken her head. "He never got into the details past that, and honestly, I didn't want to know. He gave me some of the worst years of my life. So I didn't want to give him anymore of my time. That was the last time I spoke to him, and I haven't had contact since."

She was sad for the loss of life and maybe a touch regretful, but she had nothing left for them to use other than the theory that whatever he had gotten into two years ago had probably led him to die in Darius's house now.

It had been enough for Darius, though. Rose and Deputy

Gavin had already agreed to deep dive into the man's life to try and look for some kind of connection to the Keyses. Something Darius had officially requested in Rose's office just before they had come to the break room.

"I can't give you details, but if I were doing the looking, I'd be staring at Scott Keys and his close friend, Toby Sanderson," Darius had said. "But I'd also be a bit discreet about it too."

Eve had expected the piece of advice to get a reaction out of Rose or, at least, a question or two. Instead, she had run a hand over her pregnant belly and nodded. She had already been moving behind her desk to the computer before they could leave the room.

"He's either confident or he's trying to be intimidating," Theo said now, speaking about Scott. "Which could mean he's prepared for what happened, or he's trying to send us a warning to not involve him in it at all."

Eve nodded.

Darius shook his head.

"Or he could be here to see how much we know—or don't know—about everything that's happened."

Theo conceded.

"To be fair, at this point I'm not even sure I know what we do or don't know." He touched the butterfly bandage on his cheek. "It's been a pretty wild last week or so."

He wasn't wrong.

Coming to Seven Roads had felt like a lifetime ago. Wearing a wedding dress, standing in the middle of the road and staring at the now-grown Darius had felt even further away.

And everything that had happened since?

She'd had more questions than she had answers since arriving.

It was…frustrating, to say the least.

A frustration that they all shared, even as a silence fell over them. Eve glanced over at Darius. Her cheeks heated slightly. She wanted to talk to him in private, but she wasn't sure what to say. Or even if she should say anything at all. They were in a mess.

A mess because of a man in Italian leather.

A man with a wrath that she had yet to see come out.

Even now Eve could still feel the fear of watching Scott unleash on Mitchell in that hotel room.

The hired men and woman who had come after them so far were truly scary, but there was something about the socialite that put fire ants beneath Eve's skin.

Scott Keys didn't only have rage as a weapon. He had money.

A lot of it.

When the sheriff came to see them a few minutes later, he let them know that anger hadn't been a part of his discussion with the Keys brothers. Instead, his gaze had landed squarely on Eve.

"Scott Keys wants to see you. Both of you." Then he looked at Darius. "And I'll be frank with you here—he's not asking."

FINALLY, DARIUS MET Scott Keys.

He'd seen him, sure, nodded to him and watched as deputies had taken his statement. Darius had read the news articles too, googled him and seen enough press about him during his hospital stay to *feel* like he had met the man already.

Yet now he was in the same space. Within the same four walls.

Now he could *see* the expensive suit and shoes.

He could see the winning smile and movieworthy appearance.

And none of it mattered because all Darius cared about was Eve.

Scott wanted to hurt her.

So Darius wanted to hurt him.

But first they had to do some dancing.

Eve took the seat across from Scott. Darius didn't sit at all. He stood at her shoulder instead, gaze settling on the man in Italian leather. Scott waited in silence, eyes sharp and suit wrinkle-free. If the sheriff hadn't already given them a heads-up, Darius would have traced every detail about the man at his side to try and get more information.

He would have also showed a hint of excitement.

Before they had been attacked in his house, the plan had been to find a way to talk to Toby Sanderson and, if Darius was right, the nerve that Eve and Mitchell's secret investigation had hit before the wedding had been arranged.

So to have him already seated next to the man of the hour, wearing a suit that was notably less expensive and an expression that was also notably less calm, was like hitting the jackpot.

The man they had planned to seek out had come right to them.

And he didn't seem that enthused about it either.

Toby was fiddling with a pen between his hands as Scott finally addressed them.

"Detective Williams, I'm sure you know who I am, but who would I be if I didn't introduce myself?" Scott didn't stand. He didn't reach his hand out. He didn't make to move to at all. "My name is Scott Keys. My brother is Mitchell Keys, and I currently run the Keys Foundation. Next to me is my friend, Toby Sanderson. Typically my lawyer would be in his spot… However, he's currently a part of a homicide case file that I'm sure is still on your desk."

Scott's gaze slid down slowly to Eve.

"I also happen to be the former employer of one Miss Evelyn Myers, who I am sad to say was terminated via email before arriving at the department just now."

The silence was immediate.

It fell like a guillotine had dropped between them.

And there was a tone.

One Darius didn't like being directed at Eve.

Darius gave it right back.

"I'm Detective Williams and can confirm that, along with the people who shot me and Eve and then tried to kill us again, I am currently investigating the homicide of a Gary Whittaker." Darius put his hand on the back of Eve's chair. He wanted to seem relaxed despite the anger growing inside of him. "And while I can appreciate you keeping track of my work, I should use the same reminder to point out that my time is limited. So is this a social call, or is there a specific reason you need to talk to us?"

Toby wasn't a cool cucumber. At least not like his friend. Toby's lip curled up like he was ready to snarl at them.

Scott was more eloquent with it.

His smile was picture-polite.

"Other than my brother calling me here because he's afraid that this—" he pointed at Eve and then Darius "—new development might spell out more trouble for him, I thought it might be a good idea to come in and make a few statements to the two of you. With a witness."

Toby put the pen down.

An air of self-importance seemed to expand around him.

His restrained snarl turned into a sneer.

In any other context, Darius would have mentioned that a good witness would be a third party with no clear side in mind.

But he was awfully curious.

Scott's stare settled on Eve again.

"To become an adulteress is already a questionable choice, but to leave a Keys at the altar at the first sign of trouble is an extremely disappointing thing," he said. "One of the reasons I hired you in the first place was because of your ability to think quickly and pivot in a high-intensity situation. Both traits I appreciated in your work over the last year. However, now I'm not so sure those truths still hold."

He paused. Not too long or too noticeably, but with enough space in between to change his expression slightly.

If Darius hadn't suspected Scott Keys of being a cruel, calculating man already, the subtle shift in his demeanor would have aroused suspicion. He wasn't outright threatening them when he spoke again, but there was an edge to every word.

"Starting next Monday there will be an investigation into your involvement with the Keys Foundation, the personal lives of the Keys family, and any and all connections to our beloved late Gary Whittaker." Scott cut a quick look to Darius. "Since we aren't sure where the law enforcement priorities lie, we will make sure that you *will* answer for any wrongdoings that you have committed for your own personal gain. And then you will pay for everything you have done."

The last statement hit hard.

Darius's body reacted faster than his brain.

His fist balled into the fabric of the chair back, rage no longer rising but instead crashing across his entirety.

Scott was back to looking at him again. He must have seen the change.

A whisper of a smile seemed to cross the rich man's lips.

Not only had he just clearly threatened Eve, he'd come into Darius's domain to do it.

And not only that—he'd done it in front of Darius too.

It was nothing short of infuriating.

It was also about to earn Darius's not-so-composed wrath.

He opened his mouth to say something—he wasn't exactly sure what—when another voice unexpectedly joined the chat.

"Fair enough." Eve's voice wasn't small or weak. It was loud and steady. She waited for the men across the table from her to focus before she continued.

Which is how Darius was able to read the absolute surprise in them when she spoke again.

"And when they investigate, they'll find my investigation into you."

Instead of looking at Scott, Darius could tell by the turn of her head that Eve was staring right at Toby.

His eyes widened. He opened and closed his mouth like a fish out of water for a moment.

"Me? What do you mean investigation into me? Investigation into what?"

She shrugged.

"Oh, you know, just the whole you visiting small towns before some kind of calamity happens, only to then pave the way for our White Knight here to ride in and save the day. At first I wondered if it was just a coincidence—your bad luck—but then I saw the pattern and understood that you're either one of two things, Mr. Sanderson."

Eve tapped the table's top between them.

"You're either a man who brings the plague, or you're the man who tells others to bring it. Then, after it spreads, you get to sit back and watch as your best friend, with all his resources and money, cures what you helped infect."

Toby shook his head, anger and shock deepening his frown.

"That's *ridiculous*," he exclaimed. "You think *I* have been—what?—sabotaging random towns through the years? That sounds like a bad plot to a bad movie. Can you believe this, Scott?"

The man in question hadn't moved a muscle.

His face was like stone.

As he answered, his words were just as hard.

"That's quite the accusation there, Miss Myers," he said. "If I had known you had such an imagination, I wouldn't have wasted your talents by simply hiring you as my assistant."

Most people might have heard the cold in his words—the edge that was there too—and decided against continuing to push.

But most people weren't Eve.

She pushed her chair back and stood.

Compared to the White Knight of Small-town Living, the woman dressed in plain jeans and a fuzzy sweater seemed to suddenly tower over them all.

It only added to the sudden change in demeanor when she lightly laughed.

"What can I say? You were right about me, Scott. It turns out I *am* good at thinking on my feet. That's how I found your flight logs, Toby. All of them."

Without waiting for a reaction, Eve turned and walked right out of the meeting room.

It gave Darius full view of the men sitting across the table from him.

Toby was confused, quiet with it too. The pen he had been fiddling with lay forgotten beneath his hands.

Scott was also quiet.

But his stare was burrowing a hole into Darius.

Whatever the White Knight of Small-town Living was feeling…it wasn't good.

Chapter Eighteen

There was a lot that was said in the department after that. Eve, thankfully, heard little to none of it while sitting in Darius's office with Winnie. The younger woman shared a bag of cookies with her while Theo, his father the sheriff, Winnie's father the deputy, and Darius were going room to room, doing who knew what.

All Eve did know was that she was in deep trouble no matter how she looked at what she had done.

Sometime within their stay inside of Darius's office, Eve let out a sigh that was loud, long and filled with defeat.

"I'm doomed," she said. "Big doomed. Doomed bad. Badly doomed. The worst doomed."

Winnie had been poring over information on her laptop, forgotten cookie hovering over the trackpad while she did so.

At this stream of exclamations, she looked up.

"I've seen this department come together and protect each other before, even against some pretty scary odds. No matter what Mr. Keys decides to do, they won't let anything happen to you or Mitchell."

Eve lolled her head to the side to look at the girl head on.

"I wasn't talking about this business with Scott, Toby and the hired hitpeople."

It took Winnie a second, but she finally clued in. A small smile turned up the corner of her lips.

"You're afraid of Detective Williams," she clarified. "Because you basically told the bad guys that you knew they were bad and exactly what evidence you had to prove it."

Eve dropped her head down and huffed.

"It wasn't like I was planning to do it," she defended. "It just kind of came out."

That was as true as a truth could be. Sitting there across from Scott with his fancy shoes and Toby with his nonchalant attitude had been grating. But not for the reasons it should have been.

Scott had requested to talk to her *and* Darius to threaten them. To threaten her. To fire her and make a show of it.

And he'd brought Toby to do it.

That grating against her nerves had been a noise that had transformed into absolute quiet once Eve had realized this might be her only chance to play their own hand.

They hadn't been certain that the flight records of Toby's private jet had been the reason for Scott pushing for the wedding, for Gary's murder or for the subsequent attacks.

So Eve had gambled with the piece of potential evidence.

Or, really, she had used it as bait.

Bait that had forced Darius to make his own moves.

He had put her in his office without an explanation of what he was about to do, only that she and Winnie needed to wait.

It felt like waiting outside of the principal's office in school.

She was definitely going to get a talking-to about her behavior.

Eve pushed herself forward in the roller chair, tucking

her legs up against her chest as she did so. Her shoulder hurt a little, but she had more pressing things to worry about.

"I wanted to help us skip to the end of this thing," she said. "It feels like months since Gary's body was found. And after last night, I can't stand waiting for the other shoe to drop on us. I'd rather throw my own shoe first to see what happens."

"I understand why you did it," she said. "Last night was terrifying, and I wasn't even there."

Winnie's tone was soft and caring, a far cry from how the young woman had yelled at their attacker at Darius's house. Theo's attacker. She had only fully settled down once she was sitting next to Theo after the paramedics had given him the okay.

Though, if Eve were a betting woman she would put money on the fact that Winnie's cute and gentle appearance could transform into feral at any moment. A kind of feral that would probably put the men around them to shame.

It's one reason why Eve liked Winnie so much. She felt a kinship there.

She also was starting to be so fond of Winnie for the simple fact that both she and Theo genuinely seemed to care about Darius. Even though both of their parents worked at the department, they had stayed in proximity to their detective. Theo had left them in the office as Darius's shadow earlier. Eve had no doubt he would return with the ready-to-scold-her detective too.

"Do you think he'll really be mad at me for showing my hand to Scott and maybe messing up the investigation?" Eve paused midspin to ask. If it had been Theo, he would have probably just nodded. Instead, Winnie was thoughtful with her answer.

"I think he'll raise his voice and huff at you, but I don't

think he's mad." She put the cookie in her hand down and finally closed her laptop. "I think he's just worried, you know? And not because of the investigation. He cares about you, and you just spit in the face of the monster he's trying to catch. No matter how good a detective he is, he can't predict the future. He knows that, which means he knows that he'll never be able to one-hundred-percent keep you from getting hurt. That plus the fact that both of you have already been shot probably isn't helping his frustration."

Eve let her mouth hang open a little. She hadn't expected an in-depth opinion. One that, after her accidental eavesdropping earlier, made a slow blush slid up to her cheeks.

She tried to play the feeling off.

"You make it sound like I'm more important to him than I am," Eve said. "I haven't even seen the man in over twenty years."

Winnie's smile was small and warm. Her next question caught Eve off guard.

"Have you had any serious boyfriends in those twenty-something years?"

Eve was further thrown off by how immediate her *no* was.

"I mean, there was really no time for it when I was younger," she tacked on. "I was taking care of my dad, and then I was working to pay off our debt. Then I was trying to find my place in the world, and well, I didn't have much space to do anything."

"So you've never dated anyone? Ever?"

There was no pressure or harshness in Winnie's questions. Just a genuine curiosity.

It made Eve pause a little to think about the best way to phrase her answer.

"No, I did date some," she admitted. "Though, I'm not

sure any of it counts. Most were double dates from coworkers where they dragged me along, while others were just casual meetups or as a result of bumping into someone. I tried a dating app once, went to the movies and had a nice meal, but it didn't work out. None of them ever worked out."

Winnie's gaze was expectant.

With a small sigh of defeat, Eve smiled as she continued.

"As silly as it sounds, as *pathetic* as it sounds, I think a part of me just kept looking for the boy next door."

"Detective Williams," Winnie expounded.

Eve nodded.

"Before I left, we were best friends with just a pure, innocent friendship. And yet I think Darius somehow became my standard for everything." It was true, Eve realized. Now more than ever. Sure, she'd had her first kiss. Her first time. Her first boyfriend in name and then her first breakup. She had experienced different dates and men and had tried her best to…care. But none of them had stuck. Not like the boy next door had. "I had a coworker who was a little too invested in my lack of love life and would try every day to sell me on the ideal of true love and soul mates. One day she was really, really insistent on me putting myself out there so I'd find a half."

"Find a half," Winnie repeated.

"Everyone is out there in the world looking for their other half, so when they find them they can finally feel whole," Eve said. "She said no matter how hard I was faking it, no one can be happy as a half."

Eve raised her hand to stop whatever feelings Winnie might have had about that.

"I don't think that's true," Eve added quickly. "I think people can be whole all by themselves, and if they want to be with someone, that someone can add on to their lives and be just as meaningful—"

Winnie was quick. "But?" she ventured.

Eve knew she should have felt embarrassed or shy or something at what she said next. She didn't, though.

"Since the days when Darius let me in through his bedroom window as kids, I've never been able to move on from him." No heat ran up her neck or pooled in her cheeks. No warmth surrounded her heart or flooded her belly. She felt completely unchanged. What she was saying was just a fact. "And I know it's wild to say that some boy I knew as a kid—the same boy I didn't see for over twenty years—completely changed me, but he did. I think that's why I've never really settled, at least when it comes to relationships. Part of me just…"

Eve tilted her head to side, as if movement would make it easier to find the right words.

She wasn't sure if it worked.

She simply said what she now knew as true.

"Part of me just never forgot that window. Never forgot the boy sitting inside that room." Eve ran a thumb across the side of her hand. The one she had gotten at the warehouse all those years ago. Their first matching scar. She lowered her voice, tired for the woman who had gone on those dates, trying to figure out why she couldn't make her heart move at all. Trying to find her other half but eventually giving up when she couldn't.

Now Eve understood why it had never worked.

Why it never would.

It was such a jolting revelation, and yet it didn't really feel like anything all that new.

Eve looked at Winnie and told her straight and true.

"I've never been able to find my other half out there because I've never been a half myself. Not since I met Darius. Without trying to, without meaning to, and I guess without me realizing it either, *he* made me whole."

That was the long and short of it.

The damn ridiculous truth.

Eve had grown up loving Darius Williams without reservation, without any doubt and without knowing it. And after seeing him again on the county road, her wearing a wedding dress and him wearing a badge, that love had stretched its legs and decided to walk somewhere it hadn't yet walked before.

"I guess I'm in love with him," Eve admitted. She nodded once to herself to confirm it. "And I suppose I always have been. Maybe that's why I never noticed. Like one day you open your closet and all your clothes are blue. You never realized it was your favorite color, but the evidence sure is clear once you look close enough."

Eve watched as the younger girl's gaze widened.

She couldn't help but laugh a little.

"Sorry, I didn't mean to have such a personal epiphany right in front of you," she said. "Probably not what you expected to hear."

Despite the potential awkwardness, Winnie collected herself well. She showed a smile that felt as genuine as every smile Eve had seen the girl make since they had met.

"I'll take a beautiful epiphany over drama-filled gossip any day, so don't worry. I'm actually grateful you told me. I feel honored." Her smile grew until her eyes wrinkled a little. Eve mimicked the growth. Just as she let it drop as Winnie's started to fade.

"Are you going to tell Darius?" she asked.

"Tell him what? That he's the only person I think I've ever fully and completely loved?" Eve snorted. "After the trouble I brought him—brought you and this town—I don't think I have the right to flood the waters any more than I already have. Not after I left him alone here."

The last part Eve hadn't meant to say. Truly, it had been the only part of her feelings she had hoped to keep close to her chest.

Because it was guilt.

Winnie's eyebrow arched high.

"You mean when you went to Texas with your dad to take care of him? It's not exactly like you had a choice."

That guilt in Eve soured the warmth she had finally been able to identify in her chest.

"Then, what was my excuse for the last twenty years?" she asked. "Why did I only come back when there was trouble?"

It wasn't a question that was meant to be answered. Not by Winnie and certainly not by Eve. There was no answer that would ever be enough in her opinion.

She had made a promise to Darius's mother that he was hers. For life.

Then she'd disappeared from his for twenty years.

Loving Darius Williams was one thing.

Asking him to love her back was another.

And Eve just couldn't do that to him.

Winnie opened her mouth, probably readying to encourage her, if Eve had to guess, but the attempt was cut off by a knock against the doorframe.

Eve swiveled in her chair to see Theo and his laptop bag swung over his shoulder. He shared a quick look between them before pointing in the direction of the front of the department.

"Everything has been taken care of for now, which means it's time for us to head home," he announced.

Eve stood at once, the chair rolling back behind her and hitting the desk with a little too much force.

"Is there any more news? What do we do when we get there? What happens next?"

Eve and her confession were replaced by Eve and her anxiousness to be done with Scott Keys and his potential retaliation.

Theo put his hands up in self-defense against the interrogative onslaught, but it was Darius who spoke next. He came into view with his eyes down on the phone in his hand.

"What happens next is us going to get some sleep, since none of us got anything worth anything last night," he said.

"Wait. You can't just go back to your house," Winnie pointed out. "What if another hired killer or someone else shows up to attack you? Especially now that they know about the flight records?"

Winnie the Feral Fighter of Theo-attackers was coming back up to the surface. Her words were no longer gentle and warm. Theo's eyes went to her at the change. It might have been Eve's imagination, but it almost seemed like his cheeks reddened a little at it.

Darius didn't look up from his phone as he answered.

"Everyone has a place to go that should be safe. Theo is going with you back to your dad's place, Mitchell is going with Deputy Gavin to his sister's place since she's out of town for a while, and Eve and I are going to my second house. Since only two people know about it, it's the best option for now."

"Your second house? You have a *second* house?"

Eve tilted her head to the side, once again physically moving like the act would shake an answer loose before he could give one.

Which would have been nice considering how slow it felt for Darius to answer her with a nod.

Those eyes—dark and familiar—met hers a moment later.

"If you want to find out, follow me and see."

Eve didn't need more than that. She grabbed her bag, let Winnie out into the hallway first and paused as Darius reached around her to turn off the office light. Then she followed him without hesitation out into the cold midday air.

It wasn't until they were sitting in Darius's truck that Eve spoke again.

"What if I really did put a larger target on myself?" she asked. "Are you sure that it wouldn't be safer for everyone if I stayed at the department?"

Darius snorted as he put the truck in gear.

"We'll never know, so there's no point in wondering."

Eve gave him another questioning look.

"What do you mean, we'll never know? I could stay and we could—"

Darius was quick this time. He cut her off before she had a chance to continue.

"We'll never know because leaving you isn't an option." Those dark eyes were back on her. She could see herself reflected in him as he leaned in close.

"Just so we're clear. From now until the end, I'm going to be by your side, Evelyn Myers. So I suggest you get used to it."

Chapter Nineteen

"You bought my house."

Eve was standing in the middle of the living room, bag already dropped on the floor next to her.

Darius, having finished checking all the rooms to make sure they were clear again, scooped the bag back up. He nodded.

"The man who was using it as a rental retired and went to Florida. He sold it to me at a good price, and I've been working here and there on it when I have the time ever since."

Eve's eyes and mouth were both wide.

Darius left her to her surprise and backtracked to the first room on the left.

He heard her footfalls hurrying behind him but didn't stop until he was inside the bedroom and in front of its closet. He unzipped her duffel bag before reaching for some hangers that were plastic-wrapped in the corner.

His shoulder pulled a little at the movement, but he was more interested in the woman currently standing behind him.

Darius had never once felt weird about buying the house next door. In fact, it had seemed a must for him the second he had seen the For Sale sign. However, he also hadn't expected the girl who used to live in it to come back and find out.

At least, not the way she had.

Now he tried to look at her reaction while busying his hands with her clothes.

"You bought my house and...you kept my room." She pointed to the old bed frame and then the nightstand between it and the wall. "That's mine. I mean, it *was* mine. Dad built it for me, but we didn't have the room to take it in the move. We put it by the side of the road, right?"

Eve had never been a particularly sentimental girl when it came to material things, but on that day right before they moved, Darius had seen her cry. When she had gone to the store with her dad later that afternoon, Darius had hurried to grab the piece of furniture before squirreling it away in their shed. Kid Darius didn't know what he would do with it, but he knew he didn't like seeing her cry over it.

"The previous owner kept the frame, and I kept the nightstand." Darius shrugged. "Refurbishing them saved me money in the long run. You can't argue with saving money, right?"

Eve's footsteps were moving farther away. Darius took a folded shirt from her bag and placed it on the first hanger. He glanced over his shoulder at her as he hung it up.

She had her hand placed on the nightstand's top.

"You kept this to save money but bought my house? Sounds like you lost money to me."

Darius found the second folded shirt. It was blue and worn. A T-shirt with a logo that had long since faded. He could smell the fabric softener on it.

It was nice.

"After buying *my* house, buying this one seemed like a good investment," he defended. "It is, as you might have noticed, right next door after all. Not only a good investment but an easy one to manage, since all I have to do to see it is look out of the window."

He put the shirt on the hanger and then went back to the duffel for another. There were two pairs of pants, all bunched-up together. Darius took both pairs out. He walked them over to the dresser against the wall. He wasn't going to point out that it was *his* childhood dresser.

Eve might not have been sentimental about these things, but Darius had surprised himself with his own soft spot for them. He had seen her old nightstand and couldn't help but feel like it needed something to match it.

What better piece of furniture than something from his childhood too?

"And no one knows you own it? Mitchell being held here was a coincidence?" Eve was standing in front of the window. The curtains over it were drawn save for a sliver between. The world outside had grown hazy and dark from an overcast sky. Still, she stood in the small strand of light and gazed out.

Darius finished putting her pants away before he answered, careful with his words.

"Mitchell being taken here, if I had to guess, was an act of opportunity since this place has been empty," he said. "Other than the sheriff and his friend who was the Realtor before he moved, the purchase didn't get broadcasted like other news seems to around here. The fact that Seven Roads has been through a lot through the last few years helped too, I'm sure." He laughed a little. "Compared to the rest of town, I've been the least interesting one here. If the gossip mill has found out, no one has shared the info. Who cares if the grumpy detective buys an empty house?"

Darius's attention had already slipped back to the duffel he had placed on top of the dresser. The next items he could see inside were small, black and cotton. He was already wondering if it was right for him to put them away when he heard the floor squeak a little behind him.

Two arms wrapped around his back. Eve fastened her hands at his chest to close the circuit.

Then all he felt was warmth.

The warmth of Eve as she burrowed into his back and flattened her cheek against his shoulder blade.

Her voice was small.

"I care."

Silence overlapped the two simple words. One wave coming to shore before returning to the sea. Strong, natural and then gone.

Darius took a moment to enjoy the wave before it crashed.

He put his hand over hers.

The heat came on in the living room, its buzz soft but noticeable.

Darius's phone made noise next, also soft but noticeable.

He patted her hand. She let him go.

The caller was Rose. He turned to Eve before answering the phone.

"I know you're worried about being found here, but I promise you we're safe now," he said. "This place is ours."

He meant to say it was their secret.

He didn't amend his words, though.

Instead, Darius watched as Eve nodded, a small frown at odds with the cuteness of her fuzzy little sweater.

"I trust you," she said.

Darius nodded in turn.

He excused himself to the living room, past the spot where Mitchell had been held the night before, past the living room window that looked out at his house, and answered the phone.

He listened to every word Rose said next, but part of him was still in the bedroom, Eve pressed against him in the quiet.

THERE WAS AN upset at the hospital as the afternoon rolled around. Apparently, the woman who was hired to come after them was tougher than she looked. After the surgery she'd had on the wrist that Darius had broken, she had tried to escape. Not only had she tried to do so without a weapon but also while still coming down off anesthesia.

The deputy assigned to her had been able to disable her before she could get on the elevator.

"If she hadn't tried so hard to kill us, I would be impressed," Eve decided, toothbrush in hand.

The afternoon haze had officially dissolved into the night, and Darius had finally called it quits. No more phone calls, no more researching, no more compulsively checking the security cameras on the house or the one next door.

Now it was just the two of them getting ready for bed.

"And for that same reason, I'm astounded that we still have no idea who she is," he said, putting his own toothbrush back into its holder.

While Darius had spent most of the day on the phone, Eve had spent some of her time walking the same floors she had as a little girl.

Much like his own childhood home, Darius had changed everything save a few pieces of the familiar. The tired carpet had been updated to hardwood. The guest bathroom had been painted and the hardware updated. The kitchen cabinets had been replaced and a fairly new refrigerator stood where their less-than-aesthetically pleasing former one had stood. The room that had once belonged to her father had a new bedroom suite, along with curtains that were as subtle as the new wall color. There were still some signs that the en suite was being updated, but even still nothing in it fit the memory Eve had of the room.

It was only the first bedroom on the left that she recognized with one foot in the past and one in the present.

And Eve had no idea how to feel about any of it.

Darius had bought her home and saved parts of her childhood.

What did that mean?

Did he still feel like he owed her for what had happened at the warehouse when they were kids? Had some kind of misguided guilt led him to make such a drastic decision?

Or was it really about an easy investment?

Eve huffed now at the reflection in the bathroom's mirror.

Darius must have thought it had to do with their current predicament. He walked past her to the bedroom.

"Don't worry," he said, oblivious to the almost-constant series of questions she had been listening to on repeat in her head since the discovery. "She might be good, but I'm better. We'll figure out who she is."

Eve trailed behind him, nodding.

She followed him into the guest bedroom, still nodding.

When he pulled back the covers and slid into the bed, she stopped.

Her eyebrow arched high. He caught the confusion and returned a small eye roll.

"I figured it would save you some time and energy by starting out in the same bed instead of having you creep around later." He grabbed the covers next to him and pulled them away from the sheets. "You can go ahead and just start at the end."

He was right, of course.

There had been no way—great love epiphany or not—that

Eve was going to sleep a wink without having Darius beside her. She hadn't even napped earlier despite his insistence.

Yet she hadn't actually thought about what that meant until now. Or, really, how she felt about it now that she *had* finally realized that her love for the man was no longer just loyalty or friendship. Instead it was her—a woman very much aware of how that boy had grown up well—about to slide in next to him in bed wearing her little PJ set and no makeup, and swimming in a lot of feelings.

Darius was back to looking at his phone, texting someone. Eve used the distraction to hurry to her place. She pulled the covers up to her chin. Darius continued to go through his phone.

Minutes went by, and slowly the foreign awkwardness Eve was feeling fell away. She wiggled her toes under the covers and stared at the ceiling.

The same old popcorn treatment with light from the nightstand lamp discoloring it to an off-white. She tried to remember the last time she had been in the same room. The night before the move, she had stayed in Darius's. Him on the floor, her lying on the side of his bed, hand draped over to hold his blanket.

Pure friendship. Pure loyalty. Pure love.

That was enough for her.

She could grow old with it. With him.

Like this.

In the silence.

In the same room.

In love, but knowing it wasn't her place to expect him to want anything more.

Eve let out a small breath and rolled onto her side. She reached out and turned her lamp off.

A few minutes later Darius turned his off too.

Eve could still make out the window a few feet away.

Muscle memory nearly made her move.

There was no point climbing out tonight when the boy next door was already there.

Eve closed her eyes.

And then an arm wrapped around her.

Beneath the sheets, Darius's bare arm slid across her hip and hooked up between her breasts. His hand balled into a fist, twisting her shirt in his grasp. It was a gentle hold that kept her steady as the rest of him moved into place. Every curve of her was met by every curve of him. His chest to her back, his hip to her hip, his knees to the backs of hers, his forehead to her hair.

No space was left between them.

Even as he spoke, the only place his words had to go were into the back of her neck.

"I never blamed you for leaving, Eve."

His words rumbled through his chest and into her back.

"But you never looked for me either," she pointed out.

"When you didn't reach out, I thought you were happy. I didn't want to mess that up."

Eve smiled.

"And I thought you were happy and didn't want to mess it up either," she countered. "Now look at me. I came back with nothing but baggage. Messy, complicated baggage."

Her eyes felt hot.

Guilt, anger, frustration, longing.

Years of stress and listlessness.

A broken ship on the sea, hoping to see a storm but instead lost in an endless boring calm.

A life that had been lived on autopilot.

And then suddenly seeing a familiar island on the horizon.

But it had been too long.

The landscape had changed.

It was no longer an island deserted.

There were other people and boats and stories that she had never been a part of.

Time hadn't stopped for a moment since Eve had left Seven Roads, and while she had grown up, Darius had too.

And it killed Eve so badly that she finally admitted it out loud.

"I missed everything," she managed, voice breaking. "Life passed me by and...and everyone else went with it."

Eve knew she wasn't making sense. Or maybe she was being too dramatic. But she couldn't help it.

Even as Darius slowly turned her over, careful of their injuries, and lay on his side while staring down at her, Eve couldn't help but cry.

His smile was barely visible in the light from the small opening from the curtains.

He took the side of her face into his hand and ran his thumb across her cheek, wiping away the few tears that were still there.

"Evie, I bought an entire house for one window. What part of that makes you think I was ever planning on moving on without you?"

It wasn't her first kiss.

It wasn't her second or third. Heck, it wasn't even her tenth.

But when Darius lowered his lips to hers, Eve felt like the world around them simply stopped.

He was warm; he was gentle. His tongue parted her lips and mingled with hers as Eve accepted the advance. The hand on the side of her face slid behind her neck as the tips of his fingers tangled into her hair.

Eve went with the movement and angled her chin higher.

The new position made it easier for their kiss to deepen.

The rest of the world around them might have felt like it stopped, but Eve sure didn't hesitate for a moment.

Darius might have been focusing on the kiss, but Eve had already skipped ahead.

She pulled him down onto her with hungry hands and used her legs to get the rest of him. It gave him two options: change his hold on her to accommodate a more intimate hold, or keep the kiss without giving in.

Bless him, Darius chose the former.

He let her neck go and broke their kiss long enough to rock backward.

Eve went with him.

And apparently it humored him.

"What?" she asked, barely able to catch her breath. She was now the one looking down at him. Still, she heard the smile in his voice before she saw it.

His hand flattened against her thigh at his side.

"You went from crying to straddling really quick is all," he said. "It's almost like you've really been wanting this."

Eve huffed.

"You're one to talk about really wanting this." She adjusted herself slightly on his lap. There was a notable hardness right beneath her. Her rubbing against it nearly made her lose her composure. She guessed it was a mutual struggle. Eve heard his breath catch just enough to know that he was absolutely affected by her.

"If you have a problem with me doing this, I can always just leave," she offered when he didn't immediately respond.

That threat surely did a number on the man beneath her.

The hand on her thigh joined the other as they both slid up her legs, beneath her PJ shorts and underneath her panties. He grabbed her bare hips and pulled down, applying pressure exactly on the part of him that couldn't lie about the pleasure he felt with her being on him.

This time, Eve was the one to make a little gasp.

"Where you go, I go," he said. "If you want to leave, I won't stop you. *But...*"

He bucked up against her, not enough to move her off, but enough to let her feel just how hard he wanted her.

"But...?" she asked, this time absolutely breathless.

Darius's voice also changed.

Now he was gravel and grit.

"*But* let's save us both some trouble and just spend the night in this room."

It wasn't a question, and even if it had been, Eve wouldn't have needed to give an answer.

They both knew neither one of them were leaving.

Not each other.

Not the room.

And certainly not the bed.

Chapter Twenty

Lana's world flipped upside down as the cruiser was driven off the road. One second she was strapped into the back, the next her hair and arms were dangling downward to the roof of the car.

Her first instinct was to check on her wrist, fresh from surgery, and the sling that had come loose.

The next was to escape.

She unbuckled her seat belt and thudded against the roof of the car. One of the windows had blown out, and broken glass pressed against the scrubs she had been given after her surgery. If the glass had cut into her clothes and skin, she still wouldn't have slowed. Where there was a will, there was a way, and now she could see that one of the windows that was no longer in one piece just so happened to be one she could reach.

A groan sounded from the front. One of the two deputies meant to escort her to the sheriff's department was obviously still alive.

But she wasn't going to check on him.

Lana scrambled through the pain, and the window, until her good palm felt dead grass and dirt. A line of trees wasn't too far from her. Once she got among the trees, even hurt she could outrun law enforcement.

After that?

She could disappear again.

This time, she wouldn't come back.

This time—

"I suggest you don't run just yet."

A man's voice interrupted her evolving plan. It was so even and calm that her curiosity paused her flight response.

Lana turned to see if he looked as composed as he sounded, standing at the top of road's shoulder. He wasn't too young and he wasn't too old and wore what she imagined someone would wear to a business interview. Khakis, a button-up and a thin jacket with a common logo on its chest. She had never seen him before, but he obviously knew who she was.

He pointed back to the road. The SUV that had created their crash was waiting, passenger-side door open.

"There's a new job," he said.

Lana's head swam a little as got to her feet. She made sure not to show the discomfort.

"Who are you?" she asked.

The man laughed.

He might have looked plain, but something about him made Lana suppress a shiver.

"I'm plan B."

THE SMALL SLIVER of light from the window the night before was no longer nostalgic or cute. It was annoying.

Eve swatted at the nuisance before rolling over to bury her face into the covers.

It took a few beats to realize there wasn't a man where he used to be.

Suddenly, Eve was wide awake.

She rolled onto her back and stared wide-eyed at the ceiling.

The night before had never been on a list of possibilities for Eve. And never had she thought that sharing a bed with Darius would lead to anything other than talking. Maybe an accidental cuddle after she had fallen asleep.

Not a kiss.

Not everything that had followed.

Warmth went from below her waist right up to her cheeks.

And everything certainly had happened.

Eve placed her hands on her face and did a little wiggle. She wasn't embarrassed, but she wasn't going to pretend that she was calm either.

She had already loved every inch of Darius before their time together, but now? Now she'd seen and touched most of those inches. How could they come back from that?

Did they come back from that?

Or were they not something new?

Were they together?

Or had the familiar just been the only thing they could cling to with all the chaos around them?

Eve slid her hands down her face, sighing once her lips were clear.

After their time together the night before, they hadn't talked much. At least not about what had changed between them, not about their relationship, their futures. They had showered, gotten back into bed and fallen asleep quickly.

They hadn't gotten down to the fine print of their new arrangement.

But he had to care about her, right?

Eve flung the covers off and hurried out of bed. A soreness south of her waistline reminded her that she definitely hadn't been dreaming about what they had done either.

How Darius reacted to her now would surely give her an idea of what he was thinking. If he didn't say a word about it, then she wouldn't either. If he declared his love for her? She would already be yelling hers at him. If he admitted it was nothing but a safe place to rest with someone he knew wouldn't give him grief after? Well, she would probably go cry in the bathroom when he wasn't looking.

Either way, Eve decided that it was now or never.

She *had* to have some kind of answer.

She threw her hair up high, took her jeans from the dresser and pulled on an old shirt. On reflex she patted her back pocket once she was dressed. Her phone was, of course, not there.

Remembering where her cell had been plugged in the night before, Eve turned to the nightstand, and something caught her eye at the window.

Her blood turned to ice.

The gap between the curtains was filled with a face.

Someone was looking in.

A woman.

Eve would later wonder if everything would have gone differently had she not moved. If she had screamed or called out for Darius. If she had run from the room, never once looking back.

Would things have gone better?

But in the moment, Eve didn't yell. She didn't run. She didn't scream.

Instead, she hesitated.

That's the only reason she saw the woman put her hand up to the window. And that's the only reason she noticed the writing scrawled across her palm.

Save them.

It was the woman from the steel mill. The one who had broken into the same house the day before. Eve could see the sling was still on. She could also see that the woman wasn't holding a weapon.

There was blood, though, along her hairline and dripping down the side of her face.

Maybe that was why Eve went to the window and, against all her better judgment, slid the curtains to the side.

When the woman made no immediate move to attack or show aggression, Eve took her lack of judgment even further.

She unlocked the window and slid it up a few inches. Just enough to hear her.

The woman didn't waste any time.

"A man is in your living room threatening to kill Theo Weaver, Winnie Collins, and Deputy Collins to get your detective to leave the house with him," she rushed. "He wants Detective Williams to lure *you* out, but if he finds out you're here, then he'll kill the detective without a second thought."

Like she had timed it perfectly, there was a commotion coming from the front of the house. Yelling. But no shots.

Yet.

Eve glanced at her phone.

The woman hurried on.

"They can track phones, but they can't track me," she said. "Leave with me now, and you can save them all later." The commotion from the other side of the house became louder. The woman might have been bleeding, hurt and pale, but her words were steady, her eyes clear. But that didn't mean Eve could believe her.

"Why would you help me?" she asked. "You've attacked us before."

Despite the intense situation, the woman actually rolled her eyes.

"I'm breaking my contract, and the only way to not get killed is to help you guys not get killed."

Eve's adrenaline spiked as something in the other room shattered.

Her heart squeezed.

"Why?" she had to ask once more.

The woman was nothing but serious when she answered again.

"Because when enough men keeping telling you to kill a woman, it's always a good rule of thumb to reevaluate. Now, come on so we can outsmart those idiots." The woman stepped to the side, angling her body away from the house. She looked seconds away from running.

Not attacking.

All concerns about Eve's relationship with Darius disappeared.

With no real evidence, Eve decided she believed the woman completely.

So much so that she took her cell phone off the nightstand, hid it under the blanket on the bed and grabbed her coat.

She was out the window and running before the door to the bedroom even opened.

THE WINDOW WAS OPEN, and Eve was gone.

Good girl, Darius thought, gun to his back, and the man holding it laughing behind him. *Now, stay gone this time.*

"I guess some things just don't change," the man said. "If there's a window, Eve surely will find a way through it."

The man must have shrugged. The gun moved against him slightly.

"I suppose I should have been quieter, though," he continued. "But you know what they say about hindsight. Twenty-twenty and all that."

Darius was hurting. Not only had the man gotten inside the house and beaten him good, Darius had let it happen. All because of the picture the man had showed him on his phone.

A picture of Winnie and her father, tied up and bloody somewhere nondescript.

It had been the master key to every space in both of Darius's houses.

A master key that would have broken, had Eve not fled through the bedroom window.

Darius was glad for her quick thinking so she was out of danger.

But also because of who the man was.

This time, Darius had recognized his attacker.

This time, he knew the danger had pushed them all to the brink.

"I should have kept better track of you," Darius bit out, turning to face the fourth gunman of the week. "Last I heard, you were incarcerated in Tennessee."

Jon Decanter had aged, and not just in the simplest of terms. Time had been unkind to him, taking a boy who had been Darius's age and making him a man who appeared older, more worn and grizzled. His clothes gave him the appearance of a PTO dad, but the scars along his jaw and arms spoke to a different kind of lifestyle.

His gaze, however, hadn't changed.

Hate rested there.

Angry and all too familiar.

"You track me?" Jon laughed again, the sound chilling. "Like little Evie would let you do that. After what she did, after the prank I pulled on you? I'm surprised she left you to me now, if I'm being honest. Then again, it's easy to be brave as a kid who doesn't know the world yet. Now that she's had a taste of money and fame, I'm sure she won't risk that for some lowly detective who never could move on."

Darius balled his fist.

He could disarm Jon right then and there. Get the gun

with or without one of them getting hit in the process and really give it to his personal ghost from the past.

But.

If the adult Jon was anything like the kid Jon, then there was an element of instability and callousness to him that could destroy any chances of Darius saving Winnie and her father.

Or Eve, if she decided to climb back through another window to try and save him.

Darius decided the best plan was to see what *Jon's* plan was—and quickly.

"If tying a kid up to a piece of industrial equipment to slowly get mutilated is a prank, then I'd hate to see what you think a good joke is."

Jon must not have liked the snark. He pushed the barrel of his gun harder into Darius's back. Normally, the pressure wouldn't bother him, but it just so happened to be the area that had been kicked repeatedly by the demon in humans' clothes behind him.

"Talking has always been *her* strong suit, not yours, Darius," Jon said. "You'd just get everyone killed with that mouth of yours. So I'd leave the snark to the professionals instead." He applied more pressure into the gun's barrel. "Speaking of professionals, I think it's time to leave before the colleagues I'm sure Evie has called in come running. I'd hate for you to lose the chance to save that lovely family I have all tied up, simply because the response time of Seven Roads's finest is actually impressive. Let's go."

Darius glanced at the nightstand.

Eve's phone was gone.

Relief pure and true moved through his chest.

He let Jon lead him outside to a black truck, its front partially damaged and a side mirror missing.

The relief that Eve had gotten away disappeared the second Jon cussed low.

"Looks like I underestimated Lana after all," he said. "I should have killed her first."

Darius caught his eye, his brow arching high.

Jon's mood switched gears again.

He laughed and looked back at the house.

"Hate to break it to you, Darius, but maybe little Evie didn't get away after all."

Chapter Twenty-One

Lana was fast. Even with an arm in a sling, an obvious head injury and a limp, she had her and Eve in a car and out to the steel mill's back entrance within what felt like the blink of an eye.

"This is where your friend shot us last time," Eve had to point out as they started walking to the residence halls. Caution tape could be seen across the porch of the men's building. Lana directed them toward the women's building on the other side.

"He wasn't supposed to shoot you," she said nonchalantly. "And he wasn't my friend."

Eve knew she shouldn't have followed Lana. She shouldn't have gotten into the car with her. She shouldn't have willingly come to a place no one would think to look for her. Yet, when Lana pushed open the front door and disappeared inside, Eve easily followed in step.

Like something had shifted between Eve and Darius, she could tell something had shifted behind the scenes for the criminals.

And whatever that was, it had pissed off Lana and created her own shift.

Though, Eve wasn't sure why the woman had come to her. She decided asking directly was the best way to deal with the woman who had wanted to kill her less than twenty-four hours ago.

"Why are you helping me? Helping Darius and Winnie and Price?"

Lana flipped on the lights. The inside of the women's residence hall wasn't as derelict as the men's had been. Still, Eve took care to keep closer to the wall and avoid the middle of the room until they were at a bunk bed with a mattress still intact. There was a laptop on its top, connected to a phone.

Lana sat heavily. Blood ran into her eye, and she cussed as she tried to wipe it out with her hand. The marker on her palm with her plea to Eve was a sharp contrast to the red.

"Because men are idiots," Lana ground out. "And instead of listening to the only smart one of them, they just keep calling in more men to be idiots." She blinked several times, her eye red from the irritation. Eve could now clearly see that her clothes were also torn and dirtied. She had definitely been through *something* since her stay at the hospital.

Eve had so many questions she wasn't sure which one to ask first. She decided to start with the odd choice of location.

"Why are we here, then? Why not just run if you're breaking your contract?"

Lana snorted.

"Scott Keys might be an idiot, but he's one with deep pockets and a right-hand who can control the rest of them just by snapping. I could disappear if I wanted, but there's someone I care about around here, and I don't want to spend the rest of my life running in the opposite direction."

Eve's adrenaline spiked for the second time that day.

"So Scott really *is* behind these attacks."

Lana nodded.

"Sanderson hired me, but it was heavily implied that Scott was funding my contract."

"That contract being..."

Lana reached down to a bag next to the bunk bed. For a moment, Eve felt foolish for trusting the woman. Now she was sure she was going to pay for being impulsive enough to follow the villain into the unknown.

However, all Lana pulled out was a small tin pack.

A first-aid symbol was on it.

She fumbled with the clasp, cussing lightly before responding.

"Technically, Scott wanted Mitchell dead, and you were just a piece of the story that made it all make sense. Woman tries to kill new husband for insurance money, but he kills her in self-defense before he succumbs to his injuries. Something that would be more believable after that family-lawyer guy was killed. Though, still not sure how he ended up at the wedding." Lana shook her head lightly. The first-aid kit finally opened. She pulled out a bundle of different-sized Band-Aids and set them on her lap. "But then that detective of yours kept showing up, and the rumors of you two having an affair started."

"Which is why you needed Mitchell to kill me and Darius," Eve realized.

Lana nodded.

"No matter who shot who first, the general public would have bought it," she said. "A jilted fiancé, a woman having an affair and a beloved local detective. Even if Mitchell or you survived somehow, the law around here would have come for your heads."

Lana continued to try and sort through the different-sized bandages.

"Scott already knew that Mitchell and I found evidence against him," Eve said. "That's why he pushed us to get married before we could get everything we needed. He needed it to look like I wanted the life insurance."

Lana surprised her. She didn't snort. She laughed.

"*This* is where I prove I'm a whole lot smarter than these men." Lana pointed to Eve, an unopened Band-Aid wrapper in her hand. "Scott never gave one thought to you, Miss Myers. He said Mitchell was the mastermind and that he only started dating you to gain access to Scott's day-to-day because of your job position. Scott and Sanderson? Not even for a second did they think you were important."

Eve instantly remembered what Lana had said the night before, after they had subdued her in the kitchen.

"But you realized last night that I wasn't just there," she offered.

Lana nodded.

"Mitchell killed a man to save you *and* Darius. Up until then I was under the impression that Mitchell was using *you*. Then I noticed that we had it backward. You were the one everyone kept looking at. You were in charge, even with the detective." She laughed again. "Men like Scott Keys rarely see women as anything other than pawns. Which is ironic, if you ask me."

The Band-Aid wrapper still wasn't open, and the blood along Lana's face kept dripping.

Eve sighed in frustration.

She grabbed the wrapper from the woman's hand and opened it.

"Does it really matter who found what, though?" she asked, taking the bandage out. "If Scott wants us all dead, then who cares who found the evidence? Evidence that I only have copies of, at that."

Lana's eyes widened as she pushed her hair out of the way. Eve placed the Band-Aid on the woman's skin.

She answered regardless of any surprise after the deed was done.

"It matters because they've been underestimating you," Lana said. "You're just some little pawn they want to move around to make the story of two guys fighting good."

Eve didn't like that. She patted the Band-Aid lightly to make sure it stuck. When she stepped back Lana was staring up at her with a new ferocity.

"To be underestimated is to be overlooked, and *that's* why they won't see you coming until it's too late."

"You want to—what?—ambush Scott? I won't help you kill anyone," Eve cautioned. "Even if it's him."

Lana waved the thought off.

"Scott, as far as I can tell, is untouchable for the simple fact that I'm not sure who all he's hired around here—around him," she defended. "As far as I can tell right now, you, the detective, Mitchell and that kid I beat up last night are the only ones who seem to want Scott and the rest of us behind bars. But since this new guy just appeared on the board, the only piece I could grab without getting myself tangled up was you. Everyone else is either missing or with him."

"You mean Winnie and Price Collins."

Lana nodded.

"Before this scar guy tried to kill me, he fished for some info, and I fished right on back," she said. "He took the girl, and the dad followed, and now they're somewhere in town as leverage for the detective. The detective is supposed to be leverage for you, and then *you* are supposed to be the leverage for Mitchell. Who, by the way, has really gone to ground. I don't even think Scott knows where his brother is."

Relief went through Eve at that. At least she knew Mitchell was most likely safe with Deputy Gavin. She hoped he could stay that way until everything was said and done.

Said and done with everyone she loved safe.

"But you knew I was with Darius," Eve said instead. "And this new guy didn't."

Lana laughed again.

"I noticed a pattern with the two of you," she said. "Wherever one of you is, the other is too. Something else these guys hadn't picked up on."

The relief Eve felt because of Mitchell turned to a clamp around her heart.

"We could call the sheriff," Eve tried. "Darius trusts him, and I trust Darius."

Lana didn't say no, but her skepticism was loud.

"What if Scott has someone in the sheriff's department? Or, what if there are more people like me out there, following law enforcement and reporting back?" She shook her head. "I don't know where your detective is, but I can guarantee that if Scott thinks his plan isn't working, he'll let that new boy of his kill Detective Williams quick."

Eve didn't like that.

Not one bit.

Still, she didn't understand what Lana was thinking.

"What are we supposed to do, then?" Eve asked. "Find Darius and then—what?—storm in, guns blazing? You might be good with a gun, but I've only ever shot at you."

Lana finally motioned to the laptop open next to her.

"The guy who got me out of the deputy's cruiser had this in his truck. Before I realized he was going to try and off me, I grabbed it and came here. When I saw the files pulled up on the screen, that's when I realized this must have been what had Scott and Sanderson all up in arms." She handed the laptop over to Eve. "So you tell me. How do we use five flight-plan records to push a king like Scott Keys off his throne?"

"Flight plans? There are copies on here?"

Eve was so curious she sat down next to the woman who had been her biggest enemy the night before.

"They look like they came straight from some private airfield's cataloging system, but past that I don't know what it is that's so special about them."

Lana was right.

Eve took a moment to look through the first one.

"This is actual physical evidence that has Toby flying out to areas near the towns I think Scott destroyed before saving them... It's not just someone on the phone or a blurry security picture that puts him en route."

"And this could help incriminate someone as powerful as Scott?"

Eve shook her head to the obvious surprise of Lana.

"Not just this, but we believe *this* is the start of the investigation that would uncover the truth. And seeing as how everything happened after we realized there *were* flight plans, I'm assuming we're right about it."

Lana said she didn't need any more information. Instead, she started rattling off ways they could use the information to make a deal or trap or frame Scott or *something*. Eve's attention had strayed to a detail she hadn't processed before.

"Five flight records," she said, interrupting Lana.

"What?"

Eve touched the laptop's screen with one hand and used the other on the trackpad to scroll through the pages.

"There are five here, but we were only ever able to find four records." She stopped at one file. "We nixed this one because when Toby landed, he used a rental car that took him in the opposite direction for a golf tournament."

Lana leaned in a little to look at the file in question.

"And why do we care about Toby?" she asked.

Eve opened her mouth to point out that, as Scott's right-hand man, he was someone that needed to be cared about.

But she stopped herself short.

"You never said *right-hand man*," Eve said instead. "You just said *right-hand*." She felt her eyes widen as it finally dawned on her. "And you never said *Toby*. You just said *Sanderson*."

Eve scanned the document she had once dismissed.

The same name was on all five.

Apparently, she had also overlooked someone.

TOBY SANDERSON WAS DEAD.

His wife, Maria, stepped over his body wearing heels.

Darius watched as she made her way over to him, smile rimmed with dark red lipstick.

"Honestly, I can spin this just as easy as the soap-opera storyline Scott has been trying to play out since we got to this horrible little town," she said. "Except, I'm not going to waste my time waiting for all of you to do your parts."

Maria didn't have a gun in her hand, but she did have a Jon.

He was leaning against one of the four large steel beams that had been holding up the warehouse since the last time he and Darius had been there.

Now instead of a rotary tiller, he was cuffed to a metal pole sticking out of the concrete. Whatever it used to be attached to had long since been sawn away.

"It was you who engineered the attacks on those towns—on Seven Roads—through the years," Darius said. "Not Toby."

That had become glaringly clear the second Jon had walked him inside and around the socialite's dead body. They had gotten the wrong Sanderson, and now the right one seemed to be tickled by the mess-up.

"To be honest, it's kind of nice to get the credit for once."

Maria paused next to a crate covered in dust. With her heel she hooked the handle and managed to flip it onto its side. She was elegant in the action of sitting down on it, but Darius could still see her husband's blood on the bottom of her shoes.

She caught his gaze and gave her shoe a once-over before smiling again.

"See, I've always had a knack for breaking things," she said. "Rules, boundaries, people. And wouldn't you know it, towns too."

Darius recalled Eve's notes on the first town she had suspected that Scott had purposefully crippled.

"The corruption case in Culver," he remembered.

Maria snapped her fingers, smile only widening.

"Who knew a few whispers here and there could detonate the entire infrastructure of that little no-nothing town," she said, clearly delighted. "Truthfully, I didn't even mean for it to happen. It was like playing dolls."

"Your version of dolls destroyed hundreds of innocent lives, one way or the other," Darius pointed out.

Maria waved her hand through the air, as if shooing an annoying fly that was buzzing around her.

"But then who came in and made it all better with all his money and all his charm? Scott the White Knight Keys. A hero that I had summoned for a problem that I had created."

"And let me guess. Scott thought it was his idea."

Maria nodded, her hair not moving an inch from its hairspray hold.

"That's the beauty of all of this, isn't it?" she said. "I get the power, the money and the high without the responsibility if things go south. Because who's going to look at the charming hero and the spoiled wife of his friend and think *I'm* even involved?"

Maria looked over her shoulder at her husband's body. She sighed.

"Even he had no clue what he was looking at, after your girlfriend talked about those records."

For the first time since Darius had been cuffed and Maria had entered the warehouse, the woman's mirth seemed to ebb.

The dark red of her frown made the apparent wealth she was wrapped in seem more sinister than before.

"Eve, Eve, Eve," she said. "Unlike Scott, I don't need to kill her, you *and* Mitchell all together. I can do two birds and one stone now." Maria snapped her fingers again. Jon pushed himself off the beam to stand tall. "You said she would come for him?"

Jon nodded.

"Guaranteed."

Maria swung her gaze back to Darius.

"Also unlike Scott, I don't ignore new information." Her fingernails were painted red. Darius could see them clearly as she pointed his way. "Like when Jon here reached out to our White Knight saying he could help? I didn't discount it. No, I listened to what he had to say. And, Detective, do you know what he had to say?"

Darius kept his mouth shut.

He had already profiled the woman across from him.

She was a yapper.

And yappers didn't really need feedback to keep yapping.

Maria proved him right.

"He told me that the fastest way to get Evelyn Myers is to get you." A smile twisted up the corners of her lips. She continued, sounding as wicked as she looked. "And then? All I have to do is make you scream."

Chapter Twenty-Two

Everyone's problems boiled down to one issue and one issue only.

Everyone had underestimated a woman.

Lana had realized her mistake first. So she had saved Eve from Jon's clutches, gambling that the save would also buy Darius more time.

Eve had realized her mistake second.

Maria had been the person at Scott's side the entire time. The spoiled rich socialite in designer clothes, always looking bored and annoyed and superior. Never in touch with anyone below her status. Always a passive-aggressive word or ten to people like Eve.

A woman to avoided for sanity's sake.

Scott had probably never seen her coming.

Lana had, and that's why she had jumped ship once Jon Decanter, ghost from the past, had joined Maria's forces. Lana knew Maria would be the one to clean house for Scott, and not even she thought she could outrun her forever.

Eve knew Maria had already realized her mistake since she had gone with Jon to the warehouse. If they had wanted to lure Mitchell out, they would have used another location. But Maria wanted Eve, and Jon gave her the quickest path there.

As Eve walked through the unlocked door, she saw the

satisfaction pass over Maria's expression. She stood from her seat on an old box and waved. Darius, behind her, was alive and cuffed to something.

If Eve hadn't been boiling with rage at the man between them, she would have cried in relief.

"Oh, Evelyn, how sweet," Maria started. "You really do seem to love the detective. Oh dear, I guess Mitchell was indeed just a match of convenience. Scott is going to be so upset when he finds out he was played like this. Especially when he thought his brother was the one playing you."

She giggled.

Eve ignored her.

She had taken a few steps inside the warehouse, the door closing behind her. She had no weapon. No way to defend herself. No foolproof or safe plan to free Darius and escape unharmed. No way to trap, disarm or make the secret mastermind behind the investigation that had consumed Eve's life over the last year willingly give themselves up.

Which might have been for the better.

Because the second she saw Jon, she was suddenly the same little girl she had been when she had seen him last.

Eve locked eyes with Jon.

The only human she had ever hated.

When her voice came out, not even Eve recognized it.

"What was the last thing I told you, Jon?" she growled out.

Darius said her name.

Eve took a step forward.

"Don't tell me you've already forgotten," she added. "Not after I made sure to make it memorable."

Jon's nostrils flared. She could see that clearly even from the hundred or so feet she stood away from him. Just like the scar at the side of his face.

It was small, smaller than the one on her hand. Much smaller than the one on Darius's back.

"You've got some nerve," he bit out.

Eve rolled up her left jacket sleeve. She did the other one next.

"*You're* the one with the nerve, Jon. Not even Fate would have been stupid enough to put us back together. That had to be you." Eve shared a quick look with Maria. Her mouth hung open in a confused smile. "Let me guess. He saw something about me or Darius in the news and begged to be a part of your unnecessarily complicated scheme to frame and kill us. And you decided, *why not?*"

Maria's smile faded, but her words still held confidence as she responded.

"So Jon *was* telling the truth," she said. "He has a special relationship with the two of you. How interesting." Maria took a few steps back so she could see both of them more easily. Her shifting gave Eve a clear view of a body on the floor near the opposite wall.

Toby.

His shoes weren't Italian leather, but she recognized them all the same.

Eve didn't have time to linger on him.

Just as she didn't have time to look at Darius.

Instead, she doubled down on a plan that might get her killed.

"If you really want to hear something fun, ask him how he got that scar," Eve poked. She tapped the side of her face. The same spot Jon was touching with the hand not holding a gun.

A gun that Eve was sure he was about to be itching to use.

Maria, ever a gossip, was already locked in.

"How *did* you get that scar, Mr. Decanter?" she asked. "Do tell."

Jon had always looked like a little worm of a human. As a child, he had never had a redeeming quality to him in Eve's young eyes. Nothing had changed. His face pinched, his shoulders tightened with rage, she knew that despite every effort he was most likely employing, the memory of their last meeting was replaying in detail in his head.

He didn't want to answer Maria, that much was obvious.

But Maria wasn't a woman used to being disappointed.

Her voice lowered into a command that might have alarmed Eve had it been under different circumstances.

"How did you get that scar?"

Jon's hand twitched. A smile clawed its way upward from his frown. It was as fake as a sociopath could make it.

His words came out bitter, regardless of the form of his mouth.

"Eve gave it to me when we were kids. She said it was a warning, and that, if I ever so much as showed my face in front of Darius again, she'd make sure it was a face no one would recognize after that."

Maria whirled around, full focus on Eve. The surprise affected her entire body. She was nearly dancing in delight.

"Eve!" she exclaimed. "Look at you! How vicious! Maybe I should have hired you instead of this one. Who knew you had it in you!"

It was true, and it wasn't completely true.

Eve had, in fact, tracked the kid Jon down and threatened him. But the scar on his face had been an accident. After doctoring Darius's back and her hand, they had decided to not tell anyone about the incident. It hadn't been for Jon's benefit, but for fear that the incident would get their parents to reevaluate their living situations. That, because they had been left alone so much, something would need to change. Darius had a godmother out of state; Eve could have gone to a summer program at the school. Or, if their parents hadn't decided to shuffle them off somewhere to be safe, there was always the possibility that the two of them spending so much time together would have been frowned on.

So little Eve and Darius had kept the assault and its brutality to themselves.

But that hadn't meant Eve had let Jon off the hook.

She had gotten him out of his house that night and made it sound like she would tell the adults if he ever tried to get near them again.

That had got Jon mad.

He had lunged at her. It was only good luck on her part that his grandmother's backyard was uneven and covered in dirt. He had slipped and fallen. Eve, knowing this was the only advantage she would get, had jumped on him.

Only a few minutes later, with blood covering her hands, did she realize that a rock had embedded in his cheek. Instead of pointing this out to him, instead of panicking, instead of going for help, Darius's scream of pain had echoed in her mind, and she decided to get herself one more advantage.

She had pushed the rock into his skin.

Not a lot but enough to make *him* scream.

Then, she had threatened him with those vicious words.

As an adult, Eve knew that she had been wrong to do it. That there were better ways to avenge violence.

But there was nothing she could do to change it.

So she did as she had done and leaned into the idea that she had caused the scar on purpose.

"Yet here you are," she said now. "Despite my very clear warning."

Jon let out a sound that was between a growl and a yell. He sounded possessed. Maria seemed to enjoy it all the more. She actually clapped.

"Wow, you just have to love small towns," she said. "They really are like soap operas. Everyone has some kind of tawdry back story. Surely there's something you want to add before we end this episode, Detective Williams?"

She started to turn back around, but Eve was faster.

"Maria," she called out, quickly, "do you want to know one more secret first?"

Maria paused but nodded, still clearly enjoying herself like they were at some kind of party or weird double date.

"Of course! Get it all off your chest now."

This time, Eve mirrored her smile. Her voice rang clear throughout the old warehouse.

"The tractor-supply business who owned this place? They might have gone out of business, but you want to know what they *didn't* do?" Eve's leg muscles tensed in anticipation. Her heartbeat started to gallop.

Maria was completely unaware of the change about to rock her world.

She simply raised an eyebrow in question.

Eve was happy to give her the answer.

"After all of these years, they never repaired that window."

Jon understood first. He whirled around, gun raised, but it was too late.

Eve ran for cover behind the collection of dust-covered crates closest to her just as two shots rang out.

Maria yelled.

Jon made a noise.

Then silence.

Eve scrambled to her feet again, already yelling Darius's name.

MARIA HAD BEEN RIGHT. Living in a small town sure felt like watching a soap opera sometimes.

Darius, handcuffed to a random metal pipe in an old,

abandoned warehouse, kept in check by the source of his childhood trauma, while the love of his life was in danger?

Well, it all felt very dramatic.

And maybe if the main villain had been even a little bit less dramatic and her lackey less emotional, Maria would have noticed that Eve wasn't just talking to talk. She wasn't trying to twist the metaphorical knife into the old wound of Jon Decanter just to remind him of the scarring defeat he had suffered by the hand of the little protective girl down the street.

Not that Darius had understood that himself at first, though. It wasn't until he realized Eve was purposefully not looking at him that he started paying attention to what was happening outside their past's retelling.

Someone had climbed through the window that Eve had broken during her rescue when they were kids. And it wasn't until he felt that person fiddling with the lock on his handcuff that he understood that Eve hadn't just run in as a sacrifice to try and save him.

Instead of making herself bait like she had done the day before in the meeting room in front of Scott and Toby, Evelyn Myers had made herself different once she had walked into that warehouse.

She had made herself a distraction.

And by God, it had worked.

Darius had run through Jon like a sledgehammer through a thin piece of paper.

Jon managed two shots, but they were just the last cries of a dying man.

Darius heard the crack of Jon's head hitting the cement floor before he felt it.

He knew Jon was gone as he secured the gun and turned it on Maria. Still, his body couldn't help but stay alert while standing.

"Move and I shoot," Darius yelled at the woman. The warning came out at the same time Eve yelled for him.

She didn't wait for him to answer her.

Not that Darius expected that she would wait.

The sound of her shoes slapping against the floor echoed around them as she ran past Maria and right to him.

Darius was about to warn her to get behind him when the person who had freed him spoke up instead.

"Dang, Eve, let's make sure our villainess doesn't have a weapon first before you go all gooey on our hero."

Darius tensed as he recognized the voice.

The woman known as Lana stepped slowly into view next to them. Her arm was still in a sling from where he had broken her wrist. She had a Band-Aid on her forehead.

The most surprising detail?

Eve rolled her eyes at the woman.

"Listen, I'm the one who is usually sneaking in through windows," Eve said. "Being out in the open like this is new for me."

In another surprising turn of events, Lana actually sighed.

"I don't know if anyone has told you this yet, but there are these things called doors, Miss Myers. And I'm sure no one, not even Detective Williams here, would blame you if you started using them."

Maybe it was the adrenaline wearing off, maybe it was shock at everything that had happened since he had woken up that morning or maybe it was because of the sheer amount of relief flooding his system at knowing that the woman he loved was okay that he did something out of character for the situation.

Despite himself, Darius laughed.

Chapter Twenty-Three

Scott Keys went down in a blaze of glory.

A blaze of glory that was documented so well that the news stories went viral across the country.

He had tried to make his brother look like a victim of a greedy new wife and her lover, and instead he had ended up playing the main role of the greedy millionaire versus the underdogs.

At least Maria Sanderson had been quick to take her name out of the credits.

Once the feds had gotten involved and officially opened an investigation into the Keys Foundation and the man at its helm, she had made a deal. She had sold Scott out completely before ever seeing the inside of a jail cell.

She might have skipped prison altogether had another woman not stepped forward and made her own deal.

Lana had, as far as anyone could tell—and by her own insistence—never actually killed anyone. Not in Seven Roads and not during any of her previous contracts. Darius wasn't sure he believed her, but when she provided audio recordings and physical evidence of being hired and instructed by Maria to kidnap and kill Eve, Darius and Mitchell, he couldn't help but feel a bit grateful to her. Especially when

Eve explained that Lana had been the one to get her out of the house when Jon had shown up.

"If she hadn't shown up at the window, I would have walked into the living room with the two of you like it was nothing," Eve had said, during their ride in the ambulance after the rest of the sheriff's department had come to the warehouse. "Without her, all of us might have met a much different outcome. Even if she did do it for herself."

Darius didn't push his opinion on the matter, but he did decide to thank Lana before she was taken away in cuffs.

"You could have run," Darius had told her. "Thank you for staying with Eve instead."

Lana had surprised him with a laugh.

"To be honest, if she had been my boss, I think I would have done whatever she asked of me. Evelyn is pure loyalty. Even us bad guys can appreciate that." Lana had paused before following the federal agent to their car. "I know my words don't mean much, but just in case no one has told you yet, I think you might want to marry that woman."

And Darius did.

Three months later, in between their childhood homes and the windows that had shaped their entire lives, Darius and Eve were married.

Darius wore a nice suit, Eve had a dress that poofed out at the bottom, and they even managed to find folding white chairs like Mrs. Dunphy used to have when they were kids. Which, according to Eve, had been an important detail. Her father walked her down the aisle while Theo and Winnie stood on either side of an arch her father had made by hand.

After Winnie and Price had been ambushed by Jon and the one last hired hand Maria had running around Seven Roads before being arrested, Theo and Price's wife JJ had raised hell to find and rescue them. Unlike Jon, their attacker had survived their retribution and had gone to prison, where no deals were made and no promises of an early release were given.

Since then Darius's Oil and Water duo had become somewhat inseparable.

So it only made sense when they became the new tenants of the house next door. At first Eve would pass by Darius's old bedroom window and wave at across to Winnie, who had taken over Eve's former bedroom.

Then, one day, Winnie moved out.

And right into the main bedroom with Theo.

The whole of Seven Roads was more excited for their wedding years later than they had ever been about Mitchell Keys and Evelyn Myers tying the knot. It almost felt like a holiday as nearly all the town showed up in their finest and watched as the oldest children of the sheriff's department said *I do*. Their wedding reception became a reunion all its own for the department.

The men and women who had spent their careers protecting Seven Roads to the best of their abilities gathered around for a toast about the past.

"I came to Seven Roads because I wanted quiet," Liam started. The sheriff looked at his wife, Blake, and grinned. "Now I live in the loudest house in the zip code." Everyone laughed, but no one disagreed. They had six kids, a live-in mother and father-in-law, and two dogs. *Loud* didn't cover it.

Price went next, raising his glass as his wife JJ currently held one of their surprise set of twins. Winnie had the other on her hip as she swayed back and forth with Theo on the dance floor.

"I wanted to leave the second Winnie was old enough to move out," Price said. "Now we're looking at building a house down the road."

Rose went next, her husband towering over her, a little girl fast asleep against his chest. She was the first of four who they had adopted from foster care, taking their family from three to six. Something that her husband James boasted about quite often.

"I always knew this Seven Roads was where I belonged, but I'm glad you boys finally figured it out for yourselves," Rose said, sassy as ever. "Though, I did snag the best mechanic in town, so I guess there's something I changed for us."

They all did a quick cheers for that, laughter mixed in.

Deputy Gavin went next, already grinning ear to ear.

"I went from thinking love was dead to marrying a millionaire, so I can't complain."

That got Darius really good. He and Eve couldn't hold back as they looked at the millionaire in question, currently talking the ear off JJ's brother at the bar.

Mitchell Keys hadn't only taken over the Keys Foundation once Scott had gone to prison. He and Eve had transformed it into something entirely different and absolutely impactful. Making the headquarters in Seven Roads had not only helped the town with new jobs, it had also given Mitchell and his deputy time to fall in love. A love that the department had been happy to endorse in place of his brother.

It also had made Eve jump for joy.

One night, in between the sheets, Eve had admitted to Darius that at one point, she had been afraid that she really had missed out on life.

"But now I have a best friend who I see every day, a job I really care about that makes a difference *and* I got to keep a promise I made a long time ago." She had sighed in contentedness. "I guess I didn't miss out on life. I was just waiting for you to start it."

Darius had seconded that sentiment.

Now he raised his glass, the last of them to speak, and said what he had always known to be true.

"I accepted a life in Seven Roads that only saw me growing old and grumpy by myself," Darius said. He looked to Eve. He could hear their children's squeals of laughter from the dance floor. He smiled. "Turns out I was just waiting for the drama to come back to town."

Eve was the loudest as the group around him burst into laughter at that before they all lifted their glasses together.

"It's been a wild ride these past few years with all of you," the sheriff called out. "And I wouldn't have wanted it any other way. So here's to McCoy County's finest. May we go to the dance floor now to embarrass the younger generation with dance moves that will embarrass us in the morning!"

The group all yelled and cheered and clinked their glasses together before following their sheriff to do just that.

Darius, however, caught Eve's hand before she could make it too far.

She giggled as he pulled her into his arms.

He cut that giggle off with a kiss born from a love that had never once wavered, no matter how many years had gone by.

Eve returned it with an answering love.

Then she swatted him away with laughter in her eyes.

"You better not try and get out of dancing with me, Detective Williams." She pointed at him, a beautiful smile playing at her lips. "You have to listen to me no matter what, remember? Your life is mine, after all."

It was a joke that they often exchanged through the years. The promise that Eve had made to his mother that Darius's life would forever be hers. And while no one who heard the story thought the promise made by a child had been taken seriously, he knew better.

Darius had always been Eve's.

And as he followed his wife to the dance floor surrounded by their loved ones, Darius knew without a doubt that he always would be.

*****

EXPLOSIVE EVIDENCE

CINDI MYERS

For Bernie

Chapter One

"You're sure this is the right one?" The man's voice had a pinched quality. Each word produced a puff of frost in the frigid night air. A flashlight beam played across the expanse of tan stucco wall. "I don't see any way in. Where's the door?"

"We can't use the door." The second voice, male like the first, was a low growl. "Cameras and alarms. We'll go in around back." He led the way along the side of the building and around to the rear, stopping four feet from the corner. The duffel bag he'd been carrying made a loud, clanking sound as he dumped it in the snow at their feet.

"Careful!" the first man whispered. "Somebody will hear."

"Nobody will hear. They're all at the New Year's party." He jerked his head toward the front of the building, where a bright glow lit the sky.

"Wish I was at a party." The first man stomped his feet. "I'm freezing to death out here."

"Stop whining and kill the light."

The flashlight off, the two black-clad men became invisible in the inky darkness. Then a blueish glow emanated from two feet off the ground. The gruff-voiced man had switched on a headlamp, the beam a narrow beacon shining wherever he looked. He zipped open the duffel and removed a power tool.

"What is that?" the first man asked.

"Multi-tool fitted with a diamond blade. We're going to make our own door."

"Are you out of your mind? Everyone within a quarter mile will hear the noise."

The gruff-voiced man checked his watch. "Not in a couple of minutes." He pulled out a respirator and slipped it on, added safety goggles and earmuffs. "You might want to step back. The dust this makes is no joke."

The first man opened his mouth to protest again, but just then a deafening *BOOM!* shook the air around them, followed by a chorus of *Ahhs!* and *Ohhs!* Almost immediately, what sounded like a full orchestra struck up a rousing march.

The gruff-voiced man started the saw and began cutting into the stucco and concrete of the back of the building.

The first man glanced overhead as a cascade of golden stars, red and green balls and other colorful fireworks bloomed against the night sky. More explosions sent rockets into the air, followed by pinwheels and cascades of light. Between the fireworks and the music, he almost couldn't hear the whine of the saw. Still, how long would this New Year's Eve show last? He shifted from foot to foot, as much out of nervousness as an attempt to stay warm.

"Don't just stand there. Help me get rid of this stuff." The gruff-voiced man handed up a chunk of concrete the size of a man's head.

"What should I do with it?"

"There's a dumpster on the side of the building. Chuck it in there."

"Why not just leave it all here?"

"Because we don't want anyone to notice the hole. Not until it's too late."

How anyone wasn't going to notice a hole large enough for a person to climb through, the first man didn't know, but his partner was already sawing again, making further conversation impossible.

He made six trips to the dumpster carrying heavy chunks of stucco and concrete before the second man had cut out an opening wide enough for him to squeeze through. He handed the saw to the first man. "Get that back in the bag while I get what we need." Not waiting for a reply, he crawled into the building.

The first man returned the saw to the bag, then waited. The music and the fireworks ceased, though he could still hear voices and laughter from the revelers at the annual New Year's Eve bash at SkyCrest Resort. His friends were probably there, drinking beer and mulled cider and hot toddies, waiting for the torchlight parade down the mountain that always followed the fireworks display. Last year, he had skied in that parade, carrying a flickering electric torch and wishing he hadn't had that third hot toddy, afraid he was going to wipe out in front of everybody and make a fool of himself. But he had managed to stay upright.

"Here. Shove as much of this as you can into the bag." The second man handed off two shoe-box-size parcels, and the first man wedged them into the duffel. The second man dragged out a second duffel, which sagged with a heavy weight.

"What's in there?" the first man asked.

"Everything we need to show these people who this mountain really belongs to."

The first man shouldered his duffel. "Let's get out of here."

"Just a sec." The second man felt around in his pockets and pulled out a tube of adhesive. He smeared this around the edges of the opening he had just cut. Then he unrolled a scroll of what might have been wallpaper and smoothed it over the opening. In the dim light, it blended in with the wall. The second man straightened and stepped back, then scooped up a couple of handfuls of snow and tossed them around the bottom of the opening. "Somebody walking by would never notice," he said. Then he shouldered his own duffel. "Let's get out of here."

They raced off into the dark, not stopping until they reached the side street where they'd parked the car. They threw the duffels into the back seat, and the first man got behind the wheel.

He started the car and was about to back out when something cold touched his cheek. He tried to turn his head, and the cold turned to a sharp pain.

"Hold still," the second man said. "Unless you want your face sliced open."

"Wh-what are you doing?"

"Just making a point." He chuckled. "Just remember what we talked about. A word of this to anyone, and your life will get really difficult. What's left of it." He withdrew the blade. "Now get us out of here."

"WHY DID I ever in my life think this would be a good idea?" Connor Donaldson groused to no one as he trudged from his truck to the munitions magazine on the far edge of Sky-Crest Resort. He pulled a sled behind him, the kind used to transport supplies around the ski resort, cutting a path across the expanse of empty parking lot. The small, square concrete building sat by itself at the far edge of the lot.

"This is no way to start a new year," Connor said out loud

to no one but himself. He had made it to bed about 1:00 a.m., after the New Year's Eve fireworks and torchlight parade, and he was feeling every bit of that lost sleep, not to mention the several beers he had enjoyed with friends.

At 5:30 in the morning, New Year's Day, the resort was dark and silent, only the amber glow of the security lights rimming the parking lot illuminating his path. Holiday decorations—crossed wooden skis trimmed with red velvet bows and greenery—decorated each light pole, but Connor noticed someone had draped a homemade banner over one of the poles. *Save Blaine Mountain!* was lettered in blue paint across the banner.

Security would have that down before the resort opened in a couple of hours—not that there weren't plenty of similar banners and posters all around town. While many people were excited about SkyCrest's proposed expansion into new terrain, the opposition was doing a good job of making themselves heard.

Connor had mixed feelings about the plans for new lifts, runs and condos, but it wasn't his decision to make. He only hoped the addition of new terrain would mean hiring more patrollers to help with the increased workload.

A bark from the darkness to his right distracted Connor from his personal pity party. "Farley!" he shouted and switched on a flashlight, sweeping the beam across the snow until he spotted the dog.

The goldendoodle in the red ski patrol vest had his front paws on a low wall that separated the parking lot from the street, his attention focused on movement by the dumpster. Connor took a few steps toward his dog. A furry face with triangular ears and a pointed snout peered over the top of the half-open dumpster, then the fox bounded away.

"Farley!" Connor called again. "Come!"

The dog whirled around and raced across the parking lot to join Connor, puffs of snow flying up around his paws.

"Quit messing around," Connor said. "We've got work to do."

He trudged the rest of the way to the munitions storage, Farley scampering in front of him, unfazed by the man's grumpiness. Connor took out his keys and unlocked the double locks, then shoved open the heavy steel door. He flicked on the overhead light, then moved directly to the boxes of explosives stacked along the wall to his left. Each box contained two dozen cast boosters—two-pound cylinders loaded with Pentex explosive that had the destructive capacity of several sticks of dynamite.

Connor took his time loading the sled, handling each box carefully. Even sleep-deprived and slightly hungover, the training that had been drilled into him in the United States Army didn't desert him.

He added boxes of detonator assemblies, then logged what he had taken from stock on a clipboard by the door. Every log entry for the past three seasons was accompanied by his initials. He was the munitions man at SkyCrest Resort, though the job carried no particular cachet. He was merely the man most likely to be blown to pieces if there was ever an accident. Not that there would be. But the possibility was there, adding spice to the morning.

He snapped a fitted tarp over the load, then turned to look for his dog. "Farley?"

A bark emanated from somewhere behind a stack of boxes, deep in the interior of the storage building.

"What are you doing back there?" Connor called, annoyed. "Come!"

The dog stuck his head around the tower of boxes and whined.

"Come!" Connor ordered, with more force.

The dog came, head down. He nudged at Connor's leg and whined again, plaintive and urgent.

"We don't have time for games," Connor said. He moved toward the door.

But Farley had stopped again and was staring toward the back of the building.

Connor wanted to leave, but his conscience wouldn't let him. What if some animal was trapped back there? Or worse, what if a rat had gotten in? The last thing they needed was a rodent chewing on explosives. He sighed. "All right, Farley," he said. "Show me what's got you so agitated."

Connor had to squeeze through a narrow passage between boxes to follow the dog, who led him to a void between the last row of boxes and the wall. Odd that whoever had loaded this section hadn't pushed the boxes flush against the wall but no big deal. Connor shone the beam of his flashlight over the space. At first, he didn't see anything.

Then Farley pawed at the wall. Except it wasn't wall. The dog's claws ripped right through the surface.

Connor bent and pulled at the torn material. It was paper. Paper painted the same color as the stucco outside the building. Heart hammering, he swept the light over the wall more slowly, revealing a cutout two feet wide and three feet high. Wide enough for a man to crawl through.

Wide enough for explosives to be taken out. The explosives that had probably been sitting in this empty space.

He fumbled for the radio clipped to his ski patrol vest, then thought better of broadcasting the news to anyone who might be tuned in, and pulled out his phone. He had to move out of the building to acquire a signal. He found the number he wanted and waited while it rang. And rang. After five rings, the call went to voicemail. Connor hung up and immediately hit Redial.

This time someone answered on the third ring. "What's going on?" Doug Elam, SkyCrest Resort's director of operations, sounded awake and alert.

"We've got a problem," Connor said. "A big one."

SHERIFF VAN HOWARD'S thick moustache was touched with frost as he stood in the gray dawn behind the munitions magazine. Snowflakes dusted the shoulders of his shearling jacket and that of the blue parka Doug Elam wore. Both men scowled at Connor, who scowled right back. Whatever had led to this breach of security, they weren't going to pin this on him.

"When was the last time you checked the magazine?" Howard asked.

"Two days ago. And everything was fine then."

"You said the dog pointed this out to you?" Doug asked.

"Yes, sir. Farley knew immediately something wasn't right." Connor looked down at the dog, who looked up at him with the face of a kid's teddy bear. "He was with me two days ago and acted fine, so I know this happened since then. Plus, you can see here where someone cleared away the snow from this area so they could cut into the wall." He indicated the thin snow cover on the ground around the hole.

"What exactly did they take?" Howard asked.

"I'll have to do a complete count to be certain, but from the gap they left, I'd say at least four boxes of cast boosters, twenty-four to a box. Probably some detonators, too."

The sheriff sucked his teeth. "What kind of damage could all that do?" he asked.

"You could bring down a whole mountain with that much explosive, set in the right places," Connor said.

Doug groaned. "Tell me this was just kids," he said. "Maybe they thought they were stealing fireworks."

"You and I both know that's not the case," Howard said.

Doug looked pained. "Then who? Who does something like this?"

"Somebody who wants to take down a mountain," Howard said. He glanced at Connor. "You know any of this bunch that's been protesting the resort expansion?"

Connor tensed, a dull ache pounding in his skull. "I don't *know* any of them. I've seen the signs around town and read stuff in the papers."

SkyCrest was petitioning the National Forest Service to be able to expand lift-served operations onto six hundred additional acres on Blaine Mountain, adjacent to the resort's current licensed operation.

"Only a very small group of people oppose the expansion," Doug said. "Most people see what a good thing it will be for the area—more jobs, more terrain to relieve crowding, more cash for the town coffers."

"Sure, but it's also taking away a whole section of backcountry terrain people now recreate on for free," Connor said. He probably should have kept his mouth shut, but he didn't like the idea of anyone thinking he let the resort make his opinions for him.

"You sound like you're on their side," the sheriff said.

"I can see things both ways." Connor glanced at the hole in the building. "But I don't condone anything like this. This is wrong. And dangerous."

"Have you had any other problems at the resort?" Howard asked Doug.

Doug's shoulders lifted and lowered. "Just minor stuff. Signs tacked up around the place. A bunch of lift chairs chained together one morning. Nothing like this." He stared at the hole in the magazine building, lower lip thrust out.

"Okay. Well, since explosives are missing and this happened on federal land, we'll have to call in the feds."

Doug's complexion went a shade paler. "ATF?"

"I don't know," Howard said. "I'll report the theft, and they can decide who to send."

"Just what we need," Connor said.

"What's your problem?" Doug asked.

Connor shook his head. "Don't mind me. I just had enough of government bureaucracy in the army." He checked his watch. "Right now we need to get this building sealed up, and I've got a bunch of terrain to mitigate before the lifts run."

"I'll get a security guard over here to watch the place until law enforcement is done," Doug said. "Then maintenance can do something about the hole."

"You'll need to leave everything as is until the feds can get a look at it," the sheriff said.

"When will that be?" Doug asked.

"Don't know," Howard said. "But this area is off-limits until then."

"When am I going to get the additional patrollers I've been asking for?" Connor asked. "We're down one patroller and one dog. It would help a lot if I didn't have to pull double duty handling munitions and directing patrol."

"Once we get approval from the government for the new expansion, the hiring freeze will be lifted," Doug said. "Until then, you'll have to make do. You're doing a great job so far."

Making do wasn't a good policy when it came to protecting people's lives, but Connor had made that argument more than once already and been met with the same corporate line. He whistled for Farley and left with the sled in tow.

Patroller Anders Iverson met Connor in front of ski patrol headquarters. The tall Nordic blond was red-faced in the cold. "I was just coming to look for you," he said. "Everyone's waiting."

"I got held up a little," Connor said. "Tell everyone to come out here, and we'll get started."

The team gathered around him. They were a mixed lot of young men and woman. Five of them, like Connor, had avalanche rescue dogs, but the dogs had remained inside in their kennels. The last thing they needed during avalanche mitigation work was a dog getting spooked and running in the wrong direction. They organized into two-person teams. Connor liked for the same two people to work together as much as possible. The more they knew each other's habits and tendencies, the less room for error, in his opinion.

"Before we get started, I have to tell you someone broke into the magazine last night," he said. "Cut a hole in the back wall and stole some boxes of cast boosters."

Someone in the back swore loudly. The others looked stunned.

"Keep your eyes open out there," Connor said. "Report anyone acting strangely. And keep your ears open, too, in case anyone brags about it."

"Who would do something like this?" asked Lily Alton, the newest member of patrol. The brown-haired twenty-eight-year-old had transferred to SkyCrest from a closed sister resort and immediately clicked with the team. Connor had put her with him on avalanche mitigation.

"The sheriff thinks it might be someone from the group that's been protesting the resort expansion," Connor said. "But I don't know." He uncovered the sled with that day's supply of cast boosters. "For now, we need to get to work. We're already behind schedule."

"Someone could do a lot of damage with that much explosive," Anders said. "What's law enforcement doing about it?"

"The sheriff is contacting the feds," Connor said. "I imagine they'll send someone to look into it."

Anders moved in closer and kept his voice low. "They'll want to question you," he said.

"Sure. I'll have to tell them what I found."

Anders shook his head. "No offense, but you might want to talk to a lawyer."

"Why?"

"Who do you think is going to be their number one suspect? The man who had access to the munitions magazine."

"Someone cut a hole in the back of the building. They didn't have to have a key. Not to mention, I'm the one who reported the theft."

"Yeah, but you know the resort is going to hush this up quickly. Don't let them pin this on you."

Anders and the others left.

Shaken, Connor stared after them. This definitely wasn't the way he had thought to start the new year.

Chapter Two

Avalanche mitigation had a set routine, even though each day's targets might vary. The teams loaded backpacks with canisters of explosives and detonators. Each member carried a crimper in one pocket and a lighter in the other. Always the same pockets. The idea was to be able to safety-fit the detonator, light it, then throw the canister at the target terrain in a smooth, safe routine with as little variance as possible.

The rest of the patrollers headed up the slopes in snowmobiles. Lily joined Connor as he was kenneling Farley. "That's really scary, thinking of someone out there having explosives like this," she said.

"It is," Connor said. "But there's not much you and I can do about it except be on the lookout for anything suspicious." He closed the door on the dog's cage. Farley had already curled up on his bed and closed his eyes.

Outside, Lily climbed onto the waiting snowmobile. Connor loaded his share of the cast boosters, then mounted up and set off.

With the runs deserted, he was free to race up the side of the slope, skimming past the corduroy snow laid down by the groomers last night and early this morning. He and Lily were responsible for the cornices on the ridge above the Glades, an area where heavy snow collected, presenting a danger to the popular runs below.

Connor called up a map of the terrain in his head. But instead of ski runs, his map was marked with danger zones and safe spots and the best places to launch a charge that would bring down snow most efficiently.

He parked the snowmobile out of range of any snowslide, and they clicked into their skis and made their way to their first target area.

Connor took out a charge and a detonator. "Crimping," he said as he fixed the detonator assembly in place. "Seated." He replaced the crimping tool in his pocket and pulled a lighter from the other pocket. "Lighting." He struck the flame and lit the fuse. "Fire!" He reared back and threw the charge. It sailed in a high arc over the ridge and down below. "Smoke," he confirmed as the charge landed in deep snow. "Fire in the hole."

He and Lily turned away as the bomb exploded with a loud boom that reverberated off the mountains behind them. Then they turned to watch the slide release—a river of snow flowing down the mountain. It was a beautiful sight, as long as no one was caught in it.

They moved on to the next target area and repeated the process. Connor launched most of the cast boosters, but Lily took her turn as well. He wanted everyone on the team to be comfortable with the process, safety drilled in to them over and over. All around them the sound of other explosions echoed. Sometimes they could see the resulting avalanches, clouds of white rising up from the mountain's surface.

The sun rose, bathing the slopes in gold and pink. All their charges released, Connor and Lily stopped to take in the spectacle. In the distance, a snowcat growled to life, the groomers set to clear avalanche debris that had spilled over onto a run.

"This is my favorite time of day," Lily said, her voice soft. Reverent.

"Yeah, me, too." The mountain was still peaceful, undisturbed by other people. It wasn't that he didn't like people, but people complicated everything. They broke rules. They broke things. They got hurt. He was happy to help them. Happy that he was able to do so.

But the rule breakers and the thing breakers bothered him. Like the person who had broken into the magazine and stolen explosives. They were up to no good—out to spoil the beautiful place that had given him so much peace.

THE EVENING OF January 2, Stacy Macrae sized up the man across the bar, angling her head so that she could study him through the après-ski crowd—six feet two inches, lean but muscular. Good-looking in a nonintimidating way. Brown eyes, slightly crooked nose, a scruff of a goatee. Curly, reddish-brown hair worn a little long, reaching the collar of his ski jacket in the back.

The jacket had caught her attention right away, the white cross clearly visible against the red, beneath the words Ski Patrol. He would be worth talking to. He laughed at something one of his two companions said and showed a lot of white teeth. He had nice lips, just full enough. He looked like he'd be a good kisser.

Don't go there, she chided herself, amused but not alarmed by the wayward thought. Nothing wrong with appreciating a good-looking man. But she had business to attend to.

She glanced around the rest of the Trail's End Tavern. Patrons filled the mismatched wooden tables and chairs scattered around the room, and the pool tables had a line of people waiting to play. Others stood along the walls, beneath framed black-and-white photos of people in old-fashioned ski clothes or bundled beneath blankets in horse-drawn sleighs. More patrons crowded the long bar, their reflections sepia-tinted in the antique glass of the long mirror behind the shelves of liquor. Country music provided a soundtrack for the evening and a beat for the couples who filled the small dance floor. The crowd was a mix of locals in jeans and Western wear and tourists in ski jackets and fur-topped snow boots.

Stacy wore fleece-lined leggings and hiking boots, and a black turtleneck sweater and black puffer jacket. Not fresh-off-the-slopes but not from around here, either. She leaned against a pillar in the middle of the room, aware of a few men watching her, but so far none had dared approach. She knew how to make herself intimidating enough that all but the bravest—or most inebriated—wouldn't come near.

She sipped the beer she had ordered and tried to think how to proceed. A server—brunette, pigtails, empty bar tray—stopped to talk to the redhead and his companions. The server laughed at something one of the men said, then her face clouded as a fourth man joined them.

He was frowning, waving his hands around, his words audible across the crowded bar. "I said I wanted a beer! And you're over here jawing with your friends instead of waiting on me."

The server shrank back and said something.

"I don't want your excuses," the man bellowed and clamped one hand on her shoulder.

The patroller put his hand on the man's chest and forced him back a few inches. "You've had enough, buddy," the patroller said. "Time to call it a night."

"I'll say when I've had enough." The man took a swing at the redhead, who ducked and then caught the man as he stumbled forward.

"If you can't even stand up, you've had more than enough," the patroller said and shoved the drunk into a chair.

Several people nearby applauded, then two of the drunk's friends appeared to haul him away. The patroller turned back to the bar and picked up his beer.

"Thanks, Connor," the server said.

"No problem, Summer."

Stacy smiled into her beer. Connor's two companions said goodbye and made their way to the door. Stacy decided to take her chance, crossed the room and slid into the space vacated by his friends. "Hi," she said. Big smile, friendly manner—though not too friendly. Casual.

He looked her over—not in a creepy way, but as if trying to place her.

"We haven't met," she said. "I'm Stacy Macrae." She offered her hand. "I saw you across the room and decided to introduce myself."

"Connor Donaldson." His handshake was warm and firm, his skin a little rough. A strong, masculine hand. A thrill of physical awareness raced through her, and she reluctantly released her hold on him.

"I see you're with ski patrol, Connor." She nodded to the insignia on his jacket. "How long have you been doing that?"

"Seven years." He angled toward her, elbow on the bar, one foot propped on the brass rail. "Are you here on vacation?"

"Work, actually," she said. Before he could ask what kind of work, she added, "I'm from Denver. It's nice to get away from the city. It's so beautiful out here."

"It is that." He had soulful eyes. A little sad. But very alert. He was studying her, trying to figure her out. Well, that made two of them.

"Maybe you can answer a question for me," she said.

"I can try."

"I've seen some signs around town. 'No to SkyCrest Expansion' and 'Save Blaine Mountain.' What's all that about?"

A momentary wrinkling of his forehead before it smoothed out again. He sipped his beer before answering. "The resort wants to expand their terrain," he said. "They've petitioned the government to allow them to build lifts on Blaine Mountain. Some of the locals aren't too happy with the idea."

"What do you think of it?"

He didn't hesitate with his answer. "It would be a good business decision for the resort—more terrain, something new to attract new visitors, spread out the crowds more. More jobs." His gaze slid away.

"But?" she prompted.

"But it means cutting trees, putting in lifts and closing access to national forest land that people around here have been able to recreate on for free for, well, forever, I guess."

"So you sympathize with the people who are against the development?"

"To a point."

"What point is that?"

"They're free to protest all they want. But if things get violent or they start breaking laws…that changes things."

"Some people would say preserving a pristine environment might be worth a little violence. At least, ecoterrorists say things like that."

His gaze met hers once more. Wary. "Are you an ecoterrorist?"

"No. Just someone trying to understand the situation."

He set his empty beer bottle on the bar. "Anyway, the forest isn't pristine," he said. "People have logged and mined the area for centuries. They run cattle on it in the summer."

"Hmm. But a ski resort would be different. Like you said, cutting trees. Closing access."

"I guess it's like everything else in life," he said. "If there's a choice involved, one side is always going to end up unhappy." His gaze was boring into her now.

A flutter of nervousness disturbed her stomach. "Let's talk about something more cheerful," she said. "What do you like to do for fun?"

"It's a ski town. Everybody here will say skiing."

"But you do that for work."

"It's still fun. I couldn't do the job if I didn't like skiing. But there's also hiking. Hanging out with my dog."

"You have a dog? What's his name? Do you have a picture?"

He took out his phone, scrolled for a moment, then turned the screen to face her. A curly-haired pup with an adorable grin looked back at her.

"Ohhhh!" She hadn't even realized she'd uttered the cry until it was too late. What the heck. She was a sucker for animals, especially dogs. "He's adorable. What's his name?"

He looked down at his phone, a tenderness in his eyes that touched her further. "Farley. He's a goldendoodle. Three years old." He pocketed the phone. "Do you have a dog?"

"Unfortunately, no."

"Why not?"

"I have to travel too much for my job."

"What kind of work do you do?" he asked.

"Boring work." She set aside her own beer and took his hand. "Want to dance?" The jukebox was playing a fast country song.

He allowed her to lead him onto the dance floor. He was a competent dancer, relaxed and considerate—no wild dips or gyrations, just a light touch at her back and a gentle squeeze of her hand to guide them around the dance floor.

She smiled up at him, enjoying the feel of being close to him. He struck her as smart. Sincere but guarded. A man who was able to see two sides of an argument, which could be a good or a bad thing.

"Why are you looking at me that way?" he asked.

"I'm just trying to figure you out," she said.

"Why?"

"People interest me. You interest me."

"I'm not that interesting. I like skiing and my dog. There's not a lot more to me."

"Oh, I think there's a lot more."

She hadn't meant to put so much heat behind her words but couldn't help herself. Connor was a sexy guy, and he made her feel sexy, too.

He looked away and the song ended. They returned to the bar, though they had to stand closer together now. He ordered another round for them both, and she turned to survey the crowd once more.

A group of people entered, three men and a woman. They scowled, and their gazes darted over the crowd. They struck Stacy as furtive.

"They look like trouble," Connor said, his voice low, close to her ear. "Want to go somewhere else?"

"Let's stay and see what happens," Stacy said.

They moved toward the other end of the bar, but before they reached the bartender, one of them nudged the others and nodded toward Connor and Stacy. She held her breath as they approached.

"You work for SkyCrest?" the tallest man, with dark hair and hooded eyes, his voice deep and rough, asked.

"I do," Connor said.

"How do you stand to work for those people?" the woman asked. She had a high-pitched, nasal voice.

"I have to eat like everyone else," Connor said.

"Not if it means selling your soul to a group that's going to wreck the environment," the dark-haired man said.

"It's not like they're strip-mining the place," Connor said.

"Just stealing from the rest of us to make a playground for rich folks," a pasty-faced blond said. "Those are the only ones who can afford lift tickets these days."

Connor looked away.

The blond shoved him.

"Hey!" Stacy said. "Back off."

Connor put a hand on her shoulder. "It's okay," he said. "The man's got a right to his opinion."

"It's not just my opinion," the blond said. "Lots of people think that way."

"I get it," Connor said. "Like I said, I'm just trying to make a living, like everybody else. Let me buy you and your friends a beer."

"We don't need your charity," said the dark-haired guy. He stalked away, his friends trailing behind.

Stacy leaned closer to Connor and spoke softly. "Way to defuse the situation," she said.

"I had enough of fighting in the army." His gaze met hers again. "Want to dance some more?"

She made herself push away from him. "I wish I could, but I'd better go. I've got an early morning."

"Can I get your number?"

She shook her head. "Probably not a good idea. I'm not going to be here long. But thanks." She started to move away, then leaned in and kissed his cheek. He smelled like herbal shampoo, beer and woodsmoke.

She walked briskly away, not looking back, hoping he

wouldn't try to follow. She had learned a few interesting things about Connor Donaldson tonight, but the one thing that came through loud and clear was that he was exactly the kind of man she would like to be with.

Out of the question, of course. What had he said about choices—someone was always going to end up unhappy.

JANUARY 3 BROUGHT no new snow, so little mitigation was needed on the slopes. Which meant Connor got to sleep in until 6:00 a.m. Alone. Last night at the bar he had wondered if things would work out differently. Stacy had approached him like a woman going after something she wanted but had backed off so quickly he'd been left a little dizzy. But he'd never claimed to understand women—or people in general, for that matter.

In any case, today he needed to push Doug to allow him to inventory the magazine and figure out exactly what had been stolen—not just make an educated guess. Maybe there were more voids in the stacked-up boxes. Maybe whoever had broken in had hauled away a truckload of explosives, not just a few boxes. The thought made him sick to his stomach and propelled him out of bed and into the shower.

At SkyCrest, he met with the other patrollers and handed out assignments. Farley had a runaround in the snow with Anders's black Lab, Darth, and Brian Weeks's golden retriever, Daisy, before settling into his kennel with a chew toy. Connor was on his way toward Doug's office when his radio chirped. "I need you here in my office," Doug Elam said.

"Sure. What's up?"

"You'll see when you get here."

Connor made his way past the ski lifts and shops to a high-rise amid a cluster of hotels and condos. He took the stairs up to Doug's office on the sixth floor, ski boots clattering loudly on the uncarpeted risers.

When he entered the corporate office, Doug's secretary waved him through. "They're waiting for you in there."

Who is 'they'? Connor wondered as he pushed open the heavy door.

Doug, dapper as ever in a Nordic sweater and gray slacks, his dark hair slicked back, sat behind his big desk, in conversation with a woman with long brown hair like a silk curtain around the shoulders of her cherry-red sweater.

As Connor stepped into the room, the woman turned to look at him. Stacy Macrae's expression was unreadable, but the sight of her hit him like a cannonball in the gut. What was she doing here? Had she accused him of something?

"Connor, this is Special Agent Stacy Macrae with the FBI," Doug said.

Connor heard the words, but they didn't make any sense.

Stacy smiled at him. "It's good to see you again, Connor," she said.

He tried to speak, but words wouldn't come out.

Doug looked from one to the other. "Do you two know each other?" he asked.

"We ran into each other at the Trail's End last night," she said.

"You didn't tell me you were a fed." Connor finally found his voice.

"I find that information really colors people's first impression of me," she said. "And I really wasn't expecting to see you again so soon."

"What was that all about, then?" he asked. "Last night."

"I was just getting a feel for this place, seeing if I spotted anyone I recognized."

"All those questions about the protest group." It had

struck him as an unusual conversation starter, but the protest signs were all over town, so he had accepted she was merely curious. He rapidly reviewed the conversation in his head, a sinking feeling in his stomach. "You wanted to know if I sympathized with them. Did you think I was one of them?"

"Part of my job here is figuring out connections. I saw you were with ski patrol and wanted to find out what you knew about the protestors." She obviously felt no guilt at all over having played him for a fool.

Aware of Doug watching, Connor reined in his anger.

"Stacy is investigating the theft of the explosives," Doug said. "I need you to show her the magazine and also familiarize her with the resort."

He took a step back. "I don't have time to escort her around," Conner said. "Not if you want me to inventory the munitions and get through that stack of paperwork on my desk."

"I won't take up any more of your time than necessary." Stacy stood. "It's critical that we find who stole those explosives before they put them to use."

"I don't see how I can help with that." He avoided looking at her, focusing instead on Doug.

"I think you're exactly the man to help." She moved toward him.

He thought she was going to take his arm and took a step to the side to put more distance between them.

"You heard the agent," Doug said. "Go with her. I'm sure you'll figure out how to do the rest of your work, too."

Chapter Three

Stacy led the way from the office. Connor took a deep breath and headed after her. He followed her to the elevator, even though he almost always took the stairs. As soon as the elevator doors closed, he turned on her. "I don't appreciate being lied to."

"I didn't lie to you. But it would have been foolish, even dangerous, for me to reveal who I was before I was certain you weren't involved with a terrorist group."

"These protestors are a terrorist group?"

"Not all of them. Not most of them, even. But we believe there are people involved who have terrorist leanings. We've seen this with similar groups all over the United States and Canada."

He put a hand to his forehead. "Do you mean at other ski resorts?"

The elevator dinged, and the doors slid open. "We'll talk on the way to your office, but keep your voice down."

As they exited the elevator, he fell into step beside her, shortening his stride to match hers. "I don't understand any of this," he said.

"First, let me fill you in on what we know so far," she said. "The group of people I'm interested in—the ones we've been tracking for two years—go by several different names.

The Freedom Fighters, the Society to Save America, the Sons of the Revolution—half a dozen others. The names don't matter. There are key figures at the top of the group and a lot of little cells, whose members don't know each other. Their usual mode of operation is to find a group that's protesting some issue, join the group, get into leadership positions, then advocate violence. The issues involved don't really matter to them. They've learned how to harness people's passions to wreak havoc."

"Why?" he asked.

"Their stated goal is to remake society by first breaking it down. They talk about it like a cancer—it starts small, then spreads outward. They aim to disrupt businesses, pit community members against each other and leave as much damage as possible in their wake."

"And you haven't caught up with these people yet?"

"We've identified some but not all of them. We've had the best result infiltrating small operations like this one. We take out as many of their cells as possible in hopes of eventually finding the people at the top."

"Did you really think I was a part of them?" The idea made him sick to his stomach.

"The organization works by recruiting locals. Someone like you, who works for the resort and has access to keys to a munitions magazine, would be a real asset."

"I would never do something like that."

"You might be surprised at the people who get sucked into things like this."

"So you decided to, what—seduce me?"

She stopped and put a hand on his arm. "As enjoyable as that might have been, I'm a professional. That's not how the FBI does things."

Was it her hand on his arm, or the sexy way her voice

dropped on the word *enjoyable* that sent a current of heat through him? He swallowed and stepped back. "You think there are people here in this town who are part of this group?"

"I believe so." She started walking again, and he fell into step beside her. "We have intelligence that a couple of people we've been tracking have been spotted here in town."

"You keep saying 'we.' Who else is here with you?"

A frown briefly darkened her expression, then her face became passive once more. "I'm the only agent on-site, though of course I'm communicating with my office."

"Have you seen these people—these terrorists—here in town? Who are they?"

"They go by a lot of names. And no, I haven't seen them, but we have intelligence that they're here. I'm on the lookout for them. It's one reason I was at the Trail's End last night. I'm also hoping to meet locals who are involved with the protests. The sooner I can locate the people who took those explosives, the more quickly we can stop them."

Her voice snapped as she bit off the words, and her eyes sparked. Connor didn't want to be impressed by her, but he was. But Anders's words came back to him. "Am I a suspect?" he asked.

Again, she turned that piercing gaze on him. She had earth-brown eyes fringed with long, dark lashes. Eyes he thought probably didn't miss much. "Where were you when the explosives were stolen?" she asked.

"When were they stolen?" he asked. "All I can verify is that they were there December 29 and were gone early on the first. But I didn't take them."

She nodded. "Doug speaks highly of you, and the whole charade of cutting a hole in a building, taking the explosives and then reporting the theft yourself seems overly elaborate to me. Generally, people who are good enough at this kind of terrorism to have gotten away with it for a while keep things as simple as possible."

Some of the tension went out of his shoulders. "If I'm not a suspect, what do you need me for?" he asked.

"I'm not sure yet—beyond what your boss just said. I need you to show me around the resort and introduce me to people. I need someone to tell me about the people we meet, especially if they might be involved in the protests."

"I don't know anyone involved in the protests."

"You probably do and don't realize it yet."

He stopped. "I can show you around the resort, but I have a job to do. We're already shorthanded. If I step away, I could be endangering both the other patrollers and our guests."

"I won't keep you from your work," she said. "I can shadow you. What do you have to do this morning?"

"I need to inventory the munitions and determine exactly what's missing from the magazine."

"That's a great place for me to start, too. I can help you."

"How are you going to help me?"

"If you do an inventory, that means you're counting, right?" She hooked her arm in his. Her hair brushed his cheek, and he caught the scent of flowers. "I can count," she said. "I don't even have to use my fingers and toes."

CONNOR EASED OUT of Stacy's grip. "I have to stop off at the ski patrol office first," he said. He walked faster, but she kept up, not about to let him run away from her.

She understood he was upset at what he considered her subterfuge at the bar last night, but truly she'd had no idea she would be working with him today. Maybe she had continued their conversation longer than strictly necessary, but he had been an appealing guy, and she hadn't seen any harm in dancing and flirting a little before she went back to her hotel room, alone.

He unlocked a door near the base area lifts marked Ski Patrol, and she followed him inside. The room was dimly lit and crowded with skis, toboggans, rolls of orange snow fence, a stack of orange traffic cones, a row of metal lockers and, in the corner behind a scarred wooden desk, a large inflatable palm tree.

A dog barked from the back of the room, and she followed the sound to a row of kennels. Each was occupied by a dog, some asleep, others watching her with alert brown eyes.

The door opened again behind them, and a tall woman entered. She wore the patrollers' uniform of black pants, red jacket and red helmet, a blond ponytail hanging to her midback. She stopped short when she saw Stacy. "Oh hello."

"What do you need, Nina?" Connor looked up from where he was bent over one of the kennels.

"Oh hey, Connor. I just came to get Sky to give her a little exercise, maybe run through a few drills while I'm not too busy." She moved past Stacy to the first kennel, where a red-coated golden retriever stood and was wagging her tail.

"Yeah, I'm taking Farley out, too." Connor opened the kennel in the middle of the row, and a curly-haired dog shot into the room. Stacy recognized the dog from the photo Connor had shown her last night.

"Settle," Connor said firmly.

The dog sat, though its whole body continued to vibrate, tail sweeping the floor. The blonde rubbed the dog's ears, then turned to release the golden retriever. The two dogs greeted each other with wagging tails and kisses.

The blonde, smiling, turned back to Stacy. "I'm Nina," she said, and offered her hand.

"Stacy." They shook hands. The blonde was several inches taller and, frankly, gorgeous. She had the kind of high cheekbones and full lips some people paid thousands of dollars to replicate.

"Stacy is—" Connor began.

"I'm visiting in town, and Connor agreed to show me around." Stacy flashed a warm smile at him. "We're old friends."

Nina looked from one to the other. "Well, it's nice to meet you." She snapped a leash onto her dog's harness. "Sky and I will get out of your way."

"If anyone needs me, just radio," Connor said. "I'll be over at the magazine."

"Will do." Nina waved, then left.

Stacy turned to Connor. "I should have mentioned before—I'm here undercover."

His eyes narrowed. "But you really are an FBI agent?"

"Yes."

"You never showed me any identification."

She hesitated, then unzipped her jacket, folded down the top of her leggings and slipped out her identification folder and passed it to him.

He studied it a moment, then passed it back. "Why undercover?" he asked.

"I'm hoping to get close to the protestors who are advocating violence and eventually learn the names of the leaders who have moved in from the national group we're tracking. People need to believe I'm just a regular person who believes the same things they believe."

The dog at his feet let out a low whine.

"All right, Farley," Connor said. "We're almost ready to go."

"Farley." Stacy knelt and beckoned the dog. He hurried toward her, his whole body wiggling. She buried her fingers in his soft fur and rubbed his ears. "You're even more adorable than your picture," she said. She looked up at Connor, who was still scowling at her. "It's so great you get to bring your dog to work."

"He's an employee, too. Well, an unpaid one. He's a trained avalanche rescue dog. All of the dogs are."

She turned her attention to the row of kennels. Each bore a tag with a name—Sky, Shelby, Darth, Farley and Daisy. "Do they ever have to rescue people?" she asked.

"Sometimes." He snapped on Farley's leash. "Let's go."

They threaded their way through crowds of skiers at the base of the main lift, past a row of shops and around the side of a hotel, until they reached a large, mostly deserted parking lot. Connor unclipped the leash, and Farley bounded ahead across the lot. He raced to a dumpster at the far end and began sniffing around it.

"There's a fox that likes to visit that dumpster, and Farley is fascinated by it," Connor said.

"You don't think he'd hurt it, do you?" Stacy asked.

"He might if he got the chance, but the fox is too fast and smart for that. In any case, he won't be there this time of day. We've only seen him early in the morning. We saw him New Year's day, in fact."

Farley sniffed around the dumpster, then suddenly whirled and raced toward them once more. He skidded to a stop at Stacy's feet and looked up, a goofy grin on his face.

"Good boy!" she said and patted his side. "I think he likes me," she told Connor.

"He likes everybody." He looked away and gestured toward a low stucco building. "That's the munitions magazine." He moved ahead of her, and Farley hurried to catch up.

With amusement, Stacy noted that dog and owner bore a resemblance. At least, they both had reddish curly hair and melting brown eyes.

"I'll show you where the thieves broke in," he said and led the way around the side of the building. They walked along the back until they reached a sheet of plywood screwed on to the wall. "There's a hole under there, two feet by three feet. Looks like it was cut with a saw."

"How did they saw through a wall without someone hearing?" She looked around them. There weren't any buildings close, but a sound that loud would have carried.

"If they did it on New Year's Eve, there were fireworks, with loud music."

She studied the plywood and said nothing.

"Has this group you've been tracking done something like this before?" he asked. "Stolen explosives?"

"Not explosives, but they tried to break into a research laboratory in upstate New York. They triggered an alarm, and that scared them away, but not before they did some damage."

"What kind of research?" he asked.

"Biological research. I wasn't on the team then, so I don't know a lot of details."

"That's all there is to see out here," he said. "Let's go inside."

They walked around to the front of the building, where he unlocked two locks, pushed open the door and flicked on an overhead light. Cardboard boxes were stacked along one side of the single, concrete-floored room, each box marked Danger: Explosives.

"They took the explosives from back here," Connor said and led her down a narrow aisle between boxes. At the wall, he turned and squeezed into another narrow space. "There isn't supposed to be any space between the boxes and wall here," he said. "They were able to pull the boxes right out the hole."

She studied the void. "So, how many boxes are missing?"

"I think four, but we won't know for sure until we count."

They returned to the front of the room. Connor picked up a box and shoved it at her. Surprised, she grasped it, straining against the weight.

"That's one," he said. "We're going to stack everything in the empty space on that side." He pointed behind her.

"That doesn't seem very efficient, to move every box," she said.

"If we move every one, we won't miss any. And we'll know right away from the weight of the box if they took anything out and sealed it back up."

She nodded. "I see your point." She carried her box to the far wall and set it down, then returned to accept a second box.

They worked quickly. She couldn't tell if he was really that fit or just showing off. After a while, Farley laid down on a pile of packing blankets and fell asleep. Arms aching, Stacy consoled herself that she wouldn't need to hit the gym today. Maybe not all week.

"How did you end up with the FBI?" Connor asked when they were halfway through the stacks of boxes.

"I was recruited in college," she said. No need to mention that she had already decided to apply to the Bureau when they showed up at a campus job fair.

"Were you studying law enforcement?"

"No, I was an accounting major."

He laughed.

"What's so funny?"

"I guess you really can count."

"I can add, subtract and divide too." She added another box to the growing stack. Connor was ticking off each box on a sheet on a clipboard.

"How does that apply to working for the FBI?" he asked.

"Accountants are generally methodical and detail-oriented."

"Do you like the work?"

"I do." She admired the way his shoulders looked as he hefted another box. "How did you end up as a ski patroller?"

"I was looking for a job. I like to ski."

"But how did you end up in charge of explosives?"

"Handling explosives was part of my job in the army. The resort was looking for someone with my experience, and they gave preference to veterans. It seemed like a good fit."

"And has it been a good fit?"

"Yeah. It has." He paused. She was gratified to see that he was breathing hard, his face flushed from exertion. "Three years ago, I had a chance to be part of the avalanche dog program. I bought Farley from a breeder who specializes in search and rescue dogs and started training him. I'd never get to do something like that if I had a regular desk job."

She looked at the remaining boxes of explosives. "Tell me about this stuff. What is it? What does it do?"

He tapped one of the boxes. "These contain two-pound cylinders of an explosive called Pentex. It's a chemical compound that acts like nitroglycerine. It's used a lot in mining. And for avalanche control. The explosive is very stable under most conditions, and it works even when wet—useful when you're dealing with snow. To use it, you have to install a detonator—a blasting cap—and a fuse. Light the fuse and throw the cylinder. *Boom!* Hit the right place, and you can clear a dangerous buildup of snow with one or two charges." He hefted another box. "We have almost a hundred potential slide paths inbounds here at SkyCrest, so during a big storm, we can go through a lot of these."

She accepted the box. "But whoever stole this would need the blasting caps and fuses, too."

"We'll count those, too," he said. "I'm betting we find out at least one box is missing."

In the end, there were four boxes of cast boosters and one box of detonator assemblies that couldn't be accounted for. "They could do a lot of damage with all of that," he said. "But I don't get how blowing up something will stop the resort's expansion plans."

"The people we've been tracking don't care about Blaine Mountain or the wilderness," she said. "They thrive on destruction for destruction's sake, hiding behind the idea of a just cause. It's how they get otherwise innocent people to do their dirty work. They'll think of some way to sell the explosions as furthering their cause. They've had a lot of experience manipulating people."

"So how are you going to find out what their plans are and stop them?" he asked.

"I'm going to a meeting of the local protesters tonight," she said. "Want to come?"

He shook his head. "I don't care to get near those folks. Not to mention I don't think Doug would be too happy if the head of ski patrol was seen fraternizing with the enemy."

"You're entitled to do what you want on your own time. Besides, it would be good for my cover to have you along. I can tell Doug it's important for my investigation."

"Guess you'll have to handle your cover without me for window dressing."

She winced at the bitterness behind his words. "I didn't mean it that way," she said. "We could have a good time, hanging out."

"Not a good idea." His eyes met hers, and she felt the heat of his gaze all the way to her toes. "After all, you made it clear you're not going to be around for long. I'm a man who likes to finish what he's started."

Chapter Four

"Stacy isn't with you this morning?" Nina didn't even try to disguise her curiosity, questioning Connor as soon as he entered ski patrol headquarters Thursday morning.

"Who's Stacy?" Brian asked. He dropped into a folding chair, and Daisy sat beside him, her chin resting on his knee.

"Stacy is an 'old friend' of Connor's who was hanging out with him yesterday," Nina said. "A very pretty old friend."

"Cool." Brian patted Daisy's side. "I noticed the safety fencing at the bottom of Lift Ten is down," he said. "It's fallen over into the run. Someone's going to get tangled up in it if we don't fix it."

"You can take care of that first thing," Connor said. "Do you need some help?"

"Nah. If I have to, I'll get one of the lifties to give me a hand."

Connor picked up the clipboard from his desk and scanned the list of notes he had made before leaving yesterday evening. More patrollers and dogs filed in until the room was full, men and women occupying every chair and ranged along the walls, dogs taking up most of the rest of the floor space. Connor glanced at the clock. "Looks like everybody is here, so we'll get started," he said.

The door opened again, and Stacy slipped in, a slim figure dressed in all black again, down to her black ski boots and black helmet. Every head in the room swiveled toward her. "Don't let me interrupt," she said, staying by the door.

"We're about to start our morning meeting," Connor said.

"Go ahead." She lowered herself to the floor and sat. "You won't even know I'm here."

He wanted to tell her to leave, that this was none of her business, but he wouldn't bet against her arguing with him, attracting even more attention he didn't want. He consulted his list again. "Lily, I want you and Chase patrolling the Glades this morning. Nina, you and Brian are at Buttermilk Basin. Anders, you and Raz take the runs that dump into Lift Six. Carson and David, you're at Lift Ten. I'll take Top of the Mark."

"Chase isn't here yet," Lily said.

The door burst open, letting in a flurry of snow, and patroller Chase Sergeant stumbled in, arms full of gear. "Sorry I'm late," he muttered and dropped his belongings on a bench in the corner. A sharp-featured young man with spiky black hair, he had a reputation as a dependable, if sometimes anxious patroller. He sat and removed his hiking boots, then reached for his ski pants.

"While Chase finishes dressing, I'll go over the duty charts," Connor said. He rattled off a list of tasks to be seen to, like replacing the downed snow fencing and checking the ropes marking out-of-bound areas, as well as a list of special groups expected at the resort that day, from a group of tourists from Mexico to local ski clubs.

He was wrapping up when he was interrupted by swearing from Chase. Everyone looked to the bench.

Chase sat with one foot poised above his ski boot, something white and wet dripping from his sock. "Someone filled my boots with shaving cream," he said.

Nina was the first to laugh, but the others soon followed suit. Connor had a hard time holding back his own mirth.

"It's not funny!" Chase said and turned the boot upside down.

"Don't let it drip on the floor!" Nina protested. She grabbed a T-shirt from the corner of Connor's desk and launched it at Chase. "Clean up your mess."

"Which one of you did this?" he demanded as he wiped the floor.

"Where were your boots?" Brian asked. "You carried them in with you just now, right?"

"I had my hands full of gear on the way to my car yesterday, so Cerise volunteered to keep them in the lift tech's locker room overnight. I picked them up from there this morning." Realization dawned. "You think the lifties did this?"

"Didn't you put a bag of plastic spiders in Cerise's locker last week?" Lily asked.

Chase made a face. "She loved them. She told me so."

"Maybe she thinks you love shaving cream," Renee said.

He looked down at his dripping boots. "This is going to take forever to clean up."

"Look at it this way," Connor said. "At least now they're going to smell fresher than they ever have." He looked to the others. "Anything else I've forgotten?"

Anders's hand went up. "Any news on the stolen cast boosters?" he said.

Connor glanced at Stacy, who had her head down, brushing something from her knee. Everything about her posture said, *Pretend I'm not even here.*

He turned back to the group. "I haven't heard anything. If any of you know anything, even if it's just a rumor, let me or Doug know."

"Does this have anything to do with the people who are protesting the resort expansion?" Nina asked.

"Has someone said something to make you think that?" Connor asked.

"No, but there are people who are pretty upset about it," she said. "Maybe they've decided to go from chaining lift chairs together to blowing things up."

Several of the patrollers exchanged worried looks.

"Again, if you hear anything, speak up," Connor said. "And be on the lookout for anyone acting oddly or in places they aren't supposed to be."

"If I see anyone with a pocket full of cast boosters, I'll be sure to let you know," Raz, a tall redhead, said, garnering nervous laughter from her fellow patrollers.

Stacy stood. "I'll just wait for you outside, Connor."

"Little late for that," Brian said as the door closed behind her.

"What are the local cops doing about the theft?" someone at the back of the room asked.

"They've called in the feds," Connor said.

"You mean ATF?" Brian asked. "I'll bet Doug is thrilled with the idea of a bunch of uniformed federal agents hanging around the place. Not a good look."

"I haven't seen anyone in uniform," Chase said.

"Maybe they're undercover," someone else said.

"All of that is out of our hands," Connor said. "All we can do is keep our eyes and ears open." He set aside the clipboard he'd been holding and picked up his jacket. "Let's get to work."

The patrollers without dogs filed out, while the ones with dogs set about crating them for the morning. Nina paused beside Connor on her way out. "Stacy's cute. How long have you known her?"

"A while." He avoided looking at her. He wasn't really good at subterfuge. "She's just a friend. In town for a few days."

She waited, as if expecting him to say more, but when he didn't, she shrugged. "Well, enjoy her visit."

Connor waited until everyone had left before he exited the patrol office.

Stacy was there, standing next to the ski rack. She had donned the helmet, the goggles pushed up to give a clear view of her brown eyes when she turned to look at him. "It doesn't sound like any of your patrollers have heard anything useful," she said.

"Hmm." He knocked snow from his boots and clicked into his skis.

She laid her own skis beside his and clicked into the bindings. "Where are we headed?" she asked.

"I'm going to work," he said.

"I'm going with you." At his glare, she added, "I want to talk to you about the protest meeting I attended last night."

"I don't care about the meeting," he said.

"But you should. It was very interesting."

He said nothing but skied toward the lift, bypassing the half dozen skiers who had arrived early, waiting to board at 9:00 a.m. The liftie nodded as he skied to the line to wait for a chair. Stacy slid in beside him.

"I feel like a VIP," she said as they settled into the chair. Connor didn't bother lowering the safety bar, and she didn't ask. Below them, the snow was a sea of white corduroy. "I guess you get first chair every morning, huh?" she asked.

"We do a sweep of the runs before they open, looking for any problems," he said.

"Do you ever find any?"

"I once had to postpone opening of a run because of a

lynx hanging out near the top." He glanced at her. "It didn't make me very popular with the guests."

"A lynx? Really?"

"Yeah. They're a threatened species, so we try to give them space. After an hour or so, it wandered back into the woods, and we were able to open the run."

"That's very considerate of the resort."

"Consideration has nothing to do with it." He swept a hand to indicate the terrain below them. "Except for about fifty acres full of condos and shops in the ski village, this is all national forest land. The resort leases it for the winter, but it doesn't belong to SkyCrest. The Forest Service dictates where, when and how we operate."

"And this expansion? Is that Forest Service land, too?"

"Yes. SkyCrest has petitioned the government to allow them to lease and develop the land."

"Do you think the Forest Service will agree to the lease?"

"It depends. They'll probably consider the environmental impact of development, as well as public sentiment." He glanced at her. "The protestors don't need to resort to violence to sway the decision. If they get enough people to sign petitions and show up at hearings to protest against the development—if they get people to lobby their government representatives—they have a good chance of persuading the Forest Service to rule against the resort."

"Cynics would say the resort has enough money to buy the government's cooperation."

"I never said I wasn't a cynic, but I think the system still works, most of the time."

They reached the top of the lift, and she skied out in front of him. "We're headed straight back to the bottom of this run," he said. "Then we'll ride back up and ski over to Top of the Mark—the highest lift-served terrain."

He hung back, letting her get ahead of him. She was a good skier, carving effortless turns down the slope, her stance relaxed and graceful. Her formfitting black pants and short jacket emphasized her figure, and he had trouble taking his gaze off of her. If he had ever thought much about FBI agents, he hadn't pictured one who looked like this.

At the bottom of the lift, they boarded again. "Let me tell you about the protest meeting," she said.

"Fine. What about it?"

"There were a lot of people there. Twenty or more. I saw the trio who approached you at the bar New Year's night. They were what I'd call the hard-core protestors—a half dozen people who are really angry about the resort's plan to close Blaine Mountain to free public access. The rest of the people I met are concerned, but they have other things claiming their attention, too—jobs, families. There were even some people there with their kids."

"Anybody look like they wanted to blow things up?"

"One of the hard-core types said they needed to take action to get the resort to pay attention. He didn't specify anything in particular, and the others shut him down pretty quick. But I want to take a closer look at him. His name is Nate Lee. Ever heard of him?"

Connor shook his head. "Did you see anyone you recognized? Anybody with an FBI file or whatever you call it?"

"No one. But one of the speakers alluded to people who couldn't make it that night."

"What was the result of the meeting?" he asked.

"There's another big protest planned for Martin Luther King weekend," she said. "The leaders emphasized it's going to be peaceful, but I heard mumbling before I left that some of the people were lobbying to 'make a statement,' though they didn't specify what that might mean."

They reached the top of the lift and skied away from the chair. Connor stopped beside a resort map. "What are you going to do next?" he asked.

"There's another meeting Friday night," she said. "Supposedly to talk more about activities for MLK weekend."

"You're going?"

"Yes. I want you to come with me."

He shook his head. "I already told you—"

She grabbed his arm. "They're not going to trust me. They know I'm an outsider. But they know you. You're head of ski patrol. The redhead with the cute dog. If you decided to be on their side, it would be a big deal. They'd bend over backward to include you in their plans because you would give them inside access they don't have."

"I wouldn't give them anything," he said.

"Not really. But you could make them think you would help them. That could be enough for me to find out who's really behind all of this. To find the terrorists I'm after and to stop them before they do more damage."

He shook his head. "No. I don't want any part of this." Without waiting for her reply, he took off, putting distance between her and her plans.

STACY LET CONNOR ski ahead of her, though she kept him in her sights. He wasn't going to listen to anything she had to say, but she would find a way to bring up the subject again. All she needed was the right opportunity, and she was confident she could persuade him. Watching him these past two days, she had learned a lot. He was stubborn, sure. But he had a strong sense of justice. He hadn't hesitated to put the drunk who was hassling the waitress in his place. Connor's convictions were going to be the key to getting him to help her.

"Are you up for some tougher terrain?" he asked as they exited the lift.

"Depends on how tough," she said. "Are you trying to ditch me?"

"I want to check out some of the steeper terrain. If someone decided to use those stolen explosives to set off an inbounds avalanche, that would be the place to do it."

"I hadn't thought of that," she admitted. "I assumed they would blow up a building or a road. That's the kind of thing that gets lots of attention and could put a lot of people in danger."

"An avalanche inbounds on a crowded day would put a lot of people in danger and get a lot of attention," he said.

"Then, let's check it out."

She followed him to a rope barricade. He held up the rope, and she skied under it. He stopped at the top of a narrow ridge. "Ski in my tracks across here," he said. "We mitigated up here yesterday, and there shouldn't be much danger, but better to be cautious."

She glanced up at the steep slope to their right and the snowcapped peaks above, and a shiver went through her. "You're sure it's safe?" she asked.

"Just ski in my tracks and don't stop until we get to the other side." Without waiting for an answer, he took off.

She took a deep breath, gripped her poles more tightly and skied after him.

It probably didn't take five minutes to cross the slope, but when they reached the other side her body ached from holding herself so tense.

"I didn't see any fresh tracks headed up above us," Connor said. "Climbing is the only way up there unless you drop in by helicopter, but not just anybody can fly here.

We drop charges from our own chopper when we need to mitigate that area."

"You mean you just drop bombs from the helicopter?"

"The idea is to hurl them as far as you can, but yeah. You saw the cast boosters. They're not that big. We've learned over time where to aim them for the best effect."

"So anyone who had worked with you before would know how to deploy the explosives to set off an avalanche?"

"Anyone who worked for us or any other resort."

"Any names come to mind?" she asked. "Former employees, particularly disgruntled ones."

"The only former employee I know about is the guy who had my job before this, and he left to work for C-RAD—Colorado Rapid Avalanche Deployment. He's not disgruntled, and his partner is one of the other patrollers. He's about the last person I'd see doing anything like this."

"Think about it, and let me know if you think of any possible suspects."

"Come on. Let's check out a few other locations."

They spent the next three hours on a tour of every avalanche-prone area of the resort, from windblown cornices to steep couloirs. Most of the terrain was out of bounds, the paths of the snow released in an avalanche spilling onto inbounds runs. By the time they slipped back under the ropes and onto a wide, groomed run, Stacy's muscles ached from exertion, and she had a new respect for the work Connor and his team did.

"Is anyone ever hurt on the job?" she asked. "It seems like one mistake, and you could blow off your hand. Or worse."

He shook his head. "It could happen, but I've never known it to. Everyone trains to safely handle what is basically dynamite, and we all have a healthy respect for what it can do." He tilted his head, thinking. "The first year I was working here, a couple skied up to the patrol shack where I was stationed and said there were a handful of orange canisters on the edge of a run. They were all marked Danger: Explosives. Me and the guy I was with raced over there, and sure enough there were half a dozen cast boosters scattered under the trees. Later, we figured out they had fallen out of a pack on the back of a snowmobile. We recovered them all and nobody was hurt, but I've been paranoid about securing the things ever since."

She looked out across the run to the view of snowy mountains beyond. "I'm a little disappointed we didn't see anything suspicious this afternoon," she said. "It would have been nice to catch the thieves before they hurt anyone."

"Maybe you'll learn something from the meeting Friday."

"Have you changed your mind about going with me?"

He shook his head. "Not a chance." He planted his ski poles. "Feel like one more run before we get some lunch? An easy one, I promise."

"Sure."

He led her into the trees, cutting through thick powder that felt like floating. She followed him through the white trunks of aspen, terrain like a Japanese woodcut. They had the run to themselves, the thick snow muffling the sound of their passing, enveloping them in a silence that felt magical.

By the time they emerged onto a wide, groomed run, something had shifted between them. He hadn't let down his guard completely, but she thought he was beginning to trust her more, or at least to resent her less.

Two preteen girls flagged them down. Connor skied to a stop beside them. "Do you need some help?" he asked.

"Oh no." One of the girls grinned, flashing braces with purple bands. "We were just wondering if you had any trading cards?"

"We're collecting them," said her companion, in a green helmet spangled with glitter.

"Sure." Connor unzipped his jacket and took out what almost looked like playing cards. He handed one to each girl and one to Stacy. She looked at the picture of Farley, standing against the backdrop of the mountains, flashing the tip of his pink tongue in a canine grin.

"Farley!" The green-helmeted girl squealed as she read the card. "He's so cute!"

"Thanks," the girl with braces said. "We don't have this one yet. We're trying to collect them all." She tucked the card into her jacket, and the two girls skied away.

"Farley has fans," Stacy said as she admired her own card.

"All the dogs have them. It's a way of creating awareness about the avalanche dog program. And kids like them."

"I like them." She tucked her card away. "Why isn't Farley with you now?"

"Running around on snow all day wears a dog out. We don't want them exhausted if they're needed for a rescue." He checked his watch. "But it's about time for him to get some exercise."

They skied down to the base area, and Connor unlocked the door to the ski patrol office. He released Farley from his kennel. The dog raced around, making tight turns in the small space, then flopped onto his back at Stacy's feet. Laughing, she rubbed his belly.

Belly rub over, the dog sat upright, and Connor handed him a biscuit. "I need to take him out for a bit," he said. "If you want to get something to eat, I brought a sandwich from home."

"All right. I'll meet you back here."

When she returned twenty minutes later, Farley was

sprawled in a worn upholstered chair, and Connor was at his desk, unwrapping a sandwich. Stacy sat across from him and removed the top from her cup of chicken corn chowder. "That smells good," he said.

"I could have gotten you some," she said.

"No, thanks. I'd go broke eating here every day."

"So would I," she said. "Fortunately, the government is paying for this."

He grinned. "My tax dollars at work."

Farley moved from the chair to sit by her side.

"No begging," Connor said, his voice stern.

"He's completely innocent," Stacy said. "Can't you tell by his face?"

The dog looked at her with liquid eyes. Eyes not unlike his owner's, she thought.

The door burst open, and a young man raced in. He pushed his goggles on top of his orange knit hat and stared at them, eyes wide. "There's a guy in the trees, upside down in a tree well. I tried to pull him out, but I couldn't. I'm afraid he might be dead."

Chapter Five

Connor shoved to his feet and took the frightened young man by the arm. "What run is he on?" he asked.

"T-Tessa's Trees," the boy stammered. Connor could see now that he was maybe sixteen or seventeen, the barest hint of a mustache over his thin lips, acne dotting his chin.

"Where on Tessa's Trees?"

"Maybe…halfway down? On the right side. I just saw the bottom of his board. It's, like, sky blue. I tried to pull him out, but he's stuck fast. I yelled at him to hang on, but he wasn't moving or anything. I just flew down the mountain to get here. I didn't know what else to do."

"You did the right thing." Connor put a hand on the kid's shoulder, steadying him. "Is this a friend of yours? Do you know his name?"

The boy shook his head. "I just saw the board and went over to check it out."

"Was anyone with him?" *Or her*, Connor thought. It could be a woman under there.

The boy shook his head. "Nobody."

"All right. Can you ride up with us and show us where this person is?"

"Yeah. Yeah, I can do that."

Connor was already putting on his jacket. He grabbed

his radio and keyed it as he headed for the lift, with the boy, Stacy and Farley in his wake. He could have ordered Stacy to stay behind, but he didn't want to waste time or his breath. "We've got a boarder in a tree well on Tessa's Trees," he radioed to his team. "Anyone in the vicinity, meet me over there."

Farley sat on the lift between Stacy and Connor. The boarder, whose name was Charlie, sat on Connor's other side. The kid was fidgeting so badly Connor lowered the safety bar.

"What happens now?" Stacy asked, her voice low, one hand on the dog's back.

"We have to get whoever is trapped out of there." Connor angled toward her. "Snow can collect around the base of trees, but it doesn't pack like on the runs. If someone skis or boards over it, the snow gives way beneath them. The well underneath can be deep enough to swallow up a person. The snow can collect around them, trapping them."

"But how did he end up upside down?" she asked.

"If he hit the edge of the well, the snow could give way and pitch him forward." A person could smother within minutes as the snow closed around them.

At the top of the lift, the four of them exited, Farley bounding ahead. Charlie took off, leading the way down Desi's Trees. Connor scanned either side of the run, searching for any sign of a blue snowboard in the trees.

A little more than halfway down the run, Charlie veered to the right. Connor spotted what appeared to be a discarded snowboard, upside down in the snow. He was almost on it before he recognized someone was still attached to the board.

Farley barked and began digging furiously around the trapped boarder's feet. Connor unstrapped a folding shovel from his pack and began digging. Brian Weeks arrived seconds later and began shoveling too. Within a couple of minutes, the two men and the dog had cleared the boarder almost to the waist, but the person hadn't moved or made a single sound.

"Let's try to pull him out," Brian said.

"I'll help." Chase Sergeant stepped up, along with Stacy. Connor unfastened the bindings of the board and freed the rider's feet, then tossed the board aside. He wrapped his hands around the man's thighs—he was pretty sure it was a man. "On three, pull," he said. They were taking a risk. If the man had a neck injury, they could be making things worse, but the more time that passed without him moving or speaking, the more likely it was he was already dead. If they could get him out and get him breathing again, they might be able to save him.

"One, two, three!" Everyone pulled.

"We moved him a little," Stacy said.

"Pull again," Connor ordered. "One, two, three."

The body popped free like a cork. They carefully laid the young man on the ground and cleared snow from his face. Connor felt for a pulse and thought he detected a faint one. He cleared the airway and began rescue breathing.

The body convulsed and heaved, then the young man coughed. They quickly rolled him onto his side as he retched. After a few moments, he struggled to rise. "Stay still," Connor urged. "You're going to be okay."

"I need to sit up," the man said, then shoved into a sitting position. Connor and Brian supported him, and Stacy removed his helmet, revealing straight, dirty blond hair. He coughed and trembled but gradually he settled. Then he stared at them with bloodshot hazel eyes. "What happened?" he croaked.

Chase put a blanket around the man. "You fell into a tree well," he said.

"I saw your board and fetched ski patrol," Charlie said.

The man blinked at his rescuer. "Thanks." He ran a hand through his straw-colored hair. "I remember now. I was going a little fast and got near the trees. I tried to turn, and the next thing I knew, I was upside down in the snow." He swallowed hard. "I thought I was going to die." His voice broke, and he bowed his head.

Connor gripped his shoulder. "You're not going to die. What's your name?"

"Jace. Uh, Jason. Jason Dennison." Connor thought Jace was close to thirty, about five-nine, with a stocky build. No wonder they'd had such a hard time pulling him out.

"Is there somebody you want us to call?" Brian asked.

Jace frowned. "My boss? What time is it? I'm supposed to start a shift at three. I work at the Bagel Bistro."

"It's only 1:30, but you might want to take the rest of the day off," Connor said.

"I'll be okay." His eyes met Connor's. "Can I have some water?"

Connor gave him water and checked his pulse again. It was stronger now, and the color had come back into his face. "How do you feel?" he asked. "Does anything hurt?"

Jace shook his head. "I feel okay, really." He grimaced. "A headache, but that's probably from being upside down. How long do you think I was in there?"

"Fifteen minutes, at least," Charlie said. "It must have just happened when I found you, or we probably wouldn't be talking."

Jace nodded. "Yeah. I'd like to stand up now."

The others helped him to his feet. "You doing okay?" Connor asked.

"A little shaky."

"Let's give you a ride down," Connor said. He signaled to Brian, who had arrived on a snowmobile. Chase retrieved the rescue sled that was strapped to the trunk of a nearby tree, kept handy for just such a purpose, and they helped Jace arrange himself in it and tucked blankets around him.

"I could probably board down," Jace said but without much conviction.

"Take the free ride," Charlie said. "I'll bring your board." He picked up the blue snowboard.

"Thanks," Jace said and closed his eyes.

They formed a procession down the mountain—Chase on the snowmobile, pulling the sled, Connor skiing behind, Farley loping alongside him. Charlie and Chase were together, the snowboard cradled to Charlie's chest. Stacy was last, making deliberate turns, seemingly in no hurry.

By the time Stacy rejoined them in front of ski patrol headquarters, Jace and Charlie were leaving together. Stacy watched them walk away.

"He should go to a doctor and get checked out," she said.

"I tried to persuade him to go to the clinic, but he refused," Connor said. He shrugged. "He'll probably be all right."

"He probably doesn't have any insurance," Brian said. "Except for those bloodshot eyes, by tomorrow he won't even be able to tell anything happened." He nodded to Stacy. "Thanks for your help today."

"You're welcome."

Brian glanced at Connor, then nodded again to Stacy. "I'll get back to work."

She followed Connor back into the ski patrol building. Farley resumed his spot in the chair. "Your soup is cold,"

Connor said as he settled behind the desk. "There's a microwave if you want to reheat it."

She carried the soup to the microwave, though her appetite had deserted her. "Are you really as calm as you seem right now?" she asked.

He looked up from his sandwich. "What do you mean?"

"That guy almost died. You saved his life."

"What did you think we do?"

"I thought it was all about clearing snow and getting people with twisted knees to the medical clinic."

"Some days it's about that. Other days it's tending to a heart attack victim or a lost child or someone who died after hitting a tree."

"Have you dealt with many dead people?"

"Even one is too many."

The microwave beeped, and she pulled out the steaming cup of soup and carried it to the desk. "That guy, Jace. He looked really familiar to me."

"Oh?"

"I think he was at that meeting last night. He was one of the protestors. One of the hard-core group, even."

"Do you think there's a connection between the meeting and what happened to him today?"

She shook her head. "I don't see how there could be. I just thought it was odd, to run into him again today."

Someone knocked on the door. They both turned as an older man with close-cropped salt-and-pepper hair entered. "Anybody home?" he asked.

Stacy shoved to her feet. "What are you doing here?" she demanded.

The newcomer grinned—a charming, big smile full of white teeth. "Hello, Stacy," he said. "It's good to see you again."

Connor had risen also. "Stacy?"

Stacy's cheeks were flushed, and she didn't look pleased. She remained focused on the older man and didn't answer Connor.

The man stepped up to the desk and thrust out his hand. "George Macrae," he said. "I'm Stacy's dad."

Chapter Six

The meeting Friday evening was at a pavilion at a Forest Service campground that was closed for the winter. George had insisted on coming with Stacy, and to her surprise, Connor showed up to ride with them. Stacy slid into the driver seat of her rental SUV before her dad could protest, and guided the vehicle down the narrow snow-covered road in stony silence.

Her father had plenty to say, of course. "How do you know Stacy?" he asked Connor before the man even had his seat belt fastened.

"Someone stole some of the explosives ski patrol uses for avalanche mitigation," Connor said. "I reported the crime, and Stacy showed up to interview me."

George, in the front passenger seat, turned toward Connor in the back seat. "What's your background? Former military?"

"Uh, yeah."

"I can always tell. I'm a Marine myself."

"Army Rangers," Connor said.

"At least we know he can handle himself if things get dicey," George said.

Stacy said nothing, only tightened her fingers on the steering wheel.

"She's giving me the silent treatment now," George said. "You'd think she was sixteen, not twenty-six. She lived with me, you know, after her mom and I split up. Her choice. The two of us made a great team. She's smart, like me, and gorgeous, like her mother. I ran off more than one boy with the wrong idea."

She groaned. "Dad. Connor isn't interested in any of that."

"I'm just letting him know I'm the type who does whatever it takes to protect his family."

"I can certainly respect that," Connor said.

Stacy wished she could see his face. He almost sounded like he was trying not to laugh.

"Dad, I'm not a helpless teenager anymore," she said. "I'm a trained special agent, and it looks bad to have my father—who has no business being involved in an investigation—showing up to interfere."

George looked to Connor. "I'm a special agent, too. Did she tell you that?"

"Retired," she said.

"That wasn't my idea," George said. "And I'm not going to interfere. I'm just your backup if things go south. Daughtry had no business sending you out here alone."

"Because he knows I can handle this," she said.

"I'm sure you can. But there's no harm in being careful. Pretend I'm not even here."

A choked sound from Connor. He *was* laughing now, she was sure.

George faced forward again. "Where is this place anyway?"

"Only a few more miles," she said.

"Remote, dark, only one way in," George said. "Good setup for an ambush. Are you armed, Connor?"

"No, sir."

George leaned down, then handed something over the back seat. "You can use this, just in case. I've still got my sidearm."

"Dad!"

"I'm sure a former Army Ranger knows how to handle a weapon," George said. "When you're dealing with people like this, it's good to be prepared for anything."

Stacy clenched her teeth and drove on. There was no sense arguing with her father. She could apologize to Connor later. Or not. It wasn't as if they were *involved* or anything. He was simply helping her with her investigation.

The SUV's headlights illuminated a brown Forest Service sign indicating the turn for the campground. Stacy drove until she spotted a line of cars parked alongside the road, and backed in beside the last vehicle. They got out and headed toward the glow of a lantern a short distance away.

Stacy walked fast, putting some distance between her and the two men. Connor caught up with her, her father farther behind. She glanced at him. "I thought you weren't interested in helping me," she said. "Why did you change your mind about coming tonight?" She kept her voice low, not wanting to be overheard by anyone else who might be lurking out here in the darkness.

"No way could I miss seeing you and your dad work this out," he said.

"He still treats me like I'm sixteen and I don't know what I'm doing."

"That's not the impression I got."

"What do you know about it?"

"I'm not a federal agent, but it didn't make sense to me that you were sent here to deal with supposed terrorists by yourself. Maybe your dad is on to something. Who's Daughtry?"

"My boss's boss. He was my dad's special agent in charge the last year he was with the Bureau."

"It doesn't sound like George really wanted to retire," Connor said. "So why did he leave?"

She inhaled a shaky breath, nostrils pinched, then flaring. "He was shot. The bullet went in under his arm, just slipped past his ballistics vest. He was in the hospital for two weeks." The image of him in that bed in intensive care, tubes running out of his body, his face mostly obscured by an oxygen mask, still haunted her.

"He looks okay now."

"He's a good actor. It's one of the things that made him a good agent."

"Did you join the FBI because of him?"

"I guess so. I loved hearing stories about the jobs he'd been on. He always made it seem like such honorable, important work."

"I think it is."

"It doesn't look so shiny and pure from the inside."

"Nothing does. I was in the army, remember? What we did was important, but the bureaucracy behind it wasn't always easy to live with."

At least a dozen people were already gathered around several picnic tables in the open-sided pavilion in the center of the campground. Stacy paused just inside to get her bearings, and her father caught up with them.

"See anybody you know?" George asked.

"I do," Connor said.

Stacy glanced at him. "Over there, at the table in the center. Isn't that Jace Dennison?"

The snowboarder was wearing the same pants and jacket he'd had on this afternoon, a gray knit beanie pulled down over his blond hair.

"Let's go say hello," Stacy said and started toward him. George and Connor followed.

Jace looked up, then nodded at their approach. "Hey," he said.

"How are you doing?" Stacy asked. "I'm Stacy, by the way. We didn't exactly have time to introduce ourselves this afternoon. And you remember Connor."

Connor offered his hand, and Jace shook it. "Yeah, of course. Thanks again." His gaze shifted to George.

"I'm George. Stacy's dad." George shook hands, too. "Stacy was telling me about this group, and I came out to see if I could help."

"We don't get many SkyCrest employees." Jace frowned at Connor.

Connor slid onto the bench beside Jace. "I'd probably lose my job if my boss knew I was here, but it's no secret I'm no fan of their expansion plans."

"Why not?" Jace asked. "Job security and all that."

"Hah!" Connor leaned toward Jace. "Ski patrol is already shorthanded, and they expect us to patrol new terrain without adding staff. And they're sure not going to pay us more." He shook his head. "And I live in this town, too. The last thing we need is more tourists. Corporations like the one that runs SkyCrest are ruining this country."

Stacy's eyes widened. Connor did an impressive job of sounding authentically disgruntled. Exactly the sort of man who would appeal to saboteurs looking for inside access to the resort.

"Welcome, folks." An older man with jowls like a bulldog, a canvas jacket hugging his broad shoulders and barrel chest, joined them. "I don't think I've seen you around here before."

"I'm George." George stuck out his hand. "And this is my daughter, Stacy, and her boyfriend, Connor."

"Connor works for SkyCrest," Jace said. "For ski patrol."

"So I heard." The older man nodded. "I'm Shane. I organized this group to protest the Blaine Mountain expansion."

"Shane who?" Stacy asked.

The older man eyed her warily. "Just Shane."

"We're here to help any way we can," George said, before Stacy could respond.

Shane was still studying Connor. "We're always happy to welcome new volunteers." He looked away and, raising his voice, said, "Let's get started, folks. We have a lot to talk about." He assumed a wide-legged stance at the front of the pavilion, the posture of a coach before the big game. "First of all, thanks for coming all the way out here on a cold night," he said. "We felt like we needed to get a little farther away from town because we heard rumors the sheriff's department planned to disrupt our meetings as illegal gatherings. They don't have a legal leg to stand on, but it's just another way to hassle us."

Angry murmurs rose from the crowd.

"We're all here tonight because we care about the same things," Shane continued. "SkyCrest Resort is trying to take land from the public, close it off to free access to ordinary people like us and charge for the privilege of recreating there, further lining their own pockets."

Boos rose up from several in the crowd.

Shane nodded. "They've done this sort of thing before. Back in 1968, my grandfather fell on hard times, and the resort developers took advantage of him to buy a big chunk of our family ranch for a criminally low price. They're trying the same kind of swindle with Blaine Mountain."

More boos. Shane waited for the clamor to subside. "I

won't keep you standing around in the cold," he said. "The main purpose of tonight's gathering is to plan our next protest. As you know, in a little over a week, we'll celebrate Martin Luther King weekend. It's one of the busiest weekends of the year at SkyCrest, so there will be lots of tourists in the ski village and on the slopes. It's our opportunity to make a big impact."

Stacy compressed her lips together. Did Shane intend for the word *impact* to sound so sinister, or did she only think that because she suspected the group had four boxes of explosives at their disposal?

"Tourists are all for the expansion," someone toward the back of the pavilion said. "If they're fighting the holiday crowds, they'll be even more in favor of new terrain."

"Not if we can help them see how unsafe the idea is," Shane said.

Stacy tensed.

"How do we do that?" Jace asked.

"Our new friend here has just shared that ski patrol at SkyCrest is understaffed." Shane nodded at Connor, who looked decidedly uncomfortable. "More crowds on a holiday weekend will mean more accidents. Maybe too many for patrol to handle comfortably."

"We have extra staff on holidays," Connor said. "We'll handle everything."

"Not if there are more accidents than usual," Shane said.

"What are you proposing?" George spoke up. "Are we going to booby-trap the runs or something?"

A murmur rose from the crowd. Shane held up his hands. "I'm not suggesting anything illegal," he said. "I don't want to see anyone unnecessarily hurt."

The word *unnecessarily* had Stacy on high alert.

The crowd calmed. Shane studied them. He had intense

blue eyes, and a charisma Stacy could feel. "What if everyone here tonight also decided to ski that weekend?" he asked after a long pause. "And not just those of you here. I've put the word out all over the state, inviting others to join us here at the ranch that weekend, to help protest this taking of public land away from the public."

A cheer rose from some in the crowd. Shane smiled.

"So the plan is just to have a lot of people around, criticizing the resort?" someone in the crowd asked.

"I'm suggesting people deliberately seek out the most crowded runs," Shane said. "Maybe we ski a little slower than usual or stop more often or lose our balance getting off the chairlift."

"We impede traffic, you mean?" someone asked.

"Exactly. And if anyone says anything or anyone collides with us, we complain loudly about the resort not having enough staff. They can't handle the crowds. They can't take care of the terrain they already have. Adding more is irresponsible. They're not interested in their guests. They're merely greedy."

"You know, it could work," someone behind Stacy said.

"Might be fun," added someone else.

"Sounds dangerous," said a third person.

"It does sound dangerous," Stacy muttered. George gently squeezed her arm, and she shot him an annoyed look.

"No one needs to do anything they feel uncomfortable with," Shane said. "If you don't want to ski that weekend, think about joining us in the village square for another peaceful protest on Sunday afternoon. We've got some local musicians who have agreed to play, and it will be a chance to talk to people and explain to them our point of view about the proposed expansion. All nice and friendly." He smiled. "That's all I have to say tonight. We'll have another meeting before MLK weekend. In the meantime, think about what I've said and tell your friends to join us. We can save Blaine Mountain for everyone to enjoy."

Voices rose in agreement, then the group began to break up, people making their way back to their cars.

"I want to talk to Shane some more," Stacy said and moved toward the organizer.

Shane looked up at her approach. "You're just the people I wanted to speak with," he said.

SHANE'S WORDS INDICATED he wanted to talk to all three of them, but he looked right at Connor when he spoke.

Connor met his gaze with a steady look of his own. Odd, he wasn't as nervous about this charade as he had expected to be. Maybe because a lot of what he had said reflected his true feelings. He still didn't advocate violence, but he didn't think the resort expansion was a great idea.

"You seemed pretty serious about your dislike of Sky-Crest," Shane said.

Maybe he had laid on the criticism of the resort too thickly. He'd only been trying play the part of the keen revolutionary. Time to dial back a little. "I love the ski area," he said. "But I don't necessarily like the way the corporation handles things." All true.

"I'm with you there," Shane said. "We don't want to harm SkyCrest. It's an asset to the area. It brings in lots of jobs. But the resort honchos have gotten too arrogant. They think they make or break the town, and that's not right. The people want to take back what's theirs and remind SkyCrest that it's locals who made them what they are today."

"How are you going to do that?" Stacy asked. "Are protests and rallies enough to sway corporate opinion?"

"We have something special in mind for MLK weekend," Shane said.

"Do you mean the disruptions on the ski runs?" George asked. "That is certainly going to snarl things up for skiers."

"Something in addition to that," Shane said. "Something to drive home our point about the expansion plans not being safe for visitors." He returned his attention to Connor. "How long have you been with ski patrol?"

"Six years."

"So you've done a lot of avalanche mitigation?"

The fine hairs on the back of Connor's neck rose. "Yes."

Shane stared at him, expression intent. "Then you can help us out."

"Help you how?" Connor asked.

Shane looked around. "I'll fill you in more later. Now isn't the right time." He clapped Connor on the shoulder. "I'll be in touch."

He started to move away, but Connor caught hold of his arm. "Does this have anything to do with the explosives that were taken from ski patrol?" he asked.

Shane went rigid. "What do you know about that?"

"I'm the one who found out they were missing," Connor said.

Shane shook his head. "I can't say I know anything about that."

"Then what is this special thing you want help with?" Connor asked. "And why does it matter that I've done avalanche mitigation?"

"You wouldn't have to do anything yourself," Shane said. "We just need an expert consultant."

"I can't commit until I know what, exactly, you want from me," Connor said.

"Sure. Sure." Shane pulled out his phone. "Give me your number, and I'll get in touch to explain."

Connor hesitated. Did he really want this man knowing his phone number?

"Silly. He can never remember his own phone number." Stacy slipped her hand in the crook of his arm and rattled off Connor's number.

Shane typed in the digits, then pocketed the phone. "Great. I'll talk to you later." He lifted a hand in a gesture of farewell, then hurried away.

Connor took one step after him, but Stacy tugged him back toward the road. "Let's go," she said.

This time, Connor ended up in the front passenger seat with George in the back. No one said anything until they were on the main road leading back toward the resort. "That was certainly interesting," Stacy said.

"How about criminal?" Connor asked. "Or even terrifying. He practically admitted he needed me to help with those explosives."

"He implied a lot, but he didn't admit anything," George said.

"He's certainly interested in you," Stacy said. "I was right to think you would be the perfect way to get close to these people."

"Why can't you arrest him now?" Connor asked. "Before he does something to hurt people. I mean, the whole plot to impede skiers during one of the busiest weekends of the season ought to be enough to file criminal charges. People could be seriously hurt, even killed, by such a reckless plan."

"He was careful not to give specific instructions," Stacy said. "And he emphasized they don't want to hurt anyone. And asking about your work experience is a long way from saying he has the explosives or that he wants to use them."

"He said he couldn't say anything about the theft of those cast boosters," Connor said. "That's not the same as being surprised or alarmed by the theft. Maybe he can't say because doing so could land him in jail."

"It definitely sounds like they're aiming to make a big splash for MLK weekend," Stacy said.

"Doesn't he realize he's going to be the prime suspect in anything that goes wrong?" Connor asked.

"We can suspect people all day long," Stacy said. "But without proof that will stand up in a court of law, we can't do anything to stop them. Maybe Shane thinks he's so clever he won't leave any evidence behind."

"Or maybe his belief that he's right and the resort is wrong overrides everything else," George said.

"I don't really care what he believes or doesn't believe," Stacy said. "We've got to find out his plans and put a stop to them."

"That shouldn't be a problem with Shane so keen to enlist Connor." George leaned forward from the back seat. "All you have to do is agree to a meeting when Shane calls. We'll wire you up, get the conversation on tape, and we'll know everything."

"Dad, how long were you with the Bureau?" Stacy asked.

"Thirty years, eight months and thirteen days," George said.

"In all that time, did you ever know a case to be resolved that easily?" she asked.

"No. And I didn't say this one would be easy, either. That's what we can hope will happen, but in reality, when Connor meets with Shane, you and I will be lurking somewhere nearby, listening in and ready to intervene if necessary."

"Who says I'm even going to meet with this guy?" Connor asked. "I don't want anything to do with a possible terrorist. I'm not the federal agent here. I'm not even a retired federal agent."

"You're the one with the expertise Shane wants," Stacy said. "You're the one he wants to talk to. If you didn't plan to help me, why did you even come tonight? And don't give me that throwaway line about watching me argue with Dad."

"Stacy and I don't argue," George said. "She may object to what she sees as interference, but she eventually realizes I'm her best ally in any situation."

"In *this* situation, Connor is my best ally," Stacy said.

"I'm a ski patroller," Connor said. "I just want to do that job and leave the skullduggery to other people."

"If you don't help us, a lot of people might end up hurt or killed," Stacy said.

"It's your job to stop them," he said. "I reported the theft of the explosives—the rest is up to you."

"Shane already knows who you are and what you do," George said. "If you don't help him, he might decide to target you."

Connor turned to scowl at him. "Why would he?"

"Because he's already said enough to make you suspicious. He was pretty sure he could convert you to the cause or he wouldn't have said that much."

Connor folded his arms across his chest. "I don't know how he would have gotten that idea."

"Probably from your little speech about your dislike of corporate politics," Stacy said. "You made a believer out of me."

"I never should have come here tonight," Connor said.

"But you did," she said. "And I know you want to stop these people from harming others. If Shane contacts you, at least agree to meet with him. I'm not asking you to set bombs or to cooperate with his plan in any way."

She was right. Backing out now, when he had the potential to at least find out what Shane and his cohorts were up to, smacked of cowardice. "I'll agree to meet with him," he said. "But you're coming with me."

"Good idea," George said before Stacy could answer. "Stacy is the girlfriend who recruited you to the cause in the first place. I'll come, too."

"No, Dad. Absolutely not."

"Hey, Shane has already met me," George said. "He'll think it odd if I don't butt in again. I can play the trigger-happy old guy. You two can be cautious, but I'm all for full speed ahead." He punched his fist in the air.

Connor could practically feel the irritation rolling off of Stacy in waves. Her whole body was rigid, her knuckles pale in the dashboard lights as she gripped the steering wheel. He sensed another futile argument rising. "Let's wait and see if Shane even contacts me," he said. "Maybe he'll change his mind."

"I doubt it," Stacy said. "In the meantime, I need to find out more about Shane. Why wouldn't he tell me his last name, for one thing?"

"We can run his prints," George said. "That should tell us if he has a record."

"Right," Stacy said. "I'll just ask him to let me ink him for a fingerprint card."

"You don't have to." George thrust something between the seats—a beer bottle in a plastic zipper bag. "I grabbed this off the table when Shane's back was turned," he said. "He was drinking out of it."

"Is that even legal?" Connor asked.

"Trash is abandoned property," George said. "Fair game

for pulling fingerprints, DNA, whatever else we can derive from it."

"Um, great, Dad," Stacy said. "I'll get that right off to the lab."

"You're welcome." George sat back once more. "I told you we make a great team. You've got youth and the most up-to-date training on your side, but there's nothing like experience and old-fashioned cunning to really get things done."

The triumph in the old man's voice almost made Connor smile. He understood Stacy's annoyance at her father's interference, but you had to admire the man. And Connor wouldn't bet on the side of anyone who tried to cross him.

Chapter Seven

"Where's Stacy this morning?" Nina's voice rang out as Connor unlocked the door to ski patrol headquarters mid-morning on Saturday.

"I have no idea." He pushed open the door and flicked on the light.

Nina followed him inside. "How long is she in town for?" she asked.

Connor opened Farley's kennel, and the dog stepped out and arched his back in a stretch. "I don't know that, either."

"I thought you two were friends."

"We are. But I don't keep track of her comings and goings."

"I thought I saw her yesterday afternoon with a good-looking older guy." Nina smirked. "Maybe you've got some competition."

"That was probably her dad. He's in town, too. And Stacy is just a friend. She can hang out with whoever she likes."

Nina slid one hip onto the corner of his desk. "In that case, I have a friend I could fix you up with."

"Not interested."

"Why not? She's really cute. And smart."

He met her teasing look with a scowl. "How would you

feel if I pestered you about your personal life and offered to fix you up?"

"I'd think you cared." She laughed. "Okay, I get it. I'll back off. Just call me a romantic."

"Who, as far as I know, is very much single."

"I'm living vicariously through my happily involved friends. They give me hope that maybe true love is possible."

If someone like Nina—a famous athlete and model—couldn't find "true love," that didn't leave much hope for the ordinary rest of the population. "Right now, all I'm worried about is turning in the monthly report," he said.

"I guess that's my cue to get back to work." She slid off the desk, rubbed Farley behind the ears and left.

Connor sat back and sighed. In spite of his protests that he didn't care where Stacy was right now, he couldn't get her out of his thoughts. What was she up to? Had she found out anything more about the protest group's plans? Who was Shane, and what did he want from Connor?

A knock on the door distracted him, and he looked up to see Doug, in ski jacket and helmet. "Let's take in a few runs together," the resort manager said.

"Farley needs some exercise," Connor said.

"Bring him, too."

Connor locked up, retrieved his skis, and they headed for the ski lift.

"I needed to get out of the office for a while," Doug said when they were on the lift.

"Everything okay?" Connor asked. He scanned the runs spread out below them, alert for any sign of trouble.

"You wouldn't believe the hoops we have to jump through with this expansion request. The Forest Service wants a new form or document or study every day, and now the feds have come in with this talk of possible terrorists. Corporate is riding me hard to make it all go away."

And that's why they pay you the big bucks, Connor thought. "Sounds intense," he said.

"Has Stacy learned anything more about the stolen explosives?" Doug asked.

"She hasn't said anything to me."

"You two have been spending a lot of time together."

"You've been keeping track?"

"Of her. Not you. You know, the resort comped her a place at CrestView Condos. A premium unit. The thinking was she would be impressed enough to keep us more in the loop. I need her to tell me this is all resolved so I can get corporate off my back. What is taking her so long? It's six days since the theft, and as far as I know, she hasn't even identified a suspect."

Connor thought of Shane. "I don't know," he said. "Why don't you ask her?"

Doug looked away. "I have. She won't tell me anything."

"I don't think that's unusual for law enforcement. You probably won't know anything about her investigation until it's over. None of us will."

"Keep me posted."

I'm not your spy. But again, discretion curbed his tongue. "I'm sure if there's anything you need to know, Stacy will tell you."

They reached the top of the lift just as Doug's phone rang. He swore under his breath. "I have to take this," he said and stopped to one side of the lift. "Go on without me."

"Come on, Farley." The dog raced alongside as Connor cut down one side of an ungroomed blue run named Wildcat. Fewer people braved the thick, choppy snow here, but it was also the kind of run where less experienced skiers could get into trouble. Connor had the run to himself right now and let Farley race ahead, stretching out his legs after a morning in the kennel.

He called the dog back to him when Wildcat intersected a more popular, groomed run. He slowed and steered through crowds of skiers.

"It's Farley!" a teenage girl called and waved.

The dog glanced over to her but kept pace with Connor.

"Connor! Wait up!"

He slid to a stop and looked around to see George skiing toward him.

"Good to see you," the older man said. He wore black pants, a yellow-and-black jacket and a black helmet with a single SkyCrest sticker on the back. "Hello, Farley." He bent to pat the dog.

"Hello, George." Connor looked past the older man, expecting to see Stacy.

"I'm on my own for now," George said. "Stacy wanted me out of her hair." He straightened. "Am I interrupting your work?"

"I'm just checking out a few runs, seeing if anyone needs help. And letting Farley get some exercise. You can ski with me if you like."

"That would be great. Thanks."

They made their way down the run, past groups of people having fun. No signs of distress or trouble. The sun shone brightly, warming Connor's face in spite of the brisk temperatures. This was how every day should be but too often wasn't. At the bottom, Connor motioned for George to follow him to the head of the lift line.

On the chair, George leaned back. "What a gorgeous day," he said, looking out at the expanse of white snow and blue, blue sky. "You are living the life. I should have done something like this when I was younger."

Farley settled between them, his head in Connor's lap. "You'd rather be a ski bum than a federal agent?" Connor asked.

"Yeah, well, maybe not." George grinned. "I wanted excitement, travel, to make a difference."

"And the FBI offered that?"

"Sometimes. But what's exciting when you're young can become routine drudgery when you start raising a family. All that travel was tough when Stacy was little. I missed a lot of milestones. I regret that. I didn't really get to know her as a person until her mother and I divorced when she was fourteen. I didn't know what I was getting into, taking on a teenager full time, but it was worth it."

"And she followed in your footsteps," Connor said. "That has to be flattering."

"Either that, or she was trying to show me up. I've never been sure." George glanced at him. "I suppose she complained to you about me butting in where I'm not wanted right now."

"I'm smart enough not to answer that question."

George chuckled. "It's not that I don't trust her to do her job. I know she's a good and capable agent. But she doesn't have my experience, and they should never have sent her out here alone."

"Maybe they don't think there's real danger."

"Stolen explosives sound pretty dangerous to me."

"Yeah. Me, too. I'd a feel a lot better if we could recover them."

"I got a bad vibe at that meeting last night," George said.

"I guess I don't have your instincts," Connor said. "Everyone I met seemed pretty ordinary. Do you really think some of those people are terrorists?"

"You'd be surprised how innocent dangerous people can appear. The Unabomber looked like a harmless old man to his neighbors." George chuckled. "Some people would probably say the same about me."

"Nina Rose thinks you're good-looking," Connor said.

"The ski racer?"

"And ski patroller."

"No kidding? She works for you?"

"She does."

George grinned. "I'll have to be sure to thank her."

"I hope I'm around to watch when you do."

They exited the lift. "One more run, and I have to get back to the office," Connor said.

"I need to take a break, too," George said. "Maybe I'll see if I can find Stacy."

But at the bottom of the run, Stacy was waiting for them. "What are you two doing together?" she asked when they met up in front of ski patrol headquarters.

"We're enjoying the beautiful day," George said. "What are you up to?"

"I sent off the bottle you snagged for testing. I labeled it Priority, but you know it will be days before we get any results."

"Did you find out anything about Shane?" Connor asked.

"His full name is Shane Greer. He owns a ranch in the area. Nothing particularly large or famous. Apparently, his family has been in the area for generations. The original ranch was sold a decade ago, and Shane was able to buy back a portion of it last year. He has no criminal record that I could find, but if they pull prints from that bottle we might learn something different."

"That's a good morning's work," George said. "Not that I expected anything less."

"Dad, I need to talk to Connor. Alone."

"Never say I can't take a hint." He shouldered his skis. "I'll see you later, Connor." He strode off across the plaza, never looking back.

Connor turned to unlock the door, and Stacy moved in closer. "What did Dad say to you?" she asked.

"He said he was trying to stay out of your way today."

"No. I mean, what is he doing here? In Colorado? Does he think I'm that incompetent?"

"He said you were a good and capable agent."

Her eyes widened in surprise. No poker face for her. "Then why is he here?"

"He thinks your superiors are underestimating the danger." He pushed open the door and shooed Farley inside but didn't follow right away. "And he regrets not being around more when you were growing up."

"He told you that?"

"He did. And I think he just misses you in general. And maybe he misses the excitement of being an agent working a case."

"This isn't his case to work."

"He knows that. But it couldn't hurt to have someone with his experience on your side."

She crossed her arms over her chest. "Did he pay you to say that?"

He shook his head and started to go inside, but she didn't follow. "It's busy around here today," she said.

"It's a Saturday. And everybody wants to be out on a bluebird day like today—sunshine, good snow, but not too cold."

"Hey, isn't that Jace over there?"

He turned and followed her gaze to a pair of snowboarders by the ski racks. "Yeah, I think that's him," he said. "And the guy with him looks familiar, too."

"I'm pretty sure that's Nate Lee. He's the guy who gave you a hard time at the Trail's End the other night."

The night he and Stacy had met. "Yeah. I remember now."

She put a hand on his arm. "Let's go talk to them."

Connor followed her over to the ski racks. Jace looked up at their approach. "Hey," he said.

"It was good to see you last night," Stacy said. "I was afraid I wouldn't know a soul there."

Jace glanced at his friend, who was watching them. "Go on up, Nate," he said. "I'll catch up with you in a bit."

Nate met Connor's gaze, a challenge in those dark eyes. "I think I'll stay."

Jace turned back to them. "Yeah, there was a crowd last night. I guess more people are getting upset about this expansion." He cut his eyes to Connor. "I was surprised to see you there."

"Yeah, well, don't spread it around here," Connor said. "It could cost me my job."

"The way I see it, you're either on the resort's side or on our side," Nate said. "You can't be both."

"And like I said, I have to eat," Connor said. "Besides, the existing part of the resort is here to stay. It's only the expansion we're trying to stop."

Nate shook his head, then looked away.

"What do you think about this plan for MLK weekend?" Stacy asked. "A little wild, huh?"

"A little too wild, if you ask me." Jace shifted his stance. "People are bound to get hurt, and what's that going to accomplish? I have to work that weekend anyway, so it's a good excuse to stay clear."

"Shane seems to think it will do a lot of good," Stacy said.

"Shane's a great guy," Connor said. "He wants to do a lot for the community, but I don't know if little guys like us can really fight a big corporation that owns half a dozen ski resorts."

"You're wrong," Nate said. "We're a lot more powerful than you think."

"What do you mean?" Stacy asked. "Powerful how?"

"We've got some money and resources behind this movement," Nate said. "I think a lot of people are going to be surprised by how effective we can be."

"This does sound interesting." Stacy moved a little closer to him, her expression avid. "What kind of resources?"

Nate gave her a hard look, then turned away. "I'll meet you at the top, Jace," he said. "Don't be long."

"Yeah, I'll be right up." Jace watching as Nate made his way to the lift line and melted into the crowd.

"What's his problem?" Stacy asked.

"He's just really upset about the expansion project," Jace said. "He thinks we should be doing more to stop it."

"More—like vandalism and stuff?"

"Nothing like that," Jace said. "Just...more."

"If enough people speak out, maybe the Forest Service will pay attention and deny the resort's permit," Stacy said.

"Maybe." Jace shrugged. "All we can do is try. The rally in the village square is a good idea, too. That will let visitors know what the locals think. It might make a difference to some of them. I volunteered to help man a booth to collect signatures on a petition we'll give to the Forest Service."

"That's a good idea," Connor said. "I'll look for you there." He nodded to Jace, then turned to Stacy. "I have to get back to work."

Moments later, Stacy joined him in his office, where he sat behind his desk, the work surface obscured by piles of papers, mismatched gloves, a roll of pink surveyor's tape, another of duct tape and an avalanche beacon.

"Jace says he met Nate when they worked for the same pizza place in town last summer," she said. "Nate left, but they reconnected on opening day this year when they ended up on a chair lift together. Nate introduced him to Shane and some of the other protestors."

"Anybody who might be one of the terrorists you're trying to find?" Connor asked.

"No. He said these were all other locals Shane Greer had recruited. But Shane really impressed Jace. He says Shane knows a lot about the history of the area and seems really serious about land conservation."

"Serious enough to want to blow things up to preserve the status quo?" Connor asked.

"I don't know." She sank down into a folding chair. Farley came over and rested his head in her lap. "I'm going back to the Trail's End tonight to see if I can talk to anyone else who was at the rally. I need to find out if Shane is really the one running the show or if there are other people behind the scenes."

"Will you take your dad with you?"

A teasing expression lit her eyes. "I'd rather take you."

"Seems like I'd be in the way if you're working."

She leaned toward him. "I'm not saying you wouldn't be a distraction, but we'd find a way to make it work."

Tempting. He was about to suggest she forget work for one night and go on a real date with him when she leaned away from him again. "Besides, you'd be really handy to have along," she said. "You saw how interested Shane was in your background last night. We could play up your interest and see if anyone wanted to tell you more about their plans, as a way of recruiting you."

So much for thinking she was interested in him for himself. "Your dad is probably a lot better at getting information out of people than I would be," he said.

She scowled. "Dad would end up telling me how I should handle things. He can't accept that I have my own ideas."

"Was he still working for the Bureau when you joined?"

"Yes."

"Was that hard for you? Did you worry about being compared to him?"

"Harder than I expected." She sighed. "I was naive. I always thought he was the best agent possible, and I wanted to be just like him. I found out pretty quickly that not everyone felt that way about him. Some people resented his tendency to take risks and color outside the lines—which were some of the things I admired about him. He always cared more about looking after people than following rules."

"And are you like him—taking risks and coloring outside the lines?"

"Not so much. I think my superiors are so worried I'll be like Dad that they haven't given me a chance to take the lead on anything of consequence. Sending me here on my own feels like a real chance for me to show them what I can do."

"You don't think your dad is right, and they sent you here because they don't think there's a real case?"

"There's a real case. Stolen explosives are a serious risk."

"You said yourself it's unusual to be sent into the field alone."

"Yes." She looked away. "I'm telling myself it's a vote of confidence. They know I can take care of myself. But maybe Dad's right, and they sent me out here alone to fail."

"You're not alone. Your dad is here to help you. And I'm here."

She looked up. Her eyes met his, and his breath caught,

stopped by the intensity of her gaze and the heat of his response. Maybe she only wanted him because he could help with the case, but he was already too ensnared by her to turn away.

His phone rang. He automatically picked it up and glanced at the screen. Unknown number. It was probably spam, but he needed to answer. "Hello?"

"Connor? It's Shane Greer. We need to get together and discuss some plans."

Chapter Eight

Though Connor pressed the phone close to his ear, Stacy had heard the caller's greeting. "Tell him I want to talk to him!" she whispered.

"That sounds great." Connor's faked heartiness made her wince, as did his next words. "My, um, my girlfriend wants to come, too. Is that okay?"

She couldn't hear Shane's answer.

"Yeah," Connor said. He cut his gaze toward Stacy. "Of course."

Connor listened some more, then said goodbye and ended the call.

"What was that last bit about?" Stacy asked once he had pocketed his phone.

"He asked if I trusted you."

"It's no wonder he asked, the way you stumbled over the word *girlfriend*. Is the idea so horrible?"

"No." His eyes met hers, and she couldn't ignore the warmth that swept through her. "It's not horrible."

No. A relationship with Connor Donaldson wouldn't be horrible. Confusing, complicated and maybe ill-advised but not horrible.

"You obviously haven't had enough practice lying." She laid a hand on his arm. "Or are you feeling guilty? Do you have someone in your life who's going to be upset you're spending a Saturday night with me?"

"No."

"I have to admit, I'm surprised a guy like you is single."

"What do you mean, a guy like me?"

"Young. Fit. Good-looking. So why aren't you dating someone?"

"That's a personal question."

"It is. I still want to know the answer." Sometimes personal questions were the best way to surprise a revelation out of someone.

He shrugged. "No particular reason. There are a lot of other things claiming my attention." His eyes narrowed. "What about you? Do you have someone waiting back in Denver?"

"No one."

"And why not?"

Fair enough. He had answered her question, she could answer his. "I haven't had a serious relationship with a guy since I joined the Bureau," she said. "I vowed never to date a fellow agent, so that limits my choices. And if I'm with someone else, I need to know I can trust them before I reveal everything, so that makes things difficult. I keep telling myself I'm still young. I have plenty of time to find someone. And then I wake up, and I'm another year older and still alone. Not that that's the worst thing in the world, it's just..." Her voice died away. She was babbling. Revealing too much. Talking about feelings, which she had been reassured repeatedly was a sure way to scare off most people.

"Yeah, I get it." He looked as if he wanted to be anywhere but here at the moment.

She took a step back. "I'll meet you here a little before seven, then."

"I'll pick you up at your place," he said.

"How do you know where I'm staying?"

"Doug told me SkyCrest had comped you a place in the CrestView Condos. Luxury digs."

"I hadn't noticed." Okay, maybe it had registered that the apartment was very nicely decorated and had a prime view of the ski slopes. But her attention was focused on the job, not the views. "I'll see you tonight."

She walked away, resisting the temptation to look back to see if he was watching her. She had a hard time keeping her eyes off him whenever he was near, but that was her problem, not his. As long as she didn't embarrass herself by letting on that she was attracted to him, everything should be just fine.

SHANE GREER TURNED out to live near the resort, down a long, dark, unpaved road that wound up a mountain and across a frozen creek. The headlights of Connor's truck illuminated evergreens iced with thick snow and wooden fences almost obscured by drifts. The house itself was almost hidden by trees and snow, a thin curl of smoke from a massive stone chimney visible in the moonlight.

"This looks like the setting for a horror movie," Stacy said as she climbed out of the passenger seat.

"It's just an old house." Connor led the way up a path, tromping through the snow.

Their footsteps echoed as they crossed the wooden porch. Connor rapped hard on the front door, and Stacy resisted the urge to check the pistol in a holster at her back.

"Dad knows where we are," she said. "If I'm not back in an hour or so, he'll come looking."

"I'm surprised he didn't insist on coming with us now," Connor said.

"He wanted to, but I overruled him. He only relented when I told him you were coming with me."

The door opened. "Welcome, come on in!" Shane said. He led the way down a short hall into a wood-paneled room full of furniture that would have been right at home in Stacy's grandmother's house—overstuff chintz and faded velour sofas and chairs. All that was needed to complete the look were a few crocheted doilies.

"Let me get you a drink," Shane said. "I've got beer or bourbon if you'd rather."

"Beer—" Connor began.

Stacy squeezed his arm. "Nothing for us, thank you." She sent Connor a warning look. Slipping something into a drink was the easiest thing in the world for someone up to no good. No sense taking a chance until they knew where they stood with Shane.

"Have a seat," Shane said. "Make yourselves comfortable." He sank into a chair and put his feet up on the recliner. Stacy stared at his sheepskin slippers and relaxed a little. It was hard to picture a villain in sheepskin slippers.

Connor sat on the sofa next to Stacy. "What did you want to see me about?" he asked.

"We talked about how, working with ski patrol, you're familiar with handling explosives," Shane said.

"Yes." He was sitting very straight. Stacy wanted to tell him to relax, though it was all she could do not to fidget. Maybe Shane wouldn't notice. Talk of explosives probably made most sensible people nervous.

"Have you ever worked with fireworks?" Shane asked.

"No. Why do you ask?"

"I'm planning a fireworks display for the Sunday of Martin Luther King weekend. On the square, right at dark, right after our rally. Something to really get people's attention."

"Is that legal?" Connor asked.

"You have to have a permit, but I'll take care of that." Shane dismissed the problem with a wave of his hand.

"Could I see these fireworks?" Connor asked.

"Sure. They're out in the garage." He stood and they followed him to a side door. Shane flipped a light switch, and a yellow bulb illuminated a one-car garage with a stained concrete floor. Frost decorated the single window on the far wall, and several cardboard boxes were stacked beneath the window. None of them looked like the boxes the cast boosters were stored in.

Shane crossed the space and lifted the flap on one of the boxes. "I've got Roman candles, cakes and fountains." He gathered up a handful of cardboard tubes. "Enough to make a nice showing. But I need someone who knows what he's doing to deploy them."

"Maybe ask someone with the local fire department," Connor said. "I think they handle the fireworks for New Year's and the Fourth of July."

"I thought maybe you'd help since you came to the meeting last night," Shane said. "You're sympathetic to our cause."

"I am," Connor said. "But I think handling fireworks like this is a specialized skill. I know how to safely trigger a release of snow, but that's about it."

Shane replaced the fireworks in the box and closed the top. "Never hurts to ask. Let's go back inside."

They returned to the living room. Stacy tried to get a better look at the space, but the only light came from a lamp on a table next to Shane's chair.

"You two are going to be there for the rally on MLK day, I hope," Shane said. "It's going to be a great chance to get the public on our side. We'll have people collecting signatures for a petition to present to the Forest Service, and I'm working on getting as many media people there as possible—everything from the major news networks to social media influencers. This is going to be big."

"What got you so interested in leading opposition to the ski area expansion?" Connor asked.

"My family has lived in this area for five generations," Shane said. "We lost the place for a while, but now I've got it back and plan to carry on the family tradition. That means preserving this land and the other land around it. We're in danger of every square inch being taken up by second homes and condos and private retreats where you have to pay hundreds of dollars to get in."

"So you're familiar with Blaine Mountain?" Stacy asked.

"I spent a lot of time tramping all over that mountain when I was younger," he said. "I want the next generation to have that privilege, too."

"It's a lot for one person to take on," Connor said.

"I have plenty of people helping me," Chase said.

"Oh. I guess I thought it was mainly you," Stacy said. "Or do you mean all the volunteers you've recruited, like me and Connor?"

"Lots of volunteers. And people who work behind the scenes. Some big donors, too. Some of the names might surprise you."

"Oh?" She leaned forward, smiling. "Who? Anyone I know?"

"There are some names you might have heard of. Locals who care a lot about the future of Blaine Mountain, even if they're not comfortable being in the spotlight." He straightened. "Are you sure I can't get you a drink?"

Connor stood. "We need to get going. I'm sorry I couldn't

help you with the fireworks, but I'll let you know if I think of anyone else who might be good."

"Do that. And I'll see you around, I'm sure." He walked with them to the door. "Don't tell anyone about the fireworks," Shane said as they exited. "I want it to be a big surprise."

"Don't worry," Stacy said. "We're great at keeping secrets."

They hadn't driven far before Connor said, "Fireworks. Not cast boosters."

"He could have those, too, just tucked away somewhere," she said.

"His story about wanting to keep more land out of being developed rang true to me," Connor said. "A lot of people feel that way."

"Maybe those are his true sentiments," she said. "Or maybe he's good at telling convincing stories." She stared out the windshield at the clear black sky, stars like pinholes of light. "The fireworks could be intended as a distraction for something bigger."

"That's what happened New Year's Eve," Connor said. "Someone probably used the commotion from the fireworks to cover up the noise of breaking into the munitions magazine."

"Right. So while the fireworks are going off, Shane and whoever he recruits could be blowing up something else."

"What else?" Connor asked.

"I don't know," she said. "Something big and expensive that would distract the resort from pursuing the new development?"

"How are we going to find out and stop it?" he asked.

She liked the way he said *we*. As if he really was invested in helping her now. "I'm going to keep digging," she said.

"You can talk to people, too. Find out if anyone has seen or heard anything suspicious."

"I will. But MLK weekend isn't that far off," he said. "We don't have much time."

"It will be enough," she said. "It will have to be."

"I've heard some rumors that some of those who are opposed to the ski area's expansion may increase vandalism to resort property," Connor told his patrol crew the following Monday morning.

He had been off Sunday and had spent much of the day thinking about the meeting with Shane, about the stolen cast boosters and about Stacy. He liked remembering the way she had felt in his arms on the dance floor and how he could forget everything else when he was talking with her. More than once he had thought about trying to get in touch with her but had hesitated. She was here to work and might resent his interference.

"I'm asking you all to be extra vigilant. If you see anyone in an area where they aren't supposed to be or messing around with ski resort equipment, be sure you get their name and let them know they're at risk of being banned."

"Who told you there was more vandalism planned?" Anders asked. He sat with his long legs stretched in front of him, Darth sprawled beneath him.

"Doug talked to me about it," Connor said. This was close enough to the truth he could say it with a straight face.

"We catch people all the time where they aren't supposed to be," Raz said. "They're always ducking ropes to ski in untracked snow or messing around closed lifts. And you remember last month, when I caught that guy trying to pry the window on the number four patrol shack."

"He was trying to get the phone he had dropped and

someone had turned in," Lily said. "It was locked in the shack."

"It was. But that didn't give him the right to break in," Raz said.

"Just keep your eyes and ears open," Connor said.

Lily was the last to leave after the meeting ended. She sidled up to his desk. "Everything okay with you?" she asked.

"I'm fine." Or as fine as anyone could be, knowing someone who was probably up to no good was out there with a bunch of powerful explosives at their disposal.

"You just seem distracted."

"This job does that to a person. Scott could probably tell you all about it."

She smiled at the mention of her partner, Scott Linden, former head of ski patrol. "You're doing a good job," she said. "You're much better tempered than Scott was."

He laughed. "I won't tell him you said that."

"Oh. He already knows what I think." She shrugged. "I'm not one to hide my feelings."

How do you do that? he wondered after Lily had left. *How do you lay out every emotion for possible ridicule or embarrassment?* Children could do it, but figuring out what most adults were thinking and feeling was like chipping away at a marble block. Sometimes even he didn't know what his real emotions were.

"Got a minute?"

Connor looked up to see Stacy leaning in the door of patrol headquarters. His heart did a disconcerting flutter as she moved toward him. He wasn't *unhappy* to see her, but she always made him feel off-balance. Not quite himself.

"What's up?" he asked, then winced at how lame that sounded.

"Do you have any plans for tonight?"

"Sleep?"

"Before that. Say about seven?"

"No, why?"

"Since I didn't make it to the Trail's End over the weekend, I thought I'd try tonight. Want to come with me?"

"Are you asking me out?"

She flushed. Her cheeks actually turned a bright pink. It made her look younger. Vulnerable. "I'm going to hang out there for a while and see if I run into anyone who was at the protestors' meeting Friday. I'm trying to get a line on who might be Shane's silent helpers."

"What do you need me for?" he asked.

"I don't *need* you for anything, but I thought you might like to come with me. And two sets of eyes are always better than one. Besides, people remember you. You're the man who works for ski patrol."

"The traitor to the corporation," he said.

"Is that what you feel like—a traitor?"

"No." He shut the lid of his laptop. "I'll go with you."

She smiled, and that dizzy, off-center feeling hit again. Maybe he was coming down with something.

The door opened, and George strolled in. Today he wore an acid-green ski suit, like a walking hazard sign.

"Dad!" Stacy said. "What are you wearing?"

He looked down at the suit and grinned. "It was free at the local swap box. Can you believe it?"

"That it was free, yes," she said. "That you took it—no."

"I think it's great," George said. "No one will miss me on the slopes." He looked from her to Connor. "What are you two up to?"

"What makes you think we're up to anything?" Stacy asked.

"Because you both look like you got caught with your

hands in the cookie jar." He rapped a fist on Connor's desk. "Want to take a few runs together?"

"Sorry, George. I have to get over to the terrain park. They're resetting it for a competition later in the week."

"I should try that out some time," George said. "Do some rails, try some jumps."

Stacy groaned. "Dad!"

George shook his head. "If you think your embarrassment is going to stop me from doing anything, you're sadly mistaken." He looked at Connor. "I've been making a fool of myself in front of women for fifty years. The difference is that now I'm too old to care."

Connor stood. "I'd better get to work. And I need to lock up."

George turned to Stacy. "How about you? Want to ski with me?"

"No rails or jumps," she said.

"We'll take it nice and easy," George said. "I won't do anything to embarrass you."

"Dad, you're wearing a lime-green ski suit. It's too late."

"Make fun of me all you want, but no one is going to run over me on the slopes."

The two were still bickering as they walked away.

Connor locked up and tucked away the key, then headed toward the lift. Halfway there, he was almost knocked over by a snowboarder. "Hey, careful!" He steadied the young man, then realized it was Jace. "Jace, are you okay?"

"Yeah, I'm fine." Except he didn't look fine. His face was almost as white as the snow around them, his eyes bloodshot. "I was just, uh, trying to avoid someone. Someone I don't want to run into." He looked around, then turned quickly aside. "I'll see you." Then he loped away, his board tucked under one arm.

Connor looked around but didn't see anyone looking their way.

Chase grabbed Connor at the base of Lift One. "Ride up the lift with me," he said.

"I was headed over to Six," Connor said.

"You can cut over on Runway from the top," Chase said.

"All right." Connor fell in beside Chase in the ski patrol line. The patroller was carrying a small white cardboard box. "What's in the box?"

"You'll see."

The liftie, Cerise, a shapely brunette with a heart-shaped face and big dark eyes, motioned them forward. "Hi, Chase, Connor," she said.

"I got you a present," Chase said. He held out the box.

She hesitated.

"Go ahead. It won't bite." He shoved the box toward her.

She took the box as Connor and Chase slid onto the chair.

"Go ahead and open it," Chase said.

Smiling, she shook her head.

"Come on," he pleaded. He turned to look back as the lift chair rose.

Cerise held the box out away from her and carefully lifted the lid. Nothing happened. She leaned over and peaked inside, then made a face and dropped the box. It landed on its side in the snow beside the loading area.

"Aw, man. That's edible, you know!" Chase called. He collapsed back in the chair, laughing.

"What was in the box?" Connor asked.

"A cupcake with a jelly cockroach on top. I had it made special."

"You sure know the way to a woman's heart."

"Aww, it's just Cerise. And it gets her back for filling my boots with shaving cream."

"I thought that was to get you back for the plastic spiders."

"She never should have told me she liked spiders. Anyway, it was a good cupcake. Cost me five dollars to get that bug on top."

"I'm sure knowing that will make her feel much better."

The two patrollers parted ways at the top of the lift. Connor headed down Runway toward Lift Six, but he hadn't gone far before his radio beeped. He stopped at the side of the run. "Ski patrol One," he answered.

"It's Eddie Vasquez on Lift Eleven. Got a report of a guy wiped out on Calico Hill. His friend says he's hurt pretty bad."

Chapter Nine

"I'll be right there." Connor headed for the lift. On the chair, he radioed Anders and asked him to meet him at the top of the run.

Calico Hill was a black run that featured a series of roller-coaster hills and expansive views of the distant valley. Connor collected a sled from the ski patrol shack near the top of the lift and traversed a catwalk to the beginning of the run. He spotted the crowd gathered as he came over the first rise. Someone had placed a pair of crossed skis above the injured skier to warn others to steer clear.

He had just moved in to assess the injured man when Anders joined him. Anders made the crowd move farther away while Connor knelt beside the man, who was on his back in the snow, writhing in pain. "I'm Connor with ski patrol. What's your name?"

"It's Brady." Connor looked up at a tall, thin man who spoke. He was dressed in a silver-and-red skin suit, and with his red stocking cap he reminded Connor of a pipe-cleaner figure.

"Can you tell me what happened?" Connor asked.

"I think he must have caught an edge. One minute he was skiing fine, then he just went over." He made a somersaulting gesture with his hands.

"My leg," Brady groaned. He was clutching his right leg above the knee.

"Let me see," Connor said. He laid one hand on Brady's chest. "Just take a deep breath and try to relax."

"Don't touch it!" Brady said. "It really hurts."

"I've got to get a look at it before we move you," Connor said. He looked up at pipe-cleaner man. "Help your friend stay calm."

The friend knelt at Brady's head. "I wish I had caught you on video," he said. "You were flying down that hill. It was really spectacular."

Brady closed his eyes and groaned, but he didn't try to fight Connor and Anders as they cut away his ski pants to reveal the swollen knee beneath. "Classic," Anders said.

Connor nodded. The orthopedics docs would have to confirm, but he had seen enough ACL tears in his time to recognize one. "Let's get a splint on it and get this guy transported." He radioed for Lily to bring a splint while Anders called for an ambulance to meet them at the bottom of the run.

Twenty minutes later, he was skiing down the run, Brady bundled securely in the sled. Negotiating the steep run with the heavy sled required brute strength. By the time they reached the bottom of the run, Connor was sweating and breathing hard.

"I'll run this back up to the patrol shack," Anders said, taking the empty sled.

"Thanks." Connor unzipped his jacket and took a long drink of water. His radio buzzed and he answered. "Donaldson."

"I'm over here on Maid Marion with a situation." Nina's voice was low, as if she was trying not to be overheard.

"What kind of situation?" Connor asked.

"I've got a nine-year-old girl with an injured arm. She was injured in a collision with a snowboarder who looks to be about thirteen. The snowboarder is crying. Both fathers are here, and they're shouting at each other. We're drawing quite a crowd."

"I'll be right over." He zipped up his jacket and headed for the beginner's area. On the way, he radioed for all available patrollers to report to the scene.

Maid Marion was a green run in an area dubbed Sherwood Forest which catered to families, with a treed area that featured cartoon cutouts and a ski-through play area. Connor heard shouting before he found the accident site. At least a dozen skiers encircled two men, who faced off, each with bloody noses. Nina stood between them, glaring at each man in turn. As Connor maneuvered his way through the spectators, she said, "You two ought to be ashamed of yourselves. What kind of example are you setting for your children?"

One of them muttered an obscenity, and the other man responded in kind. They lunged toward each other. Connor grabbed the nearest man by the collar, while Brian stepped up to take hold of the second man. Connor got in his captive's face. "Sit. Now!"

"He attacked my kid."

"I said sit! My job is to look after these children, not two grown men who should know better."

Both men sat, though they were still shouting at each other. Connor ignored them and turned to the children. The boy was sitting beside the girl, tears streaking his face. "I didn't mean to hit her," he said, as soon as Connor approached. "I wasn't going that fast, I promise. I didn't see her."

"It's okay." The girl, four feet tall with brown pigtails,

was pale but calm, cradling her left arm. "I shouldn't have been standing where I was." She looked up at Connor. "It was just an accident."

"Her dad said I could go to jail," the boy said, and his lip trembled.

Connor knelt in front of the girl. "What's your name?" he asked.

"Stella Chandler."

"Stella, can I take a look at your arm?"

"I think it's broken," the girl said. "I heard a pop and it hurts a lot. I think I even fainted for a minute."

The boy groaned and buried his head in his hands.

"What happened?" Connor gently took the girl's arm. Removing her jacket would hurt too much, and he hated to upset her more by cutting off her pretty pink jacket. He would leave that to the medical staff.

"I stopped to look for my dad," she said. "He was skiing ahead of me."

"Where did you stop?" Connor asked.

"Right here where we're sitting."

He looked up the slope. Anyone coming from above wouldn't have been able to see the girl until they were over the hill. A less experienced skier or boarder probably wouldn't have been able to stop in time to avoid hitting her.

"What are you going to do?" the girl asked.

"I'm going to strap your arm to your body to hold it really still," Connor said. "That way, it will hurt less. Then we're going to put you in a toboggan and wrap you up warmly, and you'll get a free ride down to the clinic where a doctor can examine you and decide what to do next. Is that okay?"

She nodded. "But what are you going to do about my dad?"

Connor followed her gaze to the man with the dark mustache who glared at him. "Mr. Chandler, we need to stabilize Stella's arm, then transport her via toboggan to the clinic at the base area," he said. "Can you ski down behind us?"

"What are you going to do about him?" Chandler jutted a finger toward the boy.

Connor looked to the snowboarder. "What's your name?"

"Aiden Welch."

"Aiden, you did the right thing," Connor said. "You took responsibility, and you stayed with Stella."

"He could have killed her," Chandler roared.

"Aiden, you know the skier's safety code says you're always responsible for being aware of skiers or boarders in front of or downhill from you," Connor said.

The boy nodded. "I know. But I didn't see her until it was too late."

"That's why it's important to be extra cautious when coming over blind hills." It was a lesson a lot of people learned the hard way.

"It really wasn't his fault," Stella said. "It's not like he plowed into me on purpose."

"Aiden, will you promise me to be more careful in the future?" Connor asked.

"Yes, sir. I promise."

"Then I'm letting you off with a warning today. But don't let it happen again."

"A warning!" Chandler shouted. "I'll sue."

"You're the one who should have been watching out for your child," Mr. Welch said. "Instead of skiing ahead of her."

Both men were on their feet again. Brian and Nina moved in.

"Need some more help?" Patroller Renee Castro knelt across from Connor. Petite and wiry, Castro was the smallest—and fastest—patroller.

"Let's get this arm wrapped," Connor said.

"I'll take care of her," Renee said. "You get the sled ready."

"Daddy!" Stella wailed.

Chandler turned toward her. "What is it, sweetie?"

"I need you!"

Chandler glanced back at Welch, who stood with one hand on the boy's shoulder, then he moved to kneel beside Stella. "It's okay, honey," he said. "It's going to be all right."

Renee wrapped the arm with a minimum of tears, and they arranged Stella comfortably in the sled. "I'll take her down," Renee volunteered. She stepped between the handles of the sled.

"Let me get my skis back on," Chandler said and hurried to follow his daughter.

Connor moved over to Aiden and his dad. "It might be a good idea to call it a day," he said.

"Are you taking my pass?" the boy asked.

"No. I'm just saying take it easy the rest of the day." Connor nodded to the dad. "Get some ice on that nose."

Welch looked sheepish. "Yeah."

By the time Connor made his way slowly to the base area, the lifts were shutting down for the day. He released Farley from his kennel, and the dog ran circles around him. The patrollers gathered for their final sweep of the runs.

"Stella's arm is in a splint, and she'll probably get a cast from the orthopedist in the morning," Renee reported. "It's a greenstick fracture, should heal fine." She grinned. "And Dad has a broken nose and two black eyes."

"I guess when your kid is hurt it's natural to see red," Connor said. "Hopefully he'll think twice before taking a swing if it happens again."

Darkness was descending by the time Connor and Farley headed home. He had just enough time to grab a bite to eat, shower and change before he picked up Stacy. Whatever happened at the bar, it would be nothing compared to the day he'd had.

WHEN THE CONDO'S doorbell sounded, Stacy raced into the living room. "I'll get it!" she shouted, then forced herself to slow to a walk. Where had that flashback to a teenager come from? She blamed it on living with her father again.

She checked the security peephole and found Connor looking back at her. She unlocked the door and pulled it open. "Hey."

"Hey." This was a different Connor on her doorstep—black slacks and an Irish fisherman's sweater, freshly shaved and hair combed and styled. He even smelled good—something spicy. "You look great," he said.

She resisted the urge to smooth the black knit dress over her black tights and short boots. "Thanks. Um, come in. I'll just get my purse."

He stepped inside, and she closed the door and went in search of her black cross-body bag.

Her father emerged from the kitchen and watched Stacy hurry past. "Hello, Connor," he said.

"How are you, George?"

"I've skied so much I can hardly walk, but I'm telling myself it's good for me."

Stacy rejoined them. "Okay, I'm ready to go."

George assumed a stern expression. "Now, son, I have to ask what your intentions are toward my daughter."

"Dad!" She swatted his shoulder.

George laughed. "Just remember," he told Connor. "She's armed and dangerous."

Connor put his hand at her back once they were out the

door and leaned close. "You're not concealing a weapon in that dress," he murmured.

A pleasant shiver shimmied down her spine. "That's what the purse is for," she answered.

The Trail's End was busy, as usual, but Connor and Stacy found a table at the back with a view of the rest of the room. "See anyone you recognize?" she asked.

"No. Do you?"

She studied the crowd. "That couple by the pool table." The man was burly, with short dark hair and full-sleeve tattoos. The woman had short red hair and wore knee-high, tooled leather cowboy boots. "Let's go say hi." Stacy took Connor's hand. The sensation of his warm, calloused fingers sent sharp awareness through her. She quickly moved away from him. *Focus!* She was here to work.

They stood as if waiting for a table to open, watching the couple play pool. When the woman looked over at them, Stacy said, "Hi. I think we saw you Friday night. At the meeting about the ski area expansion?"

"It was so dark out there, I could hardly recognize anyone," the man said.

"I remember those fabulous boots," Stacy said.

The woman said, "People always remember my boots." She offered her hand. "I'm Carly."

"I'm Stacy, and this is Connor."

"Forest," the man said.

"Good to meet you," Connor said.

"How do y'all know Shane?" Stacy asked.

"We don't," Forest said. "Not really."

"We saw a notice about the meeting online," Carly said. "We wanted to hear more about what people are doing to preserve Blaine Mountain."

"What did you think?" Connor asked.

"I volunteered to work with a woman who is gathering signatures on a petition," Carly said. "And we plan to show up at the rally on MLK day."

Forest leaned over to take his next shot. "I'm not down with stuff at the resort itself," he said. "I don't think it's cool to deliberately try to mess up people's vacations."

"I read in the local paper that people who are against the expansion have been vandalizing resort property," Carly said. "That's not right."

"I heard a rumor some people were planning something big for MLK weekend," Stacy said. "Something besides impeding traffic on the ski runs. I wondered if you heard anything like that."

They shook their heads. "Maybe they were talking about the rally," Carly said. "I heard there's going to be a band and everything."

"This sounded more sinister," Stacy said. "Maybe involving explosives."

"That sounds like something you ought to report to the sheriff," Forest said.

"You're right," Connor said. He took Stacy's arm. "We should do that." He pulled her away from the table.

"What are you doing?" Stacy pulled away from him.

"Did you see the way they were looking at us?" he asked. "They're going to be calling the sheriff themselves if you don't stop talking about explosives."

"I was trying to see if they'd volunteer some gossip of their own," she said.

"You heard them—they're definitely all about peaceful protests. And they don't know Shane or his friends."

She looked around the room for anyone else she recognized. "Maybe we should get a drink. Someone at the bar might have something interesting to say." She frowned toward the bar, where people waited three deep for a drink.

"Why don't we dance instead?" He took her arm again.

The lively two-step didn't provide an opportunity for more conversation or for studying the crowd. Stacy told herself one dance wouldn't hurt. It made her cover of being on a date more realistic. And Connor was as good a dancer as she remembered. He smiled at her, and she couldn't help smiling in return. For these few minutes, at least, she could be happy, dancing in the arms of a handsome man.

The song ended, and she released his hand and started to step away, but he pulled her close as the music started again. "One more," he said.

The song was a slow one, a love song with a soaring melody. Connor pulled her closer, and she settled against him, their clasped hands resting on his chest, his other hand at the small of her back, hers on his shoulder. The heat of him enfolded her, his scent surrounding her. "You smell so good," she said.

He dipped his head to the curve of her neck. "So do you."

She hadn't had a thing to drink, but she had the same sensation of floating a little apart from her body. She turned her head, and her lips hovered beside his, tingling as if a current arced between them. They had stopped moving, other couples twirling around them, and she could no longer hear the music or the voices of the crowd. His eyes met hers, so dark they were almost black, his gaze penetrating.

Then the raucous notes of a new song startled them apart. He moved away, and she shivered with a sudden chill. "I'll get us a drink," he said and headed toward the bar.

She stood along one wall, watching the door. No more dancing. She had forgotten herself for a moment there. Forgotten her purpose. She didn't like that out-of-control sensation.

A rise in conversation near the door heralded new arrivals. Jace Dennison entered with Nate Lee and two women Stacy didn't recognize.

"Hope beer is okay." Connor returned to her side and pressed a glass into her hand.

"Oh sure. Thanks." She nodded toward the door. "Look who's here."

"Hmm." Connor sipped his beer. "I saw Jace at the ski resort this afternoon," he said. "He seemed upset about something. He ran off before I could say much."

"Let's go talk to him and his friend." She led the way toward where the quartet had crowded around a small table. "Hey, Jace."

"Oh hey." Jace didn't look particularly happy to see them.

"And I remember your friend." Connor nodded to Nate. "But I didn't get your name."

"It's Nate."

"Hi, Nate. I'm Connor."

"The ski patroller. I remember."

"Did Shane find anyone to take care of those fireworks for him?" Connor asked.

Nate choked on his beer. He coughed and set the glass aside. "How did you know about the fireworks?"

"Shane asked me to help him with them," Connor said. "I had to turn him down. I know a lot about blowing things up but nothing about putting on fireworks displays."

"Hey, keep your voice down," Jace said. "Somebody might hear."

Connor sipped his beer. "Nothing illegal about fireworks," he said. "Or the stuff we use to set off avalanches. Not if you have the right permits."

"I'd rather talk about something else." Jace took the hand of the woman beside him. "Let's dance."

"Jace has been a little jumpy since his accident," Nate said when the couple had left. "I heard you were the one who pulled him out of that tree well."

Connor nodded. "I guess that kind of thing would shake up anyone."

"I know you said fireworks aren't your thing, but you should reconsider helping us," Nate said. "I'm sure your specialized knowledge would come in handy."

His date, a curvy dark beauty, leaned in closer. "Nate, we came to dance," she said.

"We can talk later," Nate said and allowed the woman to lead him to the dance floor.

Stacy and Connor sat at the vacated table. "What do you think?" he asked.

"I don't know. Jace is upset about something, but it might not have anything to do with the protests. Nate seems to be hinting at something, but it's easy to read too much into what people say simply because I want something to be there." She massaged the knot in the side of her neck. "Everything about this case is frustrating."

"Are your bosses pressuring you?"

She shook her head. "They haven't said a thing. But that's worrying, too. Maybe Dad is right, and they sent me here to get rid of me."

"Because of your dad?"

"I don't know."

"What happened with him? What did he do to get on the wrong side of his bosses? You said he was a rebel, but is that all there is to it?"

She almost smiled. "You've seen what he's like. He says what he thinks and does what he wants. It worked great as long as he had superiors who were willing to give him free rein. But then a new regime came in, and they had a different style. More controlling. Dad isn't easy to control."

"And maybe his daughter takes after him."

"I try to stick to regulations more than Dad ever did, but it's hard when people won't listen to your ideas. There are people in the Bureau who would rather women stuck to making coffee and filling out reports. You would think we'd be long past that now, but all it takes is one Neanderthal at the top, and it's easier for others to fall in line."

"I'm sorry you have to deal with that. For what it's worth, I don't think you're wrong about more going on with this protest group than just a bunch of fireworks."

"Thanks." She covered his hand with her own. "You're easy to talk to."

He turned her hand over so that they were palm to palm. The awareness of him that had lingered since those moments on the dance floor returned. "I don't think we're going to find out anything more here tonight," she said. Not about the protests or the stolen fireworks. Though it felt as if she was juggling something even more explosive.

"Do you want to go home?" he asked.

"Yes."

She reached for her coat, but he surprised her by coming around and holding it for her. He rested her hands on his shoulder, the weight of him making her feel heavy and languid. She wanted to turn into him, to feel his arms around her, his lips on hers.

Instead, she moved away, toward the door. But when they were in his truck, she said. "Don't take me back to the condo. Let's go back to your place."

He slid his hands along the steering wheel. His face was

turned to her, but she couldn't read his expression in the darkness. "I'm not sure that's a good idea," he said.

"Okay." She choked out the word. She would have thought she was too old to be this crushed by embarrassment. Now she didn't know where to look.

"It's not that I'm not attracted to you, it's just—"

"It's okay. Forget I said anything." What was she doing? She was supposed to be a professional. "Just take me to the condo."

She could feel his gaze still on her, though she refused to turn toward him. After a long moment, he started the truck and drove.

As soon as they were in the parking lot, she had the door of the truck open. "Thanks for your help," she said. She didn't run away, but she didn't dawdle, the soles of her boots slapping on the pavement. She had her key out and in the door lock while the truck was still idling behind her. She was inside the condo, safe in the darkness, before he could say a word.

Chapter Ten

Connor looked for Stacy all Tuesday morning at the resort. The last thing he had wanted last night was to upset her. If he could only make her understand...

Understand what? He didn't understand himself. This was why he was so bad at relationships. Instead of trying to placate a woman who already thought the worst of him, he would be much better off focusing on work and his dog. He never had to second-guess his words or his feelings with those two parts of his life.

What had started as heavy fog turned into real snow by the time the lifts started running at nine. Big, fat flakes transformed the resort into a movie scene, covering the corduroy laid down by the overnight groomers with several inches of fresh snow before noon. Fair-weather skiers deserted the slopes in favor of shopping or staying warm by the fire, but the die-hards reveled in the great conditions, whooping with delight as they plowed through the powder.

Ski patrol answered call after call that morning, from skiers injured maneuvering in heavy powder to a young woman overcome with vertigo near the top of the mountain. By noon the patrollers were cold and ravenous, grateful to take a break in a side room of the base area grill.

They pulled sandwiches from packs and pockets. Connor bit into his ham and cheese, then took a swig of water. Across from him, Chase unwrapped his lunch. A strong, vaguely familiar, meaty odor filled the air.

"What are you eating?" Anders asked. "A roadkill sandwich?"

"It's roast beef," Chase said. He eyed the sandwich skeptically. "I didn't think it had been in the refrigerator that long." He sniffed. "It doesn't smell bad. Just a little strong."

"Smells okay to me." Brian crunched a potato chip. "It's familiar somehow."

Chase took a bite. The others watched as he chewed, his expression puzzled, then horrified. He dropped the sandwich and stood, wiping at his mouth. "Cerise!" he shouted.

All heads turned. "Cerise isn't here," someone called.

Chase gulped water. "When I find that woman…"

"Why are you blaming Cerise?" Lily asked.

"She told me she was going to get back at me for filling her chair in the lift shack with snow. This is how she did it. She made me a dog-food sandwich." He removed the top slice of bread from his sandwich, and the others leaned in for a look.

"Looks like chunky beef stew," Brian said. "Daisy really likes that one."

"How did Cerise get into your lunch?" Lily asked.

"I stash my pack in her lift shack whenever I set gates for race training. It's easier to haul the drill and all the stakes without the pack. I do that every week, and she never minds."

"Except she wanted to get back at you, so she came prepared." Lily giggled. "It's pretty funny, when you think about it."

"It might be funny if it happened to someone else." Chase scowled down at his sandwich. "Now I don't have a lunch." He rewrapped the whole mess. "Guess I'll get something from the grill."

"What are you going to do with that sandwich?" Brian asked.

"I'm going to throw it away."

Brian held out his hand. "I'll take it."

"Are you feeling hungry?" Connor asked.

Brian tucked the wrapped sandwich into his jacket. "Daisy can have an extra treat. No sense letting this go to waste."

SHORTLY AFTER 1:00 P.M., Doug radioed Connor. "How's it looking out there?" he asked.

"Great snow conditions," Connor said. "You should come do a few runs."

"No time today. I'm buried under risk assessment studies."

"Better you than me," Connor said.

"Have you talked to Stacy lately?" Doug asked.

"No. Have you?"

"I managed to pin her down for a few minutes yesterday, but all she would say is that she is continuing her investigation, following up on some leads, and I shouldn't worry. Why don't you see if you can find her and get more information?"

"What makes you think she would tell me any more than she told you?" he asked.

"I got the impression she was pretty taken with you," Doug said.

"I don't think so."

"I thought I definitely saw interest there. If you run into her, see if you can find out when she expects to wrap up her investigation. I'd really like to be able to tell my bosses that there's no problem."

"Missing explosives are a real problem, Doug. You can't pretend they're not."

"If she finds them and we get them back, there won't be a problem," he said. "Just talk to her. See if you can get some bit of good news I can pass on to the people breathing down my neck."

"I can't promise anything, Doug."

"Just try." Doug didn't wait for an answer but ended the call.

Connor turned toward patrol headquarters. Time to take Farley for a run.

Freed from his kennel, Farley raced in circles, biting at snowflakes, then rolling in the snow. Then he leaped into Connor's arms, and Connor heard the click of camera shutters all around as he skied toward the lift, his arms full of snow-covered dog.

He rode the lift from the base, then headed up a second lift to Top of the Mark. A sharp ridge loomed over the runs here, popular hike-to terrain. As usual, as he rode the lift, Connor scanned the runs below for any sign of trouble. In the thick snowfall, the skiers were blurs of color glimpsed behind a white curtain.

Two dark smudges cut across his field of vision. Snowboarders, in a hurry, moving against the flow of downhill traffic. Then they disappeared into a clump of trees.

Farley barked, and Connor looked down to see Lily and her dog, Shelby, racing down the slope. Connor held onto Farley's harness. The dog had never jumped from the lift chair before, but no sense taking chances.

They exited the lift, Farley racing ahead. Connor stopped to slip his ski pole straps over his wrists. Suddenly a loud *whump!* shook the air.

"What was that?" the lift tech called out.

Connor's heart hammered painfully, and he turned to look up the ridge as a curtain of snow broke away, a fifty-foot-wide white waterfall boiling down the slope. Snow flowed like water, a cascade of white silk. It would have been beautiful if it weren't so deadly.

Connor's radio crackled, snapping him from his trance. "What's going on up on the ridge?" Anders shouted into the radio.

"Did you hear that sound?" Connor asked.

"An explosion," Anders said.

The exact sound Connor had heard hundreds of times as the cast boosters they deployed for avalanche mitigation detonated. "Get everyone and all the dogs up here now!" Connor shouted. Then he whistled for Farley and started toward the snowfield where the avalanche had run out.

Half a dozen skiers descended on Connor. "What happened?"

"Was that an explosion?"

"Is anyone hurt?"

Connor ignored the questions and raised his voice to be heard over the clamor. "Did anyone see anyone in the avalanche?"

"I saw at least one guy," a woman said. "Maybe two."

"Farley, find," Connor ordered. The dog set out. Connor shucked off his pack, then pulled out and began assembling a collapsible avalanche probe. By the time he stepped onto the field, three other patrollers and dogs were searching. It was still snowing hard, and wind blew the snow around in a vertigo-inducing wall of white.

"I've got somebody!" Anders called from the edge of the field. He and another man dug at the snow with their hands. By the time Connor reached them, a man in a bright red ski helmet and a blue jacket was sitting up.

"I'm okay," he said. Then he winced. "Except I think my leg might be broken." He looked around. "What happened? One minute I was climbing up the ridge and the next…"

"You were caught in an avalanche," Anders said.

"Was there anyone with you or near you when the slide

happened?" Connor asked. "Anyone else we should be looking for?"

The man shook his head. "I was all by myself up there. I think I was the only one crazy enough to be out here in this weather."

"We'll have you out of here in just a minute," Anders said. He raised his voice to shout, "Somebody get a toboggan over here! And a snowmobile!"

Farley and the other dogs continued to search, along with people with probes, but they turned up no one else. Most of the slide had been confined to a narrow ridge that fell away into a steep valley—not terrain favored by even the most adventurous skiers. The rest had quickly spent itself in a shallower area.

"I've talked to everybody I can find," Raz reported when they had all gathered at the edge of the snowfield. "No one else reports anyone missing. And no one saw anyone else up here before the slide let loose."

Connor stared out across the debris field. It was a relatively small area, and he was confident they had covered it all. And the sad truth was, anyone they hadn't uncovered by now was most likely dead. "I'm calling the search," he said.

Only ski patrol was left on this part of the mountain. The lift had closed as soon as the avalanche occurred and wouldn't reopen until tomorrow. Overnight the grooming crew would clean up the inbounds area. By tomorrow no evidence would remain of the slide.

"That snow didn't let loose like that by itself," Brian said.

"I heard the explosion," Nina said. "It sounded just like a cast booster."

"It had to be one of the ones that was stolen," Anders said.

"Did anyone see anyone up here acting suspiciously?" Brian asked.

Connor thought of the two snowboarders hurrying away from the area. But he had no idea who they were or if they had been doing anything other than rushing to meet friends.

"Was there just one explosion?" Lily asked.

"I only heard one," Nina said, and the others nodded.

Connor studied the avalanche path. "Just one," he said. "And whoever deployed it didn't know what they were doing."

"Good thing, too," Anders said. "Someone with experience could have done a lot more harm. We're lucky the damage was limited to one broken leg and a few hundred feet of snow fence."

The damage today. But there were ninety-five cast boosters still missing, with the potential for real disaster.

STACY CROSSED THE ski village plaza, heading for patrol headquarters. She told herself she wasn't going to hide from Connor. Just because she had misread the signals and embarrassed herself last night didn't mean she needed to avoid him. She would be sure to keep things strictly professional between them from now on.

The door to ski patrol headquarters was locked. No surprise. Connor was probably out patrolling. He would be back sooner or later, though, so all she had to was hang around the base area until she spotted him. She could get her skis and do a few runs. Or revisit the powder magazine in search of new insight about the theft of the explosives.

Was it possible Shane and his people mistook the cast boosters for fireworks? Could it really be something that innocent? She pulled out her phone and tried to look up photographs to compare the various types of explosives, but snow kept landing on her phone screen, obscuring the picture.

She stood in front of the ski patrol office, trying to decide on her next move, when a familiar figure hurried toward her. "Oh, uh, hi." Jace stopped short in front of her, then glanced toward the Closed sign on the patrol headquarters door. "I'm, uh, looking for Connor," he said.

"Are you okay?" Stacy asked. The young man was pale, eyes darting from side to side.

"I just need to talk to Connor about something." He glanced at the Closed sign again. "Could you maybe tell him I stopped by?"

"Of course." She pulled out her phone. "What's the best way for him to get a hold of you?"

"I have to work tonight. Bagel Bistro. He can stop by there after four."

"Sure." She made a note, then pocketed her phone. "You could tell me what this is about."

Jace shook his head. "I'd better go now." He hurried away, snowboard under one arm.

Stacy headed for the row of shops across from the lift—a café, two boutiques, a ski rental shop and a real estate office. She browsed the boutiques but purchased nothing. Her government salary didn't stretch to $500 ski jackets, and the faux-fur après-ski boots were adorable but didn't really fit her lifestyle.

She was crossing the plaza once more when a distant reverberation shook the air. Stacy froze. "What was that?" she asked a man walking past.

He looked up the mountain. "Sounded like ski patrol set off a charge to release snow." He shrugged. "They do that sometimes."

In the middle of the afternoon? Stacy wondered.

She headed for the lift, but a lift tech stopped her. "You can't ride the lift without skis, ma'am," he said.

"I need to get up the mountain," she said.

"You can't ride the lift without skis."

Something was happening. A new tension filled the air around the lift. Several people jogged to snowmobiles and headed up the mountain. The liftie who had reprimanded her moved to a whiteboard in front of the lift and wrote Lift Ten Closed.

"Why is Ten closed?" someone asked.

The liftie shrugged. "No idea. Probably some malfunction or something."

A skier came flying down the mountain in a racer's tuck and didn't stop until they reached the ski patrol shack.

Stacy recognized Nina and ran up to her. "What's going on?" she asked.

"I can't talk now," Nina said. She unlocked the door and pushed into the room.

Stacy followed her inside.

Nina was unlocking her dog's kennel. "Come on, Sky," she said. "We have work to do."

"Is there an avalanche?" Stacy asked.

"I really can't talk." Nina pushed past her. "And you have to leave. I have to lock up again."

Stacy moved outside. "I heard the explosion," she said. "Is Connor all right?"

"Connor is fine." Nina locked the door, then jogged away, somewhere off to the left of the building. Moments later she emerged from around the corner at the controls of a snowmobile, the dog riding behind her.

Stacy hurried to collect her own skis, then returned to ride the lift. She skied to Lift Ten but could see no reason the lift would be closed. There were a lot of people milling around, staring glumly at the Closed sign. "What happened?" she asked the man who stood next to her. "Why is the lift closed?"

"Supposedly, there's been an inbounds avalanche," said the man. He was tall, with a bushy red beard.

"I thought I heard an explosion," Stacy said.

"Yeah, ski patrol probably lost track of one of their bombs, and it went off accidentally," a lanky teenage boy said. "Somebody is going to be in trouble over that."

Her phone beeped with a message. Where R U? from her dad.

Working.

There was an inbounds avalanche.

I know. I'm on the mountain.

Where?

Bottom of Lift Ten. The lift is closed.

I know.

Frowning, she pocketed the phone once more and looked around. There had to be a way to get up to the avalanche area. She would flash her badge if she had to. But the roar of a fast-approaching snowmobile drew her attention.

The machine slowed as it neared the crowd at the bottom of the lift and stopped a few feet from her. "Stacy!" her father called and waved.

She jogged over to him.

"Get on," he said. "I'll give you a ride to the top."

She climbed on, then grabbed his shoulders as the machine surged forward. "Dad, where did you get this thing?"

"There's a whole bunch of them parked behind ski patrol, keys and everything."

"But who gave you permission?"

"I figure your badge is my permission."

She rested her chin against his back.

"You're not going to fuss?" her dad called.

"No," she said. "I'm wishing I'd thought of it first."

The cluster of ski patrollers and dogs was easy to spot. George steered the snowmobile to them and cut the engine.

"What are you two doing up here?" Nina was the first to speak.

Stacy hurried toward Connor. "I heard the explosion," she said. "What's going on?"

He gestured toward the snowfield in front of them. "In-bounds avalanche."

"Was anyone hurt?"

"One guy has a broken leg. We don't think there was anyone else around."

"Did anyone see anything? Was anyone where they shouldn't have been?"

"No one saw anything," Connor said. "How did you get here so quickly?"

"I was at the base area when I heard the explosion," she said. "Someone said it was ski patrol doing avalanche mitigation, but I didn't think you did that in the middle of the afternoon."

"What else did you hear? Does anyone know anything?"

"Someone standing around the bottom of Lift Ten speculated it was a charge ski patrol lost track of, that detonated on its own."

"We didn't lose track of anything," he said, a hard edge to the words. "No way are we going to take the fall for this."

"So you think this was one of the stolen cast boosters," she said.

"How do you know about that?" One of the other patrollers—Brian, a golden retriever by his side—spoke up. He sent Connor an accusing look.

"I know because I need to know," Stacy said.

"What is that supposed to mean?" Brian asked.

"She's law enforcement," Nina said.

Brian turned to her. "How do you know that?"

"Come on," Nina said. "Just look at her."

CONNOR DIDN'T NEED Nina to tell him to look at Stacy, since he had a hard time keeping his eyes off of her. He couldn't remember the last time he found a woman so distracting. As he focused on her now, he saw an attractive brunette who gazed back at them with a hint of a challenge in her expression. Then Stacy nodded. "Right. Now that we have that cleared up." She turned to Connor. "Did anyone see anything suspicious?"

"No," he said. "And no one we talked to immediately afterward reported seeing anything. The only person who was injured said he was by himself on the ridge."

"I'll need his name," she said. "It's possible he was up on that ridge to launch the cast booster."

"I'll get his name to you," Connor said.

"We need to put out an appeal to the public," Stacy said. "Someone knows something—we just have to find them."

"Doug isn't going to like that," Connor said. "He won't want to upset potential visitors."

"I can overrule Doug," she said.

Her father moved in beside her. "Maybe if we can figure out why this was done, that will help determine who," he said.

"To frighten people?" Lily suggested.

"Or to hurt people," Brian said.

"I think they were practicing," Connor said.

"Practicing for what?" Anders asked.

"They didn't steal one cast booster," Connor said. "They stole four boxes. They must want to blow something up. Or a lot of somethings. But if you've never used this stuff before, you don't know its capabilities. I think whoever did this today was testing, seeing what it took to set off a snowslide. They chose a steep but out of the way area, but it's just luck they didn't do more damage. Next time they'll know to adjust their aim."

"What are you doing to make sure there isn't a next time?" Nina addressed the question to Stacy and George.

Stacy glared at her, then pulled Connor away from the group. "I think Dad and I should talk to Shane."

"Undercover?" George asked. "Or as law enforcement?"

"Undercover," she said. "I'll tell him we heard about the stolen explosives and were here today when the avalanche triggered. I'll ask if his people had anything to do with this."

"Do you really think he would just tell you?" Connor asked.

"Some people would brag about it, to anyone they thought was on their side," George said.

"Shane didn't strike me as the type to brag," Connor said. "He wouldn't even reveal his last name until he met with us a second time."

"I could point out to him that Dad and I aren't the only people who've made the connection," Stacy said. "I could claim I don't want to jeopardize the success of the opposition movement."

"Do you really think a man who would orchestrate the theft of a boxes of explosives would thank you for your concern and send you on your way?" Connor asked.

"So maybe I wouldn't mention the explosives outright,"

she said. "But if I ask the right questions, I should be able to find out how much he knows."

"You can't go out there by yourself," Connor said. "It's too dangerous. Someone who would do this wouldn't think twice about killing you."

"She wouldn't be by herself," George said. "I'd be with her."

"Then I'd have to worry about you, too," Connor said.

"I'll be careful," Stacy said.

"Wait until I can go with you." Though he had been reluctant to get involved before, he was in too deep now. And he couldn't leave her unprotected, no matter how tough of an agent she was.

She looked alarmed. "Forget I said anything." She backed away. "You have a job to do here. I'll talk to you later."

He started to follow as she turned to leave, then his radio crackled. "Wait!" he called. "Let me answer this, then we'll talk."

"Come on, Dad."

But George remained where he was, watching Connor. Connor turned his back to them, speaking into the radio, the wind and swirling snow carrying away the sound of his words, making it hard to hear the transmission from the lift tech who had called. But what he heard sent ice to the pit of his stomach. He ended the call, then headed toward the snowmobile George had ridden up the mountain. "I need this," he said and climbed on. "Farley, come!"

The dog hopped onto the machine behind him.

"What's going on?" Stacy asked.

"Anders! Nina!" Connor called. "Head down to Tessa's Trees. We've got a snowboarder in a tree well." Then he started up the snowmobile and took off.

Chapter Eleven

The swirling snow and fading light only added to the nightmarish quality of the afternoon. Connor guided the snowmobile in and out among the aspen trunks, until he spotted the snowboard, a blue slash on the snow. He looked around for whoever had called in the incident, but there was no one else in sight.

Dread taking root in his gut, he parked the machine and postholed through the deep snow to the snowboard. It looked like Jace's board, but there must be others like it on the mountain.

Farley barked and began to dig at the snow. Connor pulled a shovel from his back and joined his dog. He wanted the scene to play out the way it had before—the snowboarder pulled free and revived to board again the next day, unharmed and with a story to tell.

But the stillness of the figure in the snow and the eerie silence all around added to his dread. He didn't sense a happy ending today.

Nina and Anders arrived and began digging alongside him. "Who called this in?" Anders asked. They had unearthed the legs to the knees, and he unstrapped the snowboard and tossed it aside, then began tugging at the body.

"I don't know," Connor said. He moved in on the other

side to try to dig away more snow. "There was no one here when I arrived."

"Didn't you have one of these a few days ago?" Anders asked.

Connor nodded. "I'm pretty sure this is the same guy," he said. He paused to catch his breath and ease his aching back. Digging out the packed snow was like shoveling cement.

"He's really stuck in here," Nina said. "The snow compacted around him after he fell in."

"That can happen if people thrash around," Anders said. "That's one of the things that makes these tree wells so dangerous."

"You'd think one brush with death would have kept the guy out of here," Nina said. She straightened. "Let's try again to pull him out before we dig anymore."

Connor grabbed hold of one of the man's legs. Already it felt lifeless. Unresponsive. He felt under the pants cuff and pinched the ankle, hard, praying for some reaction, but there was none.

"On three." Anders spoke from the other side of the man, arms wrapped firmly around the other leg. Nina bent awkwardly in front of them, holding onto the tail of a jacket. "One. Two. Three."

They heaved, and the body shifted. "Again!" Connor shouted.

They heaved again, and again. After the third try, Nina knelt and scooped away loosened snow from around the man's torso. Another heave, and they were able to free him.

The body emerged face down. They turned him over, and Connor stared into the blue complexion of Jace Dennison.

JACE LOOKED SURPRISED, Stacy thought as she stared into the face of the dead man. She had joined the trio around the tree well as they were working to pull the body free and said nothing until Jace lay on the ground. Only then did she remove her skis and make her way to Connor's side.

"I saw him just a little while ago," she said. "He was outside the ski patrol office, looking for you."

"Why was he looking for me?" Connor asked.

"I don't know. He said he needed to talk to you about something." She looked away. "He asked me to tell you to come by the bagel place where he works, after four."

"When did you see him, exactly?" Connor asked.

"Before the explosion," she said. "Maybe forty minutes before?"

"Was anyone else with him?"

"No. I tried to get him to confide in me, but he said he had to leave."

"Did he head to the lift? Or away from the mountain?"

"I didn't see."

Anders approached. "I called Doug, and he'll notify the sheriff. We have to wait to transport him until a deputy arrives."

Connor checked the time. "It's after four," he said. "You and Nina go on down and finish for the day. I'll wait for the sheriff. And take Farley with you."

"Come on, Farley," Nina called.

The dog looked from Nina to Connor. "Go on," he ordered. "Go with Nina."

"Farley, come," Anders said, in a fair imitation of Connor. The dog trotted after him, and Anders and Nina skied away.

"Are you okay?" Stacy asked when she and Connor were alone.

"I'm okay." He took a few steps from the body and sat in the snow. He looked wrung out.

She sat next to him.

"Where's your dad?" he asked.

"I sent him back to the condo." She wanted to touch him—to somehow comfort him. But she was afraid he would pull away.

"What about you?" he asked after a moment. "Are you okay?"

She looked at the body, then away. "I'm a little shook up. That avalanche never should have happened. I should have—"

He squeezed her knee. "Don't. There was nothing you could do."

"That isn't a good enough answer." She knelt to face him. "I have to do something. This can't happen again. Today it was just a broken leg, but next time someone could die."

"Someone has already died." He looked at Jace.

"You don't think this was an accident? He was hurrying away, maybe from the avalanche, and got too close to the trees? Maybe the snow obscured his vision."

"He wanted to talk to me about something. Minutes later someone sets off an avalanche. Next thing we know he's dead. In the same area where he was trapped last week. That feels like too big a coincidence to be believable to me."

She shuddered. Was Jace's death her fault, too? She bit her lip, fighting tears. She was a federal agent. She wasn't going to cry. Later, in the shower, when no one could see or hear her, she would give in to tears. But not now.

Connor sat up. "Someone's coming."

She stood, and together they watched the snowmobiles come through the trees. Doug and a man she didn't recognize was on one, the sheriff on the second. They parked and tramped over to Connor and Stacy.

The sheriff stared down at the body. "Do we know his name?"

"Jason Dennison," Connor said. "I pulled him out of a tree well last week. Alive that time."

The second man—middle-aged with thinning blond hair and pale blue eyes—knelt beside the body.

"This is Dr. Monroe," the sheriff said.

"I'm the coroner." The doctor was already putting on latex gloves.

Stacy turned away. Doug moved in beside her. "Was that avalanche caused by one of the stolen cast boosters?" he asked.

"I can't say for certain, but it seems likely," she said.

"Do we have any idea who did it?"

"No." She steeled herself against his protests that she wasn't doing enough. "I'm going to call my superiors and ask for more agents to be put on this case," she said. "It needs to be a priority."

"We don't want to frighten the public with an army of law enforcement officers," Doug said.

"We know how to be discreet." Though Nina had recognized her as law enforcement, and her father, too. What had tipped her off?

The coroner stood and stripped off his gloves. "You can transport the body now."

"What can you tell us about how he died?" Connor asked.

"Obviously, he suffocated in the tree well," Doug said.

"I won't know the answer to that until after the autopsy," Dr. Monroe said. "But I can tell you he also has a fractured skull."

"Did he hit his head on a rock or something when he fell?" Doug asked.

Connor moved over to the tree. "We didn't find any rocks when we were digging."

The doctor followed Connor to the tree well. "What was his position when you found him?"

"Pretty much vertical at the base of the tree."

"He was hit on the back of the head." The doctor put a hand to the base of his own skull.

"So maybe he was hit before he ended up in this hole," Connor said.

"The blow to the head might have killed him fairly quickly, or he might have fallen because of it and suffocated," the doctor said. "We'll know more after the autopsy."

"Who hit him?" Connor asked. "The man who found him didn't mention anyone else here."

"He probably fell and hit his own head," Doug said.

"You'll need to close this run until we've determined cause of death," the sheriff said.

Doug groaned. "I'm sure it was an accident."

"We still have to investigate," the sheriff said. He returned to his snowmobile and retrieved a roll of crime scene tape. Connor helped him string it up while Doug transported the doctor to the base area.

"We know Jace was one of the protesters," Connor told the sheriff. "He said he was just collecting signatures for petitions and attending rallies, but maybe he found out about other plans and threatened to tell. Apparently, he was looking for me this afternoon. He said he needed to tell me something."

"He trusted you enough to tell you a secret?" the sheriff asked.

"I saved his life. Maybe that was enough for him."

"Let me know if you find out anything else." The sheriff glanced at Stacy. "Anything you'd like to update me on?"

"Not yet," she said. "Soon." She mentally crossed her fingers.

The sheriff rode away.

"Come on," Connor said to Stacy. "I'll give you a lift."

She stowed her skis alongside his on the snowmobile

and climbed on behind him. She wanted to wrap her arms around him and lean against his back but resisted the urge. Instead, she stared out at the empty runs as they made their way back to the base area, fighting images of what this serene area might look like if terrorists unleashed a rain of bombs.

At the ski patrol shack, Connor parked the snowmobile. "How did you get here this afternoon?" he asked.

"I walked over from the condo." At the time, it had been an enjoyable walk through the swirling snow. Now it was dark, she was chilled through, and the thought of trudging the mile back to where her father waited made her shudder.

"Wait here, and I'll give you a ride," he said. He went into the shack and returned moments later with Farley, then led the way through an alley to a small lot where his truck was parked.

She climbed in and fastened her seat belt, then lay her head back and closed her eyes. "I really don't want to go back to the condo," she said. "Dad is going to ask a hundred questions, then give me a hundred suggestions for how I could be doing things better."

"Is he that bad, really?" Connor asked.

"Maybe not." She looked across at him. They were parked beneath a security light, which bleached his skin of all color and cast deeper circles beneath his eyes. She imagined she looked just as frightful. Farley lay sprawled on the back seat, watching them with alert eyes. "I just don't want to talk about what I haven't done enough of or need to do more of," she said. "I've already got that conversation going on in my head without adding to it."

"Then where would you like to go?" he asked.

She sighed. "Anywhere but to my condo."

"We could go to my place."

Just like that, she was where she had been last night, bathed in hot embarrassment, unable to look at him. "I wasn't hinting at that, I promise. I just…"

"It's okay," he said.

"It's not okay." She made herself face him, to look into his eyes, though she couldn't read the expression there. "I'm sorry I put you in that position last night," she said. "I realize you don't want me that way. It was very unprofessional of me."

He leaned across the seat and took her hand. "You're wrong," he said.

"I know," she said. "I was wrong to, um, proposition you that way." She needed to change the subject. She couldn't talk about this anymore.

"You're wrong when you say I don't want you." He slid one finger along her jaw and urged her to lift her chin and look at him again. "The problem is I want you so much, it scares me."

She opened her mouth, but all that came out was a soft, "Oh," before his lips covered hers.

His lips were warm and supple, firing every nerve in her body. She gripped his forearms, fingers digging in, as he moved his mouth against hers, deepening the kiss, inviting her tongue to tangle with his. Heat spread through her, banishing her previous chill.

He pulled away, just enough to study her. "You okay?"

She nodded, incapable of speech.

He looked down at her fingers, still gripping his jacket. "Want to go to my place now? We can talk, if that's all you want," he said.

"That's not all I want," she managed to croak. She cleared her throat. "But talking is a good start."

Chapter Twelve

Connor lived in one of the first apartment complexes built when SkyCrest resort opened in the 1980s. Five years ago, when the developer was talking of tearing the buildings down, the resort had purchased the complex for employee housing. Connor, as a member of ski patrol, was one of the first to move in.

But as he led Stacy across the parking lot to his door, he was struck by the shabbiness of the building, with its plain brown wooden facade and lack of landscaping. "It's not fancy, but it's home," he said as he unlocked the door.

Farley trotted into the apartment ahead of them and headed to the kitchen to check his food dish. It was always empty this time of day, but he always checked.

Connor moved ahead of Stacy into the small living room, clearing a towel, a shirt he had worn yesterday or the day before and an extra parka from the back of the sofa and adding them to a basket of clean clothes he had brought up from the laundry room that morning. He stuffed the basket into the hall closet, on top of a leaning pile of backpacks, a tent and a flattened inflatable kayak.

"Um, have a seat and make yourself comfortable," he said, then darted down the short hallway to the bedroom.

He flipped on the light, gathered up all the clothes on the

furniture and floor and shoved these into the closet, then straightened the sheets and pulled the comforter over everything. Not that Stacy was likely to see any of this, but if she did...

"Everything okay?" she called from the living room.

"Great." He removed his parka and returned to the living room and hung the jacket on a hook by the door. Stacy had already hung up hers. She was seated on the sofa, Farley in his bed across from her.

"Come sit down," she said and patted the seat beside her.

He sat, their thighs almost but not quite touching. "Are you hungry?" he asked. "I could heat some soup or something."

"Maybe later." She took his hand. "You have a lot of skis," she said.

He followed her gaze to the wall across from them and the six pairs of skis leaning against the paneling. "Yeah, I guess I do." There was a seventh pair in his locker at the resort. And maybe another in the back of the truck. "There are different pairs for different conditions."

"That's a lot of different conditions."

"Some of them I just own because I like the way they look."

"I've felt that way about shoes."

They fell silent again. He shifted, moving closer. What was it about this woman that left him so off-kilter?

"Do you remember the night we met?" she asked.

"At the Trail's End."

"What did you think when you saw me?"

"That you looked like a woman who knew what you wanted."

She laughed. "What did you think I wanted?"

"I was hoping it was me."

She turned toward him and pulled his head down to hers. She had the softest lips, and soft breasts pressed against his chest. Such a fascinating contrast to the steely determination with which she faced almost everything else.

He slid the tips of his fingers beneath her fleece top, satiny skin cool to his touch. She pulled away and looked up at him, flushed and breathless. "Do I really frighten you?" she asked.

"Not you," he said. "Only how I feel about you."

She was going to ask him to explain. He didn't like being a cliché—a man who couldn't talk about feelings. But he had apparently missed class the day everyone else learned to be comfortable with emotions.

"I don't know how to describe it," he rushed to add. "Just...a little out of control."

"Really?" She smiled. She slid her fingers beneath his sweater and along the waistband of his trousers. "Am I frightening you now?"

"No." He moved closer. "That's not the word I'd use." He nuzzled her throat. "I wouldn't use words at all." Then he kissed her again and slid his hands all the way up to cup her breasts over her bra.

"Don't stop now," she murmured and unfastened the button at the waistband of his snow pants.

"You're sure about this?" he asked.

She nibbled beneath his ear, sending a shiver through him. "I'm sure."

He pushed her top up further and unfastened her bra. She moved beneath him, helping him undress her until they were both naked from the waist up.

Farley let out a loud snore, and she laughed. "Maybe we should move some place more comfortable," she suggested.

He led her to the bedroom, where he switched on the bedside lamp and folded back the comforter.

"Condom?" she asked, and he took one from the box in the bedside table. The box had been there a while. How long before they expired?

"I'll be right back," he said and darted into the bathroom, where he verified that the condom was not expired, removed the rest of his clothing and brushed his hair.

When he returned, she was lying naked against the sheets, propped on her elbows. He had been right—she was a woman who knew what she wanted. All nervousness fled, banished by raw desire. He slid into bed and abandoned himself to the silken heat of her body wrapped around his.

She made love the way she did everything, he decided, with a focus that fueled his own intensity. If he was a mystery she wanted to solve, she was new terrain he wanted to spend years exploring. He wanted to study the way she moved when he passed his hands over her and memorize the pleased noises she made when he traced her curves with his mouth. There was nothing tentative in the way she touched him or in her responses, eager and joyful and urging him toward more.

By the time he rolled on the condom and pulled her on top of him they were past speech, communicating with nudges and looks. He groaned as she wrapped around him, then could scarcely breathe as she thrust against him. Then she leaned over and planted the gentlest of kisses on his mouth, and he opened his eyes to look into hers.

"You doing okay?" she whispered.

"Never better," he said and wrapped his arms around her. They moved together, sometimes smoothly, sometimes awkwardly but always with the same goal in mind. He kept his gaze locked to hers and saw there the same vulnerability and eagerness that had caught him by surprise when she had asked him to accompany her to the Trail's End to look for protestors. He watched her climax as it transformed her face, then closed his eyes and focused on his own release.

They lay together afterward, entwined beneath the comforter. He was spent but still so aware of her against him. He no longer felt out of control, merely a navigator of unknown territory, delighting in the adventure overcoming uncertainty about what lay ahead.

"Not too scary, I hope," she said, and he wondered if she had read his thoughts. Then again, maybe she had seen through him all along.

"Not scary at all," he said. He wanted to tell her that he wasn't afraid of women. That he had welcomed a lot of them—well, quite a few of them—into his bed. But that didn't sound like the diplomatic thing to say. And this wasn't about experience or inexperience. Only the knowledge that part of his brain had recognized before the rest of him had caught up—the fact that Stacy was special.

Now she had the power to hurt him, something he hoped she never realized.

STACY WAS DEEP in a dream of floating on a heated cloud. A gorgeous man was there with her, offering her chocolate. The man was Connor. And he was naked. She smiled and beckoned him to come closer.

Then loud, tinny music jarred her awake. She opened her eyes and stared into darkness, no sign of the gorgeous naked man or clouds or chocolate.

"Is that your phone?" a man asked.

"Connor!" She sat up, then pulled up the sheet to cover her breasts as cold air rushed over them. "What time is it?"

"It's after midnight."

The music had stopped, but as she groped for the switch on the lamp beside the bed, it started up again. She found her phone and checked the screen. "It's my father," she said and silenced the call.

The text alert sounded. She swiped up and read the message. You need to answer my call. The phone rang again.

"Answer him," Connor said. "He's probably worried you've been kidnapped by terrorists."

"Hello?" She held the phone tightly to her ear with one hand and gathered the comforter more tightly around herself with the other.

"Where are you?" George demanded.

"I'm okay, Dad. I'm safe."

"I didn't ask how you are. I want to know where you are."

She glanced at Connor, who was also sitting up, watching her. "I'm with Connor," she said.

"Sorry to interrupt, but we've got trouble."

"Dad?" She sat up straighter, heart racing. "What's wrong? Are you all right?"

"I'm fine. But there's a Special Agent Damien Anthony who's looking for you."

"Anthony! What is he doing here?" The last time she had seen Anthony, he had been providing far too many details about surveillance he had done on a mobster's girlfriend to a group of agents at the Denver office. "It's the middle of the night."

"He's been ordered to assume control of the investigation. I take it he drove straight from Denver and started searching for you right away."

Stacy couldn't speak. Anger choked off the words. Anthony wasn't going to wait even until morning before wresting control of this case away from her. She gripped the phone so tightly it was a wonder it didn't shatter.

"What's wrong?" Connor asked. "Is your dad okay?"

She pressed the phone to the blankets. "The FBI sent another agent to take over the investigation."

"Why would they do that?"

She put the phone to her ear once more. "Why did they send Anthony?" she asked.

"He said someone from the resort called to complain that a man had died because the FBI wasn't taking the case seriously enough. He said he's here to take it seriously."

"I am taking the case seriously!" Then she blushed. The declaration would have sounded better if she hadn't been naked in Connor's bed. But it wasn't as if she would be out interviewing suspects at this time of night. "They can't do this to me."

"The Bureau can do pretty much whatever it pleases," George said. "You can't fight these people. But you can outsmart them."

"How am I going to do that?" She kept her voice calm, though inside, she raged.

"We need to come up with a plan."

She threw back the covers. "I'll be right there, Dad."

"No. Don't come here. I'll come there. Put on a pot of coffee. It's going to be a long night."

Chapter Thirteen

Connor and Stacy were dressed and waiting when George arrived. Even Farley had gotten out of bed to greet the older man at the door. "This place reminds me of my first apartment," George said as he shed hat, parka and gloves. "Except for the skis. I had posters of motorcycles. Never had the bike, just lots of posters."

"Like some guys and supermodels," Connor said.

"Just like that." George walked over and hugged Stacy. "It's going to be all right," he said and patted her back.

"Thanks, Dad, but I'm not six with a broken toy. You can't fix everything."

"I'm crushed." George looked to Connor. "Where's that coffee?"

"In here." Connor led the way to the kitchen and filled three mugs. They gathered around the table.

"I can't believe Anthony showed up here like this," Stacy said. "At night."

"Apparently, someone lit a fire under the Bureau over this." George took a long drink of coffee.

"Would Doug do that?" Stacy asked. "Call and complain about me?"

"It was probably one of Doug's bosses," Connor said. "They're allergic to bad publicity. An inbounds avalanche and a dead snowboarder on the same day probably has them in a terror."

"Did Anthony say what's going to happen to me?" Stacy asked.

"They probably want you to return to Denver," George said. "Or maybe you'll be told to assist Agent Anthony."

Stacy scowled, then looked at Connor. "Remember I told you some in the FBI think female agents should limit themselves to transcribing interviews and making coffee? Anthony is one of them."

"How does he get away with that in this day and age?" George asked.

"He's got bosses willing to look the other way," she said.

"We just need to figure out how to outsmart him," George said.

"Damien Anthony may be a horrible chauvinist, but he isn't stupid," she said.

"When he came to the condo looking for you, I told him you were undercover at the moment, and I didn't know how to get in touch with you," George said.

"That was quick thinking." Connor stood to get more coffee.

"That was lying," Stacy said. "And he's going to find out it's a lie as soon as he learns that I was at the resort today—both after the avalanche and after Jace's body was found."

"You went undercover tonight." George slid his mug forward for a refill. "Because you had a lead on who was responsible for the theft of those explosives."

"But I don't have a lead. That's the whole problem."

"What happened when you and Connor visited Shane?" George asked. "I want more details than you blew me off with when you came home that night."

"He said he wanted Connor to help him with a fireworks

show on Martin Luther King weekend," Stacy said. "Then he showed us boxes of fireworks in his garage."

"Was anyone else with him?"

"There could have been someone in another part of the house," Connor said. "But we didn't meet anyone else."

"He lives on a ranch, right? Big property, lots of land and outbuildings?"

"I guess so," Stacy said. "We didn't get a tour, and it was too dark to see much."

"We need to go back to Shane's house and look around," George said. "Maybe fireworks aren't the only explosives at the place."

"We don't have a warrant," Stacy said.

"If we see anything interesting, we'll leave it there and figure out how to get a warrant."

"Dad, there are so many ways that could go wrong."

"I think George is right," Connor said. "When I was in the Rangers, sometimes we had to go a little out of bounds to get the results we needed."

"I don't even want to hear this." She clapped her hands over her ears.

George leaned across the table toward her. "If we go out to Shane's house and find evidence to implicate him in the thefts, you'll have solved the case and Anthony can go back to making his own coffee," he said.

She lowered her hands to the table once more. "That's a very big if."

"I have faith in you."

Her expression softened. "You really mean that, don't you?"

He straightened. "I do. Plus, I'm going with you."

"I'll come, too," Connor said.

George shook his head. "Not a good idea. If you suddenly disappear, people will ask questions."

"You have responsibilities here," Stacy said. "Plus, you can let us know if there are any new developments at the resort."

She was trying to let him down gently. But she also spoke the truth. He needed to be at the resort at 5:30 to begin avalanche mitigation, and patrol had a long list of things to do to prepare for the holiday weekend crowds. "Check in with me when you can," he said.

George pushed back from the table. "Let's all try to get a few hours' sleep. We'll set out at dawn."

GEORGE HAD DECLARED it too risky to return to Stacy's rental, in case Anthony decided to come back there to look for her. Instead, he bedded down on the sofa and said nothing when she disappeared into Connor's room.

But she lay awake next to Connor, alternately fuming over Damien Anthony's arrival and reviewing every aspect of the case, trying to see anything she had missed. Connor was restless, too. After a while, she rolled toward him, and he gathered her close.

"Are you ever afraid of getting caught in an avalanche?" she asked.

"Not afraid, necessarily," he said. "Aware. Every time we're doing mitigation work, you know there are places where a slide could come down on you any time. It's an adrenaline rush—keeps you on your toes."

"It's like that sometimes with my work, too, when I'm walking into a situation where there could be a person with a gun or a bomb who wouldn't hesitate to kill me."

"You accept the risk, but you do the work anyway," he said.

"Yes." The work had to be done, and if she was being honest, the risk was part of the attraction—the chance to test the odds over and over again and come out on top, alive. Until the day the odds won. She wasn't going to think about that. She lay her head on his chest, closed her eyes and slept.

Too soon, the alarm blared, and they all roused and met, bleary-eyed and unspeaking, in the kitchen over coffee. Connor and Farley left first. Stacy and George followed him out, down to a dirty green Jeep with a dented front fender.

"Dad, where did you get this?" Stacy asked as George unlocked the vehicle.

"I rented it from a guy down-valley." He opened the back of the Jeep and leaned inside. "I've got a bunch of supplies we might need back here. We can spend a couple of nights out if we have to."

"Where is my rental?" she asked.

"I parked it in a storage lot a few miles away," George said. "Anthony isn't likely to find it there, but if he does, for all he knows you put it there before you went undercover."

"You didn't want to use the SUV because it was too recognizable?"

"I wouldn't put it past the Bureau to have tracking software on it." He shut the hatch of the Jeep. "Better to have a vehicle they know nothing about."

She buckled into the passenger seat and gave her dad directions to Shane Greer's ranch. The sky had begun to lighten, but the sun was still an hour from showing itself. They drove through quiet streets, passing only a single shuttle bus and a cluster of three people—tourists, judging from their bright parkas and hats—outside a coffee truck.

George cleared his throat. "So you and Connor are an item?"

"Dad."

"None of my business, I know. But he seems like a good man."

"You're giving him your approval?" She couldn't hide her amusement.

"I'd rather see you with him than involved with another agent."

"For someone who was with the Bureau for forty years, you certainly have a low opinion of the organization."

"It can be a good career, with the right people," he said. "But it's a hard life. Especially with a family."

"We had a good life, Dad. I never felt deprived. And you've always been there for me when I needed you."

The silence between them was easier after that. Neither spoke until she pointed out the turnoff to the ranch. "I'm going to drive past and find someplace to stash the Jeep," he said. "We'll walk from there."

The sun was painting the clouds pink by the time they started through the woods toward the ranch house. They hadn't gone far when Stacy spotted someone in the woods. A man stood before a campfire, next to a tent.

She and her father ducked behind a fat juniper and watched. As the sky lightened, she could make out more tents, a van and one truck camper amid the trees.

Her father tugged at her sleeve and indicated they should retreat. When they were back from the campers a hundred yards, George asked, "Were those campers there when you and Connor visited?"

"No. I'm sure we would have seen them when we drove up to the house. Some of them are really close to the driveway. I don't know why they're here."

"Maybe Shane's idea to advertise for help with the protests paid off."

"Maybe." A tingle rose along the back of her neck. "They could be from the Freedom Fighters." The people the Bureau had been after for months.

"Whoever they are, we've got to get past them to reach the ranch house," George said. "We need to find another way in." He pulled off his pack.

"What are you doing?" she asked.

"I've got maps." He pulled out a sheaf of papers. He laughed at her astonished look. "Sometimes old school is still best. Let's take a look and plan our route."

SNOW HAD PILED up all day and night on the ridges above the resort. Ski patrol was out before dawn Wednesday, launching charges. At first light, Connor went up in the resort helicopter to drop bombs on a more difficult-to-reach cornice. The higher elevation lifts, including Ten, opened on a delayed schedule, but by eleven o'clock every lift was turning and skiers streamed down the mountain.

Banners hung over the plaza welcomed skiers to the upcoming Martin Luther King weekend festivities. The mid-mountain restaurant arranged dozens of bright red Adirondack chairs facing the sun and clustered around a fire pit, while Guest Services set up a large hospitality tent handing out water, maps and sunscreen at the base of Lift One. Though most visitors would arrive Saturday morning, early arrivals were already filling the parking lots and condos.

Connor had just released Farley for a morning run when Doug flagged him down. The resort director was in ski gear this morning. "I've been touring the front side," he said when Connor reached him. "Everything looks to be in good shape."

"It is," Connor said.

"No problems clearing the ridges this morning?"

"None."

"I hear we've got a new FBI agent here," Connor said.

The lines around Doug's eyes tightened. "He was waiting for me when I arrived at the office this morning. He's even more tight-lipped than that woman. Said he was here to set things straight."

"Did you call and ask the FBI for more help?" Connor asked.

"Stacy told me yesterday that she was going to do that. I would just as soon the government stay out of this. That includes the Forest Service. We've operated SkyCrest on Forest Service land for forty years. They know we're good stewards. Yet, they're giving us a hard time about this expansion."

"Since when does the government ever move quickly?" Connor said.

"We're going to have protestors around all weekend," Doug said. "The town granted a permit for them to collect petition signatures right outside ski resort property, and there's some kind of rally in the town square. You'd think the local businesses would be on our side."

"People have a right to free speech," Connor said.

Doug grunted. "I want zero tolerance this weekend," he said. "Anyone steps out of line, they're off resort property. I don't want any trouble. Understood?"

"Yes, sir."

"Security is on red alert, too. Call them if anyone becomes a problem."

"We'll have everything under control," Connor said. He only hoped Stacy and George could control things on their end.

Doug moved on, and Connor started toward ski patrol headquarters to kennel Farley. His radio crackled.

"There's someone here at the office looking for you," Lily said.

"I'll be there in five."

The man looked like a regular tourist, in dark pants and a navy parka, a black watch cap pulled low over his ears. But his rigid posture and alert attitude told Connor this was probably Special Agent Damien Anthony. "Connor Donaldson?" the man asked at Connor's approach.

"That's me." Connor leaned his ski poles against the rack and clicked out of his skis. "What can I do for you?"

"Special Agent Anthony, Federal Bureau of Investigation." Anthony showed his ID. "I need to ask you some questions."

"Come on inside."

Farley scampered around the man, but the agent ignored the dog. Inside, Farley accepted a treat from Connor and went into his kennel, but Connor left the door to the cage open. He settled behind his desk. "What's this about?" he asked.

Anthony pulled up a rickety folding chair. "Tell me about the missing explosives."

Connor repeated the story of how he had discovered the theft of the four boxes of cast boosters.

"Who has access to the keys to the magazine?" Anthony asked.

"Me. And there's another set in the resort office. But whoever stole those explosives didn't use a key. They cut a hole in the building wall. That should be in your report."

Anthony's lips tightened. "There was an inbounds avalanche yesterday."

"Yes."

"It was snowing hard yesterday. I would think an avalanche wouldn't be that unusual."

"It would be unusual in that location at that time of day. And lots of people heard an explosion shortly before the snow released. If you were at the resort earlier this morning, you would have heard the sound multiple times as ski patrol did avalanche mitigation."

"Could you have heard a gunshot? Or a slamming door?"

"It was the sound a cast booster makes when it explodes," Connor said.

"Who could purchase these explosives?" Anthony asked.

"Anyone with a license. They're primarily used in mining and avalanche mitigation."

"So a miner would have access."

"As would whoever stole the boxes of explosives from our magazine."

Anthony looked at him calmly. "We only have your word that the explosives were stolen."

Connor worked to rein in his temper. "We have a hole cut in the back of the building and four boxes of cast boosters and one of detonators that are no longer in our inventory."

"You keep the inventory records."

"Yes."

Anthony said nothing, merely looked at him.

Connor pressed his lips together. Two could play this game.

Anthony was the first to blink. He stood. "I'd like to search your vehicle and your apartment for the missing explosives," he said.

"Sure." Connor stood. "As soon as you show me a warrant."

Another peeved expression from the agent. "If you're innocent, there's no reason not to cooperate."

"There's no reason for you to accuse me of theft, either."

The two men faced off. Farley emerged from his kennel and came to stand beside Connor, silent, his gaze fixed on the agent.

Anthony glanced at the dog. "We'll talk later."

He left, and Connor knelt and hugged the dog. "Thanks for backing me up, buddy," he said. He gave Farley another treat, then pulled out his phone and texted Stacy. Everything okay?

A moment later his answer came in the form of a thumbs-up emoji. He ignored the flutter of nerves in his chest and pocketed the phone. Stacy knew what she was doing. She would be all right.

"Two skiers injured in a collision at the top of Lift Seven," came the message on the radio. "Need a couple of toboggans and some help."

"I'm headed your way," Connor messaged. He pocketed the phone, kenneled the dog and headed out the door again. He still had a long day ahead of him. Better not to think about Agent Anthony or Stacy or all the other things and people he couldn't control.

STACY AND HER dad had to hike two miles in the snow to approach the ranch house from the back side. By the time they were in sight of the house, Stacy was tired, achy and overheated from the strenuous trek. But they had encountered no one on this section of the ranch. They paused on a slight rise a few hundred yards from the house and surveyed their target.

George scanned the area with a pair of binoculars, then passed them to Stacy. "I don't see any signs of life."

"There's smoke from the chimney," she said. "Someone could be inside."

"Or they've gone out and want the house to be warm when they return." He sat back. "We'll wait another half an hour. If there's no sign of movement by then, we'll get closer."

She took out her phone. She had silenced her alerts but

could still receive messages. "Connor texted to see if we were okay," she said. She sent back a thumbs-up emoji.

"He would have been good to have along," George said. "An Army Ranger and all."

"He has a job, Dad."

"I know. And he's probably having more fun blowing up things than sitting here with us." He raised the binoculars to his eyes once more. "I remember doing surveillance one winter in Maine, up near the Canadian border. We were tracking a kidnapper. My partner at the time lost two toes to frostbite."

"Did you catch the kidnapper?" she asked.

"We did. And the little girl was safe. Her grandfather had hired a guy to take her from her father—his ex-son-in-law—and bring her over the border." He lowered the binoculars. "It was one of those cases that hit a little too close to home. I would have moved heaven and earth if anyone had tried to take you from me."

Stacy swallowed past the lump in her throat. "I worked a human trafficking case last year," she said. "Teenage girls brought to the US with the promise of an education, forced to work for an escort service in Houston. It felt good to put the creeps responsible behind bars."

"The Bureau does good work," George said. "If they could clean house of a few rotten apples, they would do even better."

"One fight at a time, Dad."

He stood. "Let's move a little closer."

She stowed the binoculars and prepared to head out once more. But they were just starting downhill when a tremendous *Boom!* shook them.

"Down!" her father shouted and shoved her to the ground.

Chapter Fourteen

"Hey, Connor. Come take a look at this."

Connor was attempting to go to lunch for the third time that afternoon when Cerise hailed him from her post on Lift Four. The busy quad lift ran from above the main parking lot to the top of the westernmost peaks at the resort. Connor detoured to meet her outside the lift operator shack. Her partner today, Saska, paused in her work of scraping collected snow away from the loading area to wave.

"Hey, Cerise," Connor said. "What's up?"

"Get a load of this." She passed him a battered cardboard box. "Open it."

"This doesn't have one of those exploding snake gags inside of it, does it?" he asked.

"No. Just take a look."

He lifted the lid on the box and stared at a cast booster, complete with attached detonator. He stared. "Where did you get this?"

"Don't freak out. It's not real. Take a closer look."

He peered into the box again. The detonator was wrong—too many squiggly wires. It looked like someone's idea of a detonator. And the can itself wasn't quite right. He picked it up and heard a rattle, like rocks or marbles. "It's a painted soda can with pebbles or something inside," he said. "Made up to look like a bomb."

"Sick, right? I found it tucked up above one of the chairs when we started up this morning."

"Did you call security?"

"I wanted ski patrol to take a look first. It would be just like one of you guys to try to scare the daylights out of me with this."

"You mean Chase."

"Tell him I'm impressed. He went to a lot of trouble for this one."

"You found it this morning?"

"Yeah. Then we got busy, and I forgot about it. Seeing you passing by reminded me."

"I'll take this back to the patrol office and talk with Chase," he said. "You two need to cool it on the pranks."

"We're just having fun."

"Then do what most people do. Go out for a beer. Play some pool. See a movie. But leave the pranks away from the job."

At the office, he radioed Chase, then studied the fake bomb. Whoever did this had at least seen a cast booster. Maybe they looked up an image online. The wiring on the detonator was wrong, but someone who didn't know better would mistake it for the real thing.

The door to the patrol office opened, and Chase came in, stamping snow from his boots. "What did you need to see me about?" he asked.

Connor gestured to the box. "Recognize this?"

Chase clomped over and looked down at the box. "Is that a fake bomb?" He picked it up and turned it over in his hand. "Pretty sweet. Where did you get it?"

"I thought maybe you made it."

"Me?" Chase dropped the fake back into the box. "Why would I do that?"

"Cerise found it above one of the lift chairs when she started her shift this morning. I know you two have been pranking each other for weeks."

"Sure, but I wouldn't do something like this. Can you imagine the panic if someone saw this and thought it was real?"

"We're lucky Cerise isn't the panicky type."

"Yeah, she's real steady that way."

"So instead of pulling her hair to get her attention like a schoolkid, why don't you man up and ask her out?"

Chase flushed. "Do you really think she'd go out with me? I mean, her last boyfriend was an MMA fighter. He looked like a Greek god or something."

"And she's all torn up about the breakup?"

"No way. She dumped him."

"Then obviously Mr. Greek God didn't impress. And she's wasted a lot of time playing with you."

"Yeah, I guess so. Maybe I'll talk to her." Chase looked at the bomb again. "So, did somebody else put that at the lift to scare her? You find out who it was, and I'll clean their clock."

Connor put the lid back on the box. "Just get back to work."

When Chase had left, Connor put the fake bomb in a desk drawer. Later, he would show it to Stacy. He thought about the idea that whoever had stolen the cast boosters had been practicing when they set off the avalanche yesterday. Was this fake a kind of practice, too? Maybe someone wanted to see if they could plant a bomb at a lift without getting caught. If anyone questioned them, they could say it was a practical joke.

Next time wouldn't be a joke. He pulled out his phone and texted Stacy. I've got a development here you need to know about.

STACY'S LEFT CHEEK was freezing, shoved into the snow. Her dad lay beside her, practically on top of her. He had drawn his weapon and was staring in the direction of the blast. A second explosion sounded, this one more muffled than the first.

She shoved at George. "Get off of me," she said. "No one is shooting at us."

He rolled off her, and they both sat. He holstered the weapon. "The explosions are coming from over there," he said and pointed to their left.

"I figured that out." She stood and brushed snow off her clothing. "I'm betting those aren't fireworks."

She moved toward the source of the explosions, her dad close behind. They kept to the trees, pausing frequently to listen for anyone nearby. Two more explosions went off before they reached the edge of a large rock-lined pit. Concealed in the bushes on the edge of the pit, they looked across toward a group of people almost directly opposite.

"It looks like an old quarry," George whispered.

"It looks like a good place to practice launching bombs." She winced as another explosion raised a cloud of dust at the bottom of the pit. When the smoke cleared, she could make out painted X's on several rocks at the bottom of the quarry. One man in the group across from them appeared to be instructing the others, waving his arms and gesturing into the quarry. "We need to get closer," she said.

They worked their way around the edge of the quarry, staying out of sight of those on the other side. Yet another explosion shook the air.

"They're wasting a lot of ammo," her father said.

"According to Connor, ninety-six cast boosters were stolen," she said. "And they only need a few to do a lot of damage. They can afford to waste some practicing." She halted when they were close enough to hear the people on the edge of the quarry.

"It's not enough to hurl the bomb," said the instructor, a gray-bearded man with a vaguely British accent. "The more accurate you are, the more damage you'll do. And the less likely you yourself will get hurt." He stepped to one side. "Nate, I want you to try again. Remember your release point and use your wrist."

The man from the Trail's End—the one who had confronted Connor the first night and been with Jace the second night—stepped up. He raised his leg in a pitcher's windup, then hurled something into the quarry.

Stacy ducked her head and covered her ears as the explosion shook the air. The crowd around Nate cheered.

"Excellent," the instructor said. "Do that Friday, and we'll all be celebrating."

The day after tomorrow. The Friday of Martin Luther King weekend. Did this mean Shane and his fellow protestors weren't going to wait until Monday's rally to make a move?

"We need to get into the house and see if we can find some indication of their target," Stacy whispered to her father.

"I can take care of that." He patted her shoulder. "I'll create a distraction while you search."

"Dad, no."

But he had already stood and was striding toward the group at the canyon rim. The others looked up at his approach.

"Hello!" George called and raised both arms. "I was told to report here to lend a hand."

"Who are you?" the instructor demanded.

"I'm George." He extended his hand, but the instructor ignored him. "Shane told me to come out here and see if I could help." George nodded toward the box at Nate's feet. "I see you're using the Trojan cast boosters. I used many of those in my mining days."

"You're familiar with these?" the instructor asked.

"Of course." George plucked a cylinder from the box. "Portable but powerful. Just the thing for shaking things up a bit."

The others closed in around George, but Stacy detected no danger. She blew out a shaky breath and retreated from the quarry rim. Clearly, her father hadn't lost any of his courage—some said recklessness—since retiring.

She set out toward the ranch house. She didn't see anyone on her way and detected no signs of recent activity. The house itself looked empty. After looking in windows and listening for noise from anyone inside, she tried the back door. It was locked, but a credit card easily defeated the simple lock. Apparently, Shane wasn't too concerned about security.

Inside, the kitchen was cluttered with the remains of breakfast: the dregs of coffee, cold in the cup. Toast crumbs in the softened butter, and a pan with the remains of eggs in the sink. The air was chilly and silent as a tomb.

The next room contained a long dining table filling most of the space. The tabletop was covered in stacks of books and papers. She glanced through old farm journals, ranch supply catalogs and two gift boxes containing shirts, the Christmas wrapping still clinging to them. No notebooks or diaries or anything to indicate Shane's plans for tomorrow.

She moved into the empty living room, then to a narrow flight of stairs. Before ascending, she drew her Glock and held it at her side. Then she started up.

CONNOR HAD FORGOTTEN to bring food from home for his lunch, so when he finally had a moment to spare, he hit up the grill below Lift Four. He collected his food and carried it to a table, then checked his phone. Stacy hadn't responded to his previous text. Which probably meant she was busy.

Or in trouble, unable to reach her phone.

He pushed the thought aside and focused on the food. He was eating his first spoonful of chili when Nina arrived with a tray.

"Mind if I join you?"

"Have a seat." He moved his helmet out of the way, and she slid in across from him.

"Busy day," she said.

"Yeah."

"You look wiped out."

As usual, she looked as if she had just stepped off a photo shoot. He should ask her some time if she'd had her patrol uniform tailored. It didn't fit anyone else that way. "I didn't get much sleep last night," he said.

She sipped hot chocolate and regarded him over the edge of the cup. "So what's the real story on Stacy? Is she really an old friend?"

He shook his head. "We just met when she came to investigate the theft of the cast boosters."

"Is she with ATF?"

"FBI."

"Ooh." Nina leaned toward him. "So, are you helping her with her investigations, or is there more to it than that?"

Last night there had been a lot more to it. In the cold daylight he was less sure. "She's only here while she's working on this case," he said.

"Where does she live the rest of the time?"

"Denver."

"That's only a few hours away."

He gave her a sour look.

She smiled. "I'm just saying. Does she like dogs?"

"Loves them. And Farley is crazy about her."

"Then she's perfect." She sat back. "Don't look so glum."

"Yeah, I'm just tired." He rubbed his hand down his face as if he could erase the weariness.

"Things are winding down," Nina said. "You should go home. Sleep while you can. Tomorrow is going to be a zoo."

"I've only got a few more hours. I'll hang in there."

After lunch he sent another text to Stacy—still no reply. His first instinct was to leave work early and drive out to Shane's ranch to look for her. And then what? As annoyed as she had been at her father for racing to her rescue, she wasn't liable to appreciate Connor's interference.

He reminded himself she was capable and trained. She knew far more about what she needed to do than he did. The best thing for him was to wait and trust her to know how to do her job.

STACY TOOK THE stairs one at a time, pausing on each step to listen. But the only noises were the rattle of wind against a loose pane of glass and her own breathing.

The upstairs consisted of three rooms and a bath. The first two rooms held neatly made beds and enough dust to indicate they hadn't been occupied in a while. The third room contained a desk, two bookcases and a beige metal filing cabinet. She slipped inside and shut the door behind her.

She quickly searched through the papers on top of the

desk, which consisted primarily of junk mail and old invoices. She moved on to the drawers. Broken pens, loose batteries and screws, a tin of snuff, a half pint of bourbon and more uninteresting paperwork crowded the first two drawers.

But in the bottom left-hand drawer, she found what she was looking for—a map of SkyCrest Resort, half a dozen spots marked with precise black X's. One of the X's was on the ridge above Lift Ten—the site of yesterday's avalanche. Other X's indicated Lifts One and Four, and ridges on the west and southwest boundaries of the resort, above networks of ski runs.

These had to be the targets the people at the quarry had been practicing to hit.

The sound of voices in the rooms below set her heart racing. She shoved the papers back into the drawer, quickly left the room and hurried down the hall to the first of the two unoccupied bedrooms. She stood with her back to the wall, weapon drawn, and waited.

Heavy footsteps sounded on the stairs, then men's voices. "You're sure about this?" the first voice—Shane?—said.

"Nate is good enough." Stacy thought this was the instructor from the quarry, with the British accent. "And that old man you sent over—George. He's got a good arm. He says he worked with this type of explosive most of his life."

"George? Who is George?"

Stacy winced. *Dad, I hope you had sense enough to disappear after you left the quarry.*

"The old guy," the instructor said. "He told me you sent him over to help. Because he worked in the mines."

"Clayton or one of the others must have sent him."

"It doesn't matter. I think we can use him. But maybe you should think about fewer targets."

Their voices faded away as they went into another room—probably the office. Stacy waited until she heard a door close, then slipped from the room. She could hurry down the stairs and out of the house, find her dad and then contact her supervisor at the FBI. She would pretend she knew nothing about Agent Anthony and ask the special agent in charge to send a team to arrest Shane and the others.

But the murmur of voices from behind the closed door drew her. Maybe she could learn more about the plans for deploying the explosives. She moved to the door and put her ear to it.

"Even if we lose half our targets, the rest will do enough damage to shut down the resort for at least a year," Shane said. "That will give me time to file suit to regain control of my family's land. And it should stop the expansion plans cold. They'll have to spend so much money repairing infrastructure and their reputation, they won't have any fight left."

"You're right. But the more people who can lead the cops back to us, the less I like it."

"We can take care of anyone likely to talk," Shane said. "We took care of that snowboarder, didn't we? And everyone thinks it was an unfortunate accident."

Footsteps moved toward the door. Stacy shot toward the stairs. She was halfway down when a voice shouted behind her. "Stop! What do you think you're doing?"

Then the whistle of a bullet passed her head.

Chapter Fifteen

Stacy yelped as the bullet whizzed past her, then ducked her head and headed for the front door, the closest exit. Footsteps pounded on the stairs behind her, and another bullet thudded into the wall above her right shoulder. She grabbed for the door, but it flew open almost at her touch.

"Hold your fire!" the man who stepped inside shouted. He was a foot taller than her and wide as the doorframe. When he grabbed Stacy by the shoulders and shook her, her teeth chattered together. "Drop the weapon," he said. "Or I'll break your neck."

Shane and the instructor pounded down the stairs. "What's going on?" Shane asked, looking from Stacy to the group of men at the door.

"We brought you a troublemaker," said the burly man who held her. "And looks like you have another one."

"Who have you got there?" Shane asked, looking past Stacy and her captor.

"Says his name's George. We caught him snooping through boxes in the garage."

"He's the miner who helped us at the quarry," the instructor said.

Stacy forced herself to stand still and not react, though seeing her father like this tore at her. Someone had given him a black eye. Standing there, arms bound behind him and head down, he looked much smaller and older.

"I know you." Shane moved in closer to George. "You were at the rally at the campground Friday night. With that ski patroller and his girlfriend." He turned to Stacy. "And you're the girlfriend."

She lifted her chin but said nothing. If they searched her, they would find her ID, but she wasn't going to volunteer the information.

"What were you doing upstairs?" the instructor asked her.

"I was looking for the bathroom," she said.

The blow snapped her head back and made her see stars. When she looked up, her father was staring at her, eyes full of fury, but he quickly looked down again.

"Who sent you here?" Shane asked.

"I came here looking for my boyfriend, Connor," she said.

"Why do you think he's here?"

"He's really unhappy about the resort's expansion," she said. "It was his idea to get involved in the protests. He felt bad about refusing to help with the fireworks and said he changed his mind."

"You're still lying." Shane pulled a pistol and aimed it at her. Some of the others took a step back. "Take her to the chicken house," he said. "When I have more time, I'll see if I can get the truth out of her."

SHANE'S MEN SHOVED Stacy and George into a small wooden building and fit a padlock on the door. Father and daughter sat on the floor where they had fallen, hands tied behind their backs. She listened to the men outside move away and wondered if one of them had stayed behind to guard them.

She looked around at the straw-filled nesting boxes and

overhead perches. "I think this is really a chicken house," she said.

"There's plenty of chicken manure." George made a face and scooted over a few inches. "I wonder what happened to the chickens?"

"They probably ate them," Stacy said. Her face ached where Shane had struck her, and she couldn't stop thinking about what he had said about *getting rid* of the snowboarder. With effort, she got up on her knees. "If we can find a sharp edge in here somewhere, we can get these zip ties off our wrists," she said.

"I don't see anything," George said. "They probably filed everything down, not wanting the chickens to get hurt."

"How thoughtful of them." She turned her attention from the walls to her father. "How's your eye?"

"Stings a little, but I'll be okay. The guy who jumped me looks worse, believe me."

"What happened? When I left, you had them all charmed."

"The folks at the quarry didn't give me any trouble," he said. "But after they left, I wandered over to the garage to see if I could find anything interesting. That big guy and his friends must have heard me in there and came in and jumped me."

"What happened at the quarry after I left?"

"The guy with the accent, Bruce, said he was in the military in South Africa and knew about explosives. I showed him I knew how to throw them and hit the target, and I was his new favorite student."

"Since when do you know how to launch explosives?" she asked.

"They taught us to throw grenades in boot camp. And I played baseball in high school and college. Third base. I was on rec leagues a few times over the years. I've still got a pretty good arm."

"I recognized the young dark-haired guy. Nate," Stacy said. "He was Jace Dennison's friend. Connor and I saw them at the Trail's End together."

"Jace is the snowboarder who died?"

"Yeah. But I'm thinking maybe Nate wasn't such a good friend. I overheard Shane talking to Bruce, saying they had 'gotten rid' of a snowboarder because he was threatening to talk."

"Nate struck me as someone with a mean personality," George said. "What happened in the house? Did they catch you eavesdropping?"

"I waited too long to leave, and Shane and Bruce caught me coming down the stairs." For a few seconds there, she had believed she was going to die. "You coming in when you did may have saved me."

"I don't like the idea of sticking around until Shane comes back to question you," George said.

She studied the chicken house again. It was large enough for a big flock, easily eight foot on each side, with a tall ceiling. There must be something in here she could use to saw through these bindings. If she moved over to the wall, she could probably stand and look around more.

"What did you find in the house?" her father asked.

"A map of the resort, with lots of places marked with X's. The ridges above ski runs and several ski lifts. From what I can tell, they plan to hit all those places Friday. Dad, do you have anything in your pocket we could use to cut these ties?"

"They took my phone, my gun, my wallet and the Jeep keys," he said. "The only thing left is lint."

"They took my phone and gun, too. If this was a movie,

I'd have a razor blade secreted in my shoe or something." Instead, that was where she had hidden her FBI identification.

"I saw a video online where a woman demonstrated how to break zip ties by contorting yourself like a pretzel and exerting pressure with your feet. Or something like that."

"No pretzels here," she said and slid on her bottom to the wall. "I'm going to try to stand up." She pressed her back to the wall and maneuvered her feet underneath her. Grunting and straining, scraping her back painfully against the wall, she managed to get to her feet. She stood for a moment, catching her breath.

"What now?" her dad asked.

"Now all I need is a knife."

"I need a cup of coffee." He closed his eyes and rested his head against the wall. His eye was an ugly purple, dried blood crusted on one cheek. He needed a shave, white whiskers glinting in the waning sunlight from the single window high overhead.

"I'm sorry I don't have any coffee," she said.

"I'm sorry I don't have a knife."

"What are we going to do?" he asked.

"Connor will call someone when we don't return tonight." But night wouldn't arrive for hours yet. She couldn't sit here waiting for help that might not come. She had to find a way out of this on her own.

CONNOR TOLD HIMSELF it wouldn't hurt if he swung by Stacy's condo on his way home. Just to check in with her. He didn't spot her car in the parking lot, but maybe she was parked around back.

He found the right door and rang the bell. No sounds from within. No answer. He tried knocking, then hard pounding on the door. Still no answer.

He looked around the area but saw no one. It was almost full dark now. Shouldn't she be back? He pulled out his phone and sent another text. Everything okay?

He stared at the screen, willing her to answer. Long minutes passed with no reply. Maybe she was busy. But had she been so busy all day she couldn't answer him?

Frustrated, he hit the button to call her number.

"The person you are calling is not available. Please leave a message…"

He hung up. Okay. She was busy. She didn't have time to talk. Never let anyone say he couldn't take a hint.

STACY'S ARMS ACHED from being pulled behind her back. Her dad leaned against the wall beside her, head back and eyes closed. He looked so pale. As she studied him, he opened his eyes.

"Don't look so worried," he said. "I'm not dead yet."

"We need to find a way out of here," she said.

"We've already looked everywhere. This place is too solid, except for that patch in the back wall." They both turned to study the rectangle of plywood in the otherwise thick siding a foot high and eight or nine inches wide.

"I could probably kick that out," George said.

"And then what?" she asked. "Neither one of us is going to fit through it."

Rattling at the door made them both tense. The door swung open, and Shane stepped inside, followed by a bearded man carrying a tray. "Hello," Shane said, his voice hearty, even cheerful. "We brought you some supper."

He took out a large pocket knife. Stacy forced herself not to flinch as he approached her.

"Don't worry, I'm just going to cut off your restraints.

Don't try anything, though. Eddie here is armed and won't hesitate to shoot."

Eddie set the tray on the floor and drew a large pistol from a holster at his side.

Shane freed Stacy, then George, then stepped back and nudged the tray toward them with the toe of his boot. "Eat up while we talk."

Stacy's appetite had vanished, but she forced herself to pick up the paper plate with what looked like a ham-and-cheese sandwich and a bag of potato chips. She set this aside and reached for the bottle of water. Her father was already draining his.

"Why are you keeping us in here?" Stacy asked.

"Because I don't like nosy people. And I don't know what your intentions are. Better to keep you out of the way until my mission is complete."

"What mission is that?" George asked.

Shane glanced at him. "SkyCrest Resort needs to learn they can't take and take from people. It's time they give back. They need to give back what they took from my family."

"Blowing up the resort isn't going to get your family's land back," Stacy said.

"You figured that out, did you? But don't worry. I won't do any more damage than is necessary to make my point."

"Even one bomb will kill people."

"I don't think the bomb will kill anyone," Shane said. "The snow might kill a few, but not too many, I hope. The only thing I'm trying to kill is the resort's expansion plan."

"Tell me about the people who are helping you."

Shane frowned. "What about them? They're locals and concerned citizens."

"Who's financing all this?" Stacy asked. "Giving you advice?"

"No one. Some people have contributed money, but most of it is mine. This is a real grassroots effort."

"What are you planning to do with us?" George asked.

"I haven't decided yet. For now, I'm going to keep you here, out of the way. Later…" He shrugged. "Maybe you'll have an unfortunate accident."

An accident like Jace had had. Stacy shivered. "People know we're here," she said. "When we don't come back tonight, they'll come looking for us."

"By 'people,' I assume you're referring to your boyfriend, Connor Donaldson." He reached into his pocket and took out a phone. *Her* phone. "He's been texting you all afternoon. Getting worried, I guess. But we'll have you out of the way before he can come looking." He pocketed the phone once more and stepped back, toward the door. "Tie their hands again," he said.

Eddie moved in and fastened new zip ties around their wrists, tighter this time, so that the hard plastic cut into her skin.

Stacy hissed out a breath against the pain and glared at the man, who didn't even look at her.

The two men left, and the lock rattled against the hasp as one of them secured it in place. Stacy glared at the closed door. It was full dark now, and the only light came from a foot-square window high in the front wall—the distant glow of lanterns and campfires seeping in to bathe the interior of the chicken house in gray.

"We might as well get some rest," her father said. "They probably won't show up again until tomorrow morning. We can decide how to handle them then." Not waiting for an answer, he lay down and rolled onto his side.

Stacy stared at the closed door, her body still tense. They couldn't even count on Connor now. Not until at least tomorrow. Her dad seemed confident they would be fine until then, but how could he be sure?

THURSDAY WAS THE last day before the holiday crowds would start arriving, and Connor and his staff were stretched thinner than usual with prep work for the influx of skiers. The day started at six with minor mitigation work. Then came a report that a new groomer had knocked down signposts for three intermediate runs and these needed to be reset right away.

Connor and Anders were working on that when their radios crackled. "I need a toboggan to the top of Free Spirit," Raz said, naming a popular black run.

"What's the situation?" Connor asked. "Who's injured?" A pause. "Raz?" Connor prompted.

"Sorry, Connor, but I'm the one injured," Raz said. "I don't know what happened, but I spotted a skier racing in and out among a group of slower skiers, and I headed down to tell them to knock it off. My ski must have caught an edge of something. I went down, and I heard my knee pop." She sounded near tears now. "It doesn't look good."

"Hang tight," Connor said. "We're on our way."

They left the sign and headed toward Free Spirit. By the time they arrived, Lily and Renee were there, comforting a pale-faced Raz. Half a dozen skiers watched from a short distance away.

"I'm sorry, Connor," Raz said as soon as she saw him. "I know we're already shorthanded, and this is our busiest weekend."

"It's okay." He put a steadying hand on her shoulder. "This isn't your fault. All that matters now is getting you taken care of."

They stabilized the knee, and Anders volunteered to ski down with the toboggan to a waiting ambulance. Connor returned alone to finish erecting the sign and was leaving that job when a lift operator called to report an altercation in the lift line. Connor headed over to break it up.

The day continued, with Connor putting out one fire after another. It was lunchtime before he had a chance to stop and text Stacy. No answer. His stomach churned as he stared at his messages from the day before and her one brief reply. Something wasn't right here.

He headed back to patrol headquarters to let out Farley and eat a late lunch. He had just unwrapped his sandwich when Chase came in. "Hey," Chase said and stomped snow from his boots.

"What's up?" Connor asked.

Chase grinned. "Cerise agreed to go out with me tonight."

"Told you," Connor said.

Chase laughed. "You did. I was just so afraid of making a fool of myself in front of her. But she said she really likes my goofiness."

"Just proves there's someone for everyone."

Chase grabbed two orange safety cones from the back of the room. "We've got an icy patch on Maid Marion I need to mark before some kid hits it and breaks something."

"Raz is out with a knee injury," Connor said.

"I heard. I guess that means someone will need to take her shifts."

Connor sighed. He hadn't even thought of that. "I guess so."

"You can put me down for my next day off. I could use the money. I want to take Cerise someplace really nice."

"She likes your goofiness. Maybe she doesn't want really nice."

"Yeah, but she deserves it, you know." Chase left, slamming the door behind him.

Connor sat back, the remains of his sandwich uneaten. Chase was set on sweeping Cerise off her feet, even if she didn't need sweeping. Was that what women wanted?

He took out his phone again and studied the text thread with Stacy. He wanted to wait for her. To respect her abilities. But he was growing more and more worried. Maybe she didn't need a knight in shining armor to rescue her, but would she appreciate the gesture?

Chapter Sixteen

Connor didn't linger after work ended Thursday. He loaded Farley in his car, checked Stacy's apartment to verify she still wasn't home and headed for Shane's ranch. He parked his truck off the road half a mile from the drive and hiked in, making note of the campers scattered in the woods around the property. At least a dozen people, mostly young, dressed in winter clothing, gathered around a fire pit near the front of the property. He parked his car behind a line of others and got out. Farley hopped out beside him. He had debated leaving the dog at his apartment, then remembered the way Farley had stood beside him as he faced down Agent Anthony and decided to bring him along.

"You need something, buddy?"

He turned to see a man with a waxed cowboy mustache, insulated Carhartt vest and a pistol in a holster on his hip walking toward him.

"I'm looking for Shane," Connor said.

"Shane's busy right now," the man said. "Maybe I can help you."

"Sure. I work at the ski resort, and Shane asked me if I could help him with some fireworks he has planned. I told him I didn't think so, but I felt bad about that. I want to do what I can to help him."

"What do you do at SkyCrest?"

"Ski patrol. You know, avalanche mitigation, stuff like that."

The man looked him up and down. "Wait here a minute, and I'll find out if Shane can talk to you."

"Sure."

Connor stood in the driveway, hands in his pockets, until the cowboy was out of sight. Then he continued up the driveway, searching for any sign of Stacy or George.

He reached the house and circled around back, hiding behind a pile of firewood with Farley when the back door opened. A man with a bushy red beard came out of the house, carrying a tray. He wore a pistol on his hip and a scowl on his face. On impulse, Connor decided to follow him.

The man walked up a hill behind the house to a small wooden shed with a cupola and egg boxes on the side. Was he going to feed a flock of chickens? He set the tray on a stump and inserted a key into a padlock on the door. The tray looked like it held two plates and a couple bottles of water. Not chicken feed.

The door opened, and the man stepped inside. "Stay back!" he barked. "Wait until I tell you to move."

Connor inched closer. He wanted to see inside, but the man's back blocked the door. Connor crouched in the shadows, watching and listening. He thought he heard the murmur of a woman's voice but couldn't make out the words.

Farley whined softly, and Connor rubbed the dog's ears, quieting him. He checked his phone as the minutes ticked by.

Ten minutes passed before the bearded man emerged from the chicken house, tray in hand, and refastened the lock on the door. Then he headed down the hill and back into the house.

Connor crept to the back of the little building to a closed, chicken-size door. Farley snuffled at the wood and whined, tailing wagging.

"Stacy!" Connor hissed. "Are you in there?"

Silence.

"Stacy! It's me, Connor."

"Connor?" Her voice was nearby but above the level of the door. "What are you doing here?"

"I got worried when you didn't come home last night."

"That wasn't me who answered your text last night," she said. "That was Shane. He has my phone."

"Are you and your dad okay?"

"We're okay," she said. "But we have to get out of here. Shane is planning to set at least half a dozen bombs at the resort tomorrow. He wants to set off avalanches and blow up lifts. Hundreds of people could be hurt."

"A lift tech found a fake bomb yesterday morning," he said. "I figured someone was practicing, the way they did when they set off the avalanche."

"Shane is big on training for the mission," George said. "Bruce told me that he had his 'soldiers'—he actually refers to them as soldiers—practice everything before they go live with the mission. It's why he had Nate and some of the others launching cast boosters in that old quarry."

"You'll have to explain who all those people are later," Connor said. "First, I have to get you out of here."

"No," Stacy said. "You have to go back to SkyCrest and find Damien Anthony."

"Anthony practically accused me of stealing the cast boosters and detonators and faking the burglary," Connor said. "He wanted to search my apartment and my car."

"Tell him Dad and I are being held captive and Shane is planning to blow up the resort. Maybe as soon as tomorrow. He won't be able to ignore that."

"I'd feel better if you could come with me to tell him."

"We're fine here until you come back," she said. "Just go. Hurry. If you stick around and get caught, too, we're sunk."

He didn't like the idea, but she was right that the longer he stayed here talking to her, the greater the risk that someone would hear and come to investigate. And Anthony had the authority, and presumably the resources, to rescue her right away. "All right," he said. "But I'll be back as soon as I can."

"Wait. Before you go. Do you have a pocket knife?"

"No. What for? To use as a weapon?"

"It would be good for that, too. But I want to cut off these ties around mine and Dad's wrists."

"I don't have a knife, but I have a multi-tool. Essential equipment for ski patrol."

"Even better," she said. "But how are you going to get it to us?"

"Are you near the chicken door?" he asked.

"The chicken door?"

"Look down near the floor. It's a chicken-size exit."

"Oh. That's a door? I thought it was where they had patched a hole."

"It's a door so chickens can go in and out. That panel should raise and lower."

More sounds of movement from inside. "It looks like it's nailed shut. And even if we could get it open, it's too small for me to squeeze through."

Even Farley would have trouble squeezing through the small opening, but it was big enough for Connor to pass her the tool. "Move back," he said. "I'm going to break the door open."

"I'm away from the door."

He sized up the small wood panel inset into the side of the building, then took a step back and kicked the center of the panel, hard. The wood splintered against the toe of his boot. He kicked a second time, then a third, until a hole opened into the chicken house.

"Here's the multi-tool," he said and passed the folding tool with its multiple blades through the hole.

She reached to take the tool, and he grasped her wrist. "Promise me you'll hang on until I get help," he said.

"I will," she said.

"Good. Because I don't want to lose you."

She was silent a moment, then sniffed. "Go! Before someone comes to investigate that noise."

"Stay safe until I get back," he said, then took off running.

I DON'T WANT to lose you. Connor's words momentarily crowded out all of Stacy's worries and fears. Even as she and her father worked to cut off their restraints, the words kept repeating in her head. It wasn't an exclamation of undying love, but it could be close. Connor struck her as someone who kept his emotions close, as was she. And right now the romantic who was hidden beneath her all-business exterior was tossing confetti and dancing around. Connor *cared*—maybe as much as she had been too afraid to admit she cared for him.

A rattling at the door pulled her out of this sugary fantasy, just as the door of the chicken house swung open. "What's going on in here?" a man demanded. "What was all that noise?"

Stacy sat on the floor, her back to the shattered chicken door. Her dad lay on his side against the adjacent wall. "Dad fell," she said. "I'm really worried he might be hurt."

The man—florid faced, with heavy jowls and thinning brown hair—looked at George. "Hey, you!" he said. "Sit up."

"I... I can't." George writhed and groaned. "My...my heart."

"Nothing wrong with your heart," the man growled. "Just quit trying to move around." He slammed the door and fixed the lock back in place with a loud metallic click.

Stacy counted to one hundred. "I think you can sit up now," she said finally, keeping her voice low.

George sat and pulled the multi-tool from behind his back. "I really wanted him to come over and check on me so I could stick him."

"He would have yelled and half the camp would have come running." She brought her arms in front of her once more and rubbed her wrists where the bindings had dug into her skin. "We're better off waiting for Anthony and whoever he can round up to come with him."

"At least now we have a weapon if they come for us," George said. "Unless you're sure you can't get out the chicken door?"

She turned to scowl at the small opening at the back of the shed. "Dad, it's only a foot high and eight or nine inches wide. Only a small child could get out that thing."

"Maybe we could enlarge the hole." He flicked through the multi-tool's blades. "I've got a saw blade here."

The blade was four inches long, with tiny jagged teeth. "If you want to amuse yourself trying, go ahead," she said.

"I don't intend to sit here like a caged bird one minute longer than necessary." He crawled toward her. She moved over, and he attacked the splintered wood with the knife blade.

She closed her eyes and said a prayer that Connor would hurry and that help would arrive soon.

I DON'T WANT to lose you. Had he been too melodramatic? Did Special Agent Stacy Macrae think the local ski bum she had decided to have a fling with was taking things entirely too far?

Sure, when he had invited her up to his apartment, he had told himself they could keep things uncomplicated. They were two healthy people who were attracted to each other. She was leaving when her investigation was done, and they could make a nice memory for both of them to look back on.

But the next morning, as he had watched her sitting there in his bed, her hair mussed and the sheet pulled up around her, he had known he was lost. What he felt for Stacey went beyond the casual desire that had stirred in him the first night they danced together at the Trail's End. This emotion went deeper and burned hotter.

He had gone and fallen in love with her. And he had no idea if she felt anything close to the same. But he couldn't sit around fretting over that big question. Right now, he had a job to do, to help her.

Finding Agent Anthony proved more difficult than Connor had anticipated. By the time he arrived back at Sky-Crest, the lifts were motionless, and everyone had gone home. Darkness was setting in.

Connor called the sheriff's office. "I have some information related to the vandalism at the ski resort," he said.

"The FBI is handling that investigation," the woman on the other end of the line said. "You'll need to contact them."

"Do you have a number I can call?" he asked.

"Try their Denver office. I'm sure they can pass on the message to the right people."

He didn't have time to wait for someone from Denver. "Can I please talk to the sheriff?"

"Sheriff Howard is off duty. I can leave a message for him when he returns tomorrow morning."

Tomorrow morning would be too late. "Can I speak with a deputy?"

"Is this an emergency, sir?"

"Yes."

"I'll put you through to dispatch."

A moment of silence, then, "Nine-one-one dispatcher. What is your emergency?" The voice on the other end of the line had the flat, mechanical quality of a machine.

"A local rancher is holding an FBI agent hostage and is going to try to blow up the ski resort."

Silence. "Could you repeat that please, sir?" Still no change to the voice. Was he even speaking to a real person?

"A local rancher, Shane Greer, is holding FBI Special Agent Stacy Macrae and her father, George Macrae, hostage in his chicken house. He's got a couple dozen people camped out on his ranch, and they're planning to blow up SkyCrest resort."

"Sir, have you been drinking?" That definitely sounded more human.

"What? No, I haven't been drinking."

"Have you taken any drugs? Unfamiliar medications? Have you eaten mushrooms?"

"No. I'm perfectly sober and in my right mind."

"You say people are being held captive in a chicken house?"

"Yes. Federal Special Agent Stacy Macrae. Ask the sheriff. He'll know who I'm talking about."

"If you leave me your number and location, sir, I'll have someone assist you."

He hung up the phone. They didn't believe him. And he was wasting time trying to convince people the danger was real.

He tried Doug again, but once more got his voicemail.

He tried the number the sheriff's department had given him for the Federal Bureau of Investigation and got a message to call back during regular business hours.

Desperate, he returned to his truck and drove to Stacy's condo, where he cruised the parking lot in search of rental cars. Unfortunately, fully three quarters of the vehicles were rented by vacationers.

Then he spotted a black SUV, identical to the one Stacy had been driving. He noted the number of the parking spot, then parked in a No Parking zone and headed for the corresponding apartment.

Agent Anthony refused to open the door when Connor pounded on it, but Connor recognized his voice. "Mr. Donaldson, what are you doing here?" Anthony asked.

"Stacy Macrae asked me to get in touch with you," he said. "It's an emergency.".

"If Agent Macrae needs to speak with me, she should call me herself."

"She can't. She and her dad are being held hostage on a local ranch." Connor decided to leave out the part about the chicken house.

Anthony opened the door and peered out through an inch-wide gap. One brown eye looked Connor up and down. Connor stood up straighter and fixed Anthony with a hard stare. "You'd better come in," the agent said after a long pause.

Dressed in knit joggers and a T-shirt, the agent looked less stuffy than he had previously. He led Connor into the living room of the rental. Connor had left Farley in his truck. "Why don't you start from the beginning and tell me what's going on?" Anthony said.

Connor wanted to drag the man out by the ear and make him come with him to rescue Stacy. But that would probably only end up with him in a jail cell. So he sat on the edge of the sofa and tried to remain calm. "Yesterday morning—or maybe late yesterday—Agent Stacy Macrae went out to Shane Greer's ranch to check out some information she uncovered in the course of her investigation," he began.

"How do you know this?" Anthony interrupted.

"Last Friday evening, Agent Macrae and I attended a rally organized by Shane Greer to recruit people for a protest against the ski resort."

"You're part of this protest group?"

"No, but I was pretending to be to provide cover for Agent Macrae."

Anthony scowled. Connor wasn't sure if this was because Anthony disapproved of this strategy or because this was his default facial expression. "What happened at the rally?" Anthony asked.

"Greer learned I was with ski patrol. He asked if I had experience working with explosives. When I told him I did, he asked for my help."

Anthony had tensed. "What kind of help?"

"He said he needed help setting off a fireworks display at a rally in the town square on Martin Luther King Day. The rally was part of his planned protest. He showed us the fireworks—bottle rockets and Roman candles and things like that. I declined to help, and he seemed disappointed. But then three days later, we had the inbounds avalanche at the resort. I thought—and Agent Macrae agreed—that it might be some members of the protest group practicing with stolen cast boosters prior to a bigger action planned during the holiday weekend."

"Why MLK weekend?" Anthony asked.

"It's one of the busiest weekends of the year for the resort," Connor said. "We usually set a record for visitors. With lots of people here, Greer emphasized that he wanted to use the opportunity to sway public opinion against the ski resort expansion."

"Did he specifically say what his plans are?"

"At the meeting last Friday night, he said he wanted people to deliberately impede skier traffic on the runs. There would also be groups collecting signatures on petitions all weekend, and on Sunday there's a planned rally in the square, with a band and, presumably, a fireworks show."

"I don't believe any of that is illegal."

"It's not. But when Stacy went out to Greer's ranch, she found people launching cast boosters at a quarry there. They said they were practicing for some big event Friday. She said Greer plans to set bombs at the resort. If they're allowed to carry out those plans, hundreds of people could be injured or killed."

"How do you know any of this?"

"When Stacy and her father didn't return to their condo last night or answer my texts, I went out to the ranch to search for them. I found them locked in an old chicken house. I wasn't able to free her and her father, but she told me what she learned and asked me to contact you."

"I spoke with her father early yesterday morning. He must have told her I was in town."

"He did. And now she needs your help."

"How do I know you're not telling me all this to set a trap? I go out to this ranch, and I'm ambushed."

"I'm not asking you to go there by yourself. Can't you get a team to go out there? Or ask the sheriff to back you up?"

"It's not like we have people on standby in the next apartment," he said. "It takes time to set up a raid. And we can't rush in without probable cause."

"One of your agents is being held hostage. Someone set

off an avalanche in the resort Monday. Someone else planted a fake bomb at one of the ski lifts."

Anthony's scowl intensified. "You didn't mention a bomb before."

"Someone planted a pretty good replica of a cast booster with fuses at Lift Four yesterday."

"But the bomb was fake."

"Yes, but I think it was a practice run for tomorrow. Someone wanted to make sure they could plant a bomb without being detected."

Anthony sat back and rubbed his jaw. "You can show me where Stacy and her father are being held?"

"Yes."

"Then let me change clothes, and you can take me there."

He rose, and Connor stood too. "Just you?" Connor asked.

"Once I've assessed the situation for myself, I'll be in a better position to mobilize more help."

"Fine. You change. I'll meet you back here in fifteen minutes."

"Where are you going?" Anthony asked as Connor headed for the door.

"I have to feed my dog. I'll be back in a few minutes to pick you up."

Connor did feed Farley, but his main reason for heading back to his apartment was to remove his pistol from the gun safe in the closet. Agent Anthony would surely be armed when they visited the ranch, and he had seen for himself that many of the people there carried weapons. He wasn't going to be left with no way to defend himself and Stacy.

Anthony was waiting when Connor pulled into the condo complex. Dressed all in black, down to a black balaclava, he looked ready for a burglary. He slid into the passenger seat of Connor's truck, then frowned at Farley, who stuck his head between the seats. "What are you thinking, bringing a dog along?"

"He could prove useful."

"He'll be in the way."

"Let me worry about him."

Anthony settled back in the passenger seat. "What do you know about this rancher?" he asked.

"Shane Greer. He's maybe fifty. No sign of a wife or kids on the place. Apparently his family owned a lot of land in this area for multiple generations but lost it over the years. Shane has been buying up parcels as they become available and is trying to establish the ranch again. Stacy couldn't find a criminal record, and he comes across as an affable, concerned citizen who wants to leave Blaine Mountain open for free recreation for everyone."

"But you don't believe him."

"I might have, if not for those stolen explosives." Connor glanced at the agent, who was turned toward him, only his outline visible in the darkness. "I've worked with these explosives for six years now. Before that, I handled munitions in the Army. You don't just casually toss this stuff around. You guard it like gold. We keep meticulous records and limit who has access to the stores. Every piece has to be accounted for every time we use them." His hands tightened on the steering wheel. "I know what kind of destruction those stolen boxes contain. I've lived through one war zone. I don't want to see another one right here."

"The ski resort representative said they thought the theft was a prank."

"The ski resort has a vested interest in downplaying any kind of danger," Connor said.

Anthony said nothing, and Connor was tired of talking. Better to let the agent see the situation at the ranch for himself. Maybe then he would believe Connor was telling the truth.

The road leading to the ranch was pitch-black, but they spotted the property long before they reached it. It was lit up like a summer fair—strings of lights in trees, lanterns, a bonfire and the glow from campers, outbuildings and the house itself. Vehicles crowded the road leading up to the ranch house.

"Who are all these people?" Anthony asked.

"Greer says he advertised all over Colorado for people to help with the protests this weekend," Connor said. "Apparently, he's allowing them to camp on his land."

"Park here at the main road, facing the way out," Anthony said. "We don't want to get boxed in."

Connor maneuvered the vehicle around, then they climbed out of the truck, Farley staying close to Connor. The dog stood very still, sniffing the air. Music and laughter drifted to them from the ranch. They made their way along the shoulder of the road toward the main entrance to the ranch. People moved from light to shadow among the trees, and the music blared louder. "Looks like a party," Anthony said.

"Sounds like one, too," Connor said. "Maybe everyone is celebrating, getting fired up for tomorrow."

"It should make it easier for us to blend in," Anthony said.

Anthony had the polished new-ski-gear look of a tourist instead of the broken-in winter wear of the locals, but Connor kept his mouth shut. Nothing said tourists couldn't be converted to the cause or just be in search of a good party.

They walked up the drive, sticking to the shadows. Farley kept his nose to the ground, following invisible scent trails for short distances but always staying close. "The chicken house where Stacy and George are being held is up behind the house," Connor said.

Anthony nodded. "A car's coming," he said.

They stepped into the trees on the side of the drive. A white pickup truck lumbered toward them. People stopped to cheer as the truck drove past. Shane had lowered the driver's window and was waving to the crowd. A man with a bushy beard and Nate, the snowboarder who had been at the Trail's End with Jace, filled the rest of the front seat.

"That's Shane Greer, driving," Connor spoke softly to Anthony. "The younger man with him is named Nate. He was friends with the snowboarder who died after the avalanche."

"Someone was killed in the avalanche?"

"Jace—the snowboarder—was killed. But not in the avalanche. He died on one of the ski runs shortly after the avalanche. The local sheriff is still trying to sort things out."

"Never mind that. Let's get to this chicken house."

Connor led the way past the house. The chicken shed sat dark and silent by itself about a hundred yards past the house. "I don't see anyone standing guard," Connor said as he, Anthony and the dog crouched behind a clump of pinion trees a short distance away.

"Maybe they've moved the Macraes to another location," Anthony said.

"Or they think the chicken house is so secure they can't escape," Connor said. He straightened. "I'm going to take a look."

He headed toward the back of the chicken house, Anthony on his heels. "Stacy!" He tapped on the wall. "Stacy, it's Connor. I have Agent Anthony with me."

The only answer was a muffled noise and a series of dull thumps. Farley growled low, his body rigid.

Anthony leaned closer. "Agent Macrae, are you in there?"

More kicking sounds and muffled grunts.

"They must be tied up and gagged," Connor said. "We have to get in there." He hurried to the front of the coop, grabbed hold of the padlock and shook it.

"Quiet!" Anthony said. "Someone will hear you."

Connor stepped back. "Then get this door open."

Anthony studied the door, then pulled out his gun. "Stand back," he said. "And be ready to grab whoever is in there and run for it."

Connor caught hold of Farley's harness. "I'm ready."

The sound of the bullet striking the lock echoed in the night stillness. Even with all the music and voices, someone would have heard that. "Let's go," Anthony said, as he pulled off the shattered lock and tossed it aside.

He opened the door, and Connor peered into the darkness. Anthony shone a light around the room.

Bright eyes stared up at them. A man with thinning brown hair and a ruddy complexion lay on the floor, wrists and ankles bound and a gag stuffed in this mouth. He gave a muffled protest as they moved into the room.

"Who is that?" Anthony asked.

Connor crouched beside the man and pulled out the gag. "Where are Stacy and George?" he asked.

"I don't know any Stacy and George. Untie me, please."

"What happened to the man and the woman who were being held captive in here?" Connor asked.

"I came to bring them dinner, and they jumped me."

Connor stood. "Let's get out of here. We have to find them."

Chapter Seventeen

Stacy kept one hand on her father's arm, afraid he was going to fall over. "How badly are you hurt?" she asked as he staggered alongside her in the darkness.

"I'm not dying, if that's what you're afraid of. I just bruised a few ribs." He sucked in his breath. "Maybe broke a couple, but I've been through worse. Did I tell you about the time in Arkansas where I walked ten miles down a mountain with a broken ankle?"

"Yes. And you were thirty then. You're a lot older now."

"I don't need you to remind me." He halted, breathing hard. "I should have anticipated that kick. I expected him to give up as soon as I stabbed him."

A guard had arrived with dinner and surprised her father trying to saw through the side of the chicken house with the multi-tool. Dad had slashed him with the saw blade, and the man had delivered a hard kick to George's ribs. Stacy had jumped the man and choked him with her scarf until he went limp. She and her father had tied his hands and feet, gagged him and left him locked in the chicken house.

"Where to now?" Her father looked around. "Everything is lit up like Christmas." Music blared from speakers in the trees, overlaid by shouts and laughter. "Sounds like they're having a party."

"Our phones are bound to be in Shane's house," Stacy said. "If I get the phone, I can call for help. And transportation back to town."

"I have a better idea," her father said. "Let's steal one of these cars and drive ourselves." He gestured to the vehicles lined up along the drive.

"We can't just drive off in someone's car," she said. "They'll see us and chase after us."

"I can drive faster than they can run."

"You're barely able to stand up."

"Headlights," her father said. "Headed this way."

They ducked to the side of the drive, into the deep shadow of the woods. A white truck rumbled toward them, Shane at the wheel, Bruce and Nate with him. "Where are they going this time of night?" Stacy asked.

"Maybe they're going to dinner," George said. "It doesn't matter. With them out of the way, it's our best chance to get to the house and retrieve our phones and weapons."

They made their way to the house, moving as fast as George's injuries would permit. Every light in the house was on, but no one moved behind the windows. Stacy tried the back door and found it unlocked.

"Maybe the door isn't locked because someone is inside," George said.

"If anyone stops us, we'll pretend to be drunk partiers," she said. "We know Shane, Bruce and Nate are gone. No one else is likely to recognize us."

They made their way unmolested to the front room and the dresser by the door. The phones were there in the top drawer, along with her Glock, resting on top of a pile of winter gloves and hats.

"Careless, leaving a weapon like that where anyone could find it," George said as Stacy slipped the gun into her coat pocket. He took her arm. "Let's get out of here. You can call from the road."

"Just a minute," she said. She turned toward the stairs.

"What are you doing?"

"I'm going to take a picture of that map with the targets marked. I should have done it before. If Shane decides to destroy it, we'll still have the photo. Wait down here. Whistle if anyone else shows up."

Not waiting for an answer, she took the stairs two at a time. The door to the office was open, the desk cleared of papers and books. She opened the drawer where the plans had been. Nothing. She rifled the rest of the drawers. The plans were gone. Had he already destroyed them?

A sick heaviness settled in her stomach. Or maybe he had taken the plans with him. Maybe that had been the scheme all along—to sneak onto the resort and plant the bombs, with some kind of timer to go off tomorrow, when the crowds were their heaviest.

She started down the stairs but stopped when she heard voices. Her father was talking, his words loud and insistent. "I just came here to see if I could get a drink. The boss man must have booze somewhere."

"There's no booze here, old man," a woman's voice said. "You need to go back to your tent and sleep it off."

"Back to my tent. Good idea." He turned toward the stairs.

"Not that way," the woman said. "Come here. I'll show you out the front door."

The rustle of shuffling feet. The door opening and closing. Stacy hurried down the stairs, past the open front door, into the kitchen and out the back. Her father met her on the side of the house.

"You were lucky to run into such a helpful woman," Stacy said.

"Helpful my foot. She tried to pick my pocket. Probably disappointed when she didn't find a wallet. And drunk as I might have appeared, I had a death grip on my phone."

She took his arm. "Come on, Dad. We need to get out of here."

They set off, skirting crowds of revelers. George detoured to a campfire and helped himself to a beer from an open cooler.

"Dad!"

"I'm thirsty." He twisted the cap off the bottle and took a long swig, then offered the bottle to her. "Would you like some?"

"No, thank you. Though I wish I had some water."

"I knew you'd say that, so I snagged a bottle for you." He pulled a bottle of water from beneath his jacket and offered it to her.

She cracked it open and took a long drink. "Ahhh." She sighed. "I might actually make it to civilization."

They made it to the end of the driveway. She pulled out her phone to call Connor. The phone rang and rang, then went to voicemail. Instead of leaving a message, she texted. I'm at Shane's ranch with Dad. Meet me at the highway intersection.

She tried calling Doug but got no answer.

She could call 911, but the thought of trying to explain the situation, and the response that might be offered by a sheriff's department with at most two deputies on duty this time of night, seemed a waste of time. Best to get to the resort, find Agent Anthony and get more help from there. She didn't even know for certain if Shane and the others had been headed for SkyCrest. They might truly have merely been going out to dinner.

"What's the plan?" her dad asked as she tucked away her phone.

"I texted Connor to meet us at the highway intersection."

"So he's on his way?"

"I have no idea. If he gets my message, I'm sure he'll show up." As soon as she said the words, some of the tension went out of her. Why was she so sure this man she had known such a short time would be there for her? Yet she believed he would not let her down.

They skirted around a bonfire, where men and women were talking and laughing, some of them passing a bottle around. "At this rate, all the protestors are going to be too hungover to show up at the resort tomorrow," she said.

"Maybe that's what Shane wants," George said. "When I helped myself to the beer, a guy standing nearby told me to take all I wanted, that Shane had paid for it, and there was plenty more where that came from."

Her stomach knotted at the words. "If he wants everyone out of the way, it could be because he has an alternative plan for tomorrow," she said.

"No organized protests, just a lot of bombs going off." George increased his pace. "We need to get out of here."

They only had another few hundred yards to go before they reached the county road, where she hoped Connor would be waiting.

At first she thought the shouting was another drunken reveler. Then footsteps pounded behind her, two figures running out of the darkness toward her.

She froze and drew her Glock.

"Agent Macrae! Don't shoot!"

"Stacy, it's me, Connor."

Shaking with relief, she returned the gun to the pocket of her coat. Connor and the man with him slowed and walked to meet them, while Farley raced toward them. She bent to greet the excited dog.

Then Connor's arms were around her, and she was trying very hard to hold back tears.

CONNOR COULD HAVE stood and held Stacy for the rest of the night. His legs were still shaking with the relief of finding her, of knowing she was okay. He had been tortured by the need to protect her from harm but was now filled with pride at her ability to protect herself. "Come on." He forced himself to pull away from her but still kept one hand on her arm. "Let's get out of here."

He led the way to his truck, putting Stacy and George in the front seat, leaving Agent Anthony to crowd into the narrow back seat with Farley.

Stacy fended off Farley's attempts to wash her face and turned to look at Anthony. "Hello, Damien," she said.

"Hello, Stacy. I assume your father told you I'm here to take over this investigation."

"That's beside the point at the moment," she said. Anthony made a noise as if to protest, and she rushed to fill the void before he could speak. "We have to stop Shane Greer from blowing up SkyCrest resort."

"Connor has given me a disjointed story of a plot to bomb the resort with explosives stolen from ski patrol," Anthony said. "I'm not sure how much I believe. So far we've spent the evening running around with a lot of drunken revelers and finding a very angry man tied up in a chicken house."

"We were locked up in that chicken house for hours," George said.

"How did you get out?" Connor asked.

"I overpowered that man you found when he came to bring our supper," George said.

"And only broke a few ribs in the process," Stacy said. "We need to get you to a doctor, Dad."

"Later. We have to stop Shane first."

"We saw Shane and two others leaving the ranch in a truck forty minutes ago," Connor said.

"I think they're headed to the resort," Stacy said. She turned toward Anthony. "Shane has the cast boosters stolen from SkyCrest. Dad and I saw him and some others—including the two men who were in the truck this evening with Shane—practicing with them at an old quarry on the ranch. I also found a plan of the resort in Shane's office that showed a number of target sites. I think he planned to set the bombs tonight and detonate them tomorrow, during one of the busiest ski days of the season."

"I thought the plan was for fireworks on Martin Luther King Day," Anthony said. "While everyone is at the rally in town."

"Maybe that was the original plan and something led him to change his mind," she said. "Or maybe that was only a distraction."

"You saw all the partying going on at the ranch tonight," George said. "Shane provided all the booze and urged everyone to have a good time at his expense."

"I think it was so people would be slower to react tomorrow," Stacy said. "A lot of them will probably still be sleeping off the night's excess when the bombs explode."

"We don't know that Greer was headed to the resort," Anthony said.

"We will if we go to the resort and check," Stacy said.

"As agent in charge, I could overrule you," he said.

"You could." Connor was driving and couldn't see Stacy's face, but he heard the steel in her voice. "But do you really want to risk hundreds of lives just so you can throw your weight around?"

Anthony said nothing, which was an answer in itself.

Stacy faced forward again.

Connor rested one hand on her thigh. "Where should we head first?" he asked.

"The plan I saw had Lifts One and Four marked."

"Both are four-passenger lifts that take people from the base area up the mountain," Connor said. "Lifts that are almost always busy. Lift Four is where the lift tech found the fake bomb yesterday."

"The resort is private property," Anthony said. "We should have a warrant. And a team assembled. It doesn't make sense for the four of us to rush in to confront these people. Especially since two of you are civilians and one of you is injured."

"I know how to handle myself," George said. "And Connor was an Army Ranger."

"And I know the resort better than any of you," Connor added.

"You're welcome to get a warrant and assemble a team," Stacy said. "But we can't afford to wait around."

"We could go in after Shane leaves," Anthony said. "Bring in a crew to disarm the bombs."

"We may have to do that," she said. "But what if we're wrong about the bombs being on a time delay? What if Shane decided to aim for maximum property destruction instead of killing a lot of people? He blows up everything tonight."

"I don't think Greer is a career criminal," George said. "He's a rancher who wants his family property back and thinks this is the way to get it."

"I was told you were sent here to track down terrorists associated with the Freedom Fighters," Anthony said.

"I thought so, too," Stacy said. "But I haven't been able to find any connection. None of the people we've met match any of the Freedom Fighters we've been able to identify. Shane Greer seems to be in charge of everything, and like Dad says, it's not a professional organization. It's more… more what someone thinks this kind of operation should be like—holding a big campout for a bunch of strangers and holding bomb practice in a gravel pit. He even put ads in area papers to recruit people. A real terrorist organization would do a better job of covering its tracks."

"If the Freedom Fighters aren't responsible for this, the FBI should never have been involved," Anthony said.

"What about the stolen cast boosters?" Connor asked. "They were stolen from Forest Service property leased by the resort. Doesn't that warrant federal law enforcement involvement?"

"Alcohol, Tobacco and Firearms could have handled it," Anthony said. "We don't need to be out here freezing to death."

"I don't care about jurisdiction," Stacy said. "We're aware of a crime, and we need to stop the criminals."

Connor turned in to the resort's main entrance. The sign of SkyCrest Resort still glowed with garlands of white twinkle lights, but the parking lots and roads were empty and silent. "We're here now," Connor said. "The rest of you can do what you want, but I'm going to try to stop Shane and his buddies." Bypassing the main parking lot, he drove onto the cobbles of the plaza, ordinarily closed to traffic.

"Where are you going?" Anthony asked.

"Lift One. And we're not the first. There are tire tracks in the snow ahead of us." His headlights swept across the tread pattern. This vehicle, too, was headed for the ski lift.

Stacy scooted forward to peer out the windshield as they approached the silent ski lift. "I don't see Shane's truck."

Connor parked in front of ski patrol headquarters. "Tire tracks lead around back, where the snowmobiles are parked," he said.

Stacy drew her gun. "Then let's see if we can find them."

Connor put out one hand. "I want to check something first."

The cold hit him like a slap as he exited the warm truck. Farley piled out after him and ran in a circle. Connor walked out to the lift. The dog quickly caught up with him, while Stacy and Anthony trailed behind. George remained with the truck.

"Are you looking for a bomb?" Stacy asked.

Connor stood under the lift and shone a light into the machinery above. "The fake at Lift Four was in a shoebox, shoved up above one of the chairs," he said.

"There!" She pointed into the shadows, where a pale shape was stuck.

"That's it," Connor said. He moved quickly to an iron ladder that led into the recesses of the machinery.

He was already reaching for the box when she cried, "Wait!"

He froze and looked down at her, her face pale in the glow of her flashlight.

"It might be rigged to explode if anyone touches it," she said.

"I doubt Shane and his bunch are that sophisticated," he said.

"But we don't know. The important thing is, we know it's here. Leave it and let's find Shane."

"She's right," Anthony said. "Leave it for the experts to disarm."

Connor climbed down the ladder. "Come on."

Anthony and Stacy followed Connor and Farley back to the truck. George climbed out to join them as Connor continued around the building to the small lot where a dozen snowmobiles were parked. Shane's white pickup sat at the far end, dark and seemingly empty.

"They took two snowmobiles." Connor indicated two

empty spaces in the row of machines, tracks leading toward the slopes.

"How did they get the keys?" Anthony asked.

"You don't have to have a key to start these things," Connor said. He lifted the hood of the nearest machine and shone a flashlight inside. "Just disconnect the electric starter." He yanked a plug loose, lowered the hood again, then walked around to the control panel, grabbed the handle of the pull start and yanked hard. The engine roared to life.

"They've got an hour's head start," Stacy said and raised the hood of a second machine. "We need to get going."

She fumbled a little but managed to start the snowmobile and took off after Connor, her father riding behind her. They left Anthony to either follow on his own or await the arrival of the sheriff, provided he could get hold of him.

"I didn't know you could drive a snowmobile," her father shouted into her ear as they zoomed up the slope.

"I didn't, either," she said. "But it's not that hard." She revved the throttle and shot forward. "Where are we going?" she shouted to Connor over the roar of the engines.

"Lift Four!"

They climbed higher on the slopes, past silent lifts like sleeping creatures crouched in the shadows. The mountains glowed silver above them, bathed in moonlight. She glanced to the side and watched, awed, as a fox tiptoed through the snow at the edge of the darkness.

At Lift Four, Connor drove right up under the lift. He shone a light up into the machinery above the chairs and spotlighted a shoebox. The box was black and would have been difficult to spot if Connor hadn't already known what to look for. "I think they set the charges on the lifts first," he said. "Before they attempted the more difficult-to-place charges."

"Where do we head next?" George asked.

"The map I found had X's on every ridge that overlooks ski runs," Stacy said.

"Let's hit the likeliest locations, then," Connor said.

They had only a short ride before Connor stopped at the base of a cliff and the others pulled in alongside him. Silence wrapped around them like a muffling blanket as they shut off the snowmobile engines. "Look over there," Connor said and pointed.

At first, she recognized nothing but shadows. Then she realized she was staring at the shape of two snowmobiles, parked in the lee of a snowbank.

"Was this ridge marked on the map you found?" Connor asked.

"There were several ridges marked," she said. "I don't have a good enough feel for the layout of the resort to know if this was one."

"There's a cornice up there that releases a lot of snow on these runs," he said. "It would be a good place to plant a bomb. We should take a look." He dismounted. "We have to hike from here. I think there's enough moonlight to see. I'd rather not use a light and make ourselves a target."

"Dad, maybe you should wait here," Stacy said. She hadn't missed his grunt of pain as he dismounted the snowmobile.

"I'm not waiting anywhere," he said and set out after Connor and Farley on the narrow trail at the base of the cliff, which seemed to lead straight up. Stacy pushed past him to get behind Connor.

They climbed for long minutes, the only sound the crunch of boots on ice and their labored breathing. Then Connor stopped abruptly. Stacy almost plowed into him but stopped herself with a hand on his shoulder. "What is it?" she whispered.

"Lights up there on the ridge."

She looked up and saw two circles of light moving steadily along the ridge. "Where's the third person who was in the truck?" she whispered.

Connor shook his head.

"If they detonate a bomb up there now, we're toast," George said.

"The ones by the lifts were unexploded," Connor said. "So maybe Stacy is right about timers. They'll make the biggest impact if they trigger the bombs while people are present."

"Would that be hard to do?" she asked. "Rig a timer on the detonator?"

"I could do it," he said. "These days there's probably a video online to show you how."

She stared at the lights moving slowly along the ridge. "Could we sneak up behind them?"

"Better yet, come in from both sides and trap them," George said.

"There's only one way up there," Connor said. "Better to wait here and ambush them on the way down."

"After they plant the explosives," Stacy said.

"If we try to climb up after them, they're sure to hear us coming," Connor said.

They fell silent, waiting. Aching cold seeped through layers of clothing. Stacy's feet and hands were numb, but even shifting her feet made a noise that seemed magnified in the night stillness.

Muffled voices drifted to them from overhead. Stacy searched the surrounding snow for any sign of the third man. And where was Anthony? They could have used him below for backup and to alert them if anyone else was approaching.

Her father breathed heavily. How badly was he hurt? Standing out here in the cold couldn't be good for him.

Shuffling noises from above sounded louder, the lights bobbing erratically.

"They just tossed a cast booster," Connor whispered.

"Did you see where it landed?"

"No."

More movement from above. "They launched a second one." He sucked in a breath. "Depending on where they landed, they could bring down half the mountain."

"They're starting back down," Stacy said. She eased the Glock from her pocket.

George was already moving away. "I'll post up farther down the trail," he said.

"Let them move past us, and I'll come in behind," Connor said.

She looked and saw that he, too, was armed, moonlight glinting off the handgun. "All right," she said.

The scrape of boots on snow grew louder as the men approached. Stacy took a slow, deep breath, trying to calm her racing heart. She recognized them now—the bearded man, Bruce and the shorter figure of Shane, a black buff pulled up over his nose. She turned her head away as the men neared, not wanting light reflected from her pale face to alert them to her presence.

Shane and Bruce were almost even with Stacy and Connor when an engine's roar shattered the night's silence.

"Who is that?" Bruce asked.

"Probably just Nate," Shane said.

"Is he finished already?"

"He's younger than us," Shane said. "And more reckless."

Bruce's answer was a grunt.

Stacy's gaze met Connor's. The arrival of a third man complicated things. She turned to follow the approaching snowmobile and saw her father moving down toward it.

Good. He could keep an eye on Nate while she and Connor handled Shane and Bruce.

She stepped down off the trail, feeling for firm footing. Connor climbed up, intending to come in behind the two men. Another foot, and Shane and Bruce would be on them. She raised her weapon. "Stop!" she shouted. "This is the FBI. You're under arrest."

Shane reached into his coat.

"Don't move," Connor said. "I'm right behind you."

"Put your hands up where I can see them," Stacy said.

"This is just a misunderstanding," Shane said. "I can explain."

"You can explain later," Stacy said. "For now, you're under arrest."

"You don't understand what I'm trying to do here," Shane insisted. "I promised my father on his deathbed that I'd do everything in my power to rebuild the legacy our family lost. I'm only trying to regain what should have been mine all along."

"Shut up," Bruce said. "They don't want to hear it."

"But if you'll just listen…" Shane began.

Bruce let out a roar and charged toward Stacy. She fired, but as she braced herself, her foot slipped, and she fell, sliding down the hill, then rolling too fast to stop.

A scream tore from Stacy's throat, silenced only when she landed, hard, at the bottom of the cliff. She fought for breath, a sharp pain in her chest. Her vision blurred, and she was unable to move.

Then someone grabbed her. "Don't move, or I'll kill you now," a man's voice said close to her ear and shoved the barrel of a gun hard into her side.

Chapter Eighteen

Stacy's shot had gone wide, almost grazing Connor. He fired and hit Bruce in the shoulder. The man staggered and turned toward him. "On your knees," Connor ordered. "Now!"

Bruce dropped to his knees. Farley rushed to his side but didn't touch the man. Shane knelt beside him.

George climbed up beside them. "Throw out your weapons," he barked.

Both Bruce and Shane tossed their guns into the snow. George picked up one of the weapons, checked that it was loaded, then kicked the other aside. Connor moved down to join them. He wanted to go to Stacy, but he couldn't leave George alone with these two just yet. In fact, what was George doing up here? He was supposed to be down the trail ahead of him.

"What about the man who just arrived on the snowmobile?" he asked George.

"It's Anthony," George said. "He's waiting below. That's what I came up to tell you."

That was some good news. "He can look after these two while we look after Stacy."

George looked around. "Where is Stacy?"

"She fell." Connor gestured below. "You didn't see her?"

George shook his head. "I'll see to these two," he said. "Go to her. You'll get there faster than I could."

Connor whistled for Farley, then headed straight down the steep slope, alternately taking giant steps and glissading on his heels. But when he reached the bottom of the incline, he found only churned snow. "Stacy?" he called, keeping his voice low.

"Don't come any closer, or I'll shoot her."

He turned and found Nate holding Stacy close, the barrel of a large pistol pressed to her cheek. Her face was in shadows, but Connor could feel her terror. Or maybe that was only his own fear, which froze him in place.

"Get your hands up where I can see them," Nate ordered.

Connor slowly raised his hands. He strained his ears, hoping to hear Agent Anthony's approach. Surely he had seen Stacy fall or heard her scream. He shifted his attention to Stacy. "Are you all right?"

"I—"

"No talking!" Nate shoved the gun in her side. He glared at Connor. "Do you have a gun?"

Connor thought about lying but didn't want to risk it. "Yes. In my jacket pocket."

"Take it out. Slowly. Toss it on the ground."

He did so. The gun landed without a sound in the deep snow.

"We're going to walk over to the snow machines now," Nate said. "Don't try anything, or I'll kill her, then you."

"I understand," Connor said. Without moving his head, he searched for Farley. Maybe the commotion had frightened him away.

Connor took a careful step back, then another. Nate stalked forward, dragging Stacy alongside him. "Turn around." Nate ordered. "Think about how easy it would be for me to shoot you in the back."

Connor turned. A few more steps brought them within sight of the three snow machines they had ridden up from the base area. "I'm going to take one of these," Nate said. "And I'm going to take the fed here with me."

"What about Shane and Bruce?" Connor asked.

"What about 'em? I don't owe them anything." Nate dragged Stacy over to the vehicle. "Get on," he ordered.

Awkwardly, she climbed onto the machine.

Nate sat behind her, then leaned over to grab the handle of the starter cord.

Stacy jerked back, hitting him hard in the chin with the back of her head. She half fell, half crawled off the seat of the machine and landed on her knees in the snow while Nate was screaming and trying to sit upright.

Barking furiously, Farley raced out of the darkness. "Farley, no!" Connor shouted.

Nate turned the pistol on the dog, but Farley was already leaping, biting at the arm that held the gun.

Stacy crouched behind one of the other snowmobiles, out of sight.

Cursing and shouting, Nate fought off the dog. There was no sign of the gun now—Nate must have dropped it. Connor ran toward him, but Nate had managed to throw off the dog and reach the controls of the snowmobile. The vehicle roared to life and headed straight for Connor.

Connor dove sideways, narrowly avoiding being hit. Farley rushed to his side and began licking his face. Connor gently pushed the dog away and struggled to his feet.

The roar of the snowmobile grew louder. Was Nate coming back to try to run him over again?

But this wasn't Nate. A man in a black balaclava raced toward Connor. Connor waved, trying to flag the driver down, but the driver veered around him. Seconds later, he heard a sickening *thump!* and the sound of the engine ceased.

Connor turned to see Nate on his face in the snow. One snowmobile lay on its side, the other idled nearby. The figure in the balaclava straddled Nate and leaned down to cuff his hands behind this back.

Then the man in black straightened and looked at Connor. "Are you all right?" Agent Anthony asked.

"Yes." Connor moved, not toward Anthony, but to the snowmobile where Stacy still crouched. She stood as he approached, then turned to watch her father walk down the trail, Bruce and Shane in front of him.

Anthony met the trio at the bottom of the trail. "I'll take over from here," he said.

"Arresting us won't stop anything," Shane said as Anthony cuffed him. "We've placed charges all over this resort, set to go off after the resort opens."

"We'll find the charges and disarm them," Anthony said.

"You'll never find them all," Bruce said.

"You'd better hope we do," Anthony said. "Mass murder carries serious penalties, including death."

Shane opened his mouth but apparently thought better of speaking and looked away.

"How are we going to get them down the mountain?" Stacy asked Anthony.

"I've arranged for someone to pick them up." A low growling rose up from lower down the mountain. Anthony turned. "I think that's their ride."

An orange snowcat rumbled up the mountains on tracks. When it stopped, Stacy had to tilt her head back to see into the cab. The door opened, and a man in black SWAT gear jumped down. A second similarly clad officer remained in the cab, along with the driver.

"Three to transport," Agent Anthony said.

"We'll take good care of them," the SWAT officer said. He took Bruce by the arm and led him to the vehicle. It took both officers to boost each shackled man into the cab, but none of the three resisted.

"We need to get those explosives off the mountain," Connor said.

"There's a bomb squad on its way from Salt Lake," Anthony said. "They were closer than Denver."

"In the meantime, we can find and mark the bombs for them to remove," Connor said. "I've already located the ones at Lifts One and Four."

"The ones on the ridges will be harder to find in all this snow," Stacy said.

"I know some experts who can help," Connor said.

"Don't tell me your dogs are trained to sniff out explosives," Anthony said.

"That would be pretty sweet, but no, they can't find explosives. But the ski patrol members know every inch of this resort. Right now, before anyone else destroys the tracks, we can find where Shane and the others stood when they launched the bombs. We know the general trajectory the cast boosters take when thrown. I think we have a good chance of finding all of them."

"The resort will have to be closed until we determine it's safe," Anthony said.

"Agreed," Connor said. Doug would hate it, but even he would see the potential disaster if they missed even one explosive that detonated and killed a guest.

"Let's get ski patrol in here," Anthony said. He turned to Stacy. "We need to question Greer and the others. Maybe we can get them to tell us how many bombs they deployed and more about the timing mechanism. And we need to get your father medical help."

"Yes, sir."

"I can look after myself," George protested, but he allowed Stacy to lead him to one of the snowmobiles. He climbed on behind her.

She didn't look back as she followed Anthony toward the base area.

Maybe it was a good sign that Anthony was including her in the interrogation, Connor thought. Maybe he recognized how badly this situation might have gone without her determination and effort.

Connor pulled out his phone and checked the time. 5:00 a.m. Most of the patrol members would be getting out of bed soon anyway. He sent a group text. Everyone report to SkyCrest ASAP. We're on the hunt for unexploded bombs.

He didn't have to wait long before the first call came in. "Is this a sick joke?" Anders asked.

"No joke. I'll explain it all when everyone is here, but we've got four hours before the resort opens to find a bunch of unexploded cast boosters wired to timers." No need to mention the resort would open late today, if at all.

"The stolen cast boosters?"

"Looks like it."

"I'm on my way," Anders said.

Massive scavenger hunt saves the day.

Nina pinned the newspaper with the headline to the bulletin board over Connor's desk. The story about the hunt for hidden bombs at SkyCrest Resort was accompanied by a photo of Farley digging furiously at the snow while Connor looked on.

"He didn't really find one of the bombs, did he?" Chase asked.

"I think it was just an accident," Connor said. "But he did dig one up. The photographer was standing right there and said it was the perfect photo op."

"He probably thought it was a toy," Raz said.

"Or maybe Farley has a hidden talent," Lily said. "It might come in handy. Every once in a while we do launch a dud and have to retrieve it. Farley could save us a lot of time."

"I'd just as soon we never lose another cast booster," Connor said.

"Have you heard from Stacy?" Nina asked.

"No." He turned away, afraid his expression might reveal his disappointment.

He hadn't spoken to her since Friday morning on the mountain, and frankly, he was a mess, though doing his best to hide it. He wanted the two of them to be together. Maybe it was impossible—the ski bum and the federal agent. But he had looked forward to the adventure of seeing what kind of future they could build. He had told himself she hadn't contacted him because she was absorbed in her work, but an ugly voice at the back of his mind had whispered that he had served his purpose and now she was done with him.

"We'd better get started," he said, with forced cheer. "Today is going to be another big day."

Martin Luther King Day had dawned clear and sunny, and skiers filled the resort, undeterred by local news stories of bombs and terrorism or the full-day closure on Friday. The protest rally had been canceled. There was still a booth collecting petitions against the resort expansion, but the effort was low-key, and protestors were distancing themselves from any hint of violence.

"First, I want to thank everyone for all the extra work

you've put in these past few days," Connor said. "Not only coming in early to search for the bombs but dealing with the record crowds on Saturday afternoon, Sunday and today. SkyCrest Resort appreciates it, too. You should see a little extra in your next paycheck."

Cheers rose around the room. Even a couple of the dogs barked. "Today is going to be another big day," Connor continued after the clamor had died. "So let's get to your assignments."

He was reading off the last of the day's tasks when the door opened, and Stacy entered.

She was dressed in the same sleek black pants and turtleneck she had worn the day they met, and his heart sped up at the sight of her. She was greeted with another round of cheers. She flushed and leaned against the wall by the door. "I didn't mean to interrupt."

"We're just wrapping up," he said.

"Tell us what happened to the bombers," Chase said.

Stacy looked to Connor.

He nodded. "Go ahead. We all want to know the news."

"Shane Greer, Bruce Finley and Nate Lee are in custody in Denver," she said. "Shane has agreed to cooperate with authorities. We've determined the plan was his idea, and he recruited Nate and Bruce and others to help. Nate stole the explosives from the resort. Jace helped him but later on got cold feet and threatened to go to the sheriff. Nate killed him and tried to make it look like an accident."

"Did they all really hate the ski resort that much?" Renee Castro asked.

"I don't know about Bruce and Nate, but Shane says he didn't hate the resort at all. He just wanted to reclaim his family's land, and SkyCrest was built on part of that land. He thought if he damaged the resort badly enough, it wouldn't be rebuilt, and he'd be able to acquire the property once more."

"So there were no terrorists?" Lily asked.

"Not the way most people think of them," Stacy said. "Though attempting to bomb a ski resort full of people is an act of terrorism."

"We could probably talk about this all day, but we need to get to work," Connor said. "The resort opens in an hour."

The patrollers filed out of the room, leaving Connor and Stacy alone. "It's good to see you," she said.

"Yeah. You, too."

"I know I've been kind of scarce."

He wanted to kiss her. To hold her close. But doing so felt awkward. The case was over. She was leaving. She was probably here to say goodbye. As much as losing her was going to hurt, he didn't want to add to his humiliation by letting her see the pain. "How's your dad?" he asked.

"Recovering from three broken ribs but in good spirits." She smiled. "He said he hasn't had this much fun in years."

"Sounds like he misses the Bureau."

"He misses being involved. Making a difference. But he has some ideas for after he's healed."

"Oh?"

"Yeah. While he was in the hospital, he read about a program here in Colorado that takes disadvantaged youth on camping and hiking and backcountry skiing and climbing trips. He's already contacted them about getting involved."

"So he plans to stay in Colorado?" Again that quickened heartbeat. She would have a reason to stay here.

"In Grand Junction," she said. "So not far away."

Even better. "How do you feel about that?" he asked.

"Good, actually." She traced a pattern on his desk with one finger. "As much as I complain about him interfering,

I've missed him. And it's kind of nice, having someone nearby who cares about me."

Pain gripped his heart, and he put a hand on her shoulder. When she looked up and met his eyes, his courage almost failed him, but he pushed on. "I care," he said. "Very much."

Then he kissed her. A long, tender kiss, one he hoped conveyed what he wasn't good at putting into words. He broke the kiss and looked into her eyes, trying to gauge her reaction.

What he saw there alarmed him. Her eyes were wet and shiny.

His throat constricted. This must be really bad if she was crying. "What's wrong?" he managed to croak.

She shook her head. "I was just thinking how lucky I am. To have come here. To have met you." She put her arms around him and moved in close.

He held her, confused but no longer panicking. "I can come to Denver to see you," he said. "Every chance I get. It'll be easier in the summer. And we can talk and text. We'll figure something out." Was he talking too much?

"Or you could come to Grand Junction," she said. "That's a lot closer."

He pulled away to look at her. "Grand Junction?"

"That's where I'll be. There's a satellite office there, under the Denver field office. I'll be a resident agent, working with area law enforcement."

"That's great. Isn't it?"

She smiled. "I think it's pretty great."

"No more Agent Anthony expecting you to make coffee or file reports."

"Damien has actually been pretty decent," she said. "He gave me credit for all the work I did tracking down Shane Greer and the others. He even alerted me to the opening in the Grand Junction office."

"Maybe he wanted you out of his way."

"Maybe. But it doesn't matter. I have plenty of reasons for wanting to be here."

"Your dad is here."

"Farley is here," she said.

Connor blinked. "You want to be near Farley?"

"I want to be near Farley's person." The smile she hit him with sent heat straight through him.

"Farley's person wants to be near you." He pulled her close in another kiss. His heart beat faster at the thought of being closer to a woman who amazed and confounded him in turn. But challenges were good, he reminded himself. And with Stacy, the risk was definitely worth the reward.

* * * * *

COMING SOON!

We really hope you enjoyed reading this book. If you're looking for more romance be sure to head to the shops when new books are available on

Thursday 23rd April

To see which titles are coming soon, please visit
millsandboon.co.uk/nextmonth

MILLS & BOON

LET'S TALK
Romance

For exclusive extracts, competitions and special offers, find us online:

- **f** MillsandBoon
- **X** @MillsandBoon
- **◯** @MillsandBoonUK
- **♪** @MillsandBoonUK

Get in touch on 01413 063 232

For all the latest titles coming soon, visit
millsandboon.co.uk/nextmonth